Anne Wyn Clark was born and raised in the Midlands, where she continues to live with her husband, plus a chinchilla with attitude. She has three now grown-up children and six grandchildren. Much of her formative existence was spent with her head in a book, and from an early age, she grew to relish the sheer escapism afforded by both reading and writing fiction.

She has a love of antiquity and a penchant for visiting old graveyards, often speculating on the demise of those entombed beneath.

Whisper Cottage is her first attempt to delve into the murky waters of psychological suspense.

You can follow her on Twitter @EAClarkAuthor

Whisper Cottage

ANNE WYN CLARK

avon.

Published by AVON
A division of HarperCollins*Publishers* Ltd
1 London Bridge Street
London SE1 9GF

www.harpercollins.co.uk

HarperCollins*Publishers*
1st Floor, Watermarque Building, Ringsend Road
Dublin 4, Ireland

A Paperback Original 2021

1

First published in Great Britain by HarperCollins*Publishers* 2021

A catalogue copy of this book is available from the British Library.

ISBN: 978-0-00-845997-0

This novel is entirely a work of fiction. The names, characters and
incidents portrayed in it are the work of the author's imagination.
Any resemblance to actual persons, living or dead, events or
localities is entirely coincidental.

Typeset in Sabon by Palimpsest Book Production Limited,
Falkirk, Stirlingshire

Printed and Bound in the UK using 100% Renewable Electricity
at CPI Group (UK) Ltd

MIX
Paper from
responsible sources
FSC™ C007454

This book is produced from independently certified FSC™ paper
to ensure responsible forest management.

For more information visit: www.harpercollins.co.uk/green

*This book is dedicated to the
memory of my dear dad.
Thank you for always being there for us.
We miss you.
Cofion annwylaf.
Caru mawr
xxx*

'What is man? A miserable little pile of secrets'
André Malraux

Prologue

Avoncote, 1964

The writing baby lay on the hearth rug, its cheeks puce, the screaming intensifying as its scrawny limbs flailed aimlessly.

'We'll let him cry it out for a bit,' she'd said weakly. She looked exhausted. She always did these days. 'He's been fed and winded, and I've changed him. Does their lungs good anyway, a nice long yell. There's nothing really wrong with him; I think he's just overtired.'

His eyes swept the room disapprovingly. Things were in disarray. He hated mess; there was comfort in order. It always used to be orderly. He could hear her now, humming to herself absently as she moved about the kitchen. He glared down at the mewling infant with contempt. Wriggling there open-mouthed on the ground. The tongue quivering in its screwed-up little face reminded

1

him of a maggot crawling through a withered windfall apple. The sight of its hands, the bud of an extra digit trembling at each extremity, made him curl his own into fists of revulsion.

How he had come to despise this pink, bald parasite. Usually clamped to her breast, the thing was like a leech, sucking the life from her, demanding all her time and attention. As he leaned over the child, the sour, sickly smell of her milk rose from its breath. It turned his stomach.

The constant high-pitched wailing was becoming intolerable, seeming to fill his whole head, competing with the shrill whistle from the kettle that was now building to a crescendo.

'Shut up,' he hissed, in a low voice. But the incessant din appeared only to amplify. His mouth was close to its ear now. 'Shut UP!'

She reappeared from the kitchen. He stood up and backed away guiltily. Maybe it was because she was so tired, but she appeared oblivious to his rage.

Letting out a sigh, she squatted down and scooped the now hysterical baby up into her arms. 'I think I'll walk him up and down outside a bit. Maybe the fresh air will help him drop off. He must be exhausted, poor lamb.'

He looked on silently as she wrapped the bawling infant in a shawl and, crooning all the while, disappeared into the garden.

The room was mercifully quiet once more. His breathing began to calm and he sat down on the sofa, watching through the window as they went down the path and past the omnipresent line of white towelling nappies flapping in the breeze. The movement seemed to have soothed the child and it had stopped sobbing. But he knew it would happen again. She had spoiled it; that's what happened when you let a baby get its own way.

The thought came into his head and he knew now with strange clarity what needed to be done.

Next time he would teach it a lesson.

A flutter of excitement began to build from somewhere within and he leaned back, his face breaking into a satisfied smile.

For he knew without a doubt that there would be a next time.

CHAPTER 1

2012

Our move to the sleepy backwater of Avoncote seemed to have been written in the stars. After four years of unwedded bliss with my partner, Jack, I had been shocked, although delighted, to discover that I was pregnant. I was apprehensive about telling Jack, since it wasn't something we had planned – at least, not at that point in time. After my initial burst of euphoria, I began to worry that he might not share my enthusiasm, or worse still, he might actually hate the idea. What if it spelled the beginning of the end of our relationship? I remember sitting in the tiny kitchen in our flat that afternoon, clutching the fateful plastic wand in my hand as my coffee turned cold, a thousand scenarios playing out in my mind. My – *our* – whole world had suddenly been turned on its head.

Hearing the door slam as Jack walked in after work,

my stomach clenched. Staring at the evidence in my hand, a lump rose in my throat.

He stuck his head round the door, his hair tousled, a smile lighting his whole face.

'Hey, you. Good day?' Miserably I lifted my eyes to meet his gaze. His brow creased into a frown.

'What's up?'

Tentatively I handed over the pregnancy test, its tell-tale blue line facing upwards.

He looked, open-mouthed, from me to the wand and back again. His blue eyes were wide and unreadable. I felt sick. My hands were bunched into fists, nails digging into my clammy palms.

The wind was knocked from me as, without warning, he lifted me off the stool suddenly, swinging me round until I was giddy. I'd never seen him so excited. I hadn't anticipated that the prospect of bringing a child into the world would mean so much to him. That I had been worried about nothing.

Two days after I had broken the news, Jack arrived home with an enormous bouquet of roses. I peeled off the cellophane and a small cardboard box fell to the floor. My stomach turned over.

'What's this?' I looked up to see him grinning broadly, his head cocked to one side, watching for my reaction.

'I've no idea. Open it and find out.'

With trembling fingers, I lifted the lid to find an unusual ring, gold, with a large diamond flanked either side by topaz. I gasped. I hadn't expected this at all.

'To match your bewitching eyes.' He smiled, a little uncertain. 'Well, what d'you reckon, Stina? Will I do?'

I was stunned. 'Is this . . . a proposal?'

He nodded. I felt my eyes fill with tears. 'Yes, of course you'll bloody do!'

At that precise moment, I think I was happier than I had ever been in my entire life. I still found it hard to believe that someone as intelligent and handsome and caring as Jack could want me – *me* – to share his life. To raise his child.

Six weeks later, we had tied the knot in a registry office – not because we felt we ought to, but because the time felt, well, right. And as neither of us were religious, a church ceremony seemed hypocritical. We agreed that we wanted it to be low-key, and rather than inviting family and friends for a big 'do', pulled in a couple of bemused witnesses from the street. We celebrated afterwards with a meal at the Italian restaurant where we'd had our first proper date. I'd never fantasised about a big white wedding, and it seemed more meaningful somehow that it was just us. I was deliriously happy.

*

The news of my pregnancy had made us both re-evaluate our priorities, and probably owing to a surge in hormones I became suddenly more anxious and obsessive about everything: crime, pollution, the general environment into which we would be bringing our precious child. I had been born and raised in Birmingham, although if the truth be told I had long dreamed of relocating to somewhere quieter and where the pace of life seemed less manic. And of escaping my past. I would have gone anywhere in the world with Jack if he'd asked me to and this was the perfect opportunity to do just that. New house, new baby; isn't that how the saying goes?

The chance of a more senior role for Jack in a well-established surgery in the Warwickshire countryside was so perfectly timed, it almost felt predestined. Everything seemed to have fallen into place. Jack was raised on a farm and had always had a hankering to return to a more rural way of life, plus neither of us were keen on the idea of raising a child in the city. And on a practical level, our second-floor flat was decidedly poky, plus there was no lift. The thought of dragging a buggy and baby up and down those stairs filled me with dread. I was working freelance from home, making enough money to keep me ticking over writing articles for various magazines, and so location for me wasn't an issue. We began to scour the local papers and the internet for an ideal area from which Jack could commute.

There were several villages within spitting distance of the practice, which was just outside Stratford-upon-Avon. Jack was enthusiastic about living close to the surgery, declaring that he could even cycle to work in the warmer weather. Eventually we had plumped for picturesque Avoncote, largely because of the house we had discovered there. We fell in love with Wisteria Cottage at first sight. It was one of two semi-detached houses, set apart on a short stretch of road towards the centre of the hamlet. Uneven cobbles winding to a frontage festooned with lilac blooms beneath a thatched roof; endearingly small and perfect for newly-weds expecting their first child. Yes, there was a good deal of work to be done and we were going to have to throw some serious money at the place

– something we could ill afford, the mortgage stretching us to the limit – but the location was ideal, and the house had such potential. We moved in at the end of April, the whole summer stretching before us, leaving several months to prepare for our forthcoming arrival.

The chocolate-box village itself, quintessentially English and slightly twee, with its small, close-knit community, seemed like the answer to our prayers. It was like something out of a Miss Marple novel. There was a village green, complete with stocks – thankfully no longer in use. It even boasted a maypole. Next to the green, a large circular duck pond was enclosed by a low wooden barrier. The spire of a beautiful old church pierced the skyline, its immaculately maintained graveyard filled with generations of the village's former occupants. Beyond the church, a canal passed through the village, the towpath providing a scenic walk towards the centre of Stratford.

The local pub, The Green Man, was an impressively wide sixteenth-century building, constructed in honeyed Cotswold stone and adorned with numerous colourful hanging baskets. A huge swinging sign stood before its doors, bearing the image of a dark green but benign-looking male face, peering through foliage peppered with red berries.

A general-store-cum-post-office and a doctor's surgery were only a stone's throw from our front door. There was a little primary school, which looked charmingly old-fashioned, its yard brightly painted with hopscotch grids, and various lines and circles for other traditional playground games.

The whole area felt timeless – a complete contrast to

the soulless, crime-ridden city we knew as home. I was brimming with excitement at the prospect of building our future in such idyllic surroundings and of giving our child the best possible start in life. No drug peddling on the doorstep, no worries about leaving the door unlocked for more than a minute in case someone burst in wielding a baseball bat demanding our life's savings. The stories in the local press before we finally waved goodbye to our former home had become increasingly alarming.

We had recently acquired a beautiful two-year-old border collie, Jobie, shortly after Jack started his new post. Jack had always been desperate to have a dog, but our flat wasn't the ideal environment. One of the other vets was emigrating to New Zealand, and although heart-broken at having to part with him, thought it unfair to drag the animal halfway round the world. Jobie was as mad as a box of frogs but a complete delight, and took to us like a duck to water – as we did to him.

Our whole existence had been turned delightfully on its head: a peaceful rural location, a dream job for Jack, a new baby on the way. It had all happened so quickly, but I was adjusting well to this change in lifestyle. It was everything I'd ever dreamed of, and I was riding high on the euphoria of it all. It felt almost too good to be true.

*

Rose Cottage, the building adjoining our new home, was beautifully maintained, which only accentuated the fact that our rusting front gate was hanging on by the skin of its teeth and the peeling window frames crying out for a lick of fresh paint.

Our neighbour, an elderly widow named Mrs Barley, lived alone, with only two caged lovebirds for company. We had met her briefly when she came out to introduce herself the day we moved in and she seemed pleasant enough. She was a small, frail-looking creature, with short, wispy white hair. There was a quiet sadness about her, which I attributed to the premature loss of her husband some years earlier, something alluded to in hushed tones by the estate agent who had first shown us round.

The rear gardens of our respective cottages nestled side by side, separated by a low picket fence. The outer edge of each garden was enclosed by a tall privet hedge, ours embarrassingly unkempt and interwoven with brambles; Mrs Barley's, in contrast, neatly clipped and bevelled. Our back gates opened onto an entry that in turn opened out onto a lane populated by a handful of quaint detached cottages, beyond which were verdant views of open, rolling fields, stretching for miles. *How* I coveted the little summer house at the bottom of Mrs Barley's lawn. Hexagonal in shape and painted pale mint green, it was a robust structure, with a proper slate roof, its varnished wooden fascia creating a sort of portico, windows to the sides and double doors at the front. It finished the garden off perfectly.

Mrs Barley's pristine flowerbeds put ours to shame. Wisteria Cottage had been a rental property for several years before the owners finally decided to sell, and the previous occupants had clearly been averse to horticulture, preferring their borders 'au naturel', leaving a forest of weeds and waist-high grass concealing any amount of wildlife. We resolved that our priority was to arm ourselves with shovels and shears and set about creating some sort of order.

The heat that first Saturday was unseasonably oppressive, making our task even more wearisome. Jobie hindered our efforts further by leaping on us playfully. He snapped relentlessly at the butterflies heading for the glorious raspberry-pink refuge of next door's buddleia.

'I'm beginning to think we should have hired a digger,' groaned Jack. 'Maybe we ought to just lay slabs over the whole bloody lot. This isn't my idea of fun.'

I prodded him playfully. 'Don't be such a misery. We want a nice garden for when the baby comes – it'll be lovely for him or her to have somewhere to play. Keep going – it'll all be worth it in the end!'

Damp with sweat, and skin prickling from the brambles and coarse ryegrass, we'd been hacking away for a gruelling couple of hours. Although still only thirteen weeks into my pregnancy, the heat was taking its toll on me and I was starting to flag. Mrs Barley appeared, balancing a tray of home-made biscuits and fresh lemonade on the fence.

'Some refreshments?' She spoke softly, with a subtle West Country burr. 'Gardening's thirsty work, I know.'

Gratefully accepting the tray, we paused to gulp down the cool liquid. I couldn't help noticing the fingerless gloves she was wearing, and the old woman obviously realised. She smiled, explaining, 'I have arthritis, my dear. Even when the weather's as warm as this, my old hands often still throb and ache. The gloves help a little with the stiffness.'

'I'm sorry, I didn't mean to stare.'

'That's quite all right. I know it must look a bit odd, especially in this heat, but it's comfort over style for me these days, I'm afraid!' She seemed unperturbed, and I was glad that I hadn't offended her.

Jack raised a thumb. 'Mmm – these are excellent,' he said, through a mouthful of crumbs.

Mrs Barley looked pleased. 'It's nice to have someone to bake for. I rarely bother these days – no point, now there's only me. Since Frank's passing, I don't do half the things I used to . . .' She tailed off wistfully. Her eyes had misted with tears. There was an awkward silence and Jack shot me a discomfited look.

'I *love* your summer house,' I said, attempting to divert her. 'And the garden's just beautiful . . .'

'Yes. Not my doing, though. It was Frank's hobby. I can't bend, you see, so I pay someone to tidy up now. I like to keep it nice – Frank was so proud of his garden.'

Pensively, she gazed at the profusion of pinks, reds, whites and mauves, each flower and shrub labelled meticulously.

'I love sitting in our summer house. Frank built it himself, you know. It's where I feel closest to him. We'd take tea there in summer and sit until sundown, just looking out at all the flowers.' She paused, lost in the memory.

'Frank always used to say you're closest to God in a garden,' she almost whispered.

*

Our day had been exhausting but ultimately rewarding. After a dinner of takeaway pizza, which meant a six-mile round trip for Jack, as the sun started to wane, we sat

13

admiring the fruits of our labour through the open French doors. The living room was bathed in a pool of rosy light, the heat of the afternoon having given way to a beautifully temperate evening. The sky was streaked pink, and a soft, warm breeze wafted through the house. There was still a long way to go, but everything now looked tidy, at least. The weeds had been cleared, the soil dug over, the lawn trimmed. I pictured the borders filled with roses in bloom, hazy purple lavender; maybe a flowering cherry, a bubbling water feature. It might not be able to compete with Mrs Barley's showpiece yet, but it was a start.

Jack went to make a pot of tea while I sat, daydreaming, Jobie at my feet. A sudden movement at the bottom of Mrs Barley's garden made me shift my gaze. Startled, I realised that a tall, dark-haired man had walked through the back gate. He wore muddy working boots, and braces over a white collarless shirt, its sleeves rolled up. He strolled slowly up the path and paused, his head bent as though carrying the weight of the world on his shoulders. I jumped to my feet and ran to the window. He didn't appear to have noticed me; he seemed to be lost in thought, staring down at the ground where our fence met our neighbour's. I felt a peculiar sensation, like an electric current passing through me. There was something inexplicably unnerving about him: his plodding, deliberate gait; his sombre demeanour.

'Jack! There's a bloke in Mrs Barley's garden.'

'What did you say? I can't hear you above the kettle.' He appeared in the doorway, tea towel in hand.

'A man – in next door's garden. Look.'

I waved frantically, turning back to the window, but

14

the intruder had vanished. Jack darted outside through the French doors. Followed by an excitable Jobie, he hurried down to the bottom of the garden and out into the entry, looking from left to right. He turned back to me and shrugged.

'Well, he must have shifted bloody quickly. I can't see anyone out there.'

I rushed to the front door and went out into the lane, looking up and down the road in case the man had gone in the other direction, but there was no one in evidence. Puzzled, I went back into the house.

'Will you go and knock on Mrs Barley's door – check if she's all right? I can't imagine he could've made it to her back door that quickly, but just in case . . .'

Jack rolled his eyes, but humoured me by going round to see the old lady. He was back in no time.

'She's fine – didn't seem at all concerned. Said it was probably her gardener. He pops in and out quite regularly, apparently. Nothing to worry about.'

'Oh. But I still don't see how he could have cleared off that quickly . . . Well, at least she's okay – that's the main thing.'

I looked back into the garden, but a shiver rippled through me. I would be keeping an eye out for the gardener, just to make sure it was him. I felt uneasy about a man being able to wander unhindered into a garden so close to our own. Having moved from an urban area where break-ins were rife, it concerned me now that maybe this wasn't going to be the bucolic haven I'd hoped for.

That night I sat up in bed, trying to read. But I felt restless, and kept going over the same paragraph time and again without absorbing a thing. Eventually, I put down my book and nudged Jack.

'Are you asleep?'

He sighed. 'Not any more. What's up?'

'I keep thinking . . . about that man in the garden.'

He rolled over and pulled me towards him.

'Stop fretting,' he soothed. 'Listen; we've had a great day, made good progress. I'm earning more, we're in our dream cottage and we've got a new baby to look forward to. Life feels . . . I don't know, full of hope. I know you're a born worrier but I'm sure that bloke out there was just the gardener or something. This is sleepy rural Warwickshire, not an inner-city den of iniquity.'

'I know. It's left me a bit unsettled, that's all.' I snuggled down beside him and he kissed my shoulder.

'Try to get some sleep. You'll have forgotten all about it by tomorrow.'

*

Early the following morning, I left Jack snoring in bed and crept downstairs. I sat at the little wooden table we had placed in front of the French doors, sipping my tea. Looking round the room, I started making mental interior decoration plans. It had plenty of character; I liked the old stone fireplace and beams were something I'd always loved, even though Jack had to duck beneath them. The unsightly flock wallpaper on the one wall would have to go, though; and as for the woodwork, which had bizarrely been painted in garish blue paint . . .

I sat up sharply as a small white van pulled up in the entry. A stockily built man, probably in his late fifties,

16

dressed in navy-blue overalls and a flat cap, opened its doors. I watched as he unloaded a petrol lawnmower. As he wheeled it through Mrs Barley's gate, he spotted me doing my nosy neighbour bit and grinned, lifting his head-gear to reveal a shiny bald dome. Sheepishly, I gave him a wave and retreated into the living room. He was the gardener, clearly. But he definitely wasn't the man I'd seen the previous evening. I thought for a moment and decided to go outside.

'Morning,' said the man, cheerfully. 'You'll be the new neighbour, then. Nice for the old girl to have a bit of company at last.' His face was deeply tanned and weather-beaten, with smiling brown eyes that crinkled at the corners when he spoke. 'I'm Bob, odd-job man extraordinaire!' He extended a grimy hand over the fence, which I shook tentatively.

I smiled. 'I'm Stina. Good to meet you. You make a lovely job of the garden. It's beautiful.'

'Aw, it's just a matter of staying on top of it. Her old fella planted everything. Quite easy to maintain, really.' He peered over the fence and nodded approvingly. 'I see you've been hard at work. *What* an improvement. Those other buggers had let it go to rack and ruin. I think they were only renting, same as the ones before them. Don't suppose it was very high on their priority list, if they were planning on moving on.'

'No, I don't imagine it was. Still, it belongs to us now and we're keen to turn things round, so hopefully once we've got a few plants in, it'll start to look a bit more respectable.' I indicated the van parked in the entry. 'Do you work alone or is there someone else who helps you?'

Bob laughed. 'No, it's just me. I'm a one-man band! Plenty of work to keep me ticking over, but I manage pretty well on my own. Why do you ask?'

'There was some chap here yesterday. He nipped in and out of the garden very quickly before we had chance to speak to him, and Mrs Barley was convinced it must've been you. I reckon he must've been on foot, because we didn't see a car.'

Bob frowned. 'Nope, definitely not me. And I don't know why she'd have thought so, either. I told her I'd be coming on Sunday this week – I had a lot on yesterday.'

'A mystery, then. No, he didn't look anything like you.' I omitted the fact that the man had been taller, younger and with a full head of hair. 'We'll keep our eyes peeled in case he turns up again – I thought it was a bit strange at the time.'

'Yes, you do that. A bit of a worry with her there all on her own and everything. But having said that, crime round here's very rare. Everyone generally looks out for one another, which is a comfort, especially for the old folk.'

I smiled. 'Yes, that's one of the reasons we moved here. It seems very safe and incredibly peaceful.'

'Oh arr, it's that all right. A bit too bloody quiet sometimes, if you ask me. Nothing much ever happens in Avoncote, nor my village – I'm in Snitterfield, just three miles up the road from here.' He gestured towards the fields that backed onto the lane. 'We moved there over twenty years ago to get out of the town, and it has its pros and cons, I'd say. They could do with a murder or two to liven things up a bit – you know, like in that

TV series with the old dear who's a bit of a sleuth on the side.' He winked, laughing raucously at his own joke.

I watched as he trundled the mower onto the lawn. 'How long have you worked for Mrs Barley?' I asked.

'Ooh, best part of the last fifteen years, I'd say. She's a funny old stick sometimes, our Mrs Barley, but I've always quite liked her. I know there are those that think her odd but I take as I find. She's never done me any harm. Can't be doing with the gossips. You'd have thought in this day and age people would have moved on from the idea that an old woman living alone isn't to be trusted.'

My skin tingled. 'What do you mean?'

'Aww, you know how it can be – or maybe you don't, coming from the city. There are some funny buggers out in the sticks. Superstitious and mistrustful. You'll find out soon enough. I'm not saying they're all like that, far from it. But there are enough of 'em to make things unpleasant if they've a mind to. Good to have more people moving in from elsewhere – new blood shakes things up a bit.'

He reflected a moment and chuckled. 'She does have some funny ways, mind you.'

'Oh? Why do you say that?'

'Well, bit of the old hocus-pocus, you know. Likes her herbal remedies and her little rituals, crystals and reading tea leaves and suchlike. Offered to do mine once, but I don't believe in all that stuff. I suppose it comes of living on her own all these years. No real harm in it though, eh?'

He winked and smiled warmly. 'Anyway, I'd best crack

19

on. The wife's getting the dinner early today as the family are coming over. Nice to meet you, Stina!'

I went back into the house. Jack had surfaced and stood in the doorway rubbing his eyes sleepily.

'Who was that you were talking to?'

'That,' I said, slightly bemused, 'was odd-job Bob.' I watched from the window for a moment and thought about what the man had said about Mrs Barley. It gave me a strangely uncomfortable feeling.

CHAPTER 2

The first day I waved Jack off as he left to begin his new job, I remember having a weird sense of foreboding. This was everything I had always wanted, but part of me wondered if there would be a price to pay. I hardly dared believe that I had married the man of my dreams and that we would be having a baby together – let alone in such a beautiful, idyllic setting. I didn't deserve it; I had this niggling doubt about it all, as though I couldn't be allowed to feel so happy. That something was sure to happen to pull the rug from under my feet. It seemed that for every positive in my life, there would need to be a massive wrecking ball of a negative to cancel it out. Jack's new role was more demanding and while the salary was a vast improvement, I knew that with the extra responsibility he would have to work longer hours, and it might upset the dynamic of our relationship. I could only hope and pray that it wouldn't be the case. I loved him so much and knew that I must do everything in my power to hold on to him.

The first time I laid eyes on Jack had been four years earlier at a house party, shortly after completing my degree at the University of Birmingham. When I think back, it's strange how fate can bring people together. I almost didn't go – I rarely socialised and have never been comfortable amongst large groups of people. But my friend Reggie had nagged me to go along with her and I finally capitulated, albeit reluctantly.

The gathering was in a huge and rather grand three-storey terraced Victorian property, in the leafy suburb of Edgbaston. Our host was an irritatingly uptight junior doctor called Zakir, the friend of a friend. The house belonged to his evidently affluent parents, who were holidaying in the Seychelles. He was anxiously following people around, ensuring that no one was spilling beer on the Persian rugs or knocking over any invaluable ornaments. And smoking was a complete no-no.

To cut a long story short, I was bored rigid. Apart from my flatmate, Reggie, I didn't know anyone, and most of the other guests were medical students, whereas my own current area of expertise was the poetry of John Donne. I felt like a fish out of water.

Reggie, who'd dragged me along insisting I'd have a great time, was in the early throes of a relationship with an aspiring forensic pathologist from Liverpool. They had disappeared upstairs, leaving me hovering like a spare part. It was a cool autumn evening, and after leafing through Zakir's dull CD collection, I'd wandered out onto the patio for a smoke (a student habit that I've thankfully since kicked).

'They're very bad for you, you know.'

Startled, I looked round to see an amused pair of piercing blue eyes peering at me from behind a huge potted spruce, still flecked with strands of tinsel from Christmas.

'I'm sorry? Oh, the fags – I know, I keep trying to quit.' I could feel the colour rising in my cheeks. I felt as though I'd been caught doing something illicit.

The owner of the eyes stepped out from behind his cover and I gave him an appreciative once-over. He was tall; well built with broad shoulders and narrow hips, his hair dark and wavy, his complexion tanned. He wore a battered leather jacket and faded jeans. I saw that he, too, had a cigarette in one hand, a bottle of beer in the other.

I raised an eyebrow. 'Hmm. Sounds like a case of what they used to call "the pot calling the kettle grimy arse"!'

He smirked. 'Oh, I only smoke at parties. Gives me something to do. I can't be bothered with the small talk, so it's a good excuse to get out into the garden.'

'Do you usually lurk in bushes like that? You want to watch out, you know. You frightened the life out of me – I might've had a heart condition. I don't suppose that occurred to you . . .' I was teasing, but he looked genuinely mortified.

'God, I'm sorry. I never thought of that. I'd been waiting for an opportunity to slip away, to be honest. Zakir's not exactly making people feel welcome. Probably not the best idea, having a houseful when your parents are away

23

– especially when they've got a priceless collection of antiques.' He paused. 'I couldn't help noticing you in there – you looked as bored out of your mind as I am.' His voice was soft but deep, with no discernible accent.

I nodded, suddenly conscious of my own Brummy twang. 'I've had enough. I don't know why I came, really. I think I may sneak away soon.'

To my surprise, his face lit up. 'Shall we sneak away together? There's a great old pub a couple of streets away and they do decent grub. I'm starving – I thought there'd be food laid on. A few crisps and nuts isn't my idea of a buffet.'

God knows why, I didn't even hesitate. I wasn't usually one for jumping head first into things, but instinct told me he wasn't a weirdo, and I was grateful for the opportunity to escape. Reggie was otherwise engaged, and no one else would miss me.

We walked the couple of hundred yards to the pub, squelching through the slippery leaves that carpeted the pavement. The sky was clear and the moon full. Our breath hung in the still, damp air as we talked. I learned that his name was Jack Mason, and that he was twenty-four, three years older than me. He had recently qualified as a veterinary surgeon in Edinburgh, and had moved back to his native Midlands to look for work.

'I grew up on a farm, so I'm a country boy, really,' he explained. 'My older brother took over the running of the place when Dad hung up his hat, so that ruled that one out. I've always loved animals, and training to be a vet seemed like a good idea. I've got an interview at a practice near the city centre tomorrow. I want to

24

build up my CV and eventually open my own surgery, if possible.'

I was impressed. Attractive and cerebral, too. I didn't know too much about medical qualifications but was aware that veterinary degrees were a slog and notoriously difficult to come by. I felt like an airhead by comparison, and my 2:1 BA in English Literature, achieved courtesy of my thesis on the metaphysical poets of the seventeenth century, seemed ridiculously trivial.

'But I love poetry,' he had said, earnestly. 'Where would we be without the lovers and the dreamers!'

Despite our different academic leanings, we clicked. The pub was busy, but the atmosphere was relaxed and the background music agreeable. We found a table by the fireplace and shared a huge pizza and a bottle of wine. I found him easy to talk to and good company. He actually seemed interested in what I had to say, which made a pleasant change. I discovered that, like me, he had eclectic musical taste and a passion for Indian and Italian food.

We talked late into the night, and before going our separate ways, exchanged phone numbers. There was no parting kiss, no clasping of hands. But his eyes – *those eyes* – had held mine and there was an undeniable chemistry between us that gave me a shiver of excitement whenever I thought about him. I hardly dared believe that someone so attractive and intelligent would actually give me a second look, but there had definitely been *something* there. I was sure I hadn't imagined it.

Naturally, even though I was itching to call, I resisted, not wanting to appear too keen. But I found I kept thinking about him, his easy manner and sense of humour. Not to mention his mesmerising blue eyes and their unfeasibly long lashes . . . I wondered, too, if he'd been successful in getting his placement at the veterinary surgery.

When I didn't hear from Jack, I felt deflated. Almost a fortnight had passed since the house party and I was beginning to lose hope of ever hearing from him again. I moped around the flat like a lost soul. As a last resort, I even cleaned my room for want of something to do.

'What's up? Your face has been tripping you for days,' remarked Reggie. She looked up from filing her nails, her long, slender legs stretched out before her, slippered feet crossed at the ankle and propped on the coffee table. She was getting ready for another date – with yet another bloke. The Scouse pathology student had turned out to be a non-starter.

'He came on far too strong,' she'd told me the day after Zakir's party. 'We'd only been together three weeks. I'm *definitely* not looking to settle down just yet and the alarm bells sounded when he started talking ideal wedding venues. Time to give him the old heave-ho.'

I checked my phone for the umpteenth time in the space of a few minutes and let out an involuntary sigh.

'Come on – spill. What's the matter?' Reggie put down her nail file and regarded me with some concern. 'You have my undivided attention.'

'It's that guy I met at the party the other week. I thought he seemed pretty keen, but he hasn't called or texted me since. Silly really – I've only met him the once but I can't stop thinking about him.'

'The vet? Yeah, he was pretty hot. Not as fit as Akhmad, mind you.'

'Akhmad?' I arched an eyebrow. This was the third different name in the space of a week.

'Sex on legs. Owns a couple of restaurants – *and* he drives an Aston Martin. What's not to love!' She uncrossed her legs and stretched. 'Why don't you ring him? It's not like you, brooding over a fella. He must have been something else.'

'Well, I thought he was. Maybe he was only being friendly. Or maybe he's got a girlfriend. Oh, I don't know. I suppose he's out of my league, if I'm honest.' I slumped into the armchair and put my head in my hands.

'Now you're being daft! Just bloody call him – find out where you stand, and then you can meet up or move on. Go on – dig his number out and give him a bell. At least you'll know one way or the other.'

'I don't need to dig it out – I saved it in my phone, and I already know it by heart. That's how much of a saddo I am. But I can't ring him. I don't want to make a tit of myself. He's probably forgotten all about me by now, anyway.'

Reggie groaned. 'I give up. I hope you're going to snap out of this.' She examined her hands and resumed the filing. 'If you want something to do, go and crack open that sauvignon blanc that's in the fridge. We'll have a glass or two before Akhmad comes to pick me up.'

*

After she had gone out, I sat watching a banal film and polished off the rest of the wine, then moved on to cider, feeling disconsolate and very sorry for myself. I kept staring at my phone, willing it to ring. I toyed with the idea of calling Jack, but was sober enough to realise it wasn't a great idea when I'd had a few drinks. I would sound like a complete idiot – and a desperate one, at that. Eventually, I fell into bed, having resigned myself to the fact that I probably needed to write him off.

The next morning, I had a thumping headache. I took a shower, swallowed a couple of painkillers and ventured out to the corner shop for milk. Conspicuous by her absence, Reggie had clearly had a good time with sex-god Akhmad. As I turned the key in the front door, my phone rang in my pocket. I fished it out, expecting to see Reggie's name flash up on the screen.

My heart quickened – it was Jack.

He began by apologising profusely as, apparently, he'd misplaced my number, which, his phone battery having died, he'd scribbled on the back of an old bus ticket. It had only resurfaced when he went to the launderette and turned out his jeans' pockets. He had just discovered he'd got the job he was after and wanted someone to celebrate with.

'Would you like to come for a meal with me this evening? I've found a cracking Italian restaurant . . .'

*

Reggie breezed in, mid-afternoon, to find me flapping about what to wear.

'So, the hot vet called you, then? Hope it works out. We'll have to go out as a foursome. Akhmad was *amazing*.' She kicked off her shoes and flopped onto the settee, exhaling in ecstasy.

'I swear to God, Stina, I've never met anyone like him.

Such a gentleman. He's a bit older, I know, but the man is *class*. I can't wait to see him again . . .'

I suppressed the urge to groan, knowing from past experience that her initial enthusiasm rarely lasted beyond the first week, the second at most. After eulogising about Akhmad and their dream date for the best part of half an hour, she suddenly seemed to have noticed that I was agitated.

'Okay, I'll shut up now. Where's lover boy taking you, then?'

'Some Italian place in the city centre. Sounds very plush and I'm not sure I've got anything suitable in my wardrobe. He's picking me up at 7.30.'

'Come on, let's see what we can find. I'm sure we can make you look presentable – you don't scrub up too badly.' Seeing my worried expression, she laughed. 'I'm *joking*. You always look great.' She chewed her lip. 'I know, I've got that gorgeous striped Missoni minidress I picked up from the show in Milan the other week. It'll be a more respectable length on you, as you're a bit shorter than I am – and it's stretchy, so it should fit a treat. Wear it with those black heels you've got and my chunky wooden necklace. You'll look like the dog's bollocks.'

I wasn't sure whether I liked the comparison, but the dress was beautiful, and after doing my hair and make-up, I didn't look too bad.

Reggie stood back to examine the finished article as I posed awkwardly in the doorway.

'There you go, you look good enough to eat. He won't be able to keep his hands off you.'

'I might not want him to . . .'

She gave a lopsided smirk and raised an eyebrow.

The doorbell rang and my heart fluttered with excitement. 'That'll be him.' Suddenly I felt panic-stricken. What if I were to get all tongue-tied and make an idiot of myself?

Seeing my face, Reggie gave me a reassuring hug. 'You'll be just fine. Off you go. Knock 'im dead, kiddo.'

I opened the front door to find Jack dressed in a slim-fitting navy-blue suit and clutching a large bunch of pink roses. He looked even more handsome than I'd remembered, and his aftershave smelled delicious. I almost swooned.

'Wow! You look . . . lovely.' He smiled, his cheeks flushing a little as he handed me the flowers.

'Thank you. You don't look so bad yourself.'

'The taxi's waiting, if you're ready . . .'

'Let me just put these in water.'

Reggie came to the door. 'I'll do that.' She extended a hand, flashing Jack a dazzling smile as she relieved him of the bouquet. I groaned inwardly.

'I'm Reggie, Stina's flatmate. I think we met briefly at Zakir's party the other week.'

My heart plummeted. I watched anxiously, waiting for the usual puppy-dog expression that seemed to glaze over the faces of most men when confronted with my friend, the goddess. To my surprise, he just nodded politely. There was no widening of eyes; no awkward body language, nor any flicker of admiration or lust.

'Sorry, I'm afraid I don't remember. I must have had a fair bit to drink. Nice to meet you – again.' He turned, fixing me with those incredible eyes. 'Shall we?'

*

The evening passed all too quickly. The restaurant was very upmarket and contemporary, all glass and chrome, with huge mirrors and fabulous spiral-shaped crystal chandeliers. But I remember feeling surprisingly comfortable in my outfit and not at all out of place. After a couple of swiftly downed glasses of prosecco, I was slightly merry, and pleasantly relaxed. We seemed to have picked up where we left off on our previous meeting, and the conversation flowed effortlessly.

I helped myself from the bowl of olives on our table while we waited for the main course to arrive. Jack watched me with amusement. I stopped eating.

'What?'

'Crikey – were you hungry? You made light work of your starter.'

'It was to die for.' And it had been – fresh ravioli, with a divine vodka and tomato sauce. 'Plus, I skipped lunch, so yes, I was starving.' I omitted the fact that I'd been unable to eat, owing to the knots in my stomach.

'That's fair enough – it wasn't a criticism, just an observation. I like to see people enjoying their food. You can help me out if I'm struggling, then.'

'I may just do that!' I smiled. Even without the alcohol, all my earlier apprehension had melted away completely. It felt like the most natural thing in the world, sitting here opposite this man who seemed to be enjoying my company as much as I was his. I look back now and see that this has always been the pattern of our relationship: totally at ease in each other's presence, appreciating our surroundings and the same simple pleasures. Almost as if we were two halves of the same whole.

'So, you finally landed your dream job?'

'Well, not exactly. It's the post I applied for and it'll do as a stepping stone, but I want to work in a rural practice eventually. It's a good start though, and I'm pretty chuffed. It'll look good on my CV.' He took a sip of his drink. 'What about you? Have you got anything in the pipeline?'

'Not yet. I'm working on it, though. I've been doing a few shifts behind the bar in my local, just to keep me ticking over while I build my résumé, then I can start applying for freelance work.'

'If you fancy writing a piece on the misadventures of a novice vet, I'm your man.'

'No offence, but I was thinking more along the lines of history and culture, rather than blood, guts and bodily fluids.'

'Damn. And here's me thinking this could be my golden opportunity for fame and fortune.'

'I could try and weave you in somewhere, I suppose; have you pop up as the local vet visiting Lady What's-her-name in her country pile to tend to her ailing corgi . . .'

'Nah. Never been that keen on corgis. One bit me on the ankle once. Vicious little bugger.'

As the evening wore on, I learned more about Jack's home life and family. He was close to his parents, although he didn't have much to do with his older brother. He had been engaged once, to a girl he was at school with, but they had parted amicably by mutual agreement a short while after he started his degree.

'We both realised we wanted different things from life,' he explained. 'We were too young, really, and grew apart. Lauren's a lovely girl, but quite materialistic, and a bit of a neat freak. I don't think she'd have coped with me working late and coming home smelling of disinfectant and cat pee. And she's not really an animal person, either. Can't cope with pet hair at all. She used to hate sitting in the living room at the farm, in case it messed up her designer clothes.' He looked suddenly anxious. 'I never thought to ask – do you like animals?'

I laughed. 'I love animals. I never had a pet of my own and always wanted to take the class gerbils home at the end of term, but my mum would never allow them in the house. I'd really like a cat or a dog, but I'll have to wait until I've got my own place. Reggie's allergic.'

'Ah. Reggie.' He gave me a knowing look.

'What about her?'

'I did remember her, actually. She's getting a bit of a name for herself, I believe.'

I felt deflated. Another closet fan. 'What, with her modelling, you mean?'

'No! With the string of men she keeps dumping. As though she thinks she's too good for everyone. She's got a bit of attitude, hasn't she?'

'Listen, Reggie is . . . complicated.'

I felt the sudden need to defend my friend. I, for one, knew the impact an unsettled childhood could have on someone, and Reggie's had been particularly troubled. An abusive father and largely absent mother had taken its toll on both her and her younger brother, Luc, who had unfortunately fallen in with the wrong crowd and now had a criminal record. Her experiences in foster care were eye-watering. She kept her acquaintances at arm's length,

33

and it had taken me some time to fully gain her confidence and find out the extent of her deep-rooted issues.

'Let people get too close and they'll always shit on you eventually,' she had told me one night after a few drinks. 'I've had more than my fair share of it and I don't give anyone that opportunity any more. It's dog eat dog out there, Stina. Look after number one – that's my motto.'

I recalled one particularly harrowing incident she had told me about involving a foster father and shuddered.

'She's had a tough start in life. I think she finds it hard to trust people – and to commit. Hopefully she'll find someone to settle down with eventually. But she's a loyal friend and a good person.'

'I'm sure she is. You're clearly a good friend, too.'

'I don't like the idea of anyone getting her wrong, that's all. Anyway, I thought most people found her pretty irresistible . . .'

'Pretty, maybe. Irresistible? Definitely not. Whereas you, on the other hand . . .'

He reached across the table and clasped my hand, looking deep into my eyes.

'I knew I'd found a gem the first time I set eyes on you. Must have been the way you tapped your cigarette ash into that plant pot.' The hint of a smile played on his lips.

'What are you implying – that I'm some sort of slob?' I was only half joking. He couldn't possibly know – he hadn't seen my bedroom . . . yet. I reflected on my housekeeping skills and cringed inwardly.

His expression became earnest. 'Sorry – I try to be

funny and it comes out all wrong. It's a nervous thing. You couldn't be less of a slob if you tried. You're beautiful.' His cheeks coloured slightly. I was a little taken aback but found it endearing.

On impulse, and buoyed up by the prosecco, I leaned across the table and kissed him full on the mouth. I was never usually so bold. I don't know what came over me. He seemed startled at first. Then, taking my face in his hands, he kissed me back, and suddenly the restaurant seemed to blur into the background. I didn't care who was looking. At that moment, it was as though we were the only two people in the world.

And so it began. From then on, we became virtually inseparable, and even though we had only been together a couple of months, I didn't have to think twice when he asked me to move in with him. I had reeled in my big fish and I wasn't about to throw him back for anyone.

CHAPTER 3

Four years after meeting Jack and with the impending arrival of a child, both our lives had changed beyond recognition, and definitely for the better. He was keen to support me throughout my pregnancy; I lost a little blood in the early weeks, something which freaked me out at the time. The doctor later explained it was quite common, but it sent Jack into a flat spin and he persuaded me I didn't need to overstretch myself by taking on too much work, saying that we could manage on his wages, at least for the next eighteen months or so. I have to admit I *was* feeling very tired, and although I didn't want to stop writing completely, I was relieved at the thought of less pressure. Being prone to anxiety anyway, anything that would alleviate this was welcome and I was grateful not to have the additional worry of work on top of that of sustaining my own health for the sake of our baby.

While the majority of my work to date had been in the form of articles for various magazines, I'd had the odd lengthier commission, which was generally a bit more lucrative but inevitably involved more research and hence a lot more hard graft. The previous year I had ghost-written an autobiography for a successful young businesswoman from the West Midlands. It was an inspiring tale of triumph over adversity – she had left school with no qualifications but built up a successful recycling firm and had subsequently generated jobs within her community, plus raised not insignificant funds for local charities. I'd taken the somewhat unusual option of agreeing to receive a portion of the royalties rather than receiving an upfront fee, and thankfully the gamble had paid off. Royalties from this book were still trickling in and meant I had a little income to contribute to the bills. The plan was that I should resume everything in earnest once the baby had passed his or her first birthday, which suited me fine.

We settled well into our new home over the next few weeks and I'd almost forgotten about the dark-haired man I had seen in our neighbour's garden. Having been into the grocery store on a few occasions, I was now on nodding terms with many of the locals, which seemed like progress. At first we had felt like interlopers. Many of Avoncote's residents had lived in the village all their lives, and their families went back for generations. They seemed slightly wary of newcomers.

The lively couple who ran the shop, Judy and Nick, were friendly and helpful. In their late forties, their children having flown the nest, they had moved into the area from the city two years earlier seeking a more sedate pace of life. Judy was fitness-conscious and stylish, in sharp contrast to Nick, who favoured oversized tracksuits to accommodate the expanding waistline that betrayed his love for ale and the tempting home-made desserts that could be found in their fresh chilled section. She would tease him mercilessly, but always in good humour and their affection for one another was obvious. They seemed well suited and their banter was entertaining. Judy had told me with a wink that people were just coming to terms with the fact that the shop was no longer run by old Mrs Cornish, who had retired to the coast after forty years' tireless service to the community.

The shop had a small deli counter, which was filled with enticing products.

'If we haven't got what you want, do let us know and we'll try to get it in for you,' Judy told me on my first visit. 'I know it's not always convenient to have to drive into town, and we do our best to accommodate everyone if we can.'

Since becoming pregnant I'd developed a strong desire for smoked olives, which Reggie had introduced me to, and Nick had ordered me in a catering-sized jar of them. One Monday morning in June, having collected my much-anticipated goodies, I was leaving the shop clutching the huge jar when I almost collided with an auburn-haired girl of around my age. We had exchanged pleasantries on a few occasions. She was open-faced and seemed approachable, and I was keen to make a friend as, Mrs Barley and Judy aside, there wasn't really anyone locally I had got to know beyond the nodding and smiling stage. At times I felt a little lost and missed Reggie, but she lived too far away, and was too busy to nip in for a coffee and catch-up as we used to.

The girl's name, I had learned from Judy, was Lucy. I suspect that Judy was a little concerned that I appeared not to know anyone my own age in the area and she was hoping that we would hit it off. Lucy had a lively toddler, Alfie, and another on the way, although her bump being much larger than mine, I suspected the birth must be fairly imminent.

Spotting the olives, her mouth fell open. 'Oh my *God*, I didn't know they sold those. I *love* smoked olives.' She looked pointedly at my stomach and grinned. 'Better than coal, eh! I know some people have *really* weird cravings.'

I glanced down at myself and laughed, realising that my leggings accentuated my neat little mound. I was almost five months into the pregnancy now, but still hardly showing – or so I'd thought.

Alfie was tugging at her arm, his blue eyes bright. 'Sweeties, Mummy?'

'No, darling, they're not sweeties. You wouldn't like them.' His little face fell. 'Sweeties are very popular,' she told me, with a wink.

Lucy's voice was not unlike mine. It had been a surprise to find that the local accent was quite similar to my own Birmingham twang. I had wrongly (and ignorantly) assumed that everyone living in the countryside tended to have the stereotypical 'country bumpkin' lilt, but many people from the Stratford area seemed to speak with a familiar, if rather less broad, Midlands inflection. I found it warm and rather comforting.

'Would you like some of the olives?' I offered. 'I do love them, but it'll take me weeks to plough through this lot. I can put a few in a container for you, if you want to come back to the house with me. And I'm sure I can find something for Alfie, too – I don't think we've got any sweets, but Mrs Barley baked us some lovely biscuits the other day.'

Lucy seemed pleased. I waited while she bought a few groceries and we wandered back up the road together to Wisteria Cottage. As we walked through the gate, within seconds of being released from Lucy's grip, Alfie had strayed into Mrs Barley's garden and, to my horror, trampled across the beautiful lupins that lined the path and onto the immaculate lawn. Lucy cursed under her breath and hurriedly caught him by the arm. She dragged him back onto our side, glancing anxiously up at Rose Cottage as she did so. Next door's curtain twitched and I noticed the old woman peering from the edge of the window. She glared in Lucy's direction, then saw me looking and promptly withdrew from sight.

'Oops,' said Lucy as we went into the house. 'That won't have gone down well.'

'Kids will be kids.' I shrugged. 'No permanent damage done.' But I winced at the thought of Mrs Barley's reaction. Her garden was her pride and joy.

Jobie greeted us effusively as we came through the door, his tail slicing the air. He bounded up to Alfie, who squealed, wrapping his chubby arms round Lucy's leg in fright. She prised him away.

'It's all right, darling, he won't hurt you. He's a nice doggy. See?' She fussed the dog, who responded by licking her hand, then Alfie's face. The little boy chuckled.

'Can I get you a cup of tea?'

Lucy pulled a face. 'No thanks. I really can't drink tea at the moment – it's one of the things that makes me want to heave just now. Not too fond of coffee, either. But a glass of water would be great.'

I tipped a decent number of the olives into a plastic-lidded container and found a cookie for Alfie, who seemed highly delighted. We went into the living room. I switched on the TV and scrolled through to the children's channel for the little boy, who sat on the rug hugging his biscuit. Lucy looked out into the garden, peering down towards the summer house.

'How are you getting on with the old dear next door?' she asked.

'Mrs Barley? She's lovely. She's been really helpful, actually. I feel quite sorry for her, living there all alone.'

'Hmm, her husband's been dead a good few years now, hasn't he? I'm twenty-eight and it was before my time.' She paused. 'I think my mum remembers him. I've lived in Avoncote all my life and Mrs Barley's always been a bit of an enigma, keeps herself to herself. When we were little, we used to pretend she was a witch and play rat-a-tat ginger on her. Dare each other to shout swear words through her letterbox. A bit mean, I suppose. But kids will be kids.'

I nodded in agreement. Children can be vicious – I knew from experience. I was an only child, the product of a loveless marriage. My self-centred father walked out on us when I was only four. I found out some years later that he had moved to the United States, to start a new life in Chicago with the American woman he had been dating. We never saw him again. Although she didn't say as much, I don't think my mother ever wanted to. When I was very young, particularly when Mum was in a bad way, I would sometimes pray that he would come for me, whisk me away like some knight in shining armour. I thought, *hoped*, that as he had chosen my name, Stina, after his beloved Swedish grandmother, I must have been special to him once. But of course, he never did return. By the time I was twelve, I had resigned myself to the fact that he wouldn't ever be coming back. It hurt to think I was of so little significance to him.

My mum suffered badly from depression and was on prescription medication most of the time. Her moods were extreme. I remembered the high phases, lying rigidly awake half the night to the sound of her pounding the floor, sometimes talking to herself, or singing along loudly and tunelessly to her music. I would hear the songs of David Bowie and T.Rex pulsating through the walls, perhaps an attempt to transport her back to a happier time, before her wildly fluctuating emotions dominated her existence. Sometimes she would clean frenetically, oblivious to the noise she was creating, opening and closing doors, switching on the vacuum cleaner. The lows were worse. My abiding memory was of trying to rouse her from her stupor, to encourage her to leave her bed, where she would lie for days on end; to coax her to eat or drink *something*. Thinking back, the situation was pretty intolerable for a child.

Mum's moods, and our life in general, were unpredictable and chaotic. She was fundamentally a decent person; I firmly believe that. But her illness too often eclipsed the positive aspects of her character. I became necessarily acquainted with the functions of various household appliances from a very early age. My clothes were dirty and shabby, and my wardrobe was woefully limited. In the lower school, I had been the smelly kid in the class, the odd one out, shunned as a games partner; the grubby little girl nobody wanted to sit next to. Kids being what they are, one bright spark latched on to my name and dubbed me 'Stinka', and of course the name stuck.

My toes curl now as I remember one occasion when, not long after starting school, our class was taken, a few children at a time, into the school hall to inspect items of lost property that had accumulated. Everything had been laid out on trestle tables, and we all filed past to see if any of the things displayed were our misplaced belongings. Not fully understanding the object of the exercise, I helped myself to a pair of gloves, a coat and a bobble hat that took my fancy. The teacher recognised the items as belonging to other pupils, and I was made to hand everything back, much to the tittering delight of my classmates.

But in the brief periods when Mum was more 'normal', she was meticulous, almost a germaphobe, and very particular about me bathing, cleaning my teeth, putting on fresh underwear and socks. I liked the novelty of smelling of soap and talcum powder. It was then I realised the importance of keeping clean, and tried my best to be presentable in the vain hope that I would eventually fit in. My clothes were washed and ironed, albeit not very well, and I learned to shop unprompted for provisions and prepare basic meals before the age of ten.

Even though Mum's behaviour could be erratic and

downright scary at times, shouting and flying off the handle at the most innocuous of things, I was terrified of being taken into care. Whenever my teachers tried to wheedle information from me about our domestic arrangements, alarm bells would start to ring in my head. For me it was definitely a case of 'better the devil you know'. Somehow, we managed to fend off social services on the odd occasion they tried to intervene. Fortuitously (at least, I thought so at the time), they only ever seemed to call when Mum was having a relatively settled period.

I remember being taunted at school, the horrible things the other children used to say about her. Although I had learned basic hygiene, I suppose I was still scruffy, the kid in second-hand clothes; the one the others looked down on. Over time, I became hardened to their jibes and could shrug it off when they sniggered and called me names, mocking my neglected appearance, but when they said my mum was a mad cow, it really hurt.

In my hormonal state now, I often found myself on the verge of tears, and began to well up at the memory. Lucy must have realised from my expression that I was getting upset for some reason, and hurriedly changed the subject.

'When are you due? Your bump's very small – I think I'm having a baby hippo. I'm only six and a half months gone and already I feel like a beached whale.'

'Oh, come on, you're not that huge! I think it's normal to get bigger more quickly with your second, anyway. I'm not due until late October, so I think you're a bit further along than me.'

'Hmm – but not much.' She poked a finger into her

45

stomach, which sank like dough. 'I'm hoping a lot of it's water – don't fancy squeezing out anything bigger than Alfie was – it stung a bit, I can tell you!' She laughed. 'Ignore me – I don't want to put you off. They throw everything at you these days, painkiller-wise. I'm telling you, take whatever you can – my cousin had an epidural and she said it was a breeze after her first, when she'd had one of those daft "natural" births. I'm definitely having the works this time. Why anyone wants to go through the pain when you don't have to is beyond me.'

I had tried to push any thoughts of the labour to the back of my mind. So far, everything was going well at my antenatal visits; I had been anxious initially, even before the bleed, but as the weeks passed, I was becoming more relaxed and confident that the pregnancy was progressing smoothly. I'd signed up for the birthing classes in the later stages, so figured that would be soon enough to find out more about my options. I nodded and smiled to be agreeable, but was eager to talk about something else.

'So, you've lived in Avoncote all your life? Lucky you. It's a real hidden gem.'

Lucy pulled a face. 'Well, it's very safe, I'll give you that. So, it's lovely if you're a small child, or if you belong to the blue rinse brigade, I suppose. But on the downside, it's a bit dead – not a lot happens here. I think we'll probably move somewhere a bit livelier when Alfie and this one –' she indicated her bump '– are older. I still want to have a bit of fun before I'm ready to be put out to pasture.'

I frowned. 'I've seen enough of the city. I was brought up in a horrible, built-up area, and trust me, having to worry whether your car's going to be propped up on bricks when you get up in the morning, or if you're going to be mugged every time you're on the way home from the corner shop, it wears a bit thin after a while. Safe and boring has a lot to recommend it.'

'I suppose you've got a point. It's just that I crave a bit of action every now and then. Maybe I'll have got it out of my system in a few years. I don't want to get to forty and feel life's passed me by. Doesn't stop my other half enjoying himself, mind you. Perhaps that's why I feel like I'm missing out. He's off out most nights, these days.'

The swivelling of her eyes spoke volumes. Clearing her throat, she looked back out of the window. 'I haven't been round the back of these houses before. Well, in spite of being an oddball, she keeps that garden very nice, doesn't she, the old biddy?'

I bristled. This seemed quite disrespectful and I felt a sudden need to speak up for our neighbour. 'She can't do it herself – she's got bad arthritis, poor soul. There's a guy that comes – Bob, he's called. He seems nice.'

'Ah, yeh, I know of him. He's from the next village. He advertises his services on the noticeboard in Judy and Nick's – not that he needs to. I think word of mouth keeps him busy enough. Useful chap.'

'I know. Wish we could afford to pay him – we've got enough on our plate with all the work that needs doing on the house itself, and Jack's not really into gardening.'

I went over to the window and was stopped in my tracks. The dark-haired man I had seen previously was coming through the back gate again. He looked tired and careworn; lost in his own thoughts. Raising his eyes briefly towards Mrs Barley's bedroom window, he turned and entered the summer house, closing the door behind him. A large crow, one wing splashed with white, alighted suddenly on the building's portico. It stood perfectly still, almost as though it were standing guard. I felt my pulse begin to race.

'Some man's just gone into next door's garden. I don't know who he is, but he was here the other day.' Frantically I tried the handle to the French doors, but they were locked. I wanted to tackle him, find out what he wanted.

Lucy peered through the glass, then threw me a strange look. 'I can't see anyone.'

'He went into the summer house.' I rattled the door handle again in exasperation. 'For God's sake. Jack's put the bloody key somewhere. I'll see if it's in the kitchen.'

I rummaged through the drawers and eventually found the key, but when I went back into the living room, the door to the summer house was ajar and the man had vanished.

'Shit!'

I looked at a wide-eyed Alfie, who was staring up at me. 'Sit!' he repeated.

I clapped a hand to my mouth. '*Oops – sorry,*' I mouthed.

Lucy snorted with laughter. 'Don't worry. He hears a lot worse from his dad.'

'I wanted to speak to that bloke. Did you see where he went?'

She grimaced apologetically. 'No, sorry – I wasn't

48

really paying attention. Alfie dropped his cookie under the chair and I was on my hands and knees looking for it. Afraid I can't move that quickly at the moment with this in the way,' she said, patting her stomach.

Just like last time. I unlocked the door and rushed to the bottom of the garden, but like before, there was no one there. It was really odd – and a bit creepy. I went back into the house, locking the door behind me. My eyes panned round the outside space but there was definitely nobody lurking.

'That's freaked me out a bit. I'm not too thrilled about the idea of strange men just wandering into people's gardens, especially when they're right next to mine.'

Lucy frowned. 'It's a bit weird, if someone walked in off the street, I'll give you that. D'you think he knows the old woman?'

'I haven't a clue. Jack mentioned it to her last time he showed up, but she assumed it was the gardener. I'll try to snap him on my phone if he turns up again. Just in case.'

Lucy stayed for another half-hour or so. The excitement of the man's appearance soon forgotten, we chatted about the joys of pregnancy and the best creams for preventing stretchmarks; fairly mundane stuff. Soon she had to take Alfie home for lunch and his afternoon nap.

'Thanks very much for these,' she said with a grin, holding the pot of olives aloft. 'I'm looking forward to tucking into them later! I expect I'll see you at the antenatal clinic – do you go on Wednesdays?'

'Yes. I don't have to go this week, though. My next appointment will be my twenty-week scan, next Friday.'

'Ooh exciting. Are you going to ask what you're having?'

I shook my head. Jack and I had debated this, as he was keen to find out, but I was adamant that I didn't want to know the sex of the baby. It felt like having a beautifully wrapped present but already knowing what was inside.

'Want a surprise package, eh? Don't blame you. Well, I daresay I'll see you at the clinic at some point, if not before. I developed gestational diabetes with Alfie so they're keeping tabs on me and I'm there every week now, until the big event.' She took out her phone. 'Anyway, give me your number and I'll text you – you can come to mine next time.'

We swapped details and I showed her to the door. She nodded in the direction of Mrs Barley's cottage as she stepped outside. 'Hey, maybe she's got a fella on the sly – you never know . . .'

Suddenly the door to the old woman's cottage opened and she appeared, almost as if she had been waiting for us. I cringed, hoping she hadn't overheard what Lucy had said.

'Oh, hello, Stina. You've had visitors, I see.' She beamed at Alfie. 'What a dear little boy.' She leaned forwards, her gloved palms resting on the front of her thighs. 'And what might your name be, young man?'

Alfie sought the safety of his mother's legs and peeped out warily from behind them.

'My name is called Alfie,' he said shyly.

'Well, that's a lovely name. I've been baking today. Would you like a fairy cake, Alfie? They've got icing and rainbow sprinkles on!'

Alfie nodded vigorously and Mrs Barley disappeared for a moment, then reappeared with two small cupcakes in a waxed paper bag. 'One for you; one for Mummy.' She smiled broadly and turned to Lucy. 'They do love fairy cakes, the little ones, don't they?'

Lucy nodded and thanked her, shooting me an uneasy sideways glance.

'Don't let me interrupt. I'm just emptying my washing machine, anyway. Nice to meet you, Alfie.' She nodded at Lucy and smiled; but the smile didn't reach her eyes. 'See you later, Stina.'

She promptly retreated back into the house and closed the door. We stared after her.

'That was a bit random,' remarked Lucy. She peered into the bag and pulled a face. 'I'm not really a huge fan of fairy cakes, but this one here will polish them both off no bother.'

She paused. 'There were rumours, you know, about the old girl,' she said, almost conspiratorially, her voice lowered. 'I remember my mum saying, years ago. They reckon they weren't married, her and her fella. Everyone found them a bit odd. They'd moved from quite a distance away and no one round here knew anything about their past. All very cloak-and-dagger. Kept themselves to themselves – never had any family or friends visiting. A bit racy for the day, don't you think, living in sin like that – if there's any truth in it. She might look all prim and proper now, but maybe she was a bit of a goer in her time!'

I was taken aback – not so much by what she said, but more the derisory way in which she'd said it. Especially

51

since the old lady had been kind enough to give her little boy cakes. Rumours could be just that, and I wasn't one for gossip. It was so petty. I watched Lucy walk up the road and closed the door as she turned the corner. She had otherwise seemed nice enough, but I felt annoyed by her comments about Mrs Barley. The old lady had been so helpful to us and I didn't like to think that people were being unkind about her. Even if she hadn't been married, it was no one's business but her own even at that time, and who on earth would care about such things these days? Perhaps this was the downside of living in a small community: small-minded individuals.

I went back into the living room, and was about to let an eager Jobie outside when my hand froze on the door handle. I looked from left to right and beyond before unlocking the door, a sudden wave of anxiety coursing through me. Maybe the grass wasn't so very much greener here after all.

CHAPTER 4

When I was fourteen, my mother's increasingly erratic behaviour had eventually led to a diagnosis of schizophrenia and bipolar disorder, and she was put into a residential home for the mentally ill. Her inability to cope with day-to-day living had meant her option of remaining independent and 'caring' for me had become untenable. It was at this point that I went to live with her estranged aunt for a few years, before going to uni. My grandparents were dead and my mother had no siblings; my father was out of the equation, and his miserable family had severed all ties with us after he left. Aside from foster care, I had really no other choice. At least she was a relative.

Auntie Jane had never married and lived alone in the little terraced council house where she was raised, on the outskirts of Birmingham. She had lost her childhood sweetheart, Gordon, in the Battle of Dunkirk, and never really got over it. She was very old-fashioned in her views, and vociferous in her disapproval of the behaviour of modern youth. I don't suppose I was her ideal house guest. I had been self-sufficient for many years and resented being told what to do and when to do it. We rubbed each other up the wrong way, and there were endless arguments about how I should conduct myself, what I should wear, what time I should be home after a night out. All the usual adolescent rebellion stuff. My mother had gone off the rails in her teens, and I think from the outset her aunt was worried that I would finish up in a similar predicament. I almost did.

We had what I'd describe as a very shaky first twelve months together, and thinking back, my behaviour was probably enough to try the patience of a saint. Finally freed from the burden of my mother's care, I felt like a caged animal liberated for the first time. For an elderly woman with no experience of raising a child, it must have been a nightmare. But in spite of everything, we muddled through somehow, and with Auntie Jane's constant emphasis on the importance of a good education and how it could open doors, I started to knuckle down and work hard at school. I was determined not to let my formative years drag me down and ruin the rest of my life. Despite feeling irked by Auntie Jane's constant, repetitive reminders of how I should speak and behave, I found myself gradually conforming to her ideal of what a young woman should be: studious, well read, well mannered. Almost a throwback to a repressed 1940s teenager who had stepped straight from childhood into the finished adult version. In a word: boring.

I was worried for a time that, given Mum's history, I might have a genetic predisposition towards developing a mental illness, but when I finally voiced my fears, Auntie Jane was quick to allay them.

'Your silly mother dabbled with drugs in her teens. LSD, I believe. It's common knowledge that it can have an adverse effect on the brain in the long run. No one else in the family ever developed the type of problems she's had to the best of my knowledge, and even though they're a rum bunch, I'm sure there's no history of psychiatric disorders on your father's side, either. Leave the drugs well alone and you'll have no cause to worry.'

And I did. Drugs had never appealed to me, and hearing this was enough to turn me off the idea of taking anything mind-altering for life.

Visiting Mum at the home had become an ordeal; she seemed suspicious of me now and refused to make eye contact. She would rant and pace incessantly, sometimes throwing things. Once, she narrowly missed my head with a heavy iron doorstop. The rest of the time she was sleeping, exhausted from her perpetual activity and the amount of medication in her system.

To all intents and purposes, Auntie Jane had replaced her as my family. While she was never demonstrative and our coexistence was not without its tensions, we tolerated one another and I suppose, in a way, I grew to respect her. For the first time in my life, even though she was not without her faults, I had a relatively positive family role model. Before retiring, she had worked in a library, and instilled in me a love of literature and poetry. I found solace and inspiration in the many books she had acquired over the years. It was this influence that led to my choice of degree.

'You can't beat a good book, my girl. They take you out of yourself,' she had told me once. 'I don't know what I'd have done without my books over the years.'

As I got older, however, I began to feel increasingly stifled under Auntie Jane's roof. Probably as a result of living alone for so long, she was intolerant of mess and noise, and liked everything to be clean and tidy at all times. She was also pedantic (to the point of being oppressive) about etiquette and grammar, constantly correcting my speech in exasperation ('it's different *from*, Stina, not *to*') and reminding me of the importance of creating a good impression when meeting new people, particularly a prospective employer. And how, despite the modern bid for gender equality, deep down a man would always want a woman to care for him and be the homemaker.

I realise now that her irritating perpetual reminders have shaped the person I have become, the way I speak and act; that her rather suffocating influence is something I will never be able to completely shake off. Spending little of my free time mixing with my peers, I suppose that having an elderly woman as my main source of company, I gradually developed an old-fashioned way of thinking. Throughout my time in the upper school (and subsequently university), tutors would often remark that I was an old head on young shoulders. I didn't take it as a compliment. Eventually, keen to gain some independence, but under the pretext of the convenience of the location, I moved out and into Reggie's flat in the final year of sixth form. I never looked back.

By the end of my second term at university, my visits to Auntie Jane had gradually dwindled and I hadn't been home for a few weeks. I went back to visit her one dismal Sunday afternoon late in March. The curtains were drawn. I entered via the back door, as usual. As I went to turn the key in the lock, the neighbour, a plump middle-aged woman called Karen who had moved in with her family a couple of years earlier, came out into her garden. She looked concerned.

'She all right? We've been away for the week and since we got home, I haven't seen her out and about at all – she's usually out there sweeping and doing – you know how she is. I've knocked a few times but there's been no reply. I didn't have your number or I'd have rung you . . .'

My heart began to thud. Karen looked on anxiously as I stepped into the kitchen and called out, but there was no response. The house was eerily silent. Gingerly, I began to make my way into the hall, Karen following close behind. A feeling of dread crept through me, my forehead beading with cold sweat.

The passageway was gloomy anyway, but the heavy curtain that hung over the front door was pulled across, plunging everything into darkness. I didn't want to turn on the light, afraid of what might confront me. Gradually my eyes grew accustomed to the dim, and I saw it then: an odd bundle, huddled at the foot of the stairs.

I caught my breath. Auntie Jane was lying on her back, limbs askew. It was as though she had perhaps overindulged and slipped into unconsciousness where she had flopped drunkenly to the floor.

But my elderly aunt was teetotal.

As I drew nearer, I covered my mouth and nose with my sleeve, almost retching. The smell was putrid, something akin to a combination of rotten meat and eggs. I could see that her eyes were partially open and her lips parted, forming a stiff oval. I pushed the curtain aside, allowing a narrow shaft of light to fall on her face. There was a purple gash on her head and a crust of blood had trickled from her mouth and dried onto her cheek. I wafted away a single fly, which was crawling across her forehead. Tentatively, I reached out to touch the crepy skin of her hand. She was stone cold, like a marble effigy. I had never seen a dead person before. I retracted my own hand in revulsion and backed away.

*

A post-mortem revealed that her neck had been broken in the fall. She had been dead for over seventy-two hours. It was deemed likely that she had lost her footing on the stair carpet runner, worn smooth and slippery over the years. I tried to take comfort from the fact that she hadn't suffered; that she would have died instantly. But the image of her like that was engraved onto my memory. I could still picture her ashen face, waxy and expressionless, her silver hair fanned out behind her on the old green and gold Axminster. It made me shiver. I hated the fact that this last sighting of her had overshadowed my recollection of Auntie Jane as she had been in life, left this ghoulish imprint on my consciousness. I was overcome with a deep feeling of self-reproach in the knowledge that she had died in such a way, and had lain there cold and alone for days. She had taken me in when I needed someone and I hadn't been there for her at the end. I felt angry with myself and a terrible sense of remorse.

I think that Mrs Barley reminded me of her in some small way, and it made me the more determined to stand up for her. Maybe in some selfish way it was to assuage my own guilt.

CHAPTER 5

I had recently begun work on a feature about Avoncote for a local magazine. Although I didn't want to embark on anything too ambitious, a nice little article was something I felt I could manage, plus it was something else to focus on, apart from the house and my pregnancy. Having approached *Avon Life*, a popular regional monthly publication, with an idea about exploring the history behind various local myths, legends and traditional festivals, the suggestion had been met with enthusiasm by the editor to whom I pitched it. It was agreed that the article would go out in the October edition to coincide with Halloween and all things spooky, and since it was only the second week of June, I had plenty of time in which to complete it.

Long-held traditions were something that fascinated me, and having attended the May Day celebrations in the village only a week after we had moved in, thoughts had started turning in my head of how these things must have developed over time.

May Day that year had brought a gloriously sunny morning and most of the villagers had been out in force on the green. There was a buzz of anticipation in the air. The pond had been cordoned off and various stalls selling local produce had been set up. Traditional fairground attractions such as a coconut shy, swing-boats and a wooden helter-skelter had been erected, with a small, brightly painted merry-go-round for the youngest children. People had gone to great lengths to adorn the fronts of their homes with flowers, scattering primroses across the thresholds (I was later to learn that this would apparently ward off evil fairies, who were said to be particularly active in the first three days of May), and at midday, a carnival procession of floats decorated with beautiful floral displays had begun to move slowly through the village. This all culminated in the arrival of the Queen-of-the-May-to-be, a petite teenage girl with long brown hair who was dressed in a flowing white gown, in a carriage drawn by two white horses.

Along with a huge number of other people, we had stood at the roadside with a sense of expectancy, still feeling very much like tourists as the procession passed by, when a hush fell over the throng lining the streets.

Beaming from ear to ear, the prospective May Queen alighted from the carriage and was guided by two small boys, who had been waiting eagerly to perform their duty, to a 'throne' of flowers set on a low podium on the periphery of the green. Another slightly older teenager, presumably last year's model, mumbled a little shakily into a megaphone and then carefully anointed the new queen with a floral 'crown', kissing her on the cheek as she did so.

A whoop went through the crowd, and the children who had been poised around the maypole clutching their coloured ribbons began to skip in an obviously well-rehearsed circle, weaving an intricate pattern with the strips of fabric, singing and jangling small tambourines as they went. The song finished and the children ground to a halt, looking round as if not quite sure what to do next. There was some sudden jostling from the onlookers, and as though this was their cue, the children dropped their ribbons and broke away from the maypole, dragging another laughing girl forward. She must have been about twelve, with long fair curls and an angelic little face. People began to applaud and the girl went to stand coyly beside the newly crowned May Queen and her previous incarnation. The three of them joined hands and everyone cheered again.

'What's happening?' I asked the middle-aged woman to my left, who was applauding half-heartedly.

'They've picked her out to be the next Queen of the May. That's my neighbour's youngest, Katie. Butter wouldn't melt to look at her, but a right little minx she can be. Her mum will be thrilled, though.'

'How exciting for her! They never had anything like this where I was brought up. It's a lovely tradition.'

I took out my phone and began to snap away, when an elderly man in front of me turned and shot me a disapproving look.

'Bad luck that,' he remarked tersely.

'Pardon?'

'Taking a picture of the three of them like that. Won't end well for the one in the middle, you mark my words.'

Baffled, I turned to the woman I had spoken to for an explanation and she wrinkled her nose. 'There's some folk believe that if you take a photo of three people together, the one in the centre will soon die,' she said in a lowered voice. 'I think it's codswallop, but maybe best not tempt fate, eh?'

The man continued to glare at me, so I put away my phone and hooked my arm through Jack's.

'Let's go and see what they're selling on the stalls. I fancy a nice cake to have with a cup of tea later.'

Hand in hand, we milled around the green for a couple of hours, attracting curious looks from some of the locals. But the atmosphere was vibrant, the sky a glorious blue, and I was revelling in our new surroundings. It hardly seemed possible that this was all being laid on only a stone's throw from our front door. The smell of frying onions and doughnuts filled the air, fuelling my appetite. There were stalls selling a variety of mouth-watering goodies, and wine from a local vineyard, which I would have loved to sample. Instead, I bought a warm samosa to stave off the hunger pangs, and for later, a homity pie, a huge home-made chocolate sponge and some blackcurrant jam.

I suddenly had the suspicion I was being watched and turned to catch one woman staring across at me from a stall selling scented candles, various polished stones and handmade Gothic-looking jewellery. Instead of averting her eyes, she continued to observe me unnervingly.

'I'm just going to have a look over there,' I told Jack,

who had sparked up a conversation with a dapper elderly man in a tweed three-piece suit, trying to drum up interest in a variety of gins from a small local distillery. Attempting to look casual, I wandered towards the woman, who was still watching me. Maybe she thought she recognised me from somewhere.

'Hello. Do I know you?' I ventured.

The woman appeared suddenly flustered and her mouth dropped open. She was around forty, dressed in a sort of kaftan, with short dark hair framing her elfin face and a tattoo depicting a crescent moon in scrollwork winding around her wrist.

'No, no. You have an unusual aura, that's all,' she said eventually.

'I'm sorry?'

'I see auras around people. Yours is . . . distinctive.'

I was taken aback. 'Oh? In what way?'

She exhaled deeply. 'Hmm. You give off mainly a blue haze, and green – which is good. But you also have a lot of dark red light around you – and there are holes in it. There's a fair bit of conflict going on there. Something bad has happened to you – am I right?'

I folded my arms across my chest. 'I'm sure something bad has happened to most people at some time in their lives.'

'Yes, but this feels like something *really* bad. Like something you're being weighed down by.' She continued to study me with interest.

I felt a little angry that this woman, who didn't know me from Adam, appeared to be looking at me as if I were some sort of specimen. 'You're mistaken. There isn't anything in particular,' I snapped. 'I'm perfectly happy, thank you.'

She held up both palms towards me defensively. 'I didn't mean to cause any offence,' she said hastily. 'Maybe I was wrong, perhaps it's just the light then. I suppose things could be a bit distorted by the canopy.' She indicated the cover over her stall.

I nodded and turned to walk away.

'Aren't you the new people in the cottage next to Mrs Barley's?' she called after me.

I paused. 'That's right, we only moved in last week.'

Her expression hardened. 'Just you keep an eye on her. Now there *is* an aura there's no mistaking.'

I shook my head and walked back towards Jack, feeling annoyed. I hoped there weren't many more people like her in the village. I had been having a lovely time and she had put a damper on my mood.

Jack looked round as I clutched at his arm.

'Can we go home now? I'm feeling very tired all of a sudden.'

He smiled and slid an arm round my waist. 'Of course.' He lifted up a carrier bag. 'That old boy was very persuasive – I've treated myself to some rhubarb gin! Come on, I'll make us a cup of tea and we can have some of that cake.'

I glanced back over my shoulder as we left the green. The woman was still staring after me.

*

I had been busily researching online for my article, and Jack had ordered me a wonderful but enormous hardback book from Amazon, hailed in its five-star reviews as 'the bible for historians of Avoncote and its environs'. I was keen to start making notes. I kept one cautious eye open for further evidence of Mrs Barley's mysterious visitor, but found it nonetheless quite therapeutic, having views out onto the garden from the table where I placed my laptop. It was a much nicer working space than the dingy, windowless box room I had used as an office in our old flat. Jobie seemed content stretched out at my feet, his chin on his paws.

Reading about the history of somewhere I could actually now relate to made the exercise more personal, and I was determined to uncover some interesting facts about the area. To be truthful, I hoped it might win me some local approval, too. I wanted to make friends within the community, and to feel that we had been accepted as fully fledged members, not outsiders. By the end of the afternoon, I had written almost a thousand words, and felt quite a sense of accomplishment.

After taking Jobie for a walk up to the pond, I lay on the settee for a while, waiting for Jack to return from work. I still kept an eye on the French doors, but there was no sign of Mrs Barley's dark-haired intruder. A large crow startled me as it landed on the fence and hopped up towards the house. It studied me with interest for a few moments, before disappearing into next door's garden. I shuddered. There was something about crows and magpies that left me with a creeping sense of unease, as though they were some sort of harbingers of doom. Probably the result of an overly fertile imagination.

Jack was later than ever coming home that day. He

walked in through the door, his shoulders sagging, and I realised immediately from his face that something was awry. Jobie rushed to greet him in his usual ebullient way and Jack stooped to scruff his fur, then wrapped his arms round the dog's neck. His eyes looked red and raw.

'Hey, what's up? Has something happened?'

He looked up at me, his face etched with misery.

'Shit day. *Really* shit day. Someone brought in a young Labrador – beautiful dog. He had run into the road and been knocked down by a Transit van. We worked on him for hours but we couldn't save him. The injuries were horrendous.'

My heart went out to him. 'Oh, that's awful. I'm so sorry. But you did your best.'

'Yes, that's just it. I did my best, but it wasn't good enough. The guy who brought him in was distraught. Someone's lost their best buddy and it's because I failed them. I feel fucking awful about it.'

Gently, I placed a hand on his arm. 'Hey, you weren't driving the van. You can't beat yourself up when something like this happens. You're a brilliant vet – so good with the animals and their owners. Look at the number of cards you get from grateful clients when things go right – which they usually do. But it's the nature of the job. There'll always be times when not everything goes according to plan. You've just got to pick yourself up and get back on that horse, because there are so many more needy animals out there that you can help – and you will.'

He forced a smile, but it didn't reach his eyes. 'Thanks for the vote of confidence. At least you still believe in me.'

I hugged him tightly and he buried his face in my shoulder. He felt rigid. I hoped that at any moment the tension would be released and the floodgates would open, but he seemed to be holding back. His pain was tangible and it was awful to see. I knew how tired he had been lately, putting in long hours to bring in some extra cash, and I suspected this had been the final straw.

'I wanted to do this job to help, to make a difference,' he said, his voice quiet and strained. 'I've lost animals before, but this one's really got to me. I kept thinking how we'd have felt if it'd been Jobie . . .'

The very idea brought tears to my eyes. I shook my head. 'Don't. Come on, I think you could do with a drink. Take your mind off it all. D'you fancy going to the pub this evening? We can grab a bite to eat in there, too – it'll make a nice change.'

He thought for a moment and let out a huge sigh. 'Yeah, you're probably right. I'll only wallow if I sit here all evening. Let me get a shower first.'

*

We hadn't been into The Green Man before, but we had heard that dogs were usually welcome, so we took Jobie along. He seemed to sense that Jack wasn't himself and was much calmer than usual, walking at his side and constantly looking up at him. As we came through the door, all eyes were on us as we made our way to the bar. I felt awkward and somewhat conspicuous. It was quite busy for a weeknight. I looked around, taking in the surroundings. The ceiling was low, with ancient oak beams bearing the remnants of strange, long-carved shapes, and there

69

were lots of interesting nooks and crannies. A welcoming fire crackled in an ancient stone fireplace, and the undulating timber-framed walls were adorned with fading sepia photographs depicting the village at the turn of the twentieth century. The interior had recently been refurbished, the soft furnishings replaced and the seating area carpeted, with the smell of paint still hanging in the air.

'Evening.' The bartender greeted us with a smile. He was a slightly built, diminutive man of about forty, unshaven, his spiky dark hair peppered with grey.

'Hello. Are you serving food?' Jack looked down at Jobie, who was gazing up at him adoringly. 'It is okay to bring the dog in, isn't it?'

'Of course – on both counts! Grab yourselves a couple of menus and find a seat, and I'll send someone to take your orders. I'm Steve, by the way. Haven't you just moved in next door to old Mrs Barley?'

Jack's bemused expression provoked an amiable laugh from the man. 'I've seen you coming out of the house a couple of times. Any unusual activity round here doesn't go unnoticed, you know. We take the idea of "Neighbourhood Watch" to a whole new level in Avoncote. There was great excitement in the village when the "Sold" sign went up.'

They shook hands across the bar.

'That's right. I'm Jack – this is my wife, Stina.'

Steve nodded at me, smiling. 'Pleased to meet you both. Hope we'll be seeing you in here often in the future – it's nice to have some fresh blood in the village.'

We found a table near the fire and pored over the surprisingly extensive menu, both of us plumping for vegetable fajitas. Jobie flopped down at the side of the table, his tongue lolling. Jack ordered a pint of locally brewed real ale and I sipped a tropical fruit juice without any real enthusiasm. Steve from the bar kindly brought over a bowl of water for Jobie, who lapped it up appreciatively. I looked over to see a middle-aged couple at the next table staring at us, but meeting my eyes, they bowed their heads and continued their conversation in lowered voices.

'Christ, anyone would think we'd got two heads or something,' I whispered to Jack. He smiled weakly, but still looked despondent.

A pretty, curvaceous young woman with long bleached blonde hair and heavy make-up brought us our food, smiling a little too flirtatiously at Jack. I was used to noticing girls furtively giving him admiring glances, and rather than feeling smug, it always unsettled me. I was full of self-doubt and always worried deep down that he was too good for me. Ever modest, I don't think Jack had any real concept of his own appeal to the opposite sex. He seemed oblivious to the effect he often had on women, which I found simultaneously endearing and frustrating.

Before we had moved to Avoncote, one of the veterinary nurses at his former practice had been overly attentive and started bombarding him with texts that weren't work-related. Although in my heart I knew that she wasn't a threat, it had caused arguments between us. It was exasperating that, initially at least, he didn't appear to have realised that she was coming on to him, nor that I might find it unacceptable. Thankfully the

71

situation was resolved when the girl eventually left abruptly and moved away. I didn't find out why she had gone, but it was an enormous relief that she had stopped pestering him.

In my current state I felt more insecure than ever, and decidedly unattractive. I glared at the waitress as she sashayed away from the table.

'You could write your name in that foundation,' I commented, cringing as I realised how bitchy it must have sounded.

'Mee-*oow*.' Jack grinned. '*You* don't need make-up.' His expression suddenly serious, he cocked his head to one side and stared at me. He reached out to touch my face. 'A natural beauty.'

I felt a warm glow, but threw my napkin at him. 'Ooh, you're such a smoothie. Eat your fajitas.'

I was glad that he had agreed to dine out. As the evening wore on, he became more relaxed and I was hoping that the unfortunate Labrador incident had been forgotten, for the time being at least. The pub had filled up even more, and the hum of conversation and the jukebox playing mellow songs from the Sixties and Seventies made for a pleasant atmosphere. We still attracted the odd inquisitive glance from some of the locals, but the novelty of our presence seemed to have worn off after a while and most people were friendly, nodding and smiling when we caught them looking in our direction. It felt as though we were gradually easing our way in.

'How was your day?' asked Jack, taking a huge bite of his tortilla.

'I've been working this afternoon, but earlier I met

a girl from the village, Lucy. She came round with her little boy this morning – he's a sweet little thing. I gave her some of those olives Nick ordered me in at the shop.'

'Oh yeah? What's she like?'

'She seems okay. She's expecting, too – due before me, though.'

He studied me for a moment. 'Just "okay" then? You don't sound very enthused.'

'No, she was nice enough, I suppose. It's just that – well, I thought she was a bit off about Mrs Barley.'

'Why?'

'Just a bit gossipy – she reckons that people round here think Mrs Barley and Frank weren't actually married. Not that it should matter to anyone. And – I don't know, the way she spoke about the old lady seemed disrespectful, that's all. There was that annoying woman at the May Day fete not long after we arrived, too . . .'

'What woman?'

I hesitated. 'Oh, just one of those New Age oddballs on a stall, she made some derogatory comment about her.' I neglected to mention the woman's impressions of me.

'Oh, right. One of those.' He raised an eyebrow.

'I can see what Bob was on about, though. He said some people don't like her; God knows why. Ignore me – I'm probably overly touchy at the moment, what with the baby and everything.'

I suddenly remembered about the man. With Jack being so upset, it had almost slipped my mind. 'That bloke showed up again this morning – in next door's garden. He'd cleared off before I could collar him.'

He put down his fajita, his face suddenly serious. 'Did you mention it to Mrs Barley?'

'No. It sounded as though she was pretty dismissive when you spoke to her so I didn't want to say anything. She might think I'm paranoid – or it might start to worry her, living on her own. I am a bit rattled by it though, to be honest. I don't like to think that there's a random weirdo wandering round the neighbourhood. I wish Mrs Barley would get a lock fitted on her gate. Even if ours isn't left open, he looks able-bodied enough to hop over the fence if he had a mind to.'

'I'm sure Jobie would see him off if he did. But if he turns up again, ring the police. And keep that bloody door locked – I'd made sure it was before I left the house this morning, I always do.'

'So, you've been worried too, then?'

'Look, I'm sure there's an innocent explanation, but when you're on your own I do worry a bit. You're very precious to me, you know. And after all, who'd walk the poor dog if someone kidnapped you?' He pushed his tongue firmly into his cheek.

I pretended to kick him under the table.

'You bugger! I'll remember that. And thanks for the kidnapping suggestion – that one hadn't even crossed my mind until now. As for Jobie, he'd probably lick him to death. I've never met such a soppy dog.'

'Which is why we love him – and why we know he'll be wonderful around the baby when he or she arrives.' He smiled, squeezing my hand across the table. 'Thanks for suggesting coming out tonight. I feel a lot better about – well, you know. I guess I'll have to toughen up a bit and put it down to experience.'

'Don't toughen up. It's good that you care so much. That's one of the things I love about you.'

His eyes locked with mine. The brief silence was broken by a shared splutter of laughter.

'Christ, listen to us,' I said. 'We've turned into a right mushy old pair. How did that happen?'

'Maybe that's what starting a family can do to you. Makes you realise what's important.' He nodded towards my plate. 'D'you want that last wrap – or can you spare it for the love of your life?'

We finished our meal, and were getting up to leave when a wizened elderly man in a flat cap, who had been sitting at the bar, hobbled purposefully over to us. His walking stick clicked against the tiled floor.

'You the new folk in Wisteria Cottage?' he enquired bluntly. One of his red-rimmed rheumy eyes had a marked divergent squint. He scanned our faces curiously, as if we had descended from another planet.

Jack looked amused. 'Yes, that's right. Why do you ask?'

The man seemed to soften. 'Oh, I knew the old owners back in the day. Ted Burrows and his wife. I went to school with him. They moved away over thirty years ago. It passed to their children after they popped their clogs, but they never wanted to move back in. Don't suppose the batty old bird next door helped matters. It's been rented out ever since. Lots of different people have come and gone, but no one's ever taken care of the old place properly. I saw the Burrows' son round there a few months ago – said it had become an albatross round his neck and he wanted shut of it. Good that someone's finally going to lick it back into shape.'

'Well, I hope we won't disappoint. We've got a list of jobs a mile long, but we'll do our best.'

'I hope you will. Whatever they say about Virginia Barley, at least she keeps that house up to scratch. We've a lovely village here and it's a shame when there's a property letting the side down. But I'm sure you'll soon get it looking decent again.' These last words were said pointedly, as though he were issuing an instruction. 'Good evening to you both.' He doffed his cap and clicked off towards the door.

We stared after him, speechless. I looked at Jack and we both shrugged. 'That's us told, then,' I said. 'We'd better pull our fingers out!'

Jack laughed. 'I'm sure he meant well. I know what he means about letting the side down, though. But we've made a start with the garden and once there's a bit more cash rolling in, we can begin to tackle the other things. I think the priority has to be that roof, before the winter sets in.'

'Don't take too much notice of old Bill. He's harmless enough,' the man behind the bar said, having obviously overheard.

I was baffled. 'Why has everyone got it in for Mrs Barley? She's been really pleasant with us. I don't get it.'

He shrugged. 'Search me. I moved here in the late 1990s and it's been a bit of a puzzle to me, too. There've been a few people who've made odd remarks about her, but no one's really gone into the whys and wherefores. I've never actually asked anyone about it. You never see the old dear out and about – I don't think she ever leaves that house any more. Even has her groceries delivered. Out of sight, out of mind.'

Jack shook his head. 'Nowt so queer as folk, as they say. Well, she's always been fine with us, so unless she puts a foot wrong, I won't be taking any notice.'

'Best policy. By the way – you were saying you need your roof doing? My mate's a thatcher – I can give you his number if you like. He's very reasonable and reliable. I've got his details in here somewhere.' Steve sifted through the paperwork on a shelf beneath the till and produced the man's business card. 'Tell him Steve from The Green Man recommended him to you. He did the roof here a few months ago and did an amazing job. He might even give you a discount.'

Thanking Steve, we stepped out into the night. It was a beautifully temperate evening. The sky was clear and littered with stars, the moon high and full. Hand in hand, we walked back across the road to Wisteria Cottage. I looked up at Mrs Barley's house, but it was already in darkness. It had turned 10.30 p.m. and I was shattered, but in a good way. As soon as my head hit the pillow, I was asleep.

*

I woke with a start and peered at the bedside clock; it was just after 4 a.m. There was a strange noise coming through the wall from next door. It was like an animal keening. I sat up, my senses heightened. I realised it was the sound of someone crying. Jack stirred slightly and turned over, but he was still sleeping. Once he had dropped off, he was usually out for the count until the bleep of the alarm sounded. The sleep of the guiltless.

I slid out of bed and padded across the floor. I pressed an ear to the wall. It sounded like Mrs Barley's voice. Between sobs she seemed to be talking – no, almost chanting to herself, although I couldn't make out the words. It was a primal, guttural sound and it gave me an awful gut-wrenching sensation. I was tempted to knock on her door, hug her; offer some human contact, some small comfort.

The voice became louder, the anguished tone infused now with anger. I only caught the tail end of what she was saying.

'But why did you do it? How could you have done such a thing?'

And then my heart all but stopped. A male voice responded, its timbre clear and deep.

'*I'm sorry.*'

A chill ran through me. I strained to listen, wondering who could be in there with her. Suddenly, the crying ceased and all was quiet once more. I wondered if I ought to go round and check she was all right. But everything seemed peaceful now. And what would I say, anyway? *Did you have a strange man in your bedroom?* I rationalised and wondered if it were possible she'd been watching TV or listening to the radio. Yes, that must have been what I'd heard. Maybe it hadn't been her crying at all. It was the only logical explanation.

I crawled back into bed and snuggled up to Jack. He

mumbled in protest as I warmed my cold feet against the backs of his legs, but he didn't wake properly. Soon I was asleep once more. I dreamed of a joyful Mrs Barley, enveloped in the arms of a dark-haired man whose face I could not see.

The next day I woke with a pounding headache – and a strange sense of disquiet.

CHAPTER 6

A fortnight had passed. I hadn't seen anyone trespassing in the garden since, and any time I had seen Mrs Barley she seemed perfectly fine, so I came to the conclusion that what I'd heard through the wall that night must have been a TV or radio programme after all.

Mrs Barley was clearly very interested in my pregnancy, which at twenty-one weeks was now quite evident. Having had various blood tests and my twenty-week scan, confirmation that all appeared to be well with the baby had allayed any initial anxieties I'd had. I was more relaxed about everything and reassured each time I felt that familiar butterfly sensation of movements from within. Mrs Barley fussed round me and kept offering to prepare various weird herbal tisanes to stave off heartburn or nausea. While I wasn't keen to take anything in case it might affect the baby in any way, it was touching that she wanted to help and she always seemed friendly and pleasant. I couldn't understand why everyone seemed to have it in for her.

Monday started as a promisingly clear late June day, but soon gave way to wet, miserable weather. I was at a loose end as my back had been playing up, an annoying side effect of the pregnancy. I had been concerned when it first began but soon accepted that it wasn't a sign of anything being wrong, just a symptom of the extra pressure on my pelvis. Nonetheless, it had left me unable to tackle any of the jobs around the house I knew I ought to be doing. I decided to read for a while and settled myself down in the living room with the book Jack had bought – *Avoncote Through the Centuries* – keeping my laptop to hand in case I felt the need to write any more notes. I had several weeks before I was required to submit my article to the magazine, but was conscious that pregnancy doesn't always go according to plan, so wanted to do as much as I could when time (and my state of mind) allowed. 'Never put off until tomorrow . . .' was an attitude fostered in me by Auntie Jane.

The wind whistled eerily through the eaves and rain battered the window. I was glad to be snug and safely indoors. I eased myself out of the chair and went upstairs to drape the clothes I had just washed over the clothes horse on the landing. A steady dripping noise stopped me in my tracks. I followed the sound into our bedroom, which overlooked the back of the house, only to discover a large wet patch developing on the beige carpet, close to the window. Looking up, I was alarmed to see brownish water slowly seeping through the ceiling near the exposed beam. Cursing, I fetched the washing-up bowl to catch the offending liquid, and dug out the number of the thatcher that Steve, the barman, had given to Jack.

The man, whose name was Kenny, was out on a job, but promised me that he'd call by later in the afternoon to assess the damage. The thought of the cost filled me with dread, but we'd known the roof needed addressing sooner or later. This had simply forced our hand.

I remained downstairs for most of the afternoon, checking periodically to see how much water had accumulated in the bowl and to empty it out. Thankfully by about 3 p.m., the rain had abated and the leak had almost stopped, but it had left a large damp patch on the ceiling.

True to his word, Kenny rapped at the door at about 4.30 p.m. He was a stocky man, maybe in his mid to late forties, bearded, with wild red hair and a gold hoop earring in one ear. He wore torn dungarees over his broad bare chest and a tool belt slung round his hips. If ever I'd pictured a thatcher, it would have been Kenny personified.

'Problem with your roof, is there?' he said amiably. 'Let's have a look, then.'

He came through the house and I showed him out into the garden. Lips pursed, he gazed upwards, a hand shielding his eyes.

'I'll need to get my ladders,' he said, 'take a proper look. Can't see owt from down here.'

I looked on as Kenny shinned up his ladder like a monkey. After closer inspection, he informed me that we needed a lot of the thatch redoing.

'There are a few gaps all over, I'm afraid,' he said, scratching his beard with stubby, ragged fingernails. 'I can do you a patch-up job where it's leaking round the

83

chimney for now, but there's some slippage and it looks like the thatch hasn't been tightly packed enough in places, so there are some hollows – you'll need the ridge and quite a bit of the rest doing before long. Definitely before the winter, anyway.'

I grimaced. 'How much will it cost?'

'I should be able to make the thatch good where it's worn by inserting more thatch material in those areas, then fix the slippage problem by fitting wire netting over the thatch to stop it sliding in future. I can do the whole lot for you for ten thousand.'

I realised my mouth was gaping. 'Oh dear. I didn't know it would be that much.'

''Fraid so. It takes a good few weeks, see. And there's plenty more out there would double that; you ask anyone round here.'

'Well, can you fix the leak for us anyway, please, and I'll have a word with my husband and get back to you about the rest.' I groaned inwardly as I contemplated the size of loan we would have to negotiate with the bank.

He nodded towards Mrs Barley's roof. 'It looks all right from the ground, but there are a few gaps in next door's, too. I can do you a good deal if I do both at the same time – d'you want to ask your neighbour, or shall I knock on the door when I finish up here?'

'I'll pop and ask – she's an elderly lady, so money may be a problem.'

*

Mrs Barley was quite concerned to learn that her roof was in need of repair. She came out into the back garden

84

and looked up apprehensively to where Kenny was busy with hammer and nails, straddling our chimney and whistling through his teeth as he fixed the flashing.

'If there's work to be done, I'd rather it was sorted before I start to get problems,' she told me, arms wrapped anxiously across her chest. 'Where did you find this chap?'

'Steve from The Green Man recommended him. He did the pub roof and made a really good job of it, apparently. It's going to cost several thousand, but if it needs to be repaired, I don't suppose we've got much choice.'

'Well, I know it's been several years since I've had any work done on the thatch, so it's probably long overdue. You tell him to go ahead and fix the lot, yours and mine. I'll pay, and you can settle up with me when you can afford it. There's no rush. I imagine money must be tight for you at the moment, with the baby on the way. Costly little things, babies.' She smiled wistfully.

I was taken aback. 'Are you sure? It's a lot of money.'

'I've still got Frank's life insurance pay-out burning a hole in my pocket. It's not like I need it so I can go off galivanting round the world or anything, is it?'

My only concern was getting the roof fixed. Her proposal seemed like the answer to our prayers, and at that moment, I could have hugged her.

'Thank you *so* much, that's really kind of you. And I promise we'll pay back every penny as soon as we can.'

'Like I said, only when you're able. Can't have you getting dripped on in the night, can we?'

*

We arranged for Kenny to come back towards the end of the week to start the work properly. Jack was amazed when I told him that evening of Mrs Barley's offer to help us out.

'Christ, we hardly know the woman really. She must be pretty comfortable if she's got that kind of money to splash about.' He looked doubtful.

'She didn't say how much she's got, but I can't imagine an insurance settlement would've been that big thirty years ago, not by today's standards. I don't suppose she needs much to live on, though. After all, she only has herself to worry about; it doesn't sound as if she's got any family to consider. Don't look a gift horse in the mouth. I said we'd pay her back as soon as we could afford to – maybe we could set up a standing order or something?'

'Yes, we must. I know we need the work doing, but I don't like the idea of owing that much money to a stranger.'

'But she's *not* a stranger – not really. I mean, I feel like we've got to know her quite well since we moved in. I think it's really generous of her.'

'I'm not disputing that. I feel a bit uncomfortable about it, that's all. I'd ask my dad, but I think he's put all his hard-earned cash into doing up their place in Spain.' He sighed. 'I'll have to put in some extra hours at the practice, then we'll be able to pay it off quicker.'

'But you're working overtime as it is. She said there was no panic to have the money back – I think it's just sitting there gathering dust, from the way she spoke.'

He gritted his teeth. It wasn't often that Jack got angry, but the muscles in his cheeks had begun to twitch. 'Look,

I don't like having debt hanging over me, all right? We'll pay it back as soon as possible. I don't want to feel beholden to her, or anyone else.'

I raised my hands in exasperation. 'You're making it into a big deal. We need the roof fixing. End of. I'm not delighted about owing anyone money either, but it was a lovely gesture and you're turning it into a massive fucking problem.'

I could feel myself welling up. Jack relented.

'Hey, I'm sorry. Don't get upset about it. We'll sort it, don't worry.' He pulled me to him. 'We'll get a standing order set up straight away. I'll go round later; get her bank details.' He looked thoughtful. 'Maybe we should have her over for dinner one evening or something, to say thank you.'

I brushed the tears away with my sleeve and tried to smile. 'Yes, that would be nice. I think she'd appreciate it.'

But his troubled eyes and the tilt of his head told me Jack still wasn't happy about the situation. And if I were to put hand on heart, I felt slightly uneasy about it all too.

*

We both went round to see Mrs Barley later that evening. She seemed distracted, saying she was tired and about to have an early night, so she didn't invite us in. Jack thanked her for her offer of help and asked for her bank details so that he could transfer some money to her. She claimed not to hold with financial institutions, and waved a dismissive hand at our suggestion of setting up a regular payment.

87

'Just pay me as and when. It's not as if I'm going to miss the money – Frank left me well provided for, and I've never been extravagant. If you'd feel happier paying me back more quickly, you can give me a few pounds whenever you're flush. I don't want a leaky roof any more than you do, and it makes sense if the man can do both houses as a job lot.'

Jack still seemed anxious. 'Do you think we should get a couple more quotes? Does that seem a decent price to you? I've never had a thatch before and I haven't a clue what the going rate is.'

'I rang Bob to ask him, and he knows of several people who've used this Kenny chap. Says he's as straight as a die and very reasonable, and does a nice tidy job, too. I think we should go ahead and let him start the work.'

Jack agreed, albeit reluctantly, that we would hand over whatever we could afford each month and thanked Mrs Barley. Kenny was to start the work on Thursday. The long-term weather forecast was favourable, so hopefully he would be able to finish it before there was another significant downpour.

'Well, at least we'll have the roof done before the baby arrives,' said Jack, as we lay in bed that night. 'We'd better keep in Mrs B's good books from now on,' he added jokingly. But something in his tone implied he actually meant it.

*

Kenny and two assistants, his sons Shaun and Nathan, both with equally unkempt red hair, arrived at the crack of dawn on the Thursday, and wasted no time in unloading the scaffolding poles and planks of wood they had brought with them. Kenny left them to assemble everything while he went away, soon to return, having reloaded the truck with bags of the new roofing material.

Jack was operating on a cat that morning and had an early start, so after waving him off, still groggy with sleep, I made myself a cup of tea and, wrapped in my dressing gown, went out into the garden to say hello. Jobie trotted beside me. He nuzzled my hand and looked up at the roof expectantly, his tail high and swishing wildly. He was always pleased to see people and I'd never known him to growl at anyone or be anything other than friendly.

Kenny must have still been at the front of the house, but the two younger boys had got off to a promising start. Despite being barely out of their teens, they clearly knew exactly what they were doing. They had begun work on our side of the building first.

Fascinated, I watched as they climbed nimbly up and down the scaffolding that they had erected, stripping away the old thatch, which was then loaded onto a trailer ready to be disposed of.

Between them, they heaved the large canvas bags, containing bundles of reeds, round the side of the cottage from the back of the vehicle and assembled them next to the wall, ready to be hoisted up and inserted into the sparser areas. The sky was clear and the sun already warm, and I was grateful that the weather had turned out as expected, enabling them to make good progress.

I went back into the house, showered and dressed. After a couple of slices of toast and honey plus a second cup of tea, I went out to ask if they would like something to drink.

'That's very kind – mine's a black coffee, two sugars, please. Lovely day for it, anyway!' called Kenny from the apex. My heart was in my mouth as he hopped about with ease, tossing down the discarded, moss-covered reeds to reveal the wooden frame beneath. Suddenly he stopped, peering down with interest into the attic between the gaps in the now exposed wooden framework.

'Ever been up in your loft? There's no dividing wall between you and next door, you know.'

I didn't know. We had never ventured into the loft space, but I'd always assumed there would be separate access.

'Is there anything up there?'

'Nothing much your side. An old roll of carpet and –' he screwed up his eyes as he leaned forward '– looks like one of them dressmaker's dummies. But it's a proper treasure trove over the old lady's bit. I reckon she must be one of them hoarders you hear about. It's going to take us a while before we finish, so we'd best get the tarpaulin in place, just in case we have any rain in the next couple of weeks – don't want anything getting ruined.'

My curiosity was piqued. I wondered what hidden delights lurked in Mrs Barley's attic. I hadn't actually been inside Rose Cottage, but from the bit I had seen through the front door and the French doors it looked immaculate, and I couldn't imagine that it would be at all cluttered.

As if on cue, the old lady came out into the garden. Seeing me, she smiled.

'Well, they're off to a flying start,' she said, raising her eyes towards the roof.

'Kenny was saying he needs to put a cover over the frame, to protect your belongings in case we have rain. He says there's quite a lot of stuff up there. I think the forecast is fine for the next few days, but it'll take them longer than that to finish.'

Mrs Barley looked alarmed. 'I can't get up into the attic these days – I haven't had the chance to sort it all out. I hadn't thought about it in a long while, to tell the truth.'

'I'm sure we could help you go through it. Maybe not at the moment, but after they've finished the work, if you'd like some help to clear it out . . .'

Her expression became suddenly stony. 'I don't expect you to be going through my stuff,' she snapped. 'You wouldn't want me rummaging through all your possessions, would you?'

She turned and went back into the house, slamming the back door behind her. I stared after her. Kenny gave a throaty laugh.

'Ooh – sounds like you touched a nerve there. Maybe there's a body in one of them trunks or something!'

I was taken aback. I wondered if I should go round and explain – I only wanted to help, not poke around her things. Kenny had obviously seen my expression. He came down the ladder.

'Don't take any notice. They can be funny, old folk. Maybe something in there from the past that she doesn't want to think about, eh? I should let her be if I were you; she'll come round.'

He was right, of course. I made myself busy doing some housework, and after lunch, chained myself to the laptop with my book and a highlighter pen once more. There was a knock at the front door.

'I've come to apologise.' It was Mrs Barley. She looked uncomfortable. 'I shouldn't have barked at you like that – it's just, well, there's a lot up there belonging to Frank, you see. I've never felt able to sort through everything – I know I should, but I can't bear to part with any of it. I'm sure you understand . . .'

I felt relieved. I didn't want to fall out with my neighbour, and her words earlier had left me feeling quite miserable. She'd been so kind since we moved in – and particularly as she had been so generous, helping out with paying for the work being done, I didn't want there to be an atmosphere between us. Especially not with us living so close.

''Course I do. I had to sort out my aunt's house after she died and it was quite upsetting. Stirs up a lot of memories.' I paused. 'I just wanted to help, you know. I wasn't being nosy or anything.'

'No, I know. Ignore me. I'm a silly old fossil sometimes. Comes of being on my own so much, I suppose. Come and have a cup of tea with me – we can sit in the summer house. I've just baked some scones.'

I joined Mrs Barley in the summer house that she loved so much. The air smelled slightly musty and damp. I looked around. The walls had been decorated with twigs arranged in unusual geometric patterns. Above the full width of the doorframe hung a knobbly branch. Following my gaze, the old woman rose and tapped the thing.

'A rowan bough,' she declared. 'Bestows blessings on any dwelling.'

I nodded but said nothing. She was entitled to her beliefs, but thinking a twisted piece of wood was capable of protecting anything or anyone seemed a little far-fetched.

We sat on cushions on the slatted bench, which sagged a little beneath our weight, watching Kenny and the boys hard at work as we drank our tea and chatted. Despite the warm afternoon sun, it felt surprisingly cool, and I wrapped my arms about me, trying to rub the gooseflesh from my bare shoulders. A sudden thud from above startled me.

'Oh my God – what on earth was that?'

Mrs Barley chuckled. 'Oh, that'll be my friend.'

I peered out of the window. At once, the same large, rather battered-looking crow I had seen before hopped down from the roof and landed in front of the doorway. It had a distinctive white flash on one wing. Tipping its head to one side, the bird stared up at me with curiously intelligent beady eyes.

'I call him Corvus. He's been visiting me for years. He must be almost fifteen now. He'll be hoping for titbits, no doubt, but he'll have to wait. Won't you?' The old woman addressed the bird who hopped closer and stood unnervingly just inside the door, watching her every move. Its movements were jerky and worryingly unpredictable. I shrank back in my seat, drawing my feet sharply beneath the bench and slopping tea into the saucer.

'So, Stina, you don't have any close family then?' the old lady enquired casually as she buttered a scone.

I squirmed. Perhaps our lack of visitors had led her to arrive at this conclusion. 'Not really. I lived with my great-aunt, but she passed away a few years ago. And Jack's parents have emigrated to Spain, so we hardly ever see them.'

'What a pity. They'll miss out when the baby is born – and little ones grow up so quickly. What about friends? Is there anyone you can turn to for support if you need it?'

I sighed. 'Unfortunately not. Reggie, my best friend, lives too far away and she travels abroad a lot with her job anyway. Jack doesn't really have much to do with his brother, and most of his university mates settled in Scotland. We're sort of on our own, really.'

Her eyes seemed to light up momentarily and I thought I detected the hint of a smile. She swatted away a fly that had landed on her plate and threw a handful of scone crumbs to the crow, who began to peck ravenously. His proximity was making me nervous.

'Oh, that's a shame.' Her expression implied otherwise. She nodded towards my stomach. 'What are you hoping to have?'

'I really don't care. A healthy baby is all I'm praying for. And Jack says the same.'

'Ah, maybe. But a man likes to have a son, you know. Someone he can take to the football, go to the pub with when he grows up. I remember my old dad . . .' She gave a strange little smile. 'Worshipped his boy, he did. I was never the favourite. Not that I minded,' she added.

94

'I understood, you see. You have to make allowances for men; they're not as strong as us, you know. Not really.'

It seemed a cryptic remark. But I simply nodded and didn't attempt to question her. She had her own ideas about things – who was I to contradict her? And equally, I didn't want to say anything that might upset her again.

She turned to look at me suddenly, her eyes twinkling. 'Would you like to know – what sex the baby is, I mean? I could read your tea leaves.' She glanced at my cup. 'Frank didn't approve, but I've never known them to be wrong.'

I felt slightly sick. My chest tightened – not at the thought of finding out about the baby, but of what else a reading might throw up. I wasn't entirely convinced there was anything in it, but it was a risk I didn't want to take.

'No, thank you. I think I'd rather it was a surprise.'

She considered this for a moment. 'Fair enough. I'd probably be the same. Makes it all the more exciting, I suppose.'

I was anxious to steer the conversation away from myself. 'Were you from a big family, Mrs Barley?'

She stared out into the garden, her focus fixed firmly on the flowers. 'My mother lost a couple of boys late into her pregnancies. I was her third child. And then my brother came along two years later. He was the apple of Dad's eye. I was always closer to my mum. We were very in tune, she and I. Taught me how to pick up on signs, to use my intuition to look into the future and people's hearts . . .' She turned to look at me, smiling sadly. 'So not a big family, no; but a close one. All gone now, though. I've only my memories of them left. Mum's health was never great and we lost her to pneumonia when I had just turned fifteen, Dad two years later. An awful road accident.' Her lower lip wobbled as she relived the memory. I was beginning to regret asking. 'What about your brother?'

My heart almost jumped into my throat as the crow let out a sudden caw, flapping its wings as though to remind us of its presence. Mrs Barley absently tossed it the remaining chunk of her scone. Taking the fragment in its beak, the bird hopped back out into the garden and rose into the sir, resuming its perch on the summer house roof. I desperately wanted to close the door to prevent it from re-entering, but resisted the urge.

Mrs Barley looked away again, staring straight ahead. Her eyes had misted over. 'What were you saying? Oh, my brother. Long passed, too.' There was an uncomfortable pause. 'Life can be cruel, Stina. You need to seize the day, as the saying goes.'

Her words made me sad. On impulse, I reached out and squeezed her hand.

'It must be lonely for you. Please don't hesitate to knock on our door if you need company. You're always welcome. I'm lonely sometimes, too. It can be a bit isolating when you work from home. And I don't have anyone I can turn to now, either – well, not really.'

My eyes dropped and I felt a stab of guilt as I thought of my mother; still breathing, maybe, but no longer a part of my life. It had been a tough call, and I felt bad about it, but I couldn't face visiting her any more. Her increasingly bizarre behaviour and violent outbursts had forced me to make a decision that I wasn't proud of; but for the sake of my own sanity and possibly even safety, especially now I had the baby to consider, I knew I had to stop going to the home.

Mrs Barley patted my cheek. 'You're a sweet girl, Stina. Please don't feel obliged to invite me round or anything, though – I don't want to intrude. I like to make myself useful, and if I can do that it makes me happy. I'm very glad that you and Jack have moved in next door. You've been a breath of fresh air after the succession of wasters that have lived there over the last few years.' She jerked her head towards Wisteria Cottage, her nose wrinkling.

'It's good to feel there's someone I can relate to in the village at last. And it's lovely to see the two of you together. I can see how much you care for one another – it warms my heart. Reminds me of how Frank and I used to be. Some people are just meant to be together.'

I shifted awkwardly in my seat. 'We don't feel obliged, honestly. You've been so considerate and helpful, and we feel lucky to have you as our neighbour. And friend,' I added hastily. 'Anything that'll repay your kindness is the very least we can do.'

She looked away. 'You don't really know me, Stina. But I would never do anything to harm you or Jack; you know that, don't you?'

Something in her tone caused my stomach to clench as she spoke, and a coldness travelled down my spine. In spite of things that other people had implied, the idea had never entered my head – until that moment. I forced a smile.

'Of course not. You've always been so good to us.'

Her lips curved upwards briefly, but dropped just as quickly.

'I've a whole lifetime of experience behind me and I have plenty to feel aggrieved about, let me tell you. Not least from some of those around here. It's a small village and there have been plenty of spiteful people in it over the years, believe it or not.' She sucked in air through her teeth, then resumed defiantly. 'But I'd never let them beat me, force me from the home that Frank and I loved. I wouldn't give them the satisfaction. And if anyone tries to take it out on you because of me, they'll rue the day.' She drummed her fingertips against the teacup, her lips setting into a hard line.

My tongue seemed to have stuck to the roof of my mouth. I swallowed hard. 'Are the people round here really so bad, Mrs Barley?'

'Let's just say they can be narrow-minded and suspicious. That's what comes of living in a small community. Oh, on the face of it, it's lovely. Pretty little place, everyone knows everyone; all very *cosy* and *neighbourly*.' Her foot rose and fell rhythmically as she uttered the words.

'But there's a lot of gossip and tall tales flying round in these backwater villages. Gives them something to talk about. They thrive on it. Just you watch yourself. They'll latch on to anything you do or say and twist it. Be on your guard. Don't fall victim to their petty prejudices – the less they know about you, the better, in my experience.'

She turned back towards the garden, her expression

suddenly hard, dark eyes glinting with a cold, flint-like quality. 'Humans,' she said quietly, 'I have come to realise, are, for the most part, not a nice species.'

The look on her face made me shudder. I finished my tea in silence. I was beginning to wonder if living out in the country was all it was cracked up to be.

CHAPTER 7

Later, I mulled over what Mrs Barley had said. Her words and the odd way she had behaved troubled me, and although I wanted to talk to Jack about it, I didn't want to worry him. It was more than a little concerning to think that we had moved into a potential nest of vipers. It had never occurred to me that rural communities could be so toxic.

I must have been unusually quiet because, after dinner, Jack pulled me onto his lap as I attempted to clear the plates from the table. He planted a kiss on the back of my neck.

'What's got into you this evening? You've looked as if you're miles away ever since I got home.'

I took a deep breath. 'I went round for a cup of tea with Mrs Barley earlier. She was acting . . . strangely. She gave me the impression that the village isn't really a very nice place to live, and that the people round here can be a vicious bunch.'

101

He shifted under my weight and turned me to face him. 'Really? Did she elaborate?'

'From everything she said, I think she's felt, well, hounded. I mean, after Lucy going on about her, and that woman at the fair, and the old boy in the pub, and what Bob said, too. It sounds as if some of the villagers have really had it in for her – and I get the impression that they've made her life a misery over the years. I don't understand why. I mean, she's a harmless old woman. Isn't she? It's really weird.'

Jack's brow furrowed. He smoothed a stray lock of hair away from my cheek. 'Maybe there *are* a lot of parochial idiots round here. Or maybe there's actually something we don't know about her. It's not impossible. I mean, I can't believe that anyone would hold it against someone in this day and age, just because they'd been cohabiting with someone. It's such a ridiculous, old-fashioned attitude. I doubt anyone really thinks that way any more. There has to be more to it.'

I shook my head. I couldn't – no, didn't want to – believe that there was something more sinister going on beneath our neighbour's kindly façade.

'But what? No, I don't buy it. She's always seemed so *nice* – I can't believe she'd be capable of anything bad. I think it's more likely that they're just that – provincial and petty. Some people can be horrible.'

He nodded, but the cogs were obviously turning in his mind. 'See if you can find out anything else from that Lucy, next time you see her. Mrs Barley's always been nothing but decent with us. Even if she *has* done something, it must've been a very long time ago. The past is a foreign country, as the saying goes.'

The past can have a way of catching up with us, though. I shuddered as the thought flashed through my head. No one is without the odd skeleton in their closet. And although I didn't want to think ill of our neighbour, a seed of doubt had been planted.

You don't really know me. That was what she had said.

But if the truth was told, *she* didn't really know *me*, either. How can anyone *truly* know what's in someone else's heart or mind – even those closest to them? I didn't mention any of it to Jack. Her words rang in my ears and I wondered if there was some oblique intimation behind them. I had an odd instinct about it all and an unpleasant sinking sensation in my gut.

That night I curled up behind Jack in bed, wrapping my arms around his girth and burying my face in the warmth of his back. I breathed in the familiar, musky comfort of his skin. From his deep, rhythmic breathing, he had clearly drifted off very quickly as usual, but sleep evaded me as I chewed over what Mrs Barley had said, and the discomfiting bitterness of her tone. A chink of moonlight passed through the gap in the curtains and I found myself mesmerised by the dancing patterns it cast on the wall. I don't know how long I lay there for, but a sudden noise overhead caught my attention. I remained still, straining to hear what it was.

Things were being moved. I extricated myself from my one-sided embrace, careful not to disturb Jack, and

103

sat up slowly. It sounded as though something was being dragged across the floor above me. I sat there, holding my breath, heart thumping in my chest. Could it be Mrs Barley, rearranging the items in her attic? But why? And how on earth could she have got up there – the ladder was steep, and certainly the narrowness of the aperture, if the set-up was the same as ours, wouldn't be that easy to wriggle through, even for someone able-bodied. Surely with her arthritis it would be impossible for her to climb through the gap, let alone shift cumbersome items.

But knowing there was no one else in the house, there seemed to be no other explanation. I lay back down, but the noise continued for what felt like hours: slow, deliberate footsteps and the bump and scrape of things being pushed or pulled across the boards. Long after the noise eventually abated, I still felt rattled, and even with my eyes tightly shut, wide awake. Thoughts about anything and everything coursed through my brain. I remembered the crying I had heard in the night; the male voice. *Had* there been someone in there with her?

By the time I eventually succumbed to sleep, first light had started to creep through and the infuriatingly joyful dawn chorus announced the onset of a new day.

I plodded downstairs and found Jack at the breakfast table. He glanced up from his cereal and almost choked.

'Christ, you look rough.' He looked aghast.

Blearily, I rubbed the sleep from my eyes and glared at him. 'Cheers. I've been awake half the bloody night. Didn't you hear anything?'

He lifted his eyebrows. 'You know me – I sleep like the dead. What was it?'

'It sounded like there was stuff being lugged about up in the attic – made a right din, all the to-ing and fro-ing. I'm assuming it must have been Mrs Barley, but it makes no sense. All I can think is that, after what Kenny said, she's taken it into her head to start going through all her things before he starts work on her side of the roof properly.'

Jacked looked doubtful. 'In the middle of the night?'

'Exactly. Why the hell would you do it under cover of darkness? I'm ever so slightly pissed off that it's cost me a night's sleep.'

'Maybe she's an insomniac.' He shovelled more cereal into his mouth, then considered for a moment. 'I'd imagine it would be tricky for her to get up there, knowing what the access is probably like. She's not exactly a spring chicken and you'd have to be pretty flexible to get through the hatch if it's anything like ours. I think people must've been a lot smaller when these houses were built.'

'Maybe she's more able-bodied than she's letting on. Maybe . . . Oh, Christ knows. It's bizarre. All I know is I've had a better night's sleep with a wild party going on next door in the past. You don't expect it from an elderly woman.'

I slumped in the chair next to him and poured myself a cup of tea.

Jack stroked my hair. 'Why don't you go back to bed? You look wrecked.'

'I'm not sure I'll be able to sleep, with the work going on. I may just put my feet up on the settee for a bit, see if I can nod off. I think I'll have a tactful word with her

105

later, though. I may need to invest in some earplugs if she's planning any more nocturnal activities.'

*

Jobie at my side, I waved Jack off, just in time to see Kenny and the boys pulling up in their truck.

'All right,' he called cheerfully, alighting on the pavement. 'Oh my days, you're not looking so well this morning. Bad night?'

I grimaced. 'However did you guess?'

Mrs Barley appeared suddenly at her front door. She always had her milk delivered and bent down stiffly to lift the new bottle from the step. She was looking remarkably fresh, considering she must have had virtually no sleep.

'Good morning, love,' she breezed. 'Another nice day for the lads to get on with the job.'

I paused. Should I broach the subject now? *Yes, never mind that, Mrs Barley, I'd like to know what the bloody hell you were doing rummaging around in your attic all night . . .*

'Mrs Barley, I was wondering . . .'

'Hmm? Sorry, can't stay chatting at the moment – I've a pan of porridge on the stove. See you later.'

She disappeared back inside. I could have kicked myself for being so reticent. I shuffled back into the house and decided to run a bath. After a nice long soak, I dressed and went out into the garden to see how work on the roof was progressing. Kenny was coming down the ladder.

'You look a bit brighter now.' He grinned.

I looked around, but Mrs Barley was obviously indoors. 'I was kept awake by a racket coming from the attic. I think my neighbour must have been going through all that stuff last night, from the sound of things.'

Kenny looked puzzled. 'No evidence of any movement that I could see. As far as I can tell, everything's all neatly stacked up exactly where it was yesterday.'

'Are you sure?'

'Absolutely. I'd had a good look when I first spotted it all. I s'pose she could've just been looking through it for something and then taken whatever it was downstairs, tidied the rest up again.' He scrubbed at his head with the heel of his hand. I found myself wondering if he actually owned a comb. 'But to be quite honest, I don't see how she could've got up there in the first place. It's a poky little hatch for an elderly person to climb through. Not unless she's one of them contortionists on the sly!'

I was flummoxed. *Someone* had been up there rooting around. And judging by the length of time they had taken, not to mention the amount of noise, the whole lot ought to have been shifted to the opposite end, or even removed. It made no sense.

I went back into the house and flipped open my laptop, then logged on. I stared at the document for a moment, my mind blank. It was pointless. I lay down on the settee. I felt irritable, queasy from lack of sleep, and knew I needed to get some rest if I was going to do anything at all with my day. I pulled a cushion over my face to shut out the light and the noise from the workers. Eventually, I managed to drift off. I couldn't have been asleep long, when a sharp tap on the window woke me with a start. I sat up, and was a little startled to see Mrs Barley peering in at me through the French doors. She'd obviously come in through the back gate.

'Sorry to disturb you – I've baked an apple pie. I thought you might like a slice.'

I smiled weakly but felt peeved that she had interrupted my nap. 'Thank you, but I'm not really hungry at the moment. Just trying to catch up on some sleep – I had a rather disturbed night.'

'Oh dear. Have to keep popping to the bathroom, did you? I know pregnancy can play havoc with the bladder . . .'

'Actually, there was rather a lot of noise coming from the attic. It went on for a long time.'

'Really? Birds, do you think? Oh Lord, I hope we haven't got mice or squirrels up there – or, God forbid, rats. I'll have to get the pest control people in.' She appeared genuinely concerned.

'No, nothing like that. It was things being moved about – like someone dragging heavy boxes from one end of the floor to the other.' I waited for a reaction, but her expression was deadpan.

'Well, I didn't hear a thing. Slept like a log all night. How strange.'

I could find no words. If *she* hadn't been moving things around, and from what Kenny had said, nothing appeared to have been disturbed, what the hell had been going on up there? I felt suddenly cold.

She stood over me anxiously. 'You've gone as white as a sheet, my love. Do you think it could've been a bad dream . . . ?'

I shook my head vigorously. 'I was wide awake. *All night*. I don't understand it.'

'Maybe the noise could have carried from elsewhere?' As she spoke, I could see she wasn't convinced by the suggestion herself.

'Or maybe I'm losing the plot,' I muttered.

'Sorry?'

'I've no explanation for it. But I know what I heard.'

She smiled – patronisingly, I thought. 'The mind can play tricks on us, especially at night. Every little creak can seem like something sinister. But if the noise starts again, you must come and knock on my door – or ask your Jack to go up there and have a look. Did it wake him too?'

'Nothing wakes Jack. He could sleep through a hurricane.'

'Ah.' She inclined her head slowly, her mouth twitching.

I was beginning to feel annoyed. I suspected she didn't believe that I had actually heard anything; that I was exaggerating. I resolved that I might do just that if it happened again – knock on her door, to prove I wasn't imagining things.

'If you'll excuse me, Mrs Barley, I don't want to be rude, but I really need to try and catch up on some sleep. I've got some work to do and I can't concentrate when I'm feeling like this.'

'Of course. I'll leave this pie in the kitchen – I daresay you might fancy some later. I'm sure Jack will, too. What is it you have to do – maybe I could help?'

'That's very kind, but it's nothing anyone else can do for me, I'm afraid. I'm doing some research for an article I'm writing – about Avoncote, actually.' I nodded towards my laptop, still open on the table. 'It's for a magazine. About local history and folklore.'

Her eyes followed my gaze. She pursed her lips. 'Folklore, you say?'

'Yes, it's very interesting. But I need to rest or I'm going to be writing a pile of rubbish.'

She stared at the laptop for a moment, then turned back to me and beamed. 'You settle back down then, love – I can let myself out. And if you have trouble sleeping again, just you let me know. I can mix you up a nice herbal draught – I know my stuff and it's quite safe in pregnancy, so you won't need to worry on that score.'

I thanked her, but still had no intention of taking any herbal preparation she offered me, whatever assurances she may have given.

Eventually I managed to doze a little, but despite my best attempts to block out the light and noise, I could still hear banter and laughter from Kenny and the lads, and the thud of their work boots as they climbed repeatedly up and down the scaffolding and across the roof. In the end I gave up, and after a mug of milky coffee decided to resume my research into Avoncote, hoping that I might get a decent sleep the following night through sheer exhaustion. Frustratingly, it proved impossible to concentrate. The deadline was still over a fortnight away, but I was beginning to think I wouldn't make it. My head felt as if it were stuffed with cotton wool. In the end, I decided I might be best taking a walk and getting some fresh air in an attempt to put all thoughts of the previous night's events behind me.

I put on Jobie's lead and wandered up to the village green. A mother duck, followed by seven fluffy ducklings, was waddling across the far side of the grass towards the pond. The dog began to strain eagerly in their direction and I had to use all my strength to pull him back.

'Someone being a bad lad this morning?'

I looked round to see Lucy walking slowly up the road. Her abdomen had ballooned, making her gait comical. She had reins on a squealing Alfie, who looked equally keen to head for the ducks. I smiled and nodded.

'I don't think Jobie would hurt them; he's such a softie. But he seems to find them very interesting!'

We watched as the little feathered family reached the water and bobbed purposefully across towards the opposite side. Alfie continued to tug at the reins, so Lucy scooped him up.

'How are you keeping?' I asked. 'Sorry, I've been meaning to text you. Can't be long now.'

She patted her bump. 'Yeh, a bit over six weeks to go now. I can't wait. Not for the birth,' she added hastily, pulling a face. 'Just to get back to some sort of normality, you know. I'm okay though, thanks. How's things with you? I see you're having some work done. Bet that's not cheap. We don't have a thatch – I know they look lovely, but it seems like a lot of hassle.'

'It's a pricey do, I can tell you. We weren't expecting to have to get it done quite so soon. But at least once it's finished, we can forget about it for another few years.'

'Are you busy? You can come round to mine for a bit if you like.'

111

I hesitated initially, but then thought I might take her up on the offer. The day felt like a write-off anyway – it wasn't as if I could get on with anything much at home. 'Thanks, that would be nice. Is it okay to bring Jobie?'

'Sure, we can all sit out in the garden. Just ignore the weeds!'

Lucy lived in a row of seventeenth-century terraced cottages on the road out of the village. We stopped en route for her to buy milk from the shop. Judy seemed pleased to see us together.

'Nice that you've found some company of your own age,' she said to me, as Lucy went to use the cash machine at the back of the store. 'How are you settling in?'

'Fine, thank you. We're having some work done on the roof at the moment – I wanted a rest as I had a rough night last night, but with the racket the thatchers are making, I gave up.'

'You do look tired. Make sure you take it easy. It's surprising how exhausting pregnancy can be, even in the early stages.' We wished Judy a good day and meandered up the road to Lucy's house. Alfie was keen to lead the way, and Jobie trotted alongside us obediently.

Lucy's front door opened straight into the living room. The room was smaller than ours, painted cream, with dark exposed beams and a pot-bellied stove sitting on the hearth, in front of which was spread a brightly coloured rug. Washing was airing on an old-fashioned rack suspended from the ceiling.

She hurriedly gathered up the toys and books that were scattered across the varnished wooden floor, shoving them into a large plastic container in the corner. We walked through to the kitchen, where the sink was piled high with dirty crockery, evidence of the morning's breakfast all over the work surface.

''Scuse the mess. I s'pose it'll get even worse soon – the things we let ourselves in for, eh.' She grinned, but her cheeks flushed a little. 'Do you want a cold drink, or would you prefer something hot?'

'I don't mind. Whatever you're having.'

'My mum made me some ginger beer – I find it helps with the sickness. That do?'

'Yeh, that's great.'

We went out into the garden, which was in a marginally better state than ours had been when we first moved in. It was long and narrow, enclosed on all sides by a high wooden fence, with a tall wrought-iron gate at the bottom. The paved area outside the back door was strewn with weeds, as were the borders. But there was a decent-sized lawn for Alfie to play on.

I let Jobie off the lead and Lucy and I sat at the moss-covered wooden table on the patio, sipping our drinks as we watched Alfie climb onto his plastic sit-on tractor and chase the excited dog up and down.

'My hubby's not much of a gardener,' Lucy said, almost apologetically. 'He inherited this place from his nan, so you'd have thought he'd show a bit more interest. He cuts the grass now and again, but he's not really bothered about planting anything. We lost my dad a couple of years ago. He used to come round and do it for us, but now he's gone we've let it go a bit, I'm afraid. I just don't have the time with Alfie.'

'Sorry to hear about your dad. It's hard work with a

113

toddler, though. Your priorities are different when you've got small children.'

'Eddie's priorities revolve around going to the pub and playing bloody darts, or whatever it is he gets up to with his mates. He's out most nights. It's like living with a lodger.' She gave a sigh of resignation, staring down at the glass, which she was rotating on the table in front of her. 'What about your fella? Is he handy round the house?'

'Jack does try, but I don't expect him to feel much like doing anything after work as he puts in such long hours at the surgery – did I mention he's a vet?'

'No. Oh, well at least he's got a decent job. I used to do the admin for a small construction firm in town, but the company folded and there was no job to go back to after my maternity leave – and then of course I fell pregnant again. I've felt pretty rough this time around as well, so I'm having an extended break right now!' She laughed, stroking her bump. 'Eddie's only doing some casual work at the moment, on a building site just outside the town. Brings home the bacon, I suppose, but it's not exactly the career he dreamed of. But if he'd worked a bit harder at school, he might've finished up doing something more exciting. Probably why he's so keen to go and drown his sorrows.'

She looked rueful and I felt suddenly sorry for her. Eddie didn't sound as if he was much help. I wondered how she'd cope once there was another baby on the scene.

'Oh gawd, Alfie – don't do that!' Lucy had looked up in time to see the little boy about to pop a wriggling worm into his mouth.

114

'Why not? The birdies does.'

'Well, we're not like the birdies. We don't live in the trees, do we?'

Alfie looked skyward, as though considering the possibilities of this statement. We both laughed.

'Oh, the joys of motherhood.' She grinned. 'You've got all this to come. No wonder he had such an upset tummy after we came round to see you. God knows what he puts in his mouth. I did wonder if it might've been the cakes the old dear gave him, but he'd probably eaten something off the floor, knowing him.'

My stomach lurched. I recalled the coldness in Mrs Barley's eyes when she'd looked at Lucy, and how Alfie had trampled all over her precious garden. Surely she wouldn't have put something in the cakes? No; it was a ridiculous notion. But I thought of what Lucy had said about there being rumours about the old woman, and remembered that Jack had suggested I do some digging.

'I was wondering, do you know why people round here seem to have it in for Mrs Barley? She's always been very good to us, but I'm curious to find out if there's something we ought to know.'

She chewed her lip, looking thoughtful. 'She was always a miserable old cow when we were kids. Banging on her window, telling us to clear off if we were hanging around anywhere near her garden wall, that sort of thing. And woe betide anyone who dared to knock on her door on Halloween. She's hardly ever left that house, from what I can gather, even when her fella was alive.'

'Really?' I'd assumed that Mrs Barley had become more reclusive since Frank died.

She nodded vigorously. 'I've always found her a bit creepy. Like I told you, we used to play that game – rat-a-tat ginger we call it round here – you know, when kids rap on someone's door and run off. One of my mates was sure she heard her talking away to herself through the window when she went up the path once – said it sounded like she was chanting or something. Weird. It freaked her out.' She pulled a face. 'And then, there were the rumours about the cats . . .'

'What rumours?'

'I remember my mum telling me. Years ago, before her husband died, the Burrows family – the people that used to own your house – had an old black cat, and it used to go into her garden to do its business. She kept complaining to them about it – but you've no control over where a cat chooses to roam, have you? Anyway, one day the animal went missing. They found the poor thing eventually. It was dead. Someone had strung it up in a bush, in the entry behind the house. It had been sliced open and all its innards were hanging out. Really gross.'

'And they think Mrs Barley was responsible?' It felt as though ice was being dripped down my spine.

'Apparently so. Of course, she denied it, and they couldn't prove anything, but it all seemed too much of a coincidence.' She shook her head. 'I mean, who would do something like that to a cat? Bloody nutter if you ask me. And then a couple more moggies from further up the road disappeared too, soon afterwards. Everyone assumed they'd finished up the same way, but their bodies were never found.'

My stomach twisted in revulsion. If it had been Mrs Barley, this was a really disturbing revelation.

'Maybe it wasn't her. I really hope not. God, that's a shocking thing to do.' I shuddered, picturing the unfortunate lifeless animal suspended somewhere near the back of our home.

I loved cats. Auntie Jane used to have a lovely, placid old tabby called Rufus. He would curl up on my bed at night purring, and I was devastated when he was killed on the road. I didn't want to believe that Mrs Barley or anyone else was capable of such a monstrous act.

'I don't suppose we'll ever know for sure,' Lucy said. 'But I'm glad she's your neighbour and not mine!' She laughed, but I wasn't amused. I wondered whether I should ask the old woman about the allegation, but if it *wasn't* true, I would sound as suspicious and damning as the rest of the village. And chanting, too. What was that all about? A horrible tingling sensation began to stir somewhere deep inside me.

'I'd better get back. I'm supposed to be working on an article, but I needed to get some exercise and clear my head.' I rose from the table and called to Jobie, who raced across the lawn to meet me, his tail thrashing. 'Thanks very much for the ginger beer. It's really nice.'

'Glad you like it. My mum's own secret recipe! I've been drinking gallons of the stuff. The olives were delicious, by the way.'

'I've still got plenty. I'll give you some more next time you come round. Drop by any time.' I paused. 'Listen, will you ask your mum if she knows anything else about Mrs Barley? This whole thing about the cats has given me a really sick feeling. I'm wondering if there's anything else she's supposed to have done. It's not a nice thought, living next door to someone who could do a thing like that.'

'Sure. But listen, don't go worrying. I probably shouldn't have said anything. You know how it is in small villages – people gossip. I bet there's nothing in it.'

From her expression, I suspected she was just trying to make me feel better. She and Alfie watched from the door as we walked back down the road. My head was still full of the disturbing image of the poor murdered cat and the thought of what gruesome fate had befallen the others. It sounded almost like some ghastly satanic rite, and however long ago it may have occurred, I didn't want to dwell on the fact that it had happened on our doorstep.

*

Kenny was outside, leaning against his truck as he chatted on his mobile, when I got back. He looked up and waved, finishing his call.

'Just ordering some netting. We're making good progress. Did you get to the bottom of the attic mystery?'

'No. Mrs Barley claims she heard nothing and doesn't seem to know anything about it. But there was definitely *something* going on up there. If it happens again, I'll get Jack to go and have a look.'

He looked suddenly serious. 'Yeh, don't you get trying to climb up there yourself. We don't want you falling in your condition.'

I smiled. 'No, I won't.'

118

He lowered his voice, tipping his head towards Rose Cottage. 'By the way, while you were out, I could hear the old lady rattling away to herself in there. I'd just come down off the roof and the window was open. She seemed to be chanting or something, and she was burning a candle, like she was performing some kind of . . . I dunno, ceremony or something. She wasn't talking to no one else – she's definitely on her own in there. Sounded a bit *weird*, like.' He gave a slow nod, as if to emphasise this last observation.

I remembered what Lucy had said and a shiver passed through me. 'Could you hear what she was saying?'

'Not really; just the odd thing that sounded like a word, but even then I haven't got a clue what it was. That was the thing, it sounded sort of, well, foreign I s'pose. Not chanting like when someone's praying or anything. It was a bit like, you know, when you see them horror films.' He leaned forwards gleefully. 'Hey, you don't reckon she's one of them devil worshippers, do you?'

I must have looked horrified, as he quickly back-tracked.

'I'm only kidding. She's probably talking to herself because she's lonely . . . Can't be much fun when you don't see a soul from one day to the next. She don't have any family, does she?'

'Not that I know of, no. I've seen a man coming into the garden a couple of times now, though. We thought at first he was her gardener, but it wasn't. We've mentioned it to her, but she was pretty dismissive, so it doesn't sound as if he's a relative.'

119

Seeing my worried face, he forced a grin. 'Probably something and nothing.'

'Hopefully not.' My stomach began to churn. I was starting to think, more than ever, that it might be something to be very worried about. Now on top of the strange man in the garden and unexplained noises in the attic, there was a dead cat and a chanting neighbour to add into the mix. I went back indoors, my mind whirring. Sitting down at the table I frantically googled 'spells and rituals'.

'*Incantations and fire can be used to bring harm or death to another,*' I read aloud. '*Performing magic rituals requires the use of secret language sacred to the user.*'

For God's sake. What was I doing? This was ludicrous. Mrs Barley was no more a witch than I was, just a slightly eccentric, lonely old woman. I was so tired, and hormonal into the bargain; everything seemed suddenly magnified. Giving myself a mental shake, I put the laptop on standby and rose from the table. I knew I would feel more rational after a solid night's sleep and would simply have to try to get through the day without having a meltdown. My mouth felt suddenly uncomfortably dry.

I cleared my throat and called out into the garden. 'Would you like a cuppa?'

'Thought you'd never ask!'

I made drinks for Kenny and the boys and, after a glass of squash and a cheese sandwich, felt a little more human. In an attempt to purge my thoughts of dead cats and Mrs Barley's chanting, I sat at the table and logged on once again, flicking through the book about Avoncote to the chapter about its pagan festivals. I was interested to read about a May Day celebration called 'Jack o' the Green', where a man would head a procession of villagers and musicians, dressed from head to foot in a huge conical wicker frame decorated in flowers and foliage, with only a tiny slit out of which to see. Coming from the city, this sort of thing was alien to me. In truth, I found it vaguely sinister – I had never really understood the appeal of Morris dancing or bizarre customs like rolling enormous cheeses down a hill, either. According to the information in the book, the role of 'Jack o' the Green' had been dropped from Avoncote's May Day festivities some fifty years earlier. The 'Jack' was traditionally played by a chimney sweep, and the last unfortunate man to be cast in the role, a local sweep in his twenties by the name of Leonard Wiseacre, had met with a mysterious and untimely death shortly after his performance. With locals being naturally superstitious, no one was keen to take on the part thereafter. Everyone had concluded that the custom brought with it bad luck, and the following year the May Queen became the main focus of the celebrations.

My own Jack and I had found this year's event entertaining, aside from my uncomfortable exchange with the aura-reading woman. I hadn't seen her since and wondered where she actually lived. Maybe she was from another village.

Turning the page, I was slightly disturbed to read that the local pond had once been used to 'duck' suspected witches. Worse still was the revelation that on the outskirts of the village was the site of the still-unsolved twentieth-century murder of an elderly local man, suspected by many of witchcraft. He was found at the foot of a hill, pinned to the ground by a pitchfork, a trouncing hook through his neck and a cross carved into his flesh.

The idea that men or women who lived alone, maybe offered herbal remedies and told fortunes, were viewed with such unfounded suspicion and mistrust was abhorrent. Not so very long ago, somebody like the woman I encountered on May Day or even Mrs Barley could quite easily have become the focus of one such campaign, to round up those who were deemed different or a threat. I thought of their fate and it made me shudder. This really wasn't improving my mood at all.

I flicked forward to some more recent information and peered at the various black-and-white images of past annual festivities, such as the midsummer carnival, which went back as far as the 1920s.

A photograph from 1958 caught my eye. A young man, standing outside The Green Man watching the procession go by, seemed remarkably familiar. I looked more closely. The hair was dark and swept back from his face, and he had a closely cropped beard. The facial hair aside, and possibly thirty years younger, he bore an uncanny resemblance to the man I had seen in Mrs Barley's garden. His father – or even grandfather, maybe? It was possible. Then he must be from the area. I wasn't sure if this was a comforting thought or not.

Aware I was becoming distracted from the task in hand, I typed a few more paragraphs, saved the document and snapped the laptop lid shut. I was still tired and the effort of constructing coherent, let alone interesting, sentences was proving taxing. It was pointless trying to continue.

I stood up and stretched. It was approaching three o'clock and I felt as if my day had been largely wasted. I hated feeling so lethargic. I'd just have to write it off and hope for a better night's sleep later. My mobile pinged and I checked to see who was texting me. It was a message from Reggie.

'*Long time no c! In town this wkend. U up 2 a visitor?*'

*

My best, and truthfully only friend, Reggie – short for Régine – had never struggled to find men. With her shock of dark curls, caramel skin, courtesy of her mother's Antiguan heritage, and limpid brown eyes, she oozed confidence and seemed to draw the opposite sex – and even her fair share of other girls – like a magnet.

Reggie and I had met at sixth-form college, and hit it off straight away. I suppose we were polar opposites: she, outgoing and confident; me, the typical wallflower, the quiet swot in the corner. But she always did her utmost to bolster my self-esteem, and was fiercely protective of me if anyone ever took the mickey or made an unkind remark.

The first time I saw Reggie was during our inaugural English lesson. That morning, I had been hopeful of not finding any familiar faces amongst the other students pushing their way through the corridor. School had generally been something of an ordeal for me, and I hoped fervently that sixth form might be better if I knew no one. Maybe I could reinvent myself.

I was first into the classroom. The teacher, a scruffy, fortyish man with receding hair and a greying beard, was shuffling papers on the table in front of the whiteboard. He looked up briefly.

'Morning! Take a pew. We'll have the introductions when everyone's arrived.'

I sat at the back, observing the others as they filed in and found desks. I counted twenty-one heads in all, with a fairly even gender ratio. My stomach dropped as I recognised a particularly unpleasant boy who had attended my primary school. I tried to keep my head down, and prayed that he wouldn't notice me.

'Fuck me! It's Stinka.'

I felt my cheeks burning, as all eyes in the room seemed to have swivelled and settled on me. Ryan Corbett, the boy in question, leaned back, rocking in his seat. He was tall now, and had filled out into his once-spindly frame. But his wiry red hair and freckles were instantly recognisable.

'Well, well.' Gleefully, he looked me up and down. 'You haven't changed much. I see the years haven't done much to improve your dress sense.'

I was about to reply when a tall, startlingly attractive mixed-race girl breezed in. There seemed to be an intake of breath from every male in the room.

'Sorry I'm late.'

Ryan's mouth fell open. 'Well, hello, gorgeous. There's a chair here if you want to park your lovely bum.'

Her lip curled with distaste. 'Uh, no thanks.'

I was surprised when she turned to me.

'Were you saving that seat for anyone?'

I shook my head mutely.

'D'you mind if I . . . ?'

'No, it's fine.'

'I'm Reggie, by the way.' She smiled, extending a slender, manicured hand. I shook it shyly.

'Hi. I'm Stina.'

Ryan spluttered. 'Hope you haven't got a strong sense of smell, sweetheart.'

Reggie sat down next to me. She looked at him with contempt. 'I'm sorry?'

'It'll be overpowering by the end of the afternoon.'

'What's your problem, mate? I thought I'd signed up for the sixth form, not the Reception class. They should put up a sign: *Immature Twats Needn't Apply*.'

The group erupted into laughter. Ryan blushed crimson to the tips of his ears. He opened his mouth, but could find no suitably witty response and sat gaping like a goldfish.

The tutor, thus far oblivious to the interaction, looked up suddenly and clapped his hands.

'Right. If I could have everyone's attention . . .'

They all turned back towards him and the hum of conversation lulled.

'I can't stand arseholes like that,' Reggie said to me in a low voice, her Midlands accent even more pronounced than my own. 'Let's hope he drops out. I don't know anyone here. How about you? Apart from the ginger prick, of course.'

I shook my head.

'What other subjects are you taking?'

'French and History.'

'Well, that's settled it! Same as me. We must have a lot in common. Shall we sit together in the other lessons too, and then we'll both know someone, won't we?'

I looked at the back of Ryan's head, his ears still flushed, and felt smug. It felt good to see someone put the idiot in his place.

I warmed to Reggie at once, and as we got to know one another over the coming weeks, I started to see her socially, too. I think most people thought of me as her little sidekick, but I didn't really mind. I felt she was the first true friend I had ever had. She did some modelling work on the side and earned enough to rent her own place, and when things became increasingly difficult for me at home, eventually I moved in with her in our final year of sixth form. I never looked back.

Later, things really took off for Reggie. Without a second thought, she had dropped out of uni, having been snapped up by a prestigious model agency. By now she was earning a ridiculous amount posing for magazines and on the catwalk. And no wonder. She moved like a gazelle, the epitome of grace and elegance. I felt like the dowdy supporting actress to her exotic and infinitely more glamorous leading lady. Any time I had ever brought anyone home, their interest in me, if ever there had been any, waned noticeably as soon as they saw Reggie. It wasn't her fault, but it did little for my self-confidence, however much she tried to reassure me. With my poker-straight, medium-length mousy hair and slim but unremarkable figure, I felt decidedly average, and had all but given up on finding someone who found me either attractive or interesting. My only real assets, I had been told, were my almond-shaped, hazel eyes, inherited apparently from my father. One smooth-talker (who had lasted a whole two dates) had described them as 'the hypnotic eyes of a she-wolf'. I wasn't sure if that was a good thing or not, but it clearly hadn't been enough to keep him coming back for more.

Even before we moved to Avoncote, I had been seeing less and less of Reggie, as her modelling commitments took her away from home for long periods of time. We chatted regularly on the phone and she had congratulated me half-heartedly on the nuptials. Although she didn't say as much, I suspected that she was even less enthused about the idea of the pregnancy. She and Jack were civil to one another, but didn't really get along for some reason. They had very different priorities and I think their personalities clashed.

Reading between the lines, I think that deep down she thought I was making a mistake. Reggie was my friend, and I knew that she had my best interests at heart. I loved her dearly, and was saddened that the two people who meant the most to me in the world couldn't be friends. But I knew Jack was the one for me, and nothing would persuade me otherwise.

CHAPTER 8

While part of me wanted to see Reggie and hear all her news, I was slightly uneasy about her visit. It felt as though we had grown apart as my relationship with Jack blossomed and I almost felt disloyal to him, since there was obviously some unspoken animosity between them. And she represented my past, the old Stina; something which I was keen to shake off. I did miss our chats though, and wanted to tell her all about Avoncote and the weird goings-on in our house. We always used to shared everything and I missed talking to her and her infectious energy.

When not hopping on a flight to some far-flung location, she was languishing in a smart penthouse apartment in the centre of Birmingham. She'd sent me photos – it was huge, very modern with lots of glass and stainless steel, and views over the city skyline. It was all being funded by Akhmad, who, it turned out, was married. He'd always seemed rather an elusive figure, so it wasn't entirely a surprise; I'd only met him on the one occasion, when they hadn't been seeing one another long. He had called to the flat to collect her for a date, and on first impressions, I didn't think much of him, in all honesty. He was in his mid-thirties, expensively dressed, tall and very good-looking, with intense dark eyes and slicked-back hair. He had seemed aloof and impatient, pacing up and down the living room as he waited. When she emerged from the bedroom, he had disapproved of the outfit she had chosen to wear, so reluctantly she had changed into something more to his taste – which, personally, I found a little tacky, considering Reggie's impeccable dress sense. It surprised me that she had obliged him – she was usually so single-minded.

I had tried to be friendly and make conversation, but he was abrupt and clearly not interested in talking to me. Once or twice subsequently, Reggie had suggested going out as a foursome with Jack and myself, but I made excuses. I could just imagine the uncomfortable atmosphere, and knew Akhmad and Jack would never be on the same wavelength, either. Thankfully she stopped asking. But he kept her in the lifestyle to which she had always aspired, and the arrangement seemed to suit her. When she'd first told me about his wife, I didn't pretend to approve. I knew she wouldn't be remotely concerned about my, or anyone else's opinion, anyway. But she was my friend and in spite of everything, I still thought the world of her. Whatever happened, that wouldn't change.

*

Saturday morning came around quickly and I had a cursory tidy-up, although I knew Reggie wouldn't be fussed. We had shared a flat for over three years and she'd always been very casual about housework. I suspected Akhmad would probably have employed a cleaner for her. Maybe it was a reaction to having to care for my mum when I was young, but I loathed housework myself. I did what was necessary – most of the time, anyway – but I wasn't really house-proud. Thankfully Jack didn't seem to mind.

Kenny and his boys were still working on the roof and were round at the back of the property, but Jack had gone into work for the morning, so I was looking forward to having a good girlie natter. Remembering Reggie's allergy, I had put Jobie on his long lead and tied him to a fence post in the back garden, leaving him a big bowl of water by the door. He looked up at me dejectedly and I felt guilty.

A sleek red Audi convertible pulled up on the road and Reggie stepped out, all sunglasses and heels, her hair tied back with a multicoloured bandana, wearing cropped navy trousers and an ivory silk blouse. She was swinging a massive gift bag as she sauntered up the path. I rolled my eyes. She just had to make an entrance wherever she went.

I greeted her at the door and she gave me a huge grin. We shared a hug and I noticed her wince a little.

'Are you okay?' I asked.

'Oh, I'm fine; overdid it at the gym yesterday and my muscles are a bit sore, that's all.'

I heard a wolf whistle from above and looked up to see Kenny staring down.

'Morning!' He flashed her an enormous grin and she waved back flirtatiously. I couldn't help but smile.

'You'd better come in before he falls off the roof.'

Her familiar perfume filled the air as she stepped into the hallway.

'How are you, hon? It's been too long. And just look at you – all mumsy! The bump really suits you.'

'Hmm – I'm not too sure about that. But I'm good, thanks. No more morning sickness, so touch wood it's all going well; at the moment, anyway. I feel like a blob. How about you? You're looking great. Love the motor, by the way.'

'Oh yeah, a present from Akhmad. He likes to splash the cash. But then, he's got plenty of it to splash.' She grinned. 'It really is the ideal arrangement, you know. No strings, I can carry on living my life without having to worry about putting dinner on the table every night, or being at his beck and call. I'm not in his pocket. I still see other people.'

Her eyes moved skyward and she sighed theatrically.

'And my God, Stina. The *sex*. I've never known anything like it . . .'

I grinned. 'I see your priorities haven't changed! Come on, I'll get the kettle on.'

I made tea and we went through to the living room. Reggie took off the bandana and ran her fingers through her hair, then flopped back onto the settee.

'Oh God, that feels better. It's Gucci – cost a packet but it's got an itchy label and it makes me sweat. It was starting to get on my bloody nerves.'

She kicked off her shoes and swept up her legs. Her eyes panned round the room, the slight disappointment in her expression betraying her thoughts, but she nodded in polite approval. 'This is really lovely. Very . . .'

'Rustic?'

We both laughed.

'Probably not to your taste, I know, but we love it. It's so quiet here and it'll be a fantastic place to bring up a child. Still, there's a lot of work to be done before we get it how we want it.'

'I know I always go for more modern stuff, but this house has certainly got bags of character. It'll be fab once you've done it all up. It's very *you*.'

'What – dishevelled and in dire need of attention?'

'Don't be daft. You know what I mean. Oh, I almost forgot.' She reached down and passed me the gift bag. 'Belated house-warming pressie.'

Peering into the bag, I found two rectangular packages encased in bubble wrap. Eagerly, I peeled off the plastic, revealing two beautiful carved olive-wood bookends in the shape of owls. They were polished to a sheen, with huge amber glass eyes.

'Oh, they're gorgeous! Thank you so much.'

She smiled, pleased by my reaction. 'I remembered how much you loved that big old carved "mummy and baby" elephant I brought back from Thailand, and I know you and all your books. Thought these might appeal to you.'

'They can go in the alcove next to the fireplace – once I get Jack to put my shelves up. I'll sit them on the hearth for now. There are so many jobs to do, unfortunately.'

'How *is* Mr Wonderful? Still putting in the hours, I imagine.' There was an undisguised whiff of sarcasm in her tone. I didn't rise to it. 'Yes, he works hard.'

'Any more unwanted admirers at this new surgery?'

I grimaced at the memory of the annoying veterinary nurse. 'Thankfully not. All the female staff are older ladies with grown-up families, as far as I know. And that's just how I like it.'

She nodded, pursing her lips. 'Luc was asking after you, by the way.'

I squirmed. God knows why, but Luc, Reggie's younger brother, had developed a crush on me when we were first introduced. The feeling wasn't reciprocated. He was far too young – and something of a loose cannon. Luc's troubles with the police were a great source of worry to Reggie, who had always been protective of him. He had been very taken with me and annoyingly persistent, asking me to go out with him several times. Eventually I had to be quite blunt with him. I still felt awkward about it, more because I was worried about offending Reggie than anything else.

'And how is Luc?'

'Back on the straight and narrow, thank God. Akhmad's been brilliant – he found him a job in one of his restaurants. He's training to be a chef and he's not half bad, actually. My little bro! Who'd have thought it, eh?'

She got up and went to the window. Jobie was sprawled on the lawn, his head down, tongue lolling. He looked bored, and I felt guilty for excluding him. Mrs Barley was walking slowly up her path. She looked up sharply, clearly surprised to see an unfamiliar face. Reggie gave her a little wave, which she didn't return. Instead, the old woman paused for a moment, scrutinising my friend with narrowed, hostile eyes. As she disappeared back into the house, Reggie stuck up two fingers.

'Miserable old sod!'

'Oh, she's not so bad. Maybe you gave her a fright.'

'What, *moi*?' She laughed. 'You've got the makings of a nice little garden out there. Ooh – she's got a summer house next door! I've always fancied one of those. Eugh – don't think much of the weather vane, though.'

I looked out to see Corvus atop the summer house roof, surveying the ground below.

'Oh, it's that bloody crow. Freaks me out a bit, but it seems quite tame. It likes coming to see the old lady, anyway.'

Reggie shot me a look. 'That's just too weird. A crow? They're bad luck, aren't they? Sounds like something out of a creepy fairy tale. She got a cauldron in there too, or what?' She laughed. 'What are your other neighbours like?'

'There's only the old woman, Mrs Barley. She's a widow, no family. People round here don't seem to like her much for some reason. She keeps herself to herself most of the time. But she actually seems very nice when you get to know her. She's been a real friend to us, to be honest – even helped us out paying for the roof to be rethatched.'

Reggie pulled a face. 'You want to be careful. Don't get too chummy; you might finish up being her carer. You'll have enough on your plate with a sprog to look after. Rather you than me, on both counts.'

I threw a cushion at her. 'Don't be awful. You're such a cynic.'

She grinned. 'I'm a realist, love.' As she plonked back down onto the chair, her sleeve billowed up, revealing a huge purple welt on her forearm.

'Ouch. What happened there?'

'Akhmad . . . likes to play rough.' She gave a tinkling laugh, but her eyes avoided mine. I made no comment, observing as she fidgeted self-consciously with her cuff.

She reached across and patted my stomach. Diversion tactics. 'So, how long have you got to go now?'

'Too bloody long. I feel like a proper heifer already.'

'You look fine, really. Blooming.'

'That's a tactful way of telling me I'm fat. I'm eating far too much, I know. I'll need to come along to the gym with you once in a while, after the baby's born. I mustn't let myself go completely.'

'You are *not* fat. But yeah, that would be good. We don't see nearly enough of each other. I really miss our chats.' She looked suddenly pensive.

'Everything is . . . okay, isn't it?' I asked. Her expression made something twist uncomfortably inside me.

'Of course. Never been better.' She shook back her curls, avoiding eye contact as she surveyed the room once more. 'Life is treating me *very* well.'

We chatted for a couple of hours. She spoke a little about Akhmad, but eventually let slip that she also had a regular girlfriend, too; another model. She was keen to show me her photograph – a statuesque, striking girl with ebony skin, cropped hair and chiselled cheekbones.

'Her name's Maryam,' she told me, her eyes shining. 'She came over from Somalia with her family when she was twelve. We met on a shoot a couple of years ago, but we've grown really close these last few months. Her family were dirt poor and she's had a difficult upbringing. But she's kind and *so* smart – she actually has a degree

136

in philosophy – and she's got a great sense of humour, too. She's off here, there and everywhere at the moment, though, so I don't see her as often as I'd like to; but her career's really taking off, so it's great.'

Reading between the lines, I suspected that there was more genuine enthusiasm for the blossoming relationship with Maryam, but Akhmad was obviously funding things, and from what I could gather the arrangement was mutually convenient. I had the niggling feeling though, that, in spite of everything, deep down she wasn't really happy.

I told her about the noises in the attic and disrupted sleep, and she listened with wide-eyed interest.

'Get that bloody man of yours up there to have a proper look. It all sounds a bit iffy to me. I'd go up myself, but I'm not really dressed for it.'

I was glad that she didn't seem to think it was my imagination. 'There's been this bloke in the old lady's garden a couple of times, too. It's really odd. We can't get to the bottom of who he is.'

'Maybe she's hiding a fancy man in her loft! Two mysteries solved in one hit.' She glanced at her watch. 'Oh God, I'm afraid I'm really going to have to go, hon. I've got a casting call at 2 p.m. No rest for the wicked.'

As she opened the front door to leave, I was startled to find Mrs Barley standing on the doorstep, about to knock. She wore a pained expression and her lips were pinched into a thin line. She scowled at Reggie.

'Oh, hello, Mrs Barley – this is my friend, Reggie. She . . .'

'I just wanted to say – that car really shouldn't be parked on the kerb like that. It could block the way if

137

anyone passes by with a wheelchair – or a pram, for that matter.'

Reggie grimaced. 'Oh, sorry. I'm leaving now, anyway.'

'You should think about how you park in future – it's most inconsiderate.'

Before I could say anything, the old woman went back into her house, slamming the door.

Reggie raised her eyebrows. 'Fuck's sake! What was that all about?'

'Don't take any notice. She's a bit funny at times. I don't think she means anything by it – she can be very nice when she wants to be.'

'Well, I hope it's more often than when she doesn't. Grumpy old mare.'

She leaned in to give me a hug. 'Anyway, I really do have to get off or I'll be late. Don't be a stranger,' she told me. 'Keep in touch, and I want updates about the weird happenings in your loft.' She bobbed her tongue out in the direction of Mrs Barley's cottage and laughed. 'And keep *that* one at arm's length!'

I walked up the path to wave her off with a slightly apprehensive feeling. There was something a little desperate about the way she squeezed me as she left, and I suspected that everything in her world wasn't as rosy as she was making out. I wondered what the set-up with Akhmad was really like, and whether there was more to that bruise than overenthusiastic foreplay. I wondered too if he was aware that he wasn't her only love interest. But Reggie was a strong woman. I had to trust that she was in control of her life; that if things weren't right, she would have the good sense to cut her ties and move on. Wouldn't she?

No amount of luxury was worth being miserable. And certainly not being anyone's punchbag.

'You know you can tell me anything, don't you, Reg? I'm always here if you need to talk.'

Reggie hesitated as she was about to climb into the car. I wondered for a moment if she was on the verge of sharing something, but then she painted on that famous smile, the one she reserved for the cameras. 'Sure, hon. I know that. But I'm fine – never better. You don't need to worry about me – I'm a born survivor. You concentrate on yourself and that baby.'

'We must have lunch in town soon – let's keep in touch more, eh?' Then, as an afterthought: 'I've really missed you, you know.'

'You too, babe. But I've *really* got to go.'

As she drove away, I turned back towards the house and saw Mrs Barley staring from her upstairs window after Reggie's disappearing car. The look on her face was what I can only describe as one of loathing. It chilled me to the bone.

Jobie was delighted to be allowed back into the house, and I gave him an extra bone biscuit and lots of fuss. Ridiculously, I felt quite wrung out after all the talking and lay down on the settee. I could hear Kenny and the boys calling to one another outside. There seemed to be some excitement. Groaning, I eased myself off the chair and went to see what was going on.

'Well, we've had an interesting find, if you can call it that.' Kenny, who had just descended the ladder, turned to me as I stepped outside. 'What do you make of this, then?'

139

I recoiled as he held out what looked initially like a bundle of rags. On closer inspection, I saw that it was an old bath towel or something of a similar size, the once-white fabric filthy and shredded, wrapped round the remains of some poor dead animal, about two feet in length. As Kenny peeled back the cloth, it revealed what looked like a mummified cat. The skin was pale and parchment-like, stretched taut over the delicate, protruding bones. The unfortunate creature's ears were pressed back, the teeth bared, its mouth gaping open as though desperate for air. It was quite disturbing.

'Oh, that's awful. Where did you find the poor thing?'

'It was wedged in the old lady's chimney, just above the rafters. Some of the bricks were loose and I'd taken a bit of mortar up there to repoint it. Got a bit of a shock when I pulled one out!' He offered the animal forward as if to demonstrate the point. 'I've heard of this before – never found one myself, mind. People years ago had some odd beliefs – thought that burying things alive in their walls would ward off evil, apparently. I've seen a few witch markings in my time, though – even found a witch bottle once.'

'*Witch* markings?' The term sent an awful coldness through me.

'Oh, folk would carve things into beams – star shapes and such – to protect their homes from wicked spirits.'

I suddenly recalled the strange shapes I had noticed carved into the beams in The Green Man and felt quite light-headed.

'The bottles are *proper* fascinating,' he went on. 'The one I found was a real work of art – stoneware, all decorated with little flowers and bearded faces. I gave it to a local museum in the end – the wife wouldn't have it in the house. I s'pose I can understand why. Full of teeth and little bones and bent pins, it was – and fingernail clippings. And to top it off, there was pee in there too. Bloody stank to high heaven, it did. The idea was that the urine would draw the witch into the bottle when she came down the chimney, Christ knows why, and then the sharp things would trap her there. Poor old Santa had better watch his arse, eh!' He laughed bawdily. 'It all sounds daft to us, I know; but it still goes on in some places, or so I've heard.'

'*Jesus Christ*. There's another one, Dad.' From the roof, Shaun, the older of Kenny's two boys, held a similar bundle aloft, his face contorted in distaste. He climbed down and placed the dead creature carefully on the lawn. We all stared down at it. The cat's appearance was much the same as the first, its front legs extended as though reaching out for something. The eyes were open but dried out, the thin tail stiff and string-like. It was like something from a horror film.

'So you say people used to do this years ago?'

'Oh arr, back as far as the 1600s, I think.'

I peered dubiously at the two pitiful bundles, now placed side by side at my feet. My initial revulsion replaced by curiosity, I looked more closely at Shaun's discovery. Again, the cat was wrapped in a rectangle of indeterminate material, although it was in a marginally better state of repair than the first. I suddenly noticed a small, frayed square of cloth protruding from its outer edge.

'That looks remarkably like a label to me. I don't

think they put labels on things hundreds of years ago, did they?'

Kenny scratched his head. 'No, I don't imagine they did.'

He bent down to scrutinise the tiny scrap of fabric, turning it from side to side, then looked up at me with a smirk.

'You're right. And I'm bloody sure they didn't have Woolies then, either.'

'Sorry?'

'Woolworths. Winfield – that's what it says. You can just about make it out. That was their brand name. I remember my old gran having a lot of stuff from there.'

'So these poor things probably haven't been in the chimney all that long, then.' I was thinking aloud, remembering what Lucy had said about cats going missing in the area, and felt suddenly nauseous.

'Not hundreds of years, that's for sure.' Kenny tipped his head towards Mrs Barley's house. 'Maybe the old dear can shed some light, if you'd care to ask her.'

I didn't respond. I had no wish to interrogate the old woman about the contents of her roof space. The more things that came to light, the more uneasy I was beginning to feel about her. It was all deeply unsettling.

After Kenny and the boys had left, I kept Jobie in the house, leaving the mummies on the lawn to show Jack.

When he returned, the medic in him was fascinated with their state of decomposition, or rather the lack of it. He knelt down on the grass to get a closer look.

'The preservation is incredible. They've somehow become naturally desiccated. I've never seen anything

142

mummified in the flesh before – if you know what I mean.'

'Yes, it's all very interesting, I'm sure. But what worries me is how the hell the poor things got there in the first place.'

'If it hadn't been for the cloth, I'd have said misadventure. But someone's gone to a lot of trouble to conceal them. I think we need to ask our Mrs Barley if she knows anything.'

I still felt slightly queasy. I watched as Jack strode back into the house. Moments later he returned, and Mrs Barley came out of her back door. She hobbled down her path, looking flustered as she craned her neck to look over the fence.

'Oh, my! So these were inside my chimney?' She cupped her hands round her cheeks in horror, her eyes wide. 'Oh, how awful. What a shocking thing to find. To think they've been up there all these years and I'd no idea. I wonder if the old man who lived in Rose Cottage before us put them up there? He was a strange chap and no mistake. He had to go into a home and they pretty much had to drag him kicking and screaming, from what I heard.'

Jack and I exchanged glances. The old lady appeared genuinely appalled. Maybe she really didn't know anything after all.

We buried the cats at the bottom of the garden. I felt saddened that someone had probably lost their pets and that the animals had met with such a tragic end. But more than anything, exactly how that end must have been brought about played on my mind.

CHAPTER 9

That night I lay awake once more, mulling over the events of the day. I wondered initially about Reggie. What exactly was going on beneath the façade of her outwardly perfect existence? And what had provoked such an extreme reaction towards my friend from Mrs Barley when she didn't even know her? My mind soon became a jumble of witchcraft, the unfortunate mummi-fied cats, the man in the garden. So much was going round my head I felt it might explode.

A low squeaking sound shook me from my thoughts. It had started again.

My heart in my mouth, I strained to listen as the floorboards groaned slowly overhead. I considered waking Jack, but he was snoring loudly and reluctantly I thought better of it. I desperately wanted him to hear what I had been hearing, but he'd had a long day and looked exhausted that evening – it seemed unfair to disturb him. I wriggled to a sitting position, holding my breath. Not as loud or obvious as on the first occasion, but something was definitely moving in the attic. I got up and padded out onto the landing where the hatch was immediately above me, illuminated by the light of the full moon pouring through the bathroom window. I wouldn't attempt to climb through it, but I could have a peep . . .

There was a torch in the kitchen. I groped my way downstairs and rummaged through the drawer. The floor felt cool beneath my bare feet, although the air was warm and humid. All was silent except for the background hum of the fridge. Jobie stretched and came trotting to greet me from his basket, but I coaxed him back gently, closing the door behind me. Adrenaline coursed through me as I climbed the stairs. I fetched the wooden storage stool from the bathroom. Brandishing the flashlight, I pulled myself up, poised to release the catch that opened the trapdoor, and quivering in anticipation. For a moment, I thought I heard whispering from above and stood, perfectly still, hardly daring to breathe as I tried to make out the words.

I don't know what happened. I can only assume I must have become dizzy. The next thing I knew, I was lying on the landing, Jack frantically rubbing my arm.

'Stina! Are you okay? What the hell were you doing?'

With his support, I eased myself up to a sitting position, still dazed. My head throbbed; I had somehow cut my leg and there was blood seeping through my pyjama trousers. The distorted beam of the torch was angled towards the bathroom. Its lens must have cracked when it fell to the floor.

'I heard noises again – up there.' Wincing, I waved a hand towards the hatch.

'For God's sake, you could have broken your bloody neck if you'd fallen down the stairs.' He helped me to my feet, regarding me with a mixture of concern and exasperation as I staggered a little. 'I'm taking you to A & E – you need checking over.'

I protested that I was fine, but he was insistent.

We spent over two hours in the hospital waiting room, but thankfully, an egg-sized lump on the back of my head and the cut shin aside, I was relatively unscathed. More importantly, the baby's heartbeat was strong and it was kicking wildly to make its presence known. An emergency ultrasound confirmed that everything looked fine. I almost cried with relief.

'Don't you *ever* do anything like that again,' Jack warned me as we lay in bed later. I felt tearful and foolish, thinking of the damage I could have done to our baby.

'I'm sorry.' My voice was as small as I felt.

He sighed, turning and pulling me to him. 'You gave me such a scare. That could've ended really badly. You do realise that?'

'I know, it was a stupid thing to do. But I was sure I heard someone moving around again, and then voices up there, too. It's driving me crazy.'

'Listen, I'll take the morning off, go in a bit later,' he said, then seeing my surprise that he'd be going in at all, added, 'I know it's Sunday, but it's been really busy this week and I had promised to do a few hours. I'll go up into the attic and have a proper look, see if there's anything obvious going on. Hopefully it'll put your mind at rest. In the meantime, try to get some sleep.'

Drained by my ordeal, I nestled gratefully into the safety of his arms and soon drifted off, the rising sun spilling across us where we lay. I dreamed fitfully of multitudes of panic-stricken cats, clawing at the walls of our home in a bid for freedom; of Kenny's witch bottle, tumbling down the chimney and spewing its revolting contents onto the living room floor; of Mrs Barley chanting over a candlelit shrine.

And of the menacing shadow of a man's hand, reaching down towards me through the ceiling.

*

My head banging, I woke to hear voices outside. Jack was talking to Kenny. I groaned, remembering he had said he would be calling briefly, to finish tying the area he had been working on the previous day. Inevitably it would mean more noise.

Aching and a little bruised after my fall, I eased myself from the bed and made my way over to the window, looking down at them in the garden. Kenny was rubbing a hand across his chin, looking bemused, but their conversation was too muffled to decipher. Feeling slightly woozy, I went slowly downstairs and into the kitchen to get a glass of water. Jack came in through the French doors.

'Morning, Trouble. How are you doing?' He kissed the crown of my head. I still felt sheepish.

'I've been better.'

'Well, you'll be pleased to learn that I could find no evidence of anything untoward in the attic. It was a bit of a bugger getting through that hatch, mind you. It does look as though there's been some movement up there, but I'm willing to bet that it's being caused by visitors of the furry kind.'

'What d'you mean?'

'Squirrels. The loft's been insulated at some point with that loose-fill stuff, and there's quite a pile of it that's been heaped up. It's fairly common, apparently. Looks like they've started building a nest. Kenny says it wasn't like that the other day. He'll move it all back, and once the netting's in place, it'll stop them getting in again. They chew everything, so apart from damaging the joists, they can be a fire hazard if they start nibbling through cables.'

'But it was so loud – heavy, like footsteps. And what about the whispering?'

'They can be noisy, so I understand. I remember one of the chaps who worked for my dad saying he had an infestation in his roof a few years back. He reckoned it sounded like a herd of elephants running around up there. I suppose everything's amplified when it's coming through the ceiling. And as for the whispering you thought you heard – well, things can sound distorted, can't they – especially in the dead of night. It could've been water trickling through the pipes, or anything.'

I wasn't convinced, but decided not to push it. I *knew* the type of noise I'd heard couldn't possibly have been caused by squirrels – could it? Or was it feasible that there was indeed a perfectly mundane and rational explanation for it all, and that my mind was playing tricks on me? I thought suddenly of my mum, and a feeling of panic began to well inside me. Before it grew more serious, her mental illness had begun as neuroses. Could my own pregnancy have triggered something similar in me? It didn't bear thinking about.

Jack went into work right before lunch. I didn't have the energy to even take a shower or get dressed. Half-heartedly, I sat myself at the table to resume work on my feature. I wanted to focus more on the mundane and less on folklore or anything remotely away from the norm, not wishing to dwell further on the more sinister aspects of Avoncote's past. I opened the document and stared in horror at the screen. Beyond the title page, it was blank. Frantically I scrolled through, but there was nothing there. *Completely* empty. What the hell had happened? I *knew* I'd saved it. In desperation I went through all my files, but it had definitely gone. Weeks of work, for nothing. Stupidly I hadn't even backed it up – maybe I'd been lucky in the past, but this had never happened to me before. I could have cried.

A sudden yell from outside made me look up with a jolt. Kenny was running down the path as though the hounds of hell were after him. I went outside to see what was happening, in time to see him accosting Bob, who was just about to come through Mrs Barley's back gate. The poor man looked mystified and ruffled as Kenny held him firmly by the arm, like someone making a citizen's arrest. I hurriedly made my way down the garden.

'This the bugger who keeps loitering?' Kenny turned to look at me, his eyes flashing with anger, and I was worried he might actually hit Bob.

'No, no. This is Bob, Mrs Barley's gardener.'

Kenny released his grip, his face relaxing as he examined

Bob more closely. 'Sorry, mate. I didn't get a proper look at you – thought I'd better grab first and ask questions later. Stina says there's been some dodgy bloke hanging around – can't be too careful, eh?'

Flustered, Bob rearranged his overalls, trying to muster some composure.

'No, but you could've asked first.'

'I'll buy you a pint when you've finished up here. No hard feelings, eh?'

Bob grinned good-naturedly. 'No, I suppose not. And you can throw in a whisky chaser for good measure.'

Kenny looked sheepish. He shook Bob by the hand and went back to the scaffolding.

Mrs Barley appeared, disturbed by the activity.

'What's going on?'

Bob was wheeling his lawnmower through the gate. 'Case of mistaken identity, Mrs B. Nothing for you to worry about.'

I turned to her. 'We have squirrels, apparently. Jack went up into the loft after I heard more noises last night.'

She clapped a hand to her mouth in exaggerated alarm. 'Oh, dear. At least he's found out what was making the racket that kept you up, then. Mystery solved!'

After returning from the hospital, I had changed my clothes, but blood oozing through the dressing on my leg was evident. The old woman peered at me over the fence.

'Ooh that looks nasty. What happened, love?' Her brow furrowed in concern.

I pulled a face. 'Stupid of me, really. I was trying to look through the hatch into the loft and fell off the stool I'd been standing on. I think I must have blacked out.'

'Good Lord! You poor thing. And how's your head?'

I put a hand to the lump. It was tender and bigger than ever.

'A bit sore. My own silly fault, though. It could've been much worse.'

'Don't you go trying to do anything like that again, will you? You need to have a restful day. I bet you're properly shaken up. I'll be baking later, so I'll drop a cake round, cheer you up a bit.'

She disappeared back into the house.

It was only afterwards that it dawned on me. I hadn't mentioned my head. How could she have known? Maybe she had noticed it when I turned round; it was quite swollen, after all.

I tried to dismiss the thought and returned with a heavy heart to my article. Thankfully I'd made copious notes and could remember at least some of the content, but I was so rattled by everything that it was futile. Soon I had to abandon the idea, since even the tiniest creak had me leaping from my chair in anticipation of an uninvited and potentially malevolent guest. I couldn't shake the feeling that something was very wrong in my home.

CHAPTER 10

A fortnight passed, and work on the roof was finally complete. There was brief excitement when we thought that there had been a glimpse of Mrs Barley's mystery man one afternoon a few days earlier by Shaun, when a dark-haired man had appeared on the old woman's doorstep. When the boy tore down the ladder to demand to know what he wanted, however, the startled man turned out to be from the electricity board and had only come to read the meter. It had now been some weeks since I had seen the intruder and I was beginning to hope we'd seen the last of him. I was even starting to question whether he had actually been a figment of my imagination. I wasn't sure which explanation was the least appealing: the prospect of someone lurking, or the fact that I could no longer rely on my own judgement.

I felt quite isolated and missed having Reggie to confide in. I wondered how she was getting on and still had a nagging feeling that all wasn't right with her. I needed to set aside my irritation regarding her feelings about Jack – she had always been there for me in the past. Even if it wasn't possible to see one another as often as we used to, I felt determined that we shouldn't lose touch – if she was too busy to drive over, maybe we could meet up for lunch in Brum one day.

I was almost sorry to say goodbye to Kenny and the boys as, in spite of all the noise, they had been good fun, and a comforting presence while Jack had been at work, particularly with a strange man prowling the neighbourhood. As they were putting their tools back in the van, I went to the shop to buy them some beers by way of a parting gift.

I was being served when Nick came in.

'I've just seen Eddie. Lucy had the baby last night – nearly a month early, so a bit unexpected, but all's well with both mother and baby, apparently. Another little boy.'

'Oh, that *is* good news. I know she was getting really fed up – as long as everything's okay, maybe it's for the best. Those last few weeks can be hell.' Judy winked at me. 'Ooh – you'll be next, eh! Lovely to have more little ones in the village. God knows when *our* kids are going to produce some grandchildren for us.'

'Something for you to look forward to in future!' I said, smiling.

Leaving the bottles on the counter, I went to select a suitable card from the revolving rack for Lucy. I was glad that she and the baby were safe and well, and wondered how Alfie was going to feel about sharing his mummy with the new arrival. I hoped he would cope with no longer being the centre of her universe.

*

Kenny and his sons were about to leave when I got back. They seemed most appreciative of the beer.

Kenny shook me by the hand. 'Good luck with the baby and all. And you watch out for that weirdo – something very fishy there. You want to train that dog of yours up to attack.'

'Fat chance of that! But thanks.'

I waved them off and went inside to write the card for Lucy, then walked back up the road with Jobie to post it through her door before Jack returned from work.

I hadn't intended to knock, but Lucy's husband Eddie, wearing only a vest and boxer shorts, opened the front door as I was walking away. We'd never actually been introduced. He wasn't particularly good-looking, but broad-shouldered and muscular, with numerous tasteless tattoos. He looked dishevelled and rather surly. I could hear Alfie wailing plaintively from upstairs, and wondered if I should have waited a while.

'Sorry – I didn't mean to disturb you. It's just a card to say congratulations about the baby. How's Lucy doing?'

'She's all right. Bit knackered as you'd expect – I am, too. I've been trying to get the littl'un to have a nap, but he ain't having any of it. We were up all sodding night. Luce and the bab'll be back home tomorrow.' He looked me up and down. 'You'll be Stina, then? She's mentioned you a couple of times.' His blatant lack of enthusiasm made me wonder what she'd said.

'Yes.' There was an awkward pause. 'Well, congratulations to you both, anyway. Tell Lucy I was asking after her and hopefully I'll see her soon.'

He grunted and tilted his head back slightly, his stubbly chin jutting, then disappeared into the house. Feeling slightly annoyed, I made my way home.

I let Jobie out. Mrs Barley was pottering in the back garden, wielding secateurs in her fingerless gloves. I often wondered if she even slept in them. I groaned inwardly; I wasn't in the mood to talk to her.

'Well, it's all done now, then. They've made a decent job of it, at any rate.' She waved up towards the roof.

'Yes. No more leaks, with a bit of luck.' Even though I wasn't keen to engage her in conversation, I thought I would tell her about Lucy. 'I've just heard that my friend from up the road has had her baby; a few weeks early, too. I'm next in the queue.'

'Oh yes, that girl with the little lad – Alfie, wasn't it? I don't know her name, but I've seen her walking past now and again – and when she came to see you, of course.' She appeared to ponder for a moment, then enquired casually, 'Is all well with the baby – quite healthy, is it?'

It wasn't an unreasonable question, but there was something about the way she said it that set an alarm ringing somewhere within me. 'Yes, as far as I know everything's fine with both of them.'

She nodded. 'Good, good.' I couldn't be sure, but thought I detected a hint of disappointment in her voice. She shuffled her feet. 'Well, she'll have her work cut out, with two of them.'

'Still, lovely news though.'

'Yes, I suppose it is.' She gave a half-hearted smile. 'What did she have?'

'Another little boy. Nice that Alfie will have someone to play with when he's a bit older.'

All pretence dropped away now; her voice became suddenly harsh and her eyes cold. 'Let's hope they get on, then. Not all siblings do, you know.'

Without another word, she retreated into the house. It struck me as an unnecessarily negative and unkind remark. But it was her peculiar, almost contemptuous expression that troubled me most. At times Mrs Barley's behaviour was undeniably erratic and disturbing.

CHAPTER 11

We were now well into August and the days were gradually shortening. Autumn and consequently my due date were on the horizon. Since work on the roof had ceased, so had the strange noises from the attic. My sleep pattern still wasn't good, but I was glad not to have any additional nocturnal disturbances. Despite Jack's insistence, I remained unconvinced about the squirrel theory. What I had heard was definitely human footsteps, not the scurrying of industrious little creatures preparing for the arrival of their offspring.

It was almost as though the activity had unsettled something, but whatever it had been was now calm once more. My imagination going into overdrive, I had been googling frantically, finding several instances where building work and renovation had caused disruption of a paranormal nature in old houses. I always used to sit firmly on the fence with regard to belief in the supernatural, but with everything that had been going on – and the more I was discovering – I had become increasingly open to the idea that there might actually be something else out there. And I was desperate to have some sort of explanation, however implausible. Maybe some dormant spirit had been upset by the removal of the old thatch? Whatever the cause, the main thing was that it had stopped as abruptly as it began. Equally strangely, the man in the garden hadn't put in any further appearances, either. Everything seemed more settled, somehow; Mrs Barley had become much more consistent and pleasant of late, and I was feeling more positive about things generally. I wondered about Lucy and how she was getting on. I felt bad that I hadn't seen her for a while, but with everything that had been going on I'd been preoccupied. I made a mental note to pay her a visit when I got the chance. From everything she'd said, I couldn't imagine Eddie was being much help.

I had thought too about contacting Reggie to tell her about the dead cats, as she'd clearly been fascinated by what was happening in our home. She'd texted me the day after her visit asking if she'd left her designer bandana behind, but there was no sign of it so I assumed she must have dropped it on the road or something. She had said flippantly that she'd just have to get Akhmad to buy her another one. I hadn't heard anything from her since. I wondered, too, how things actually were between her and Akhmad, and whether he'd got wind of the fact that he had competition. I tried her mobile, but it went straight to voicemail. Maybe she was on location somewhere. I left a brief message saying it was nothing urgent, and hung up.

Now that the house was quiet once more, I needed to polish my article about Avoncote so that I could finish it before the deadline, which was looming. I'd managed to negotiate an extension to the original submission date with my contact at the magazine, who said it would be a shame to miss the Halloween issue but if I couldn't manage it, they would print it in the subsequent edition. I was extremely grateful. I hadn't dared admit I'd been stupid enough not to have my work backed up. I felt a bit guilty about it, but fibbed, saying that I'd been unwell due to my pregnancy. It was a lesson well learned.

Thankfully, I felt less tired and more focused for once. I worked all morning and, having made good progress, was almost ready to hit 'send' to the editor I had been liaising with at the magazine. I felt quite elated, but decided to pause for a sandwich before a final proofread, with the intention of submitting it by the end of the afternoon.

I cleared up after lunch, and was sitting on the settee finishing a mug of tea before resuming work. It was a still, mellow afternoon. I looked out into the garden and could see Mrs Barley in the summer house. She looked deep in thought.

My mobile rang, and Reggie's name flashed on the screen.

'Hey, you! I tried to reach you earlier . . .' I was cut off in mid-sentence by a quavering male voice.

'Stina, this is Luc.'

My innards clenched and a shiver of dread passed through me.

'Luc? What's happened? Is Reggie okay?'

161

There was a horrible silence, then he emitted a strangled sob. 'Reggie's . . . gone. She's dead.'

I felt as if I had been punched. My head began to swim. The mug fell from my hand, smashing on the hearth.

'What d'you mean? No, no she can't be. Oh God, has there been an accident? This can't be happening.' I wanted to be sick.

His voice was strained, barely more than a whisper. 'I found her. I came round earlier as I hadn't heard from her for a few days. She was lying there, next to the fireplace. Stone cold. The police are here now. I don't know what the fuck to do.'

'Luc, I'm so sorry. I just can't take it in. What the hell happened?'

'It looks as though someone's caved her head in and she's got two black eyes. I think the bastard's finally flipped. She should have got out months ago. I knew something like this would happen.'

Akhmad. What was it that she'd said? That he liked to 'play rough' – but it had clearly been much more than that. I had known something was wrong. Why hadn't I tried to contact her sooner? I was her closest friend. Maybe I could have made her see sense, persuaded her to leave him. It was all so preventable, so tragic. I felt overwhelmed with guilt.

'He treated her like shit. The guy's a control freak. She'd been wanting to call it a day for ages. I feel terrible. I think she only stalled because he'd given me a job, and she was worried about messing things up for me. She must've finally told him . . .'

162

The wave of anger and hatred I felt towards a man I hardly knew momentarily eclipsed the feelings of shock and grief.

'Stina? Are you still there?'

'Yes, yes; I'm sorry. It's just – I can't get my head round it. She's always so full of life. I can't believe she's gone.' My heart went out to Luc; poor Luc, who had always relied so heavily on his sister's support. Always impetuous and cocky, but underneath I recognised that he was insecure and full of self-doubt. What would become of him, without Reggie to bail him out or even give him a metaphorical kick up the backside now and again; her comforting arms when he needed a shoulder to cry on?

The tears came now. My lovely, audacious friend. Her life cut cruelly short by someone who was supposed to care for her. It was so unnecessary, so unfair.

'Luc, I have to go. I can't think straight at the moment. Can I call you back later? Text me your number. Look after yourself, sweetheart. I'm so very sorry. I really can't believe it.'

He mumbled a goodbye and hung up. Jobie sat at my feet, looking up at me quizzically. I buried my face in his silky fur and sobbed. He nuzzled my hand gently, his expression suddenly sad, as if he could read my mind. I felt a rush of love for him. The empathy animals can feel is extraordinary.

I needed to talk to someone. I wondered about messaging Lucy but it didn't really seem appropriate, given the fact that she was probably worn out and busy with the baby. She didn't need my own troubles on top of her own. There was no one else around I could tell,

163

only Mrs Barley; I wasn't sure I wanted to share the news with her, but I desperately needed to be with someone. I stumbled out into the garden, tears streaming down my face, the dog close behind me.

Seeing me, the old woman came anxiously out of the summer house. Corvus, her crow companion, must have been sitting with her. He followed her out and, seeing Jobie, took to the air.

'Whatever is it, love? Are you all right?'

The words I didn't want to believe tumbled out. 'Oh God, Mrs Barley, I've just had some terrible news. My friend is dead. She's been killed. It's so horrible.'

'You poor thing. What an awful shock. Was that your friend who visited a few weeks ago with the red car?'

I nodded, shaking violently as the sobs tore through my whole body. The pain was physical, a deep ache within the solar plexus.

'Come on, let me make you a cup of tea and you can tell me all about it.'

We sat in the summer house, Jobie at my feet, his concerned eyes never leaving my face. Everything poured from me almost involuntarily. I told Mrs Barley about Akhmad; about poor Reggie's miserable upbringing and how she had worked so hard to put it behind her. I told her about her kindness, her sense of humour and how she had been such a good friend to me; how I had been able to trust her enough to share secrets about my own past with her, even things I could never tell Jack.

'And now I'll never see her again. I can't get my head round it. She was a force of nature – always so full of energy. It's just not fair.'

164

Mrs Barley's voice was quiet and measured. 'It's a terrible blow, when someone is taken from us so suddenly. It will take a while for it to sink in properly, I'm afraid. There are all sorts of emotions to struggle with. You'll need time. But eventually you'll remember the good times you shared, even smile about the silly things that you argued over.' She squeezed my hand. 'It may not feel like it now, but the pain will lessen. You will make other friends.'

Her closing remark seemed insensitive. I didn't want to make other friends. I just wanted Reggie back.

She stared into space, lost in thought. I realised then that this was not about Reggie or my own grief at all: it was, as ever, Frank she was thinking of. At first, my sadness was overridden by anger. But then I thought how grateful I should be that I still had my lovely Jack, and all I wanted to do was have him hold me in his arms and make it all go away.

*

Luc looked older and much thinner than when we'd last met a couple of years earlier, the strain of recent events evident in his drawn face. In spite of his best efforts to make the occasion a joyous celebration of her life, Reggie's funeral was desperately sad. The chapel was packed to capacity, with several people forced to stand outside. Fortunately, it was a sunny and pleasantly warm early September day. Everyone had been told to wear bright, cheerful colours, but the misery exuded by the mourners told a different story. Many of those present were breathtakingly beautiful models and acclaimed designers that Reggie had worked with over the years, but everyone seemed to be struggling to maintain a semblance of dignity as the flower-bedecked coffin was carried through the door.

Luc delivered a faltering yet heartfelt eulogy, to the sound of muted sobs. Jack was solemn and supportive, holding my hand tightly throughout the service. I felt as though I were in a bubble. None of it seemed real. I looked at the lonely coffin, perched on a trolley at the front of the chapel. Reggie's smiling face stared out from a photograph propped on its lid. I could not connect this box, this inanimate, functional object, with my beautiful friend. She had been in her prime; so full of life, her future stretching promisingly before her. I could still hear her wicked giggle, picture the grin that so often lit up her face, hear the dirty jokes that she loved to shock people with. I thought of the gentle side to her nature: her kindness, her loyalty to those she loved. It all felt like a bad dream.

Afterwards, people assembled in sombre clusters, looking on as hundreds of helium-filled balloons were released outside the crematorium. Luc switched on a portable speaker, and Reggie's favourite song, Coldplay's 'The Scientist', filled the air. The finality of it all was almost too much to bear.

Seeing us through the crowd, Luc came over as people gradually began to disperse. He hugged me and shook Jack by the hand.

'I'm so glad you could come. Reggie thought the world of you, you know.'

'And I thought the world of her, too. Oh, Luc, she's

166

going to leave such a gap in our lives.' I fought back the tears as I thought of the last time Reggie and I had met. If only she'd opened up to me, told me what Akhmad was really like. If only I'd listened to my own instinct that something was actually very wrong – asked her outright whether he was violent. Maybe I could have helped, although how, I wasn't sure. How do you persuade someone to leave an abusive partner unless they've made that decision for themselves? There were so many what-ifs. It was torture.

He nodded miserably, his eyes swimming with tears. Suddenly noticing someone behind me, he beckoned wildly. 'Have you met Maryam?'

I looked round to see a willowy, elegant black girl weaving her way towards us. She was extraordinarily beautiful, but looked exhausted and utterly desolate.

'Maryam, this is Stina, and her husband, Jack.'

Maryam smiled sadly, shaking Jack hesitantly by the hand. She bent forward to give me a tentative squeeze. Her slight frame felt so thin, I worried her bones might snap. I recognised Reggie's signature perfume and hot tears sprang to my eyes.

'I've heard a lot about you, Stina. It's good to meet you at last. Reggie spoke very highly of you.' Her English was perfect, the accent still heavily influenced by her African heritage.

'She told me all about you, too. You made her very happy.'

'And she brought me such happiness. We had so many plans . . .' She broke down suddenly, burying her face in her hands.

I felt so sorry for the girl. I put my arms round her, and she wept as if her heart would break. Jack looked on awkwardly as we stayed like that for some time. Eventually she drew back, composing herself. She dragged the back of her hand across her eyes.

'May I call on you?' she asked me. 'I'd like you to have something of Reggie's – for a keepsake. I know you were very close.'

'Of course. Luc will give you my number. You can come and spend a few hours in the country!'

'I'll look forward to it. I'm sorry we've had to meet under such circumstances.'

I watched her wend her way back towards a group of tall, expensively dressed girls waiting by a parked limousine. She turned to wave as they all climbed into the car and were whisked away.

Protesting his innocence, Akhmad had been arrested and was 'helping police with their inquiries'. Reggie had sustained a fatal head injury. It appeared that she had fallen backwards and landed against the edge of the hearth, resulting in a basilar fracture of her skull, which in turn had caused a massive bleed on the brain.

The whole horrible incident had actually been on the regional news. Reggie was something of a celebrity in the area, and naturally the story had been pounced on and sensationalised by the local newspapers. Her lovely, smiling face, captured in an informal photograph taken by Maryam, had made the front page of one. It was surreal.

Someone in a neighbouring apartment had regularly heard shouting and things being thrown, but nothing had ever been reported to the police. Their rows had been frequent and violent. Reggie had told Luc the week before she died that she intended to leave Akhmad for good, to start afresh and move in with Maryam. Clearly, the news had not been well received.

I was relieved that Akhmad was in police custody, since I knew Luc would have killed him in a heartbeat. I, too, would have been happy to see the man dead, quite frankly, but I didn't want Luc to lose his freedom. Reggie had been so pleased that he seemed to have turned his back on a life of criminality. I really hoped he would pursue his dream of becoming a chef, and had told him so.

The wake, paid for by Reggie's model agency, was held in a smart, modern hotel in the city centre, all marble floors and glittering chandeliers. Jack clasped my hand reassuringly as we went through the imposing double doors into the function room, and I was so grateful for his presence. It was a vast space, but the mourners filled it easily. We showed our faces for an hour, but I felt like a fish out of water. Champagne flowed, and waiting staff proffered trays of exotic-looking canapés. Of course, I couldn't drink, and really had no appetite, either. The atmosphere was understandably sombre and the conversation stilted. There must have been over two hundred people present, and I didn't know anyone, apart from Luc. I suddenly realised how compartmentalised Reggie's life had been.

Poor Maryam had had to fly off for a photoshoot in Spain. I thought how terrible it must have been for her, having to pose and pout when all she must have wanted to do was curl up in a corner and cry. I went into the toilets and found a small group of models cutting lines of cocaine by the sink. It seemed so inappropriate and disrespectful. I just wanted to get away from there. We made our excuses and left.

The misery in the air that day was tangible. The brutal actions of one man had affected the lives of so many people. I prayed that my friend would get the justice she deserved and hoped that Akhmad was finding incarceration sheer torture. I thought about the man's wife, and wondered if she might actually be glad to see the back of him. Monsters like that rarely reserve their brutality for only one woman.

*

By the time we returned home, I felt emotionally drained. Jobie greeted us enthusiastically as we entered the house, and after we'd given him plenty of fuss, Jack let him out into the garden. I slumped into the chair. My head was buzzing with the memory of the day and the devastating knowledge that I would never see Reggie again. I felt empty and exhausted.

Jack looked at me, his head cocked to one side. He gave a sympathetic smile.

'I'll get the kettle on,' he said gently. 'I think we could both do with a cuppa.'

'Come here a minute.'

'Hmm?'

I eased myself from the sofa and wrapped my arms around his neck. At that moment I felt such an incredible surge of love for him, it almost took my breath away.

'I couldn't have got through today without you. You really are my rock.'

He pulled back for a moment, looking earnestly into my eyes, then drew me to him and kissed me on the lips. That lingering kiss told me that I was loved and wanted. It was enough to lift me from the depths of despair; to remind me that, in spite of everything, life goes on.

*

A few days after the funeral, I had just come in from Jobie's morning walk when my mobile rang. I answered in a rush without checking the caller's identity, and was surprised to hear Luc's voice as I picked up. He sounded agitated.

'Stina, I've had a visit from the police – I thought you should know. It's going to be in the papers anyway, but probably won't make the front page now. It's turned out it wasn't actually murder.'

I felt as if all the breath had been knocked from me. '*What?*'

'I know. I can't get my head round it either. Akhmad was out of the country for a few days on business at the time Reggie died – the cops had been waiting for confirmation, but he had a rock-solid alibi.'

I was stunned. 'So . . . he had nothing to do with her death? And they're quite sure – I mean, he's not faked it or anything?'

'It certainly looks that way, yeh.' A breathy sigh travelled down the line. 'I don't know how to feel about it. I mean, it was all kind of sorted in my head, but now . . .'

'But he did used to knock her about, didn't he? I don't

171

suppose he'll ever receive any sort of punishment for that. He's a total bastard who made her life a misery but he's got off scot-free.' I sank into the chair. Jobie sat at my feet, staring up at me quizzically.

'Pretty much. There'll still be an inquest, but it looks as though the verdict will be accidental death. There was a lot of alcohol in her system, and God knows how, but it sounds as though she must have slipped and hit her head. They've re-examined the pathologist's report and reckon the black eyes were due to the basal fracture, apparently.'

My mind began to dart. Somehow this put a whole different complexion on everything. 'I don't know what to say. I suppose it should be a relief in a way, but I still hate him for the way he treated her.'

There was a long pause from the other end of the line. Luc's voice was quiet and resigned. 'Nothing will bring her back, though, Stina. Whatever happened, it makes no difference now.'

I hung up with a heavy heart. I don't know why, but somehow having someone to blame for Reggie's death, someone who was going to be punished for their part in it, had helped to rationalise it in my mind. All I was left with was a sense of emptiness and a huge question mark over what had actually happened to my friend that fateful night. I buried my face in my hands and sobbed. It was like losing her all over again.

CHAPTER 12

The weeks rolled by. The realisation that I would never see Reggie again had begun to sink in. I felt guilty initially that here was I, getting on with my own existence and looking forward to the baby's arrival, while my lovely friend's life had been cut cruelly short, even if it hadn't been at the hands of someone else. With time I was growing to accept it, although there were occasions that something would remind me of her: a song on the radio, a weepie film shown on TV that we had watched together with a box of hankies and a bottle of wine. I would wallow for a time and have a good cry. But gradually I was coming to terms with her loss, something I never thought that I would do at first. If we had been as close as we used to be, particularly when we were still living together, I would have felt it much more keenly. But I was about to move into a new phase of my life. I tried to keep busy and push any thoughts of Reggie to the back of my mind. I owed it to Jack and the baby not to allow myself to slide into depression. I had seen what it did to my mother and there was always the nagging fear that I had the propensity to finish up the same way.

I texted Lucy to check if it was okay to pay her a visit. I was conscious that I hadn't seen her baby yet and thought it might be nice to see her and Alfie again. I felt a little deflated by her response.

'*Bit busy just now. Could we do it another day?*'

Given Eddie's reaction when I had gone round to the house, I began to wonder if she wasn't that keen to be friends after all. I decided not to push it; if she wanted to see me, she knew where I was. Besides, it wasn't as if we had been bosom buddies or anything.

In spite of our occasional differences of opinion, I was growing more accepting of Mrs Barley and her quirky ways. However eccentric she might be, as I got to know her better, I was beginning to find it hard to believe that she was capable of killing cats or putting hexes on people, or whatever it was the locals suspected her of doing. I had come to the conclusion that she had been badly affected by the loss of Frank, and this, coupled with spending so much time alone, had made her turn to her somewhat unorthodox pastimes and beliefs. If it gave her comfort, where was the harm? I knew too that it was just in some people's nature to be suspicious of anyone who didn't conform to what was considered the norm, and that tenuous rumours and spiteful gossip spread like knotweed through small communities.

Nobody ever visited the old lady and it made me feel bad to think how lonely she must be since losing her beloved Frank so long ago, and of the shoddy treatment she'd received at the hands of the community.

She was eager to assist me as my pregnancy progressed, helping with chores, and regularly presenting us with home-made goodies, often even a lasagne or cottage pie. I was grateful, since my increasing size seemed to have drained my energy resources, and it was nice for Jack to have a proper meal waiting for him after working all day.

She would often appear at our door, brandishing a cake or a tart that she had baked. I suppose some people might have found it intrusive, but being alone much of the time myself, I was usually pleased to have the company. Though initially reticent, over time, she gradually opened up to me, talking at length about Frank and their years together. I learned that they had moved to Avoncote as newly-weds, from Dorset, from where they both hailed originally.

One wet, windy afternoon in early October, there had been no sign of Mrs Barley since the previous morning. I rarely had cause to knock on her door, but was a little concerned and thought I should perhaps pop round to check on her. I'd just been to the shop to pick up a copy of the magazine in which my article was due to appear; in spite of my earlier concerns about the deadline, I'd actually completed it before Reggie's funeral and submitted it with a couple of weeks to spare. Aside from my own contribution, the Halloween issue contained plenty of other information about the locality and I thought the old lady might like to read it.

She seemed delighted to see me; she explained that

she had developed a bad headache, but after taking one of her herbal remedies and spending the rest of the day in bed, was starting to feel much better. She invited me in and ushered me into her living room while she went through to the kitchen to put the kettle on.

I shook the rainwater from my jacket, draping it over one of the dining chairs, then placed the magazine strategically on the table for her to see. Coming in from the driving rain, the warmth of the room was welcome, and I sank into the comfortable seat-pad of the small, wooden-framed settee near the window. A tap on the glass made me jump. I looked round, to see Corvus staring in. He seemed to observe me for a moment, then flew off. He didn't even need to *do* anything; his very presence left me uneasy for some reason.

Perched in their cage to my left, the lovebirds preened one another incessantly, chirruping their mutual devotion. I thought fleetingly how devastated the other would be, should anything happen to its mate. It made me wonder if, to Mrs Barley, they were in some way a symbol of the love she had shared with Frank. Then my thoughts turned to Jack, and the certainty that at some point in the future one of us would almost inevitably leave the other behind. I thought of Reggie, and how unreal it felt that someone could be so full of life one minute and then gone forever the next. The sudden realisation of the transience of our existence overwhelmed me with sadness. The pregnancy was playing havoc with my emotions; even the sight of roadkill remains had the power to reduce me to tears.

In an attempt to divert myself, I scanned the room,

taking in the cornucopia of items accumulated by Mrs Barley over the years. Opposite the door leading into the hallway, shelves from floor to ceiling, crammed with books, stood along one wall at the far end of the room. In front of this was the small dining table and four chairs. Various trinkets sat along the mantelpiece, above which hung a sturdy-looking circular mirror framed in ebony. A large wreath of dried flowers, a wicker pentacle across its diameter, hung on the wall of one alcove. An intricately woven corn dolly tied with red ribbon spiralled from the other, next to which dangled a clear glass orb, filled with what looked like bits of moss and potpourri. Four white candles in descending sizes were spaced out across the hearth. The furnishings were old-fashioned; all heavy, dark wood and itchy tapestry cushions, but beautifully maintained, and everything was spotlessly clean. The tick of the mantel clock was almost hypnotic.

A small, low table covered with a bottle-green velvet cloth stood in the alcove beneath the wreath. At the edge of the table, a curious little figure was propped against the wall. It was about six inches in height, faceless, and fashioned from knotted natural-coloured wool, with darker strands sprouting from its head. It was dressed in a simple hessian smock, the front pocket bulging with acorns. Next to it lay a huge, ancient-looking book, its threadbare cloth cover embossed in gold with what looked like runic letters, and a large candle in a brass holder. A band of brightly coloured fabric poked from between the pages of the book, as if it were being used as a page marker. The pattern nudged a twinge of familiarity.

Before I could take a closer look, Mrs Barley appeared with a tea tray. Noticing my interest in the table's contents, she whisked the items hurriedly into one of the sideboard's cupboards. As she went to close the door, I noticed a collection of similar dolls, all lined up inside, along with several large glass baubles. She placed the tray and its contents on the tabletop. I wondered for a moment whether I had seen something I shouldn't have.

'I've always liked making my little dolls,' she told me, studying my face for a reaction. 'My mother showed me how, and I used to make them as a child. I call that one Hecate. I made her years ago – for Samhain.'

I tried to remain nonchalant. 'Who's that?'

Her lips twitched in amusement. 'No, not who; *what*. You'd call it Halloween.'

I realised it was her pronunciation that had confused me – *Soween* – I was familiar with the written word but had never heard it spoken before.

'The time we remember those who have gone before us.' She paused, her face clouding for a moment. There was brief silence as she seemed to have lost her train of thought. 'I've several others I've made over the years – for Beltane, too – or May Day, as it's known these days. There are eight festivals in the Wheel of the Year, and I've a doll for each, you know.'

Oh yes?' I had seen the term *Wheel of the Year* during my research about local folklore, but hadn't actually made it a focus of my article. Mrs Barley was in full flow now and clearly eager to share the extent of her knowledge.

'It's a way of marking the cycle of nature – the sabbats,

we call them. The winter solstice, the summer solstice, Ostara in the spring, Mabon in the autumn, and so on. The wheel depicts the birth and death of the seasons.'

'So, you're very in tune with nature, then?'

'Absolutely. Always have been, and it's given me a focus since Frank's passing. We owe everything we are to the earth. We come from it and one day we all go back to it. I'm a great believer in the power of talismans, too.' She seemed to light up from within suddenly. 'I don't find it so easy these days with my hands, but I could still make one of my dolls for you if you like – bring you good luck for the baby.'

'Thank you.' I felt uncomfortable. Truthfully, I wasn't keen on the idea of my unborn child having one of these strange little pagan figures created for him or her, but didn't want to offend Mrs Barley, who was clearly passionate in her belief. I told myself that it was all harmless hokum, but while I found folklore interesting, there was something about symbolic figurines and wiccan tenets that felt slightly macabre.

I sensed a sudden shift in her manner. The intense way she was observing me made me keen to steer the dialogue towards something more prosaic.

We sat drinking tea, made the old-fashioned way, poured through a strainer into china cups. Possibly after all the talk about the little figures and, although I may have felt like it initially, I hadn't thrown up my hands in abject horror, Mrs Barley had become unusually animated. As was often the case, the topic of conversation turned to Frank. I didn't mind and was glad that her witchy dolls seemed no longer to be uppermost in her thoughts. I often found myself thinking about Reggie and felt a bit emotional that day anyway, so at least it was a distraction.

Having lived for so long with Auntie Jane, I had always been comfortable in the company of the elderly and found the old lady's little anecdotes fascinating. I thought how her descriptions of times gone by might have made a wonderful biography. It crossed my mind that this could be a future project. Having been raised in the countryside, she described a world very different from the one in which I'd grown up.

'There wasn't any work,' she explained. 'Frank landed a job in the quarry nearby, so we moved here; autumn 1955. I'd just turned twenty-one. Bet you can't imagine me ever being that age!' She smiled ruefully. 'Here, let me show you something.'

She lifted the tea tray onto the floor, then went to another cupboard in the sideboard and produced an old, leather-bound photograph album, opening it carefully on the table. She put on her glasses and leaned forward, squinting a little at the picture on the opening page.

'That's me. I'd be about thirty.'

The photograph had been taken in the garden on a summer's day. She was standing by the fence, a quizzical smile on her face, her huge brown eyes staring intently, perhaps teasingly, at the camera. The image bore no resemblance to the stooped, gossamer-haired creature she had become. Mrs Barley had been voluptuous and striking; thick, dark locks tumbled in waves past her shoulders.

'Oh my gosh, you were *beautiful*, Mrs Barley!'

She smiled sadly. 'It doesn't seem so long ago, you know. Frightening, how quickly the years have flown.'

Continuing to turn the pages, she gave a sudden gasp as though seeing something for the first time. '*Here's* Frank.'

I looked at the picture, then examined it more closely, my heart quickening. Mr Barley stood leaning on a spade, shirt sleeves rolled above his elbows, his dark hair combed back. He had indeed been handsome in his youth; tall, wiry, with piercing dark eyes. But the moment I saw the picture I knew who he was. Because I had seen him before – and not just in a photograph. He was, without a shadow of a doubt, the man I had seen in Mrs Barley's garden.

I looked up at her open-mouthed. Should I say something? I felt a sudden unpleasant chill surround me and gooseflesh prickled my arms. But Mrs Barley appeared oblivious to my discomfort. She was lost in the past, a faraway look in her eyes. She stroked the picture lovingly with her forefinger.

'He was *gorgeous*. Had eyes for no one but me, though – nor I him. The only person I ever had to share him with was Jesus. His faith always very important to him. Said his prayers every night.' She shook her head. 'It was one thing we never really agreed on. Can't say I was ever particularly religious in that way myself, and even less so after his passing. Where was God when he needed him?'

She sighed, turning the pages slowly, her eyes glistening with tears. The remainder of the album was devoted mainly to Frank, and most of the time, he had been captured in the garden. I was mesmerised by the images before me. The man exuded an air of brooding intensity, which was apparent in all the photographs. Something about his haunted expression made me uncomfortable.

I couldn't bring myself to raise the subject of ghosts. It seemed, I don't know, inappropriate – and I suppose she could have been offended, although given her pagan interests she would probably have been quite open to the idea of a visitor from beyond the grave. But the love she had for him still burned so brightly, and even though she had to live with the knowledge every painful day, it would somehow have felt wrong to remind her that he was no longer living. He was evidently very much alive in her heart. My teacup rattled against its saucer and I realised that I was trembling. My curiosity got the better of me.

'How long . . . have you been on your own?' I asked, my eyes never leaving the picture staring out from the album.

She sighed. 'You mean when I lost Frank? It'll have been thirty-two years this Christmas; 1980. Not long after his forty-fourth birthday. It still hurts as though it was only yesterday.'

I thought for a moment, but didn't like to ask the cause of his death. I gathered that it had been sudden, so assumed it was probably a heart attack. They seem to be frighteningly common in middle-aged men.

I went back to the start of the album, re-examining the pictures of Frank as a younger man. There was one taken with another slightly shorter man of a similar age, with his arm somewhat possessively round Frank's shoulder, outside the front gate of Rose Cottage. The pair of them were smiling and laughing.

'Who's this, Mrs Barley?'

She peered at the image with distaste. 'That's Len. He was a sort of – well, a pal of Frank's, I suppose. Never cared for him much. He died young . . . but they say what goes around comes around, don't they?'

'Why didn't you like him?'

She glowered. 'He liked his whisky a bit too much, kept calling for Frank to go out with him several nights a week. I was being left on my own a lot and it couldn't carry on. The bugger only wanted a drinking partner, if the truth be told. Anyway, it was the ruin of him in the end – you can't climb a roof drunk and not expect there to be consequences.'

'Oh dear.'

Mrs Barley began to drum her fingers on the album. I hastened to steer the discussion away from the subject of the errant Len.

'You – you had no children, then?' I ventured falteringly.

The old woman's eyes narrowed and her face hardened. I realised I'd touched a nerve and could have kicked myself.

'I'm so sorry. It's really none of my business. I didn't mean to pry . . .'

She paused, avoiding my gaze. 'It's natural that you should wonder. We weren't . . . blessed in that way. But we had each other. Even if it wasn't forever. I'll always be grateful for that.'

The atmosphere had become almost oppressive. I stayed for another ten minutes or so, making small talk, then made my excuses to leave. From the doorway, I indicated the magazine I had left on the dining table.

'By the way, I brought this for you, Mrs Barley – I thought you might like to read the feature I wrote about the village.'

Her eyes narrowed. 'You finished it, then?'

'Eventually – I did have a bit of a computer glitch, but I managed to get it done, thankfully.'

She stared at the magazine with a face that could have turned milk sour. Her reaction was baffling.

I cleared my throat. 'You could probably have given me a few interesting facts and figures yourself – I should've interviewed you!'

This prompted a scowl. 'No one round here would want to hear anything I've got to say. Or they'd rubbish it.' She put on her glasses and squinted as she leafed through to the relevant pages.

'Oh, there are photographs.' She looked up at me almost accusingly. 'Where'd you find these?'

'You can find a lot of information online – and Jack bought me a wonderful book about Avoncote. The history of the place is fascinating.'

She thrust the magazine back at me. 'Yes. Well, I don't think I want to know any more about this place, thank you all the same.'

I must have looked wounded – I certainly felt it. Her expression softened.

'Please don't take it personally. I don't really read magazines, if I'm honest. But well done for having your piece published. Oh, just a minute . . .' She raised an index finger. 'Before you go. There's something I'd like you to have.' Going back to the sideboard, she took out one of the baubles I had noticed earlier and pressed it into my hands. 'To bless your home.'

I examined the object, holding it up to the light. It was made from deep blue glass, with a hole in the top, and it was strangely beautiful. 'Thank you. What is it?'

She gave an odd little laugh, as though I should have known. 'It's a spirit ball. A charm to keep you safe. Hang it by your fireplace and it will bring you luck.'

Leaning forwards, she patted my burgeoning midriff.

'You're carrying very low, my dear. Baby'll be here any day now, you mark my words.'

'But I've a good fortnight left . . .'

'Oh. Well make sure you've a bag packed, that's all I'll say.'

The old woman's silent, knowing smile left me uneasy.

*

'I'm telling you, Jack, it was him. It was Frank Barley that I saw in the garden all those times. I'm absolutely *one hundred per cent* certain.'

We sat at the dinner table that evening, Jack scratching his head in disbelief.

'There must be some other explanation. I mean . . . I'm sorry, I don't believe in all that paranormal bollocks. It's just . . . fanciful. Maybe . . . I don't know, maybe it was a visiting nephew with a strong family resemblance – or the husband could've had a long-lost son she didn't know about who turned up out of the blue. I'm looking for a rational explanation here. Have you had your eyes tested recently?'

I wanted to throttle him. It was exasperating.

'There's nothing wrong with my eyesight! And she never seems to have any callers. You know that as well as I do. The only person I've ever seen round there apart from Bob has been the mysterious visitor, and she denies all knowledge of him. And if he's actually a ghost, it would explain a hell of a lot.'

'We don't watch her house 24/7 – it's not impossible that someone else has been round to see her once or twice.'

'For God's sake.' I raised my palms skyward in frustration.

'Look,' he said gently, taking my hand, 'I'm not trying to patronise you, but I think you're being a bit irrational. I mean, I know you're anxious – and that's understandable. Apart from the fact that you're not sleeping well, the pregnancy must be taking its toll on you and you've lost your best friend. That's a hell of a lot for anyone to have to deal with.'

I rolled my eyes. He tilted my face towards him.

'Listen to me. Whoever he was – is – the man clearly meant no harm. I mean, she's always been fine, hasn't she? We've never seen any evidence that she's been harassed by anyone. Perhaps that's it – her husband sowed his wild oats and produced a long-lost son that she doesn't want to admit to. Or perhaps they had a child and gave him up for adoption – they *were* pretty young when they came here. He could've tracked her down. It happens. Maybe the Barleys were running away from something. That's a fair bet. People of that generation can be guarded when it comes to stuff like that. It would've been a stigma in their day.'

I shook my head. Reasoning with him was futile. I pulled my hand away sharply. 'Let's drop it, shall we? I know what I saw. You can think what the hell you like.'

We sat in silence for the rest of the evening. I was certain that the man I had seen was Frank Barley. And nothing was going to persuade me otherwise.

*

That whole afternoon with Mrs Barley had been unsettling and now Jack had upset me further by implying I was delusional. Reflecting on Mrs Barley's attitude, maybe I was being hyper-sensitive, but I felt quite put out that she hadn't wanted to read my article. I thought, too, about the creepy little dolls; the photographs of Frank. It was all very eerie.

Later that night, I lay rigidly in bed staring at the ceiling, unable to sleep for all the thoughts weaving through my head. Jack, of course, lay sprawled and breathing heavily beside me, having virtually passed out the moment his head hit the pillow. At that moment, his ability to switch off so readily infuriated me. It was as though everything just washed over him and he clearly wasn't taking anything I said seriously.

Eventually I decided to get up and make myself a chamomile tea. Jobie padded after me into the living room and settled himself by the back door, staring out into the darkness. It was a clear, cold night and the wind was beginning to pick up. I slipped the throw from the settee around my shoulders and sat at the table, sipping my drink. Picking up the copy of *Avon Life*, I flicked through and absent-mindedly began to pore over all four pages of my magazine feature, if only for the novelty of seeing my work in glossy print. The editor, herself a local history enthusiast, had managed to source a couple more photographs from an old family friend, apart from those I had submitted. I skimmed through the text, by now all too familiar, and admired the digitally enhanced photos of old Avoncote. Scrutinising the picture of the man I now knew to be Frank Barley, I shuddered.

My head was still buzzing with everything I'd seen in Mrs Barley's house that day. However much I tried to distract myself, I couldn't stop thinking about it all. For some reason, the piece of material I'd noticed tucked between the pages of her book was worrying me. Maybe it was just because it was late and lying there in bed I'd had too much time to chew everything over, but it kept resurfacing to the front of my mind. The familiarity of it was bugging me; I definitely knew it from somewhere.

And then, like a bolt from the blue, I remembered Reggie's multicoloured bandana – the one she thought she'd lost when she visited. *Was that it?* Was that what Mrs Barley had, sitting there amongst all her other weird belongings? But why would she have a piece of my friend's scarf – and why would she have secreted it between the covers of that sinister-looking tome? Ridiculous as it seems, now I look back, the desire to know at that moment was overpowering.

Without really thinking it through, and fired up by the need to see what my neighbour might be hiding, I unlocked the back door, guiding a disappointed Jobie gently back inside, and closed it behind me.

I crept down the garden and through Mrs Barley's back gate. I'd remembered that she kept a spare key beneath a plant pot outside her French doors *'for emergencies'*. Rose Cottage was in darkness and all was quiet. Trying desperately not to make a sound, I made my way up the path, taking exaggerated steps like a cartoon burglar. Heart banging like a kettle drum, I checked my surroundings cautiously, then lifted the heavy ceramic tub and slid out the rusting key with my foot. I stooped to pick it up, my fingers trembling so much I almost let it slip between them, but managed to retrieve the thing before it hit the paving slabs. Inserting the key into the door, I held my breath and turned. With a little force, it eventually clicked open. I hesitated, wondering about the prudence of what I was about to do. But curiosity got the better of me. The door creaked a little as it opened and I froze, expecting to hear footsteps from above. But after a minute or so of silence, I felt emboldened, and ventured over the threshold.

For a moment I was rooted to the spot, unnerved by the shadowy recesses of the room. As my eyes grew accustomed to the gloom, I looked for the side table in the alcove that had held the little doll and the book, then remembered that Mrs Barley had put the things away in a cupboard. I edged my way gingerly over to the sideboard. My stomach turned a somersault as I heard a scratching noise behind me. I spun round, but exhaled in relief as I realised it must have been the lovebirds, whose cage was covered with a cloth. I eased open the door to the left of the sideboard and felt inside. It was empty! Why would she have removed the contents?

I opened the other side: the photograph album was still there, but there was no sign of any of the things that had been sitting on the little table earlier. Exasperated, I looked around in case she had put the book elsewhere. Maybe it had been replaced on the bookcase at the far end of the room. In desperation I picked my way gingerly across the floor and began to scan the shelves. There were so many books, and in spite of the moonlight creeping though, the lighting was too dim to make out the wording on their spines. It was hopeless.

But what did I expect to find, realistically? Even if the material *had* come from Reggie's bandana, what of it? Mrs Barley could have found it on the road – she might have had no idea where it came from.

I stopped suddenly and took stock of the situation. *What on earth was I doing?* This was madness. What if my neighbour came downstairs suddenly and found me searching through her belongings? She could call the police – and quite rightly; I could even give her a heart attack – after all, she was an elderly woman. I realised now that my behaviour was absurd – and seriously ill-judged. As quietly as I could, I made my way back into the garden and carefully pulled the door shut, replacing the key beneath the plant pot. I glanced up at the house, but mercifully there was no sign of life.

I edged down the path and back into my own home. Stoked with adrenaline, my heart was hammering like a steam train at full pelt. I was more wide awake than ever. A brandy would have been welcome, but I knew I couldn't drink. I made another chamomile tea and hugged the mug in my frozen fingers, wrapping the throw tightly around myself as Jobie hovered, watching me uncertainly from the kitchen doorway. I took deep breaths as I sat at the table once more, torturing myself with what might have happened had I been caught. I felt stupid and reckless. My mind still darting, I went back to the magazine and leafed through other items but couldn't resist returning to my own feature.

A chill ran through me as I looked again at the brooding picture of Frank Barley. I quickly turned my attention to the other recently added photographs.

One of the editor's new images made me sit up and take notice. A street scene of the main road from May 1964, but it was in colour! The roads were empty of cars, the trees in blossom; only the occasional pedestrian and a girl on horseback. And there was our very own Wisteria Cottage. I was excited to see a couple standing side by side just inside the gate – presumably Mr and Mrs Burrows, the former owners. It was interesting to think that these people had once lived in our home, raised their family within our walls. I suddenly remembered the magnifying glasses that Jack used for ophthalmic examinations. His veterinary bag was beside the armchair, so I rooted through to look for them. I took the magazine over to the lamp, to see if I could make out the couple's features more clearly. Then I noticed something else. In the upstairs window of Rose Cottage, an unsmiling face, framed by short dark hair, was staring down at the street below.

But it was neither Mrs Barley, nor Frank.

It was the face of a young boy.

*

191

The following morning was exceptionally breezy. Jack brought me a cup of tea in bed before leaving for work, but I was still miffed with him and disinclined for conversation. And I daren't tell him that I had broken into our neighbour's house on a wild goose chase. Reflecting on my actions in the cold light of day, they seemed utterly deranged. If *I* was beginning to doubt my own sanity, God knows what anyone else would have thought. At least no one had seen me. I decided it was best kept to myself, and pushed it to the back of my mind.

'We'll have to agree to differ on this one, I'm afraid,' he said gently, before planting a kiss on my head. 'Put your feet up and have a rest today. You're looking very tired, you know.'

No wonder. Even after going back to bed eventually, I'd lain awake half the night thinking about the insane thing I'd just done, the conversation with Jack and then the photograph I had seen. The frequent need to get up for the loo, plus the incessant noise of the wind rattling and wailing through the rafters, hadn't helped either. My head swam with it all.

I got up shortly after he had left and sat to eat breakfast in the living room, staring out into the garden. The sky was a bleak dove grey. I saw Mrs Barley walking down the path, as she so often did, to put food out for the birds. I thought again of my actions the previous night and felt ashamed. What the *hell* had I been thinking of? I was beginning to wonder if I was on the verge of some sort of breakdown. It actually frightened me that I had acted so impetuously.

Corvus was waiting expectantly on the apex of the

summer house roof, squawking as Mrs Barley approached. I watched him alight on the ground near her feet. She stroked his head as he ate and I flinched, thinking how unnatural it looked. Her bizarre connection with him actually made my flesh crawl. But he was only a harmless bird – it felt irrational that it should provoke such an extreme reaction in me. Seeing me, she waved as she went back into the house. Again, I recalled Mr Barley's haunted countenance in the photographs and shuddered. It gave me a bad feeling – as though his appearance was in some way unpropitious. And who was that little boy in the window?

For God's sake, what was *wrong* with me? My mind birling, I resolved to make myself busy, try to restore some sense of normality. There was so much going through my head I felt as though I was losing my grip. I stripped the bed and put on the washing machine, before showering and dressing. I felt an uncomfortable heaviness in my stomach, and rested on the bed for a moment until it passed. We needed bread, so I forced myself to take a stroll to the shop. Jobie was keen to accompany me, but I hadn't the energy to be pulled along at a rate of knots. He looked deflated when I stopped him at the door, so I patted his head and consoled him with a bone biscuit before stepping out into the street.

Judy smiled as I entered. 'Bit of a blowy one out there today.'

I nodded. I felt too tired to chat and was monosyllabic in response.

'You're looking shattered, love,' she remarked. 'You should go home and put your feet up. Can't be long now, eh?'

'Still a couple of weeks yet. It's getting quite uncomfortable now, though.'

'Yes, I remember it well. Still, you make the most of it before the baby arrives. Your feet won't touch the ground afterwards!'

I smiled thinly and wished her a good morning. The sycamores lining the road bowed and creaked, their discarded leaves dancing in a whirling vortex across the pavement. The sound of distant gunshot rang out, quickening my pulse, and a family of rooks scattered skyward from the shelter of a nearby tall leafless tree, circling and cawing loudly.

It was uncanny. I felt suddenly acutely aware of my surroundings, as though everything was portentous of some event looming.

My hair whipped about my face as, breathless, I arrived back on my doorstep, turning the key in the lock. Even the short walk up the lane had felt like a marathon and the heavy sensation in my abdomen had returned.

I made a mug of coffee and eased myself into the armchair, switching on the television. The morning programmes seemed to be filled with glamorous, reed-thin women having beauty treatments and modelling the season's latest trends. My thoughts turned to Reggie and a lump rose in my throat. Plus, in my current barrage-balloon-like state, it did nothing for my self-confidence. I sighed and turned off. Hearing the washing machine bleep, I went to empty it.

Excited by the gusting leaves, Jobie raced up and down the garden like a mad thing. I struggled to prevent the wind from claiming the laundry I was attempting to peg out. Stretching to retrieve a wayward sock from the privet hedge, a searing pain gripped my stomach. A sudden, unexpected gush of warm water soaked through my jeans.

Seized by panic, I cried out. Within seconds Mrs Barley had appeared in her garden. Taking one look at me, she knew immediately what had happened.

'I'm coming, love; I'll telephone for an ambulance.'

She was marvellous: the epitome of calm and practicality. Helping me into my living room, she spread towels beneath me, mopping up the alarming amount of fluid that continued to seep out. She found me a change of clothes, then made chamomile tea, rubbing my back and talking in a quiet, reassuring voice; telling me how to breathe. For someone who had never had children, she seemed to know exactly what to do; what I needed.

The pain in my stomach had now extended to my back and it felt as though it were about to break. I moved this way and that, but there was no respite. I had been led to believe that pain ceased between contractions; this appeared to have been a myth. It was unbearable. I was starting to feel nauseous and faint. I felt an excruciating pain in my pelvis. The increasing pressure led to a sudden irresistible urge to push. It was all frighteningly quick, not the twenty-four hours or so of labour I had been anticipating.

'Mrs Barley, I think the baby is coming!'

'Shush, now. Don't give in to it just yet. Take short breaths, try to pant when you want to push.' Her voice was soothing, measured. I was trying my hardest to resist but it was becoming almost impossible. I really feared my pelvis might be in danger of being ripped apart. The old woman began to mumble softly, her voice almost a monotone. I had no idea what she was saying and was in so much pain I was beyond caring.

There was a sudden sharp rap on the front door. Mrs Barley seemed shocked back into the here and now. She ushered the two paramedics, a man and a woman, into the room and looked on anxiously.

The female paramedic, a tall, kindly woman of about forty with a Jamaican accent, sat me down and took my blood pressure, then strapped a foetal heart monitor around my abdomen. She frowned, turning to ask her colleague and Mrs Barley to leave the room. She explained that she had trained originally in midwifery and needed to examine me internally to establish how imminent the birth was. Her manner became noticeably more urgent.

'We have to get you to hospital quickly, child. You're not dilating properly, but baby's quite distressed, and the quicker we get him or her out, the better. I think you may need a C-section.'

I was vaguely aware of something being injected into my thigh, but hardly felt anything. The sensation was eclipsed by the agonising pain in my abdomen. The stocky male paramedic lifted me with ease onto a stretcher. I remember being fixated on the angel tattooed on his solid forearm. Mrs Barley waved from the pavement as I was bundled into the ambulance. I have a dim recollection of the sirens blaring, but everything else after that is a blur.

Elodie Régine arrived, sixteen days prematurely, by emergency Caesarean section at 9.53 on October the third.

Blearily, I awoke to the sight of Jack standing at my bedside. He was nursing what looked like a tiny bundle of rags, with tufts of fine, dark fluff protruding from the top. He leaned forward and kissed me gently on the forehead, his eyes glistening with emotion.

'Hello, sleepyhead. Welcome back to the land of the living. Someone here would like to meet her mummy.'

Very carefully, he placed the baby on my chest. I cradled my daughter to me, absorbing the sweet, delicious scent of her downy head. I gently stroked her peach-soft cheek. She was pink and warm, and so impossibly small. Above a tiny button nose, deep blue eyes squinted back at me. Tears blurred my vision. The rush of maternal love I felt, the sudden, fierce instinct to nurture and protect, was like nothing I had ever experienced. I was completely overwhelmed. We had created this minute, perfect being – and the thought of anything harming her or taking her from us was more than I could bear.

I recalled Mrs Barley's words: '*We weren't blessed.*' Only now could I truly appreciate what she'd meant. Because this time, I was old enough to understand.

*

At fifteen, relocating to the other side of the city had been liberating. I'd moved to a school where no one knew me; they knew nothing of my past. I was desperate to feel part of something for once in my life. I formed new friendships, if you could call them that, and started seeing boys. Looking back, I was only ever on the periphery of things, never really properly accepted. But at the time, I was swept along with whichever group I had briefly attached myself to. I see now that my actions were wildly and guilelessly misjudged.

I didn't know I was pregnant. Well, not for sure. I tried my best to ignore the symptoms, put the lack of periods down to the fact that my cycle had always been a bit erratic. Lying in bed at night, I'd run a hand over my stomach, wondering in my naivety if its slightly swollen state was water retention, or weight gain, due to the improved nutrition I was receiving under Auntie Jane's roof.

He was seventeen, two years older than me; dark and gorgeous. At least, I thought so at the time. He rode a motorbike and would take me on the back, speeding through the streets as I clutched onto his waist. I loved the sense of freedom, the rush of exhilaration, my hair billowing out behind me. I had no helmet and no thought for safety. My heart lurches now at the thought of my youthful stupidity.

It was exciting that someone more mature could find me attractive and I was flattered. Of course, I was no more than a brief distraction for him and he moved on to a girl in the year above me all too readily. But there had never been a proper relationship to mourn, and after the initial disappointment, I got over it quite quickly. Some months later, I had heard that he'd been sent to prison for two years, for aggravated burglary. I wasn't particularly upset.

The pain had been sudden and violent. I woke in the night not knowing what was happening. At first, I thought it must have been something I'd eaten, but the cramps grew stronger and stronger, like bad period pain. I went to the bathroom and realised that I was losing a large amount of blood. I vomited and was doubled over in agony. I don't know how long it went on for – it felt like hours. Hunched on the bathroom floor, I caught sight of my reflection in the mirror: my face was grey, my eyes hollow. I resisted for some time, but it was frightening and I knew I needed help. Eventually, I called out for Auntie Jane.

She came through from her bedroom, her eyes heavy with sleep. From the look of shock on her face, she must have known what was happening. Whether she'd suspected anything before, I don't know.

She stayed with me until it was all over. The baby was a boy. His head seemed disproportionally large but he was tiny, less than a foot long. He was mine – and he was perfect. But he never drew breath. I couldn't have been more than around five and a half months gone. He could never have lived.

Auntie Jane wrapped him in a towel and took him away. She ran me a warm salt bath and I sat in there, hugging my knees to my chest until the water had gone cold, the blood dispersing to turn it a shade of orange. I was shivering and bewildered, shaking with the horror of what had just happened. She said very little. What was going through her mind, I don't know; maybe she thought it was a life lesson I had to learn, to give me the kick up the backside that I so obviously needed.

She helped me get dry and put on a fresh nightdress, changed the sheets and tucked me up in bed, bringing me brandy with sugar and warm water for the trauma. God knows how, but I slept eventually.

The following morning was grey and miserable, one of those days when the cold seems to seep into your very bones. My mind still careening from my experience, I lay in bed, staring up through the open curtains at the veil of mist hovering ominously above the rooftops. I realised smoke was rising from the garden. I rushed to the window, only to see Auntie Jane stoking the old incinerator. At once, I understood what she had done. I tore down the stairs and ran outside, screaming hysterically, but she restrained me and led me back into the house. Her face was stony; emotionless.

'This is how we always did things in my day,' she said coldly, her eyes never meeting mine. 'I watched my father do the same, twice, when my mother had miscarried. The child was never to be. There will be others in future, when the time is right. But not this one. The less said about it all, the better.'

We never spoke about it again, but I knew I could never forgive her for what she had done. I buried the memory and told no one. Years later, after a few drinks too many one night, I blurted the whole story out to Reggie. She had told me so many things about her own past, and I knew that I could trust her to keep it to herself. But it was something I knew I could never share with Jack: not now. Initially, I worried that it might change things between us, that he might look at me differently. As time passed, I didn't want to drop a bombshell that could jeopardise the close relationship we had built. And so I decided that it was something he never needed to know.

*

The four days in hospital seemed interminable. Mrs Barley had helped Jack to prepare the house for my return. The 'Welcome Home' banner secured above the front door, with pastel pink and white balloons at either end, made me weep. Everything was spotlessly clean and tidy as I eased myself across the threshold, a sleeping Elodie securely in a sling against my chest.

I felt a hormonal rush of emotion. Tears were never far away at this time, a whole spectrum of thoughts running through my mind. It was all so bittersweet. I loved my baby so much that it hurt, but I had to live with the certainty that one day she would grow up and leave me. The thought was incredibly, irrationally painful.

The table was laid with sandwiches and fairy cakes, a vase of beautiful pink and white carnations placed in the centre. An animated Mrs Barley busied herself making tea. Exhausted, I lowered myself gingerly onto the settee, resting Elodie's head on my shoulder.

Mrs Barley placed a steaming mug on the side table next to me. She tilted her head to one side, gazing at Elodie with evident adoration.

'She's just beautiful. Such a little dot. You are so lucky.' Her face clouded for a moment. 'So lucky,' she murmured again, as if thinking aloud.

My heart went out to her. Mrs Barley was all alone in the world, with no children or grandchildren of her own to dote on. It was so sad. 'Would you like to hold her?' My voice wobbled with emotion.

I straightened, wincing as I felt a pull on my stitches.

'Just you be careful, now. You need to look after yourself, get your strength back for the sake of this precious bundle.' She leaned forward and gently took Elodie from me, her eyes never straying from my daughter's face. Elodie's tiny hand curled tightly round Mrs Barley's extended finger as she nestled in her arms.

'Oh my, she is *so* perfect.' She spoke in a whisper. Looking up at me, her eyes swam with tears. 'You wonder how anyone could ever be cruel to a helpless little soul such as this. The world can be a terrible place.'

It was not a thought I wanted to dwell on, having just brought my daughter into it. I watched as Mrs Barley rocked Elodie, humming a strange, haunting little melody to her as she did so. She carried her to the window and stared out into the garden. I could hear her talking softly but the words evaded me. Maybe she was showing Elodie the flowers.

Jack sat beside me on the sofa, sliding an arm round my shoulders. He leaned in and brushed my cheek with his lips.

'How are you doing? You look shattered.'

My breasts were engorged and sore, and I felt the sudden wetness of milk leaking through my top. I looked at him and instantly burst into tears, burying my face in his chest. It was all too much.

He laughed, but not unkindly. 'I think you could probably do with a few hours' sleep. Try and give Elodie a little feed now and then go and have a nap. I'll take care of her for a while – I can bring her up to you if she needs feeding again. Things will feel a whole lot better when you're not so knackered.'

Mrs Barley, having heard his words, turned towards us with a knowing smile.

'A good rest can work wonders,' she agreed. 'And don't you worry, either of you. I'll always be here to share the load.'

CHAPTER 13

CHAPTER 13

Jack's parents had announced that they were coming to visit us the following Friday. We rarely saw them as, after retiring from farming, they'd bought a flat in Spain and spent the majority of the year enjoying sunnier climes. But the lure of meeting their new granddaughter had brought them over to England for a couple of weeks. They had already arrived in the UK and were staying at their old farm near the village of Enville, in Staffordshire, with Jack's brother, Matt, and his family, some forty miles away. Old habits dying hard, Jack's dad had been helping out with the cattle, but they were planning on staying the one night with us after coming for dinner, as he didn't want to drive back to Enville in the dark.

I was anxious that the cottage was a mess, since I hadn't the energy for housework, nor was I physically able, as with the aftermath of the C-section I was weak and sore, and my movement restricted. I didn't like to ask Jack to start cleaning, since he'd been working longer and longer hours right up to Elodie's birth and was still having to pop in to the surgery now and again, despite being on paternity leave. I had wanted this to be quality time for the three of us, but everything seemed to be piling up. The fact that his parents' arrival was imminent was causing me real stress. Jack, however, was annoyingly flippant about the state of the house.

'It's fine, they won't care if it's a bit untidy. It's not like we're living in a hovel. They're coming to see Elodie – and us, of course – not to pass judgement on our domestic skills. After all, they lived on a bloody farm – they're used to muck.'

But I had my pride and I *was* worried. I didn't want anyone, particularly Jack's mother, Sylvia, whom I wasn't entirely sure liked me, thinking that I was inadequate in any way, or not coping. His father, Harry, was laid-back and easy to please and we got on well. She, on the other hand, seemed rather more judgemental. She had always been perfectly pleasant, but on the few occasions that I'd been in her company over the years, there were odd moments when I had caught her looking at me in a slightly hostile way that made me uncomfortable. I suspected she thought Jack could have done better for himself.

Mrs Barley called round the morning before the visit. It was 9.30 a.m. – Elodie had finally gone to sleep, but I was exhausted after walking her up and down in the night and was on the verge of tears, as I so often seemed to be at that time. The sleeplessness and the discomfort after the birth were getting me down and I could really have done without the in-laws descending on us. Apart from everything else, I felt like a physical wreck. I had begun to dread every feed, which – cracked, painful nipples aside – induced unpleasant cramping in my stomach. I needed a bath and hadn't washed my hair for days. Lack of sleep had left my eyes sunken and my skin sallow. It was as though I had aged about ten years overnight. I hated the sight of my ugly scar and my stomach looked like a wrinkly, deflated balloon. I wondered if I would ever regain my figure, and worried that Jack would never find me attractive again.

I kept thinking about my mum, too. Was this how things started for her – did her mental health deteriorate after my arrival? Maybe she had been on the brink anyway and then everything completely went to pot as a result of some sort of post-partum psychosis. Was that the beginning of the end of her relationship with my father? He must have loved her once. And now she had been abandoned by both of us. I thought about how devastated I would feel if Elodie turned her back on me and was consumed with guilt. Then I thought about Jack and was suddenly terrified that I might descend into mental illness and that he might leave me one day. My mind was darting wildly from one thought to another and I felt as though I was losing control.

'Whatever is it, love?' Mrs Barley came in through the French doors, looking concerned.

'Jack's parents are coming to see us tomorrow – I haven't got the energy for entertaining and the house is a bloody tip. I look a complete mess, too. I'm just too tired to do anything, but I can't put them off. They've flown over from Spain – it would look rude. And Sylvia hates me, I know it.' I began to sob, burying my face in my hands. It was as if everything had come to a head and the floodgates had opened.

She placed a soothing hand on my arm. 'I'm sure it's all in your imagination. No one could hate you – you're such a lovely girl. And you look fine – just tired, which is what you'd expect in the circumstances. It will soon get better, believe me. You go and sit down and I'll make you a nice cup of tea. Then you can tell me what needs doing.'

Her arthritis apparently forgotten, she set about tackling everything with gusto. She got on top of the washing and ironing that had steadily piled up, cleaned the bathroom, mopped the kitchen floor and damp-dusted everywhere. She prepared a casserole and baked a Victoria sponge for our guests' arrival. Being useful and needed seemed to have tapped into some hidden energy reserves, and she amazed me with how much she was able to do in such a short space of time. I could have hugged her.

'Mrs Barley, you're an angel. I'm so grateful.'

'Not at all. It's never a problem – you only have to ask. I've nothing much to do, let's face it, and I like to keep busy. Besides,' she said with a wink, 'we want to make sure you don't fall foul of your mother-in-law.'

I laughed. 'Is it a cliché, or are all mothers-in-law like mine – watching you like a hawk to make sure you're treating their little boy properly? What was yours like, Mrs Barley?'

She seemed to flinch. 'I didn't have a mother-in-law. That is to say, I never knew mine. She died when Frank was in his teens.' There was marked tension in her voice. 'I believe she was a good mother, though.'

'Oh, I'm sorry to hear that. But I'm sure you made up for it later by taking care of him. You've been a godsend for us, you really have.'

'I'm happy I can still make myself useful. Well, I'd better get home to my poor birds – they'll think I've forgotten them.' She turned to leave but stopped in the doorway, her face pensive. 'I hope I did, you know. Look after Frank properly, I mean. He deserved it.'

*

The following day, Harry and Sylvia arrived late in the afternoon, an hour earlier than expected, but thanks to Mrs Barley's efforts everything was presentable. Jack had finished work early, but had barely walked through the door when their car pulled up. I had just bathed Elodie and she looked gorgeous in her teddy-print pinafore dress and soft lacy jumper. I needn't have worried about the house – all eyes were on Elodie, and the proud grandparents couldn't get enough of her. Jobie was vying for everyone's attention and lay at Harry's feet, gazing up at him adoringly. I noticed the dog didn't seem as keen to sit by the newly fashion-conscious Sylvia, who, despite being accustomed to 'muck' as Jack put it, had upon arrival declared her concerns about him jumping up on her new trouser suit with dirty paws.

'I'm sorry, but I've had enough of our four-legged friends to last me a lifetime,' she declared. 'It's so nice not to have to worry about mud and fluff, and snags in my clothing any more. I can actually feel presentable whenever I go out these days.'

I noticed surreptitious eye-rolling from Jack and his

dad, and looked away, trying not to snigger. I wondered how Harry was adjusting to his new role as a man of leisure, and more than once while we were seated round the table that evening, noticed a faraway look in his eyes. I imagined that being around Sylvia for long periods of time could be quite oppressive.

Jack had once told me how, before her marriage, his mother had aspirations to be something rather more glamorous than a farmer's wife, and that although she had eventually embraced the role when she had fallen for Harry, it was not without a degree of reluctance. From various sniping remarks, it was now glaringly apparent that much of her existence, and what she clearly considered drudgery, at the farm had been under sufferance. Perhaps their new lifestyle in Spain was, in her eyes, helping her to claw back some of those lost years, but I wondered at what cost to her relationship with her husband.

Eventually Elodie became tired and grisly, and I decided to put her down for a nap.

'So how are you enjoying being a mum, Stina?' Sylvia had joined me in the kitchen later after dinner, as I washed up the plates. I could feel her eyes boring into the back of my head, as though she were watching my every move. Jack and Harry were in the living room, absorbed in conversation about the merits of different types of animal feed. I think Jack would have liked to take over the farm, but I was secretly glad that he hadn't. Farming seemed to require even more of a person's life than being a vet – at least he could take a day off now and again, even if he did work long hours.

'I'm totally in love,' I confessed, drying my hands. 'Elodie's adorable. I never thought I could feel so protective – it's quite overwhelming, actually.'

'Just you wait until she's older – when you have to let her go out without you. Nothing really prepares you for the worry. I still fret now. Even though the lads are two big brutes, they're still my babies.' She smiled. 'The kind of things that concern you when they're small pale into insignificance – at least you can tuck them in at night and know they're safe and warm. When you have to let them go out into the big wide world, you're in a constant state of anxiety.' She sighed. 'Oh, you've got it all to come.'

Her tactless words did nothing to reassure me. I thought of my beautiful Elodie, and then of poor Reggie's fate, and a sudden feeling of dread crept through me. I didn't want to contemplate the dangers of the wider world as my daughter grew. It was more than enough to worry about the needs of a tiny baby for the time being.

She continued, oblivious. 'We couldn't be prouder of Jack, you know. He's worked so hard to get where he is today. And you have to be pretty clever to become a vet, I can tell you. Our Matt's doing a great job of running the farm, too. It was hard for Harry to let go, but he can sleep easy at night. We've been so fortunate to have such capable, hard-working sons.'

I wasn't sure how to respond. I thought of Lucy's Eddie. 'Yes, there are plenty of wasters out there.'

'Oh dear, did you have a bad experience before you met Jack, then?'

'No, nothing like that – it's just that I've got a friend

211

whose husband doesn't seem to take his responsibilities very seriously. He pretty much leaves her to get on with everything, too, and she's got a toddler *and* a new baby. It puts things into perspective, when you see what some people have to put up with.'

'Well, Jack seems to be really hands-on with the baby. You're very fortunate. I don't think Harry ever changed a nappy!' She tapped her fingers on the table, and there was an awkward pause. 'And how are you, anyway? No postnatal blues or anything? I mean, it must have been a worry for you both, with your mum's mental trouble . . .'

'What do you mean?' I felt suddenly defensive. 'What has my mum's mental state got to do with me?'

'I just thought that, well, you might have been more susceptible – you know, as there are mental health issues in your family . . .'

'For your information, there are no *issues* as you put it in my family history. My mum's problems aren't genetic – they're the result of something she took when she was younger. Before you ask, *I've* never done drugs. And in answer to your question, no, I haven't got postnatal depression. I'm perfectly okay, thank you.' I was seething at her suggestion, even though it was something I had often contemplated myself. But I had to believe that my mother's problems were drug-related. The thought that they could be hereditary, that I might be at risk of going down that same precarious road, was just too terrifying.

Jack appeared in the doorway. 'Everything all right in here?' he enquired anxiously.

'Yes, yes – we're fine, love. Just having a healthy discussion, that's all.'

I glared at her. 'Excuse me, I'll go and check on Elodie.' The baby monitor would have alerted us if there was a problem, but I needed to get away from Sylvia before I said something I might regret. Her tactlessness was astonishing. It was at times like this that I wished I could have picked up the phone to call Reggie for a vent. She would have said something to make me laugh, defuse the situation.

Angry tears stung my eyes. I pushed past Jack and went up the stairs. Elodie was fast asleep in her Moses basket, snuffling softly as she moved her head. She looked so beautiful. Her eyes were tightly closed and I gazed at her long dark lashes. Just like Jack's. I felt bad then that I had reacted to Sylvia's jibe; bad because she was Jack's mother and, even if I didn't care for her very much, I certainly didn't want to upset my husband. I could hear raised voices downstairs and realised that Jack was grilling Sylvia to find out what had gone on. I stroked Elodie's cheek and crept from the bedroom.

Taking a deep breath, I stepped back into the living room. 'I'm sorry – I'm overtired and it's taking its toll on me. I shouldn't have reacted like that. I'm a bit touchy at the moment. You'll have to excuse me.'

The words almost stuck in my throat as I said them, but I didn't want an atmosphere. Sylvia and Harry would be returning to the farm tomorrow, and back to Spain in a couple of days. We wouldn't have to see them again for ages and I didn't want them to leave thinking badly of me, for Jack's sake. I would have to grit my teeth and try to be on my best behaviour until they left.

'That's all right, love. I'm only concerned for your well-being, that's all.' Sylvia's smile was syrupy. She

213

patted the seat next to her. 'Come and sit here and tell me all about your neighbour. Jack was telling his dad what a help she's been. She's getting on a bit though, isn't she? I hope it isn't too much for her . . .'

I tried to relax and enjoy the evening, not get too het up by her insensitive remarks, but was massively relieved when they eventually turned in for the night. Conversation had been a strain thereafter, particularly when Sylvia had started talking about Mrs Barley and how it wasn't a good idea to get too friendly with neighbours.

'It's fine when things are going well. But if you have a falling-out, well, you can't avoid them, can you? It can make for an uncomfortable existence when someone lives right on your doorstep and there's been a disagreement. Best to be civil but not get too involved; that's what I always say. We've got some nice new neighbours in Spain – a retired couple from Kent who've bought the flat upstairs. The chap's asked Harry to go for a pint a couple of times. But we won't be getting too pally with them, will we, love?'

Harry threw her a withering look. 'If you say so, my dear. Anything for a quiet life.'

Sylvia gave a high-pitched laugh. 'Oh, you. You know it makes sense really.'

From Harry's face, it was clear that the chance to escape his domineering wife for a while might have made a welcome change, but apparently he wasn't going to have that option. At least while he was still running the farm, he had been out most of the day. He must have been finding their change in circumstances claustro-phobic. I felt increasingly sorry for him.

'Oh, Jack – did we tell you that Lauren got married last month? Matt went to the church service. The whole village turned out for it, apparently. He said she looked beautiful. Well, she always did look a picture, didn't she?'

I bristled. The mention of Jack's perfect ex-fiancée was something Sylvia seemed unable to resist slipping into the conversation at some point whenever we saw her. I glanced at Jack, who appeared irritated.

'Yes, I think you did mention it. Best of luck to the chap – he'll need it.'

Sylvia looked deflated. I smiled to myself and gave a mental air punch.

*

They left around mid-morning the following day. After helping them to load the car, we were assembled on our front step about to wave them off, when we heard the rattle of a chain and Mrs Barley's door opened. She looked pleased to see us all.

'Hello, you must be Jack's parents. I'm Virginia Barley. Lovely to meet you at last.'

Harry smiled and went across to shake her by the hand. 'We've heard a lot about you, Mrs Barley. I believe we have you to thank for our delicious dinner last night. Jack and Stina were saying how wonderful you've been. We're very grateful – I wish we could do more, but we're so far away now it's impossible . . .'

'Oh, it's nothing. I like to help. It's been lovely having this pair next door – and now little Elodie, too.'

'Yes, she's just beautiful,' chimed in Sylvia. 'Don't go

getting too attached though – our Jack's a high-flyer. They'll probably be moving on to bigger and better things soon enough.' She gave her annoying laugh again, but her eyes were cold as she looked the old woman up and down.

I felt angered by her lack of sensitivity and had to bite my tongue.

Mrs Barley smiled sweetly. 'Ah well, I'll have to make the most of them while they're around, then!' She peered at Sylvia's arm and bent forward suddenly. 'Oh, just a second; you have a loose thread on your sleeve. Let me catch it for you before it pulls.' She disappeared into her hallway for a moment, then returned with a pair of nail scissors, and gave a sharp snip at the offending strand of cotton. Stepping back, she beamed. 'There, that's better. It would be a shame to spoil such a lovely coat.'

Sylvia smiled tightly and mumbled a begrudging thank you.

'Have a safe journey, both of you.'

Our neighbour went back into her house.

Harry turned to his wife in disbelief. 'What on earth did you say that for? These two are probably the best thing that's happened to the old dear for years. She won't want to think they're going to up sticks and leave when they've only been here five minutes.'

'Oh, Harry, I was just making conversation. Besides, it's true – she shouldn't get too used to them being around. It'll only be an upheaval for her when they move on.'

'*If* we move on,' interrupted Jack. 'And we've no plans to go anywhere for some time. Avoncote is the perfect place for Elodie to grow up in and we love it.'

'Of course you do. But time changes things. You might feel differently when she's a bit older – and when you're earning a bit more, which no doubt you will be very soon, if I know you. You've always worked so hard. And then helping with the baby on top of all the pressure of your job . . .' She turned to me. 'I know he's my son and I'm biased, but you're such a lucky girl, Stina.'

'I know,' I conceded, smiling through clenched teeth.

Jack looked mortified. He had actually been marvellous, but it was almost as though Sylvia thought I should be worshipping him for it. We were a unit; we shared things. Elodie belonged to both of us, and while I knew that I was ultimately responsible for feeding her, Jack was her father and I expected him to pull his weight when possible. If it had been left to his mother, I think I'd have been waiting on him hand and foot and bringing him his pipe and slippers at the end of the day. It was as if I should simply be grateful that he had chosen me and ask no more of him.

We said our goodbyes and I felt my whole body relax as their car pulled away. Closing the front door, Jack pulled me to him and stooped to kiss my cheek.

'Thank you. I know she can be a pain in the arse, but she means well. I think it's a bit of a ball ache for my poor old dad, though. Anyway, we won't be seeing them again for a while, so you can breathe now!'

'I'm sorry if I was tetchy. I know your mum has a good heart really – I just wish she hadn't said that to Mrs Barley. And I'm not too sure she likes me sometimes, either.'

He looked surprised. 'Don't be silly! She thinks you're wonderful. And why wouldn't she?'

I laughed. 'If you say so.' I wasn't going to justify my thoughts and left it at that. I felt bad for Mrs Barley and hoped she hadn't been upset by Sylvia's thoughtlessness. I was grateful that we didn't have to see Jack's mother too often or I think I might have exploded.

It was Saturday and although Jack usually went in for morning surgery, he had been able to take the whole day off. The weather was cold but bright, and he was keen to get me out in the fresh air. I had been advised that gentle walking would be helpful after the C-section, but was a little reluctant nevertheless. We wrapped Elodie up in her pink quilted snuggle suit that Jack's parents had bought for her, and tucked a warm blanket round her in the pram.

'Let's walk up the towpath by the canal. Just see how far you can go comfortably – I don't want you to overdo it.'

'I don't think there's much danger of that – I doubt I've got the energy to get further than the end of the lane,' I remarked, grimacing as I pulled on my coat and gloves.

'Don't be defeatist – you might be able to do more than you think. But go at your own pace – we'll only walk as far as you're happy with.'

We stepped out, Jobie trotting proudly alongside the pram.

Elodie's cheeks were flushed with the cold, and anxiously I kept stopping to check she was warm enough.

'Hey, how are you? Ooh – let me see the new arrival.'

I looked up to see Lucy crossing the road towards us.

She was carrying her baby in a sling across her chest. A despondent-looking Alfie clutched her hand, dragging his heels at her side. She peered down into the pram, cooing at Elodie. Leaning forward, she revealed a creamy trail of dried baby sick from her shoulder down the front of her navy-blue coat. I felt a pang of guilt, not having seen her for weeks. After she had declined my request to call round, I had dropped her the odd text to see how things were going, but her replies had been brief and, I had thought, a little dismissive. If I'm honest, I'd felt slightly annoyed. It occurred to me now that she might have been so up to her eyes in things after the baby's arrival that she simply didn't have the energy or the inclination to do much else. Maybe I should have just swallowed my pride and gone round unannounced.

'We're good, thank you. A bit knackered as you'd imagine, but this one's only nine days old so things could be worse! Haven't really been out much yet and thought we'd get a walk in while it's dry. I don't think you two have met, have you? Lucy, this is Jack.'

Jack smiled and extended a hand. Lucy shook it diffidently.

'Pleased to meet you, Jack.'

'You too.'

There was an uncomfortable pause, as if no one knew who was supposed to speak first.

'How are you?' I ventured.

Lucy looked exhausted, her eyes circled with bruise-like mauve rings, her face pale and drawn. Aside from shedding the baby weight, she had clearly lost more besides, and looked painfully thin.

219

'Georgie's teething at the moment – he's started early, just like his big brother did – so I'm not getting a lot of sleep. Alfie's a bit j-e-a-l-o-u-s –' she spelled out the word, looking pointedly at the glum-faced little boy '– so I'm trying to keep in his good books by taking him to get sweeties.'

'Where's Eddie this morning?'

She rolled her eyes. 'Late one with the lads last night. I've left him in bed.'

I felt angry; not least with myself. The poor girl looked not just tired but ill, and she was obviously trying to juggle the needs of both children without their father's support. It wasn't fair.

'Are you okay?' I asked. 'You look shattered.'

'Yeh, it's the lack of sleep, you know? Gets to you after a bit. Comes with the territory though, I suppose. I knew what I was letting myself in for, so I've only got myself to blame.'

She smiled shakily. For an awkward moment I thought she might burst into tears, but she straightened resolutely. 'It'll get better. I'll just have to weather the storm a bit longer – only another two years or so.' She gave a bitter little laugh, then shook it off and smiled weakly.

'Congratulations, anyway. I'm guessing from all the pink it's a little girl? What have you called her?'

'Elodie. After Jack's grandma.'

'Nice. She's beautiful. I'm sorry – I meant to pop a card through the door. I need to get my act together.'

'Don't worry. You've got enough on your plate.'

'I'll be more organised once this one starts to get into more of a routine.' She rubbed the baby's back and smiled down at him lovingly. 'He's still demand-feeding at the moment. I feel like a dairy cow.'

A pouting Alfie began to tug at her sleeve.

'All right, Trouble, let's go and get those sweeties. See you all again soon, I hope.'

We watched her cross the street and amble wearily towards the shop. My heart went out to her. At least Jack was doing his bit to help, in spite of his work commitments.

'Poor girl,' he said in a low voice. 'She looks done in. Sounds like that Eddie's a waste of space.'

'You can say that again. What an arsehole.'

We continued up the road as far as the pub, but it was bitterly cold and I really wasn't getting any pleasure from our excursion.

'Shall we go back? I'd love a hot drink.'

Jack put an arm round me. 'Sure. You've done really well, anyway. Little and often is best. Maybe we can come out again later, if you feel up to it?'

'Hmm. Maybe not. I'll try again tomorrow.'

*

I thought a lot about Lucy over the next few days and wondered how she was getting on. Although still very sore and achy, I was gaining a little more strength daily; Elodie was feeding well, and I was getting more used to the breastfeeding. It had been something of a shock initially, and I hadn't anticipated the ferocity of the suction that could come from such a small mouth. Thankfully it was less uncomfortable than it had been over the first week or two, and although it was difficult to gauge how much milk I was producing, she was clearly getting enough, having already regained her birth weight and a little more besides. She seemed contented and it was a relief that she didn't cry all the time like some babies, mainly only when she was hungry.

I listened to the advice of the kindly midwife and made sure that I took a nap during the day when Elodie was sleeping. Feeding her myself was convenient and I was glad that I had persevered; during the night I could just lift her into the bed from her crib, which I kept beside me. It was far easier than having to get up and start mixing bottles. So far, so good. Apart from the sleeplessness, and my fluctuating moods, which I'd assumed were par for the course, I felt very fortunate.

The following week, Jack Skyped his parents to see if they were okay, and to check whether they'd settled back into life in Spain after their flight home. Sylvia had gone shopping, the first time she had left the house in days, apparently. Harry said he was fine, but unfortunately Sylvia had been ill with violent stomach pains and vomiting for the first couple of days after leaving our house, which had started on the journey back to the farm in Enville.

'You might know, she blamed it on the casserole the old lady made,' he told us with a dismissive shrug. 'Can't have been that, obviously, as the rest of us ate it and didn't have any problems. But she's got it in her head that's what caused it and nothing will persuade her otherwise. You know how she can be sometimes.'

We did know how she could be. It was ludicrous to blame Mrs Barley's cooking and as mean as it may have been, part of me felt the tiniest bit of schadenfreude that Sylvia had been unwell. I was fed up with her self-righteous attitude and it almost felt like someone or something had been teaching her a lesson.

'But she's fine now?' Jack asked, biting his lower lip as he glanced at me.

'Oh yeah, no long-term damage. She's lost a bit of weight if anything, so it's probably done her a favour. You know how she is, always on some bloody diet or other.' He laughed, looking over his shoulder jokingly and saying behind his hand, 'You'll have to ask the old dear to make it again next time we visit – I really enjoyed it!'

I wouldn't mention it to Mrs Barley. It had been very good of her to help us out, and it wouldn't do for her to think that someone was questioning her food hygiene. And I'd seen her kitchen – it was always immaculate. As usual, Sylvia was being theatrical and ridiculous. It made me even more glad that they lived so far away.

Later that afternoon, I felt completely wrung out. While Elodie was, all things considered, a remarkably good baby, the constant round of breastfeeding, nappy changing and not getting a solid night's sleep was beginning to take its toll. I was frequently weepy and the least little thing would set me off. I tried to tell myself how lucky I was to have such a beautiful baby and a supportive partner, but sometimes it was hard to stay positive.

I had fed Elodie and thankfully she was now dozing. I had laid her carefully in her basket, switching on the baby monitor, and crept back downstairs. Jack was in the spare room catching up on some paperwork. I was about to curl up on the settee when I saw Mrs Barley coming up our garden path, carrying a basket with a tea towel draped over the top. My heart sank. I knew she was only trying to help but I had hoped to have some time to myself, and it seemed my plans were scuppered. I waved half-heartedly as she slowly made her way up towards the house, and went to open the French doors for her.

A flicker of movement suddenly drew my eyes towards the summer house. My stomach turned over as the door opened and a dark-haired figure slipped through the gap and headed for the gate. I shrieked hysterically to Jack, who came running from upstairs to see what was wrong.

Mrs Barley heard me yell and almost dropped the basket. She looked about her anxiously just in time to see the figure disappearing through the gate and out into the entry.

'There! Did you see him?' I turned to Jack triumphantly.

'Whatever is it, love?' Mrs Barley had arrived breathlessly at the back door.

'That . . . man – he was in the summer house . . .' I looked from Jack to Mrs Barley, who in turn were looking at each other in bewilderment.

'I didn't see anyone,' said Jack eventually. 'Did you, Mrs Barley?'

The old woman looked doubtful. 'I didn't see a soul and I'm sure I'd have noticed if there was a stranger in my summer house. Are you quite sure you saw someone, Stina?'

I stared at both of them in disbelief. 'But you must have

– he was right there – seconds ago! How the hell can I have been the only one to see him?' It was exasperating.

Mrs Barley cocked her head to one side sympathetically. 'Listen, love, I know this will probably sound daft, but you're worn out – and your hormones are all over the place. I wonder if your eyes are playing tricks on you. Lack of sleep can do funny things to the brain.'

I felt suddenly angry. Jack may have been a fraction too late, but I couldn't believe that Mrs Barley hadn't seen anyone. The man, or ghost, or whatever he was, had been going out of the gate as she turned – surely she couldn't have missed him?

Jack placed a hand gently on my shoulder. 'Mrs Barley's right, you know. I remember Matt saying how confused his wife was after their eldest was born. She was doing all kinds of odd things – dishing out the breakfast cereal and pouring boiling water onto it instead of the milk, putting shaving foam on her toothbrush, wearing her clothes inside out – that sort of thing. It's surprising how badly sleep deprivation can affect some people, particularly when you're still getting to grips with looking after a new-born into the bargain.'

They were both looking at me pityingly as if I was some sort of imbecile. Gritting my teeth, I shook him off, tears of frustration welling in my eyes. No matter what I said, I couldn't persuade Jack that I had definitely seen someone.

But I had a suspicion that Mrs Barley had and – for whatever reason – she wasn't prepared to admit to it. It gave me a strangely unsettled feeling.

*

Jack returned to work properly when Elodie was just over three weeks old. Since the practice were short-staffed (owing to one of the other vets having to go into hospital for a long-scheduled procedure), he had reluctantly agreed to go in for emergencies during his paternity leave, but for the majority of those first weeks he had been a constant presence at home, which had been an enormous relief to me. He was a little anxious, but I reassured him that I'd be fine. Nursing Elodie, I stood at the door to wave him off, feeling slightly apprehensive, but determined that I wasn't going to have a meltdown, too.

'Don't forget, call me any time if there's a problem. Anything at all. I don't want to come home to find you in floods of tears,' he had instructed me.

I laughed. 'I think we can manage for a few hours, can't we, Elodie?'

I couldn't admit as much to Jack, but part of me felt slightly panic-stricken at the thought of being left entirely alone with a tiny baby. Having sole responsibility for her welfare was a daunting prospect. What if something went wrong? It was a comfort to know that Mrs Barley was always willing to step in if I needed help. But I was still baffled about her claiming not to have seen anyone in the garden that day; I knew what I had seen and nothing was going to persuade me otherwise. I may have been sleep-deprived, but I felt certain I wasn't hallucinating. Although I began to wonder if the old woman genuinely hadn't been looking in the right direction at the right moment and had failed to see anything. It was all very odd.

The weather was cold, but bright, and I felt in need

of some fresh air. After breakfast and the baby's feed, I wrapped her up warmly and put on Jobie's lead. He looked up at me hopefully, his tail held high.

'Come on, let's go for a walk, shall we?'

I looped his lead around the pram handle and we slowly made our way up the road. It was still relatively early, only 9.30. I wondered if it was too soon in the day to call on Lucy. I decided to amble for a while first and then go and knock on her door. We walked up to the shop. I thought I might take the baby to introduce her to Judy and Nick.

I left Jobie and the pram at the entrance and carefully carried the sleeping Elodie into the shop. Towards the back, near the cash machine, I noticed Lucy's husband, Eddie. He was leaning forwards, almost leering, his hand propping up the wall, talking in hushed tones to the curvaceous waitress from The Green Man, who was pinned beneath the line of his outstretched arm. Every now and then, she emitted an irritating girly giggle. She was gazing into his eyes, a red-taloned hand stroking his shoulder. Seeing me looking over, she quickly drew back and cleared her throat.

Eddie's head whipped round. He fixed me with a challenging stare as he promptly made his way towards the door, the blushing girl, eyes cast downwards, in his wake.

Judy looked on with folded arms from behind the counter. She glared after Eddie as the shop door closed behind him and his companion.

'He should be ashamed of himself. And that little tart. Poor Lucy. She has a dog's life with him. And I don't think she's got any idea what he gets up to. It's the talk of the pub, you know.'

I didn't know. I felt angry, and disgusted with Eddie, although not entirely surprised. But I couldn't tell Lucy – she was clearly fragile at the moment. I certainly didn't want to be the bearer of news that would make her feel worse than she already did.

'I was on my way over to see Lucy and the baby, actually. I thought I'd bring Elodie in for you to meet her.'

'Oh, what an adorable little soul. And you look so *well*. Congratulations to you both.'

'Thank you. I'm still pretty sore and knackered to be honest – I shouldn't complain as I know some people don't get a minute to themselves and she is sleeping fairly well at the moment, considering she's still so young. I'm bracing myself for the teething though!'

Beaming, Judy came forward to give me a careful hug. She called through to the back of the shop.

'Nick, come and look at Stina's beautiful baby.'

Within seconds, Nick appeared, brandishing a bottle of sparkling wine, a pink bow tied round its neck.

'Congratulations,' he said, grinning broadly. He held up the bottle. 'We'd heard your good news. I'll pop this in the pram, so you and Jack can have a drink on us. Lovely to meet the new arrival.'

'Thank you so much, that's very kind. I'm feeding Elodie myself, but I'm sure I can allow myself a glass or two after her last feed at night!'

We made small talk for a few minutes, but all I could think about was Lucy and her selfish idiot of a husband.

I made my excuses, thanked them once more, and left the shop. I wondered whether to go straight home again, but then decided not to be so cowardly. I didn't have to mention that I'd seen Eddie. Lucy could really do with some moral support right now; more than she knew.

CHAPTER 14

Puffy-eyed, Lucy came to the door wearing a filthy dressing gown, her hair matted and unwashed. A sleeping Georgie was draped over her shoulder. He was breathing heavily and sounded wheezy. Alfie appeared, still in his pyjamas, his face smeared in what looked like dried egg yolk. He peeped at me shyly from behind her legs.

'Look at the state of me. Come on in, just ignore the carnage.' She gave an awkward laugh.

'Are you sure? I can come back another time if it's not convenient.'

'No, no. We're not going anywhere, are we, Alfie?'

The little boy shook his head and looked at the floor miserably. I unclipped Jobie's lead and let him enter ahead of us. Alfie's face lit up, and he giggled as Jobie gave his hand a sloppy lick.

Lucy smiled, but tears glistened in her eyes. 'We'll put your coat on in a minute, sweetheart, and then you can play with the doggy in the garden.' She turned to me.

'There's not a lot of room in here at the moment, I'm afraid. You can bring the pram in if the little one's asleep, though.'

I manoeuvred the pram and squeezed into the little living room. There was barely standing room, the floor littered with toys and baby paraphernalia. I looked around, wondering if I should attempt to sit down. Lucy hurriedly shifted a pile of folded washing from the settee onto the coffee table, its surface sprinkled with crumbs and sticky with a puddle of spilled juice.

'Here, take a pew and I'll get the kettle on. I've drunk so much tea since this one was born – I'm making up for all those months when I couldn't stand it!'

Elodie began to stir. She screwed up her face as if about to yell, so I hastily located her dummy in the changing bag and lifted her from the pram, sitting her on my lap and rocking gently. She was instantly soothed, her eyes taking in the unfamiliar surroundings with interest.

Lucy returned from letting Jobie and Alfie out into the back garden. The baby, still hanging from her limply like a rag doll, gave a throaty cough but did not wake. His face was slightly flushed.

'Well, isn't she a little darling. And you're looking great. I feel such a bloody mess.' Her eyes filled with tears again. 'If I could just get one solid night's sleep . . . It's really getting me down.'

'Isn't Eddie helping out?' I already knew the answer, but felt compelled to ask.

'The only way he's helping is by keeping out of my hair. It's like having a third child when he's at home.'

'Is he working today?' I wasn't about to say I'd just

seen him but wondered if Lucy had any inkling of what he was up to.

'I don't know where he is, and to be quite honest I don't much care at the moment. We had a massive row last night. He's been acting like a total dickhead.' Her eyes dropped, a hand self-consciously smoothing her hair suddenly. 'Georgie's had an awful cold and he's been really whingy. I asked Eddie to watch him while I went for a bath and he kicked off, saying he has to go out to work, so why should he have to do babysitting duties too? He stormed out and didn't come home, the prick. His mum's got wise to his strops and she won't let him stay at hers any more, so I suppose he must have slept on a mate's sofa.'

So, he'd been out all night, then. What a complete shit. I looked past her into the kitchen and saw that the dishes were piled up. The poor girl was obviously sinking under the strain of everything.

'Look, why don't you run yourself a bath now and I'll keep an eye on Alfie. We can have that cup of tea in a bit. Elodie's happy enough at the moment, and if you pop the baby in his cot, I'll listen out for him.'

She hesitated. 'I don't expect you to . . .'

'Go on. You need a few minutes to yourself. Go and have a soak – it'll perk you up a bit.'

'If you're sure. I've started topping him up with the odd bottle – there's one already made up in the door of the fridge, if he wakes up. And the Calpol is on the kitchen side – he's due a dose in about half an hour, but hopefully I'll be done before then.'

'Take your time. I'm not in any rush.'

'Thank you. I could do with it. I feel disgusting.'

Taking Elodie, I went into the kitchen and looked out into the garden. Alfie was happily running up and down, Jobie hot on his heels. Looking at the dirty pots and pans in the sink, I thought I'd better try to clean up a bit. I managed to move the pram into the kitchen doorway and lay Elodie down. She had been fed right before we left home, and seemed quite content chomping on her dummy. Her eyes began to close once more. I went through the kitchen like a whirlwind, anxious to restore some sort of order before Lucy had finished her bath.

Thankfully Georgie didn't stir, and by the time she came back downstairs, I'd washed and dried the mountain of crockery and wiped down the work surfaces, plus the sticky coffee table in the living room. The effort had left my stomach uncomfortable and I was glad to sit down.

'Oh, you're a diamond. Thank you.' She had put on clean clothes and her damp hair was wrapped in a towel. She looked more relaxed and a little colour had returned to her cheeks. 'I've just checked on Georgie – he's still asleep. I know he's due a feed soon, but I didn't want to disturb him. He could probably do with the rest. He's awfully warm, though.'

We sat drinking tea, popping out from time to time to see what Alfie was up to. I had given him Jobie's rubber bone, which I carried on the pram's shopping tray, and the little boy was attempting to throw it, although he hadn't quite got the hang of it. Jobie was clearly enjoying the attention and amenably retrieving the thing each time, even though it was only landing about three feet in front of him.

Lucy and I chatted about this and that, but mainly about breastfeeding, sore boobs and exhaustion. She was obviously feeling very fragile and seemed grateful that I had gone round.

'It's good to talk to someone who's in the same boat. You can feel quite isolated when they're tiny. My mum comes round when she can, but she has to work. Some days I feel as though the walls are closing in on me.'

There was a sudden whimper from upstairs. 'Oh, Georgie's awake at last. I'll go and bring him down.'

She returned moments later clutching the baby, a look of panic on her face.

'He's gone all floppy. And he's burning up; feel his head.'

I touched the baby's forehead. His skin was pale and clammy, and unnaturally hot. Georgie's eyeballs had rotated upwards, leaving only the whites visible through their half-opened lids. He seemed oblivious to his surroundings and his limbs were jerking in an alarming way. His breathing sounded worryingly erratic.

'I think you'd better call an ambulance.'

Lucy had begun to shake. Her eyes were wide with fear. She seemed incapable of action, and stood, immobile, staring down helplessly at the twitching baby in her arms.

I took out my mobile and dialled 999. After being connected to the ambulance service, the call handler asked me a whole list of questions, then told me to remain calm and that someone would be with us as soon as possible.

'What d'you think's wrong with him? Oh my God – d'you reckon that old witch next door to you could have had something to do with this?' Her eyes were wild, her face filled with panic. 'She hates me, I know she does. I've seen her looking out at us when we walk past. She frightens the life out of me. And I'm sure she was at the back of Alfie's upset stomach that time. I think she tried to poison him. D'you reckon she's put some sort of, I dunno, hex on us?'

I was appalled. The idea that Mrs Barley could launch an attack, psychic or otherwise, on an innocent baby was horrific. Mrs Barley wasn't capable of such a thing. Then I remembered the old woman's words when I'd told her about Georgie: *Is all well with the baby?*; the look on her face as she had asked. A cold dread began to stir from somewhere deep within me.

'Oh Christ, where's fucking Eddie when I need him?' She began to pace up and down, as much as the lack of floor space would allow, the baby's slack head bobbing involuntarily with her movement.

I was lost for words. Alfie suddenly burst through the door, squealing with laughter as Jobie almost knocked him over with an exuberant nudge. I steered them back outside and checked on Elodie, who had mercifully been sleeping throughout the proceedings.

The ambulance arrived within minutes. The paramedics introduced themselves as Lynn and Shoba, then came straight into the living room. They exuded an air of calm and efficiency as they took over. Lucy lay Georgie carefully on the settee, looking on anxiously as Shoba, the younger of the two, examined the listless infant, whose breathing was thankfully beginning to sound more normal. He had stopped twitching and seemed more aware of his surroundings.

'I suspect he's had a febrile convulsion,' she explained. 'Little ones can't regulate their own temperature like adults, and if they overheat when they have a virus or something, this sometimes happens. It's like a safety valve. It can be pretty scary, I know, but they're rarely dangerous. Keep a close eye on him and give him the paracetamol suspension to keep his temperature in check. If it happens again, lay him on his side and stay with him – just observe how long it goes on for. If it's passed within about a quarter of an hour, that's definitely all it is. It's just one of those things – some are more prone to it than others. You'll need to look out for it, now he's had an episode, as unfortunately it's not usually a one-off. But they all outgrow it by the time they're about five or six.'

Lucy stared at the baby, almost as if she couldn't quite believe he was still breathing.

'So, he's going to be okay? He doesn't need to go into hospital or anything?'

'He'll be fine. But you did the right thing calling us, always better to be safe than sorry with a little one.' She studied Lucy with evident concern. 'What about you? Are you all right, love?'

Lucy looked embarrassed. She nodded mutely. There was a pause and the women exchanged glances.

We thanked the paramedics, and I showed them out. Lucy dissolved into tears. I put an arm round her shoulder.

'It's okay, Georgie's going to be okay. Don't worry.'

'But what if he hadn't been? What if it had been something really serious? I needed his bloody father here right now, even if he is a tool, and I don't even know where he is. I tried his mobile earlier and he's not picking up. I've had enough, Stina. I need someone I can rely on. I can't cope with this any more. I don't know where it's all going to end. I'm going back to my mum's.'

I helped Lucy to pack an overnight bag for herself and the boys. She rang her mum to ask if she could come and collect them once she had finished her shift at work. I stayed for another half an hour or so, until her mum was on her way, then told her I had to get home. She thanked me for my support.

'I'm so glad you were here. I was really losing it for a bit there. Please, ignore what I said earlier about the old woman. It was stupid of me. I realise I must have sounded like a total fruitcake. I was so scared for Georgie. I don't know what I'd have done if . . . No, I can't even think about it.'

I went home with a sinking feeling in the pit of my stomach. Lucy was right: it could have been so much worse. I was hugely relieved that Georgie was all right. I felt bad, too, that I had actually wondered if there was something in her suspicions about Mrs Barley. It seemed crazy now to think she could put curses on people, but Alfie had been so poorly after eating the cakes, and the angry look she had given Lucy that day – I knew I hadn't imagined it. But surely it was ridiculous to think that an old woman could stoop so low as to give a child food poisoning . . .

Even if it meant breaking her family up, I felt that Lucy was doing the right thing leaving Eddie. As if it wasn't bad enough that he did nothing to support or help her, the fact that he was cheating on her – and so publicly – was unforgivable. It worried me, too, what being brought up in that kind of atmosphere might do to little Alfie. Children pick up very quickly on hostility between their parents. Sometimes it was better for them to live apart than to be in a constant war zone.

Whether it would bring Eddie to his senses or not was another matter. But in my eyes, a waster like that didn't deserve a second chance. Right now, Lucy needed looking after. Someone who would step up to the plate, share the load, treat her with love and respect. And he clearly wasn't man enough for the job.

*

That Thursday was Halloween. While Elodie was obviously far too tiny to know anything was going on, we still enjoyed keeping up the tradition. Jack brought a pumpkin home and hollowed out its centre. I carved a grinning face, then positioned it in the front window. I wasn't sure whether we could expect trick-or-treaters but had bought plenty of sweets from the shop just in case, and at dusk we lit a candle to place inside the pumpkin. The weather had been cold but dry, and as night fell, the full moon against its inky black backdrop seemed to set the scene perfectly.

At about 7.30 p.m., there was a rap at the front door. Three young children, aged between about five and eight and all in suitably creepy costumes and masks, hovered expectantly at the door while their bored-looking father stood waiting on the pavement just outside the front gate. Holding Elodie, I steered the excited Jobie back into the kitchen and looked on from the doorway as Jack offered them the tub of sweets, from which they each eagerly took a handful to drop into the bucket the eldest was brandishing. The children thanked him and retreated back up the path. I noticed that the father had grabbed the youngest child by the collar of his vampire cloak and yanked him back when he attempted to enter Mrs Barley's garden.

The man leaned forward, looking up warily at the cottage. 'No, we don't go to that one; I've told you before. It's where that funny old woman lives.'

The children all stared as they hurried past our neighbour's cottage. I wondered why their father had been so vehement. Mrs Barley's curtain twitched, and within moments her porch light had been lit. The front door opened abruptly.

'No better than begging, it is,' she announced, her tone angry as she watched the children and their father making their way back up the road towards the centre of the village.

Jack raised his eyebrows and shot me a look, but said nothing.

I was quite shocked. 'It's just a bit of fun, Mrs Barley. They're only kids.'

She turned to look at me and I could see that she was riled. 'Samhain is an important date in the Wheel of the Year, not one for silly fancy dress and playing cruel tricks on people,' she said sharply. 'Children should be taught the true nature of it, not encouraged to go bothering people and expecting something for nothing. It's demeaning.'

Without another word, she closed her door abruptly and the light went out once more.

'Good grief, what was that all about?' Jack remarked as we went back inside. 'D'you think someone's played a nasty prank on her in the past or something? Bit extreme.'

'Very. She's a real puzzle at times. I'd love to know what goes on inside her head.'

We went back indoors. There was a steady stream of other trick-or-treaters for the next hour or so, but then it was obviously past the children's bedtime. We extinguished the candle, and after I had fed Elodie we settled down to watch TV for an hour or so before bed.

A sudden noise from outside made me sit up and listen. Jobie, who had been lying at my feet, jumped up at once and gave a little bark of warning. I shushed Jack and muted the TV. Loud voices and laughter could be heard from the front of the cottage. We went to the window and peered out in time to see a group of five or six jeering teenage lads disappearing at speed up the road.

'Fuck off on your broomstick, you old witch!' was one's parting shot.

Jack switched on the hall light and opened the front door. Eggs had been pelted at all of Mrs Barley's front windows; yellow goo was left dribbling down the glass, shells lying smashed on the ground beneath.

Mrs Barley appeared at her door. She came out onto the path and inspected the mess, her face white with anger.

'Little bastards,' she growled. 'Every year it's the same. They'll live to regret it one day.'

'I'll help you clean it off tomorrow,' Jack told her, glancing at me and grimacing. 'Kids, eh.'

She turned to look at us, her expression almost murderous. 'The next generation just the same as the one before. All scum, with no respect for their elders. I've had a bellyful of it.'

She slammed her door so hard that the reverberation could be felt in our own walls. Jack and I looked at one another in stunned silence. A sudden wail from above told us that the disturbance had woken Elodie.

I groaned. 'I'll go.'

I made my way upstairs. It was gone 10 p.m. by now and I decided I might as well turn in for the night, leaving Jack to walk Jobie and switch everything off.

'Suffice to say Halloween's not Mrs B's favourite festival,' said Jack, as he climbed into bed beside me a little while later. 'They *really* don't like her, the locals, do they?'

'It's so odd. I mean, I know kids do that sort of thing, but why target an old lady? Mind you, she obviously doesn't like the modern take on Halloween. Maybe she's been abusive to people and that's why they've got it in for her. I feel sorry for her, though. I think she's a decent person at heart and no one round here seems prepared to give her a chance.'

'Well, all we can do is try to be supportive and let her know we're on her side, even if she can be a bit, well, out there at times. Anyway, let's try to get some sleep. I'm bushed – and no doubt Elodie will be waking us up again in a few hours. Plus it looks like I'm going to have to don my window cleaner's hat tomorrow. Deep joy.'

*

In those early weeks after Elodie's birth, I was permanently exhausted, but had begun to dread night-time. I would dream regularly about Reggie, seeing her lying gaunt and motionless in her open coffin, even though it wasn't a sight I had actually witnessed. I often woke with a start, either in a cold sweat or with warm tears trickling down my face. The more tired I became, the more amplified any minor issues seemed to be, along with my anxiety levels. It was a vicious circle.

Like clockwork, Elodie stirred at half one for her feed that night. By then, however, I was already wide awake and had been for some time.

My sleep pattern wasn't good even before my pregnancy and Reggie's loss, but now it was as though I was pre-empting Elodie waking and didn't fall into a deep sleep at all. Despite feeling shattered, I had lain awake for almost an hour beforehand. Just before one, I decided to go downstairs and make myself a hot chocolate. I fumbled for my slippers with my feet and pulled on my dressing gown, then slipped from the bedroom as noiselessly as possible.

Jobie was pleased to see me as ever. He padded from his basket and followed me into the living room. I sat at the table, flicking the switch on my laptop. Maybe I could do a bit of online grocery shopping – at least it would be something useful.

As it was booting up, my attention was drawn to the French window where Jobie was moving the curtain aside with his nose. I wondered if he wanted to go to the loo, so got up to open the door for him.

Small, evenly spaced globes of light could be seen

shimmering through the summer house window. There was someone out there. My heart thudding, I eased the double doors slowly open and peered through the gloom down Mrs Barley's garden. Jobie darted through the gap and straight onto the lawn to relieve himself. My whole body quivering, I watched in trepidation as a dark shadow paced back and forth across the window of the summer house. I realised now that the lights from within were cast by several low candle flames, waxing and waning with the draught passing through the partially opened door.

Should I wake Jack? In a split second I decided against it; with hindsight it was probably reckless of me, but from somewhere I mustered the courage to investigate myself. I was determined to catch someone in the act and be able to prove to myself – and my doubting husband – that there was indeed an intruder, whether from this world or the next, and that it wasn't a figment of my imagination. In case it *was* the former, I looked around the room for something to use as a weapon and picked up one of the wooden owls that Reggie had given me. Looking back now, it could all have ended very badly, but I wasn't thinking rationally at all.

Hardly drawing breath, I ducked down below the fence, clutching at my stomach in irrational fear of rupturing my scar and moving stealthily in a semi-crouching position down the garden, the cold moisture from the grass soaking through my slippers and pyjama bottoms.

One by one, the candles were snuffed out and a silhouette appeared in the summer house's doorway. Thankfully

Jobie was busily sniffing the ground and hadn't betrayed my presence. I continued to observe from just beneath the level of the fence. It sounded as though someone was chanting. Quaking with fright and the cold, I almost gasped as the door was pushed fully open. It had become apparent that there was no intruder after all.

I watched as Mrs Barley, her face expressionless, began to make her way back towards the house. She seemed almost in a trance and was muttering something unintelligible to herself. It was a strange, repetitive sound and made my skin prickle. I watched as she disappeared into the darkness of her living room, waiting for the light to go on. It didn't.

Calling Jobie softly, I went back into the house and locked the door. What on earth had she been doing out there at such an unearthly hour? It was most discomfiting.

From above I could hear Elodie's muffled cries and the creak of the floorboards as Jack rose to soothe her. So much for my intentions to order the weekly shopping. I switched off the laptop once more and made my way back upstairs, holding out my arms to take the baby from Jack. He felt my hands.

'Bloody hell, you're freezing. Have you been outside?'

'I – yes, I couldn't sleep. I went down and let Jobie out for a wee.' I wriggled off my wet pyjama trousers and slipped under the duvet, pulling it up around me as best I could while Elodie latched on and began to suckle greedily. I was still shivering, both from the cold and the memory of what I'd witnessed.

'Jack, I've just seen Mrs Barley in her summer house. She'd lit a load of candles. God knows what she was up to out there. She was doing that chanting thing again. It's made me feel quite odd hearing her.' I shuddered again. Elodie paused and looked up at me for a moment, then resumed her feed.

He looked annoyed. 'Did she wake you? I'll have to have a word if she did – it's bad enough being woken by the baby several times a night, let alone being disturbed by our neighbour for no good reason.'

'No, I was awake anyway. But when I went down, I could see lights outside so I went to have a look. Christ, it looked like she was performing some sort of ritual or something.'

Jack sniggered. 'Summoning up a demon or two to get her own back on those kids, I shouldn't wonder.'

'Don't even joke. It's really not funny. You should've heard her. It was . . . eerie.'

'Probably an innocent explanation. I shouldn't worry about it. You can ask her tomorrow – everything always seems more logical in the cold light of day. She wants to be careful lighting candles in there, though – the whole thing could go up in flames if she forgets to put one out.' He sighed. 'I'm sorry – I'm going to have to try and get some sleep – I'm in surgery in the morning.' He squeezed my hand and stroked Elodie's cheek lightly. ''Night.'

''Night.'

Jack turned over and was soon snoring again. I sat upright for another ten minutes or so until Elodie had fallen asleep. I slid a finger into her mouth and lifted her gently from my breast, holding her over my shoulder and rubbing her back vigorously for a few minutes, then carried her carefully back to her crib.

I tossed and turned for a while but eventually sheer exhaustion kicked in and I fell asleep. Elodie woke for another feed at around six, but thankfully went straight back to sleep afterwards, as did I. I didn't wake again until daylight had begun to creep through. From downstairs I could hear Jack moving around in the kitchen but Elodie was still sleeping beside me, snuffling softly and fidgeting a little. I watched her and felt a surge of love. Sometimes I still found it hard to believe that she was actually mine and Jack's; that she was here to stay. She was such an adorable little being, and we had created her. It was mind-blowing.

Initially I had forgotten about Mrs Barley and the strange goings-on in the summer house the previous night, but peeling back the curtains, I looked out into the garden and was reminded immediately. The thought of the old woman's strange mumbling and its implications invoked an unpleasant tingling sensation throughout my whole body.

Jack appeared in the doorway with a steaming mug of tea. He smiled, speaking softly so as not to wake Elodie.

'Morning, sleepyhead. Thought you could use this. I've got to hit the road as I'm operating first thing. Why don't you pop and see Lucy later if you feel like a bit of company? I'm sure she'd love to see you.' He smirked playfully. 'You can compare notes on embroidery or knitting, or whatever it is young ladies like to talk about . . .'

'Aren't you the comedian? Sod off.' I took a mock swipe at him. 'Yeh, I might just do that. Think I could do with getting out of the house for a bit. I reckon I'll need a kip later though. Can't have had more than four hours last night after all that business with Mrs Barley.'

'I'd ask her outright what she was doing. I'm sure there'll be a reasonable explanation.'

'I hope so.'

He planted a kiss on my mouth. 'You take things easy today. See you this evening.'

*

I drank my tea, then texted Lucy to see how she was doing and if she would be free later. I thought how I would have loved to ring Reggie to tell her what had happened. She would have been buzzing about it all. It was times like this that I really missed not being able to pick up the phone and hear her voice at the other end of the line. I felt tears threaten and gave myself a shake before I began to wallow in nostalgia. I managed to shower and dress before Elodie woke, then started to worry that she'd slept too long, and kept putting a finger beneath her nose to make sure she was actually breathing. To my relief, she soon screwed up her little face and began to cry.

I changed her nappy, and put her into a fresh Baby-gro. I sat on the bed and put her to my breast, scrolling through my phone as I did so. Uncannily an old message from Reggie popped up. *'Hope you're having fun whatever you're up to.'* It felt very strange, yet poignant and a tear ran down my cheek. I missed her so much.

My phone pinged suddenly. It was Lucy, responding to my message with quite a lengthy text. She had gone back home but the relationship with Eddie was over, and she was in the process of moving a lot of stuff to her mum's, which was at the other end of the village. Her mum was out at work, and she'd given the address, asking if I wanted to go round there for lunch. I replied that I'd love to and said I'd see her later.

*

Elodie was awake but quite contented, staring up at the mobile dangling from the hood of her pram in the living room. I went to pick up the post from the doormat and through the small frosted pane could see movement outside the front door. It was only 8.30 a.m., but already Mrs Barley was out at the front of Rose Cottage with a bucket of soapy water and a sponge, trying to remove the mess from her downstairs windows. The eggshells had been swept into a dustpan. She looked pale and worn out, and I felt suddenly sorry for her, in spite of her peculiar behaviour during the night.

'Mrs Barley, Jack said he would do that for you later.'

She stopped what she was doing and turned to look at me, wiping her forehead with the back of her rubber glove. 'That's very good of him. I'd be grateful if he could do the upstairs – I'm not going to even attempt climbing a ladder at my age.'

'No, you mustn't. Here, let me help.' I rolled up my sleeves, took the sponge from her and started to scrub at the window. She watched me for a moment.

'I'll get a chamois; dry them off.'

Between us we cleaned the glass until all evidence of the previous night's assault had been removed, from downstairs at least. That left three upstairs windows for

Jack to do later. My hands were red and numb with cold.

'Thank you, love. That's been a great help. Come round the back, I'll make us a hot drink. I've made an apple cake for Samhain.'

I thought about her nocturnal activities in the summer house and hesitated. But then maybe this would be an opportunity to talk to her properly, ask what she had actually been doing.

'Okay. I'll see if Elodie's dropped off – I'll wheel her round in the pram if she has.'

Elodie was fast asleep, so I pushed the pram down the garden and back up to Mrs Barley's house. She had already opened both doors for me to get the pram over the step and called through from the kitchen.

'Have a seat, I'll be with you in a minute.'

I wasn't quite prepared for what met my eyes. The little table that had once held the doll and the candle was in the centre of the room, now covered with a black silk cloth and adorned with an array of objects. A silver-framed photograph of Frank as a young man had been placed in its centre, surrounded by flickering tealights. Sprigs of rosemary had been twisted around the frame and a pocket watch sat in front of it. There was a large, oval-shaped polished black crystal to one side of the photograph and a jagged, myriad-coloured one to the other. A little brass bell had been placed on one corner of the table, and what looked like a lock of dark hair, tied with a black ribbon, sat at another. The clear intention was to create some sort of weird shrine to her husband. It was eerie and part of me wanted to turn and run.

The assortment of candles on the hearth were all lit

and an incense burner released a potent, cloying smell into the air. The atmosphere was strangely heavy and it didn't give me a good feeling. Even the little lovebirds seemed subdued, perched in their cage like statues in solemn silence as though sedated by the heady fumes. A sudden fluttering startled me, and I looked round to see Corvus immediately outside the window. His sharp little eyes seemed to follow me with contempt. He tapped the glass impatiently with his beak and I was glad that I had closed the doors behind me.

Mrs Barley appeared in the doorway at the far end of the room, which opened out into the hall nearer the front of the cottage. Seeing the crow, she laughed. 'He's already had plenty today, greedy boy. Come and sit up here, Stina. We'll have more room at the dining table. You can leave the pram there if you like.'

Elodie was still sound asleep, so I put on the brake and went to sit at the table. There was an arrangement of dried flowers and berries in the centre and more lit candles. I was surprised to see that there were three places set.

'Oh, I'm sorry – are you expecting company?'

'Possibly.'

Mrs Barley smiled knowingly as she handed me a side plate with a huge slice of cake and a mug containing a warm, spicy-smelling brew. I sipped tentatively. It was a delicious apple and cinnamon concoction.

'Samhain is a special time,' she explained. 'A time to give thanks for the fruits of the harvest, to prepare for the winter and also to remember our dead. I've laid a place for Frank, you see. I always feel him drawing close on this day every year.' As she spoke, her eyes settled on the photograph on the small table. 'I speak to him all the time anyway, but he seems to answer me on Samhain. You should try to talk to your loved ones who have passed, too. To your auntie, maybe?'

I noticed she hadn't mentioned Reggie. I felt suddenly cold. I had no desire to try to speak to my dead aunt. The very thought gave me goose bumps.

Mrs Barley was studying me with interest and I began to feel unnerved.

'I don't really . . . it's not my thing, in all honesty.'

She nodded, an odd smile twisting the corners of her mouth. 'Ah well, there we have to agree to differ. I've always felt it's so important to commune with people who have passed to the other side. Especially those who have meant a lot to us. It might . . . help you.'

I didn't want to dwell on the subject of Auntie Jane. I needed to steer the conversation back to Mrs Barley.

'I don't want to sound nosy, and I hope you don't mind me asking, but what were you doing in the summer house last night? It's just that, well, I was awake and thought there was an intruder, but then I saw you in the garden.'

She inclined her head and gave me a wry smile. 'Ah. Well, I'm sure you must have guessed by now. Frank loved his summer house and I always feel closest to him in there. So I light candles for him, and say prayers of sorts. It's a kind of tradition I have, to set the scene for the following day. Samhain started yesterday and goes on until late tonight, and that's when the magic is strongest. Some people even celebrate it for a few days.'

This seemed plausible. Mumbo jumbo it may have been, but it explained what she had been up to. I glanced at the little altar she had erected in Frank's memory. It was alien to me, but I suppose if it brought her some comfort to think Frank was communicating with her there was no actual harm in it. Nevertheless, it still felt slightly macabre.

I felt I needed to broach the subject of the attack on her house.

'Do you get much bother from the kids in the village? It was pretty rotten, what those lads did.' I wanted to choose my words carefully here. 'I appreciate it's against what you believe, but maybe if you met people halfway – offered the little ones sweets or something, they'd be a bit more understanding.'

The smile faded. 'It's gone on far too long for that. I've been a target for them for years; from one generation to the next, the parents condone their children's behaviour and try to say it's just high jinks. I'll never build any bridges in this village.'

She flicked crumbs from the table top absent-mindedly with one hand, staring towards the window that looked out onto the road. 'It's too late for them to change their attitude to me, and I feel so bitter about the way I've been treated over the years. And trivialising an important festival makes me angry. They know better than to knock on my door. No, I'm not going to try to accommodate them, any of them. One day they'll all be sorry.'

Her mouth had set into a hard line and I knew better than to pursue any attempts to reason with her. We finished our drinks and cake in awkward silence.

253

Elodie began to stir and I thought this could be my excuse to leave.

'I'd better get her back. She'll be needing a feed shortly and I've got to empty my washing machine, too.'

The old woman eased herself from her seat and went over to the pram, gazing down at my daughter for a moment.

'She's such a good baby.' She turned back to me. 'Any time you need someone to take care of her for a while, you know where I am.'

I thanked her for the refreshments and rose to leave.

'Wait.' She went to the mantelpiece and chose a bright green crystal that had been sitting at the end of the shelf, then placed it beneath the pram's mattress. 'Malachite. For protection. I'm a great believer in the power of stones.'

She watched as we went back down the garden and then closed her door, disappearing from sight and leaving me with a most uneasy feeling niggling in my stomach. As I was about to lift the pram over the threshold, I looked down at Elodie, who was now fully awake and squinting up at me. I glanced across the fence and reached down to stroke her face. 'Well, my darling,' I whispered, 'it looks as if we might actually be living next door to some sort of witch.'

*

I was relieved to go round to see Lucy later and have a more normal conversation. She seemed a little subdued, but was resolute in her decision to leave Eddie and was trying to put a brave face on things. Alfie was excited to see Jobie and eager to play with him in the garden, so we sat in Lucy's mum's conservatory eating jacket potatoes with baked beans, watching them through the glass, both Elodie and Georgie sleeping in their respective prams at our sides.

'How are things with you?' she asked, rocking the pram with one foot as the baby began to stir.

'I'm permanently knackered at the moment. The scar's healing nicely but I'm still getting some discomfort from it. Jack does his bit I suppose, but of course he can't breastfeed, so all the getting up in the night is still down to me. How about you?'

'I'm getting there. Eddie was never any help anyway, and at least Mum can take Alfie off my hands for a bit when she's here.' She paused for a forkful of beans. 'So how're things coming along with the house?'

'Very slow progress – everywhere still needs decorating and Jack's been working long hours, so he doesn't feel much like getting the paintbrush out at the weekend. Hopefully we'll get a bit more done in the spring.'

'You'll get there eventually. That's the thing with houses – always something that you need to do. How are you getting on with the old girl next door?'

I winced. I really wanted to tell her all about Mrs Barley's unusual pastimes but felt it would be disloyal. Plus, I didn't want to add fuel to the local suspicions about her. I tried to be diplomatic.

'She's – interesting, shall we say. A bit unpredictable with her moods, but she's been very helpful since Elodie was born. We haven't really got anyone else we can call on to help us out and I've been so grateful – she cooks

255

us things, and she even helped to clean the house when Jack's parents came to visit.'

She looked thoughtful. 'Just be careful, that's all. I did ask my mum – you know, if she knew anything else about her.'

'And did she?'

'She remembered my gran talking about a fella that used to live in the village years ago, who was mates with her husband; a chimney sweep he was. My granddad would have a pint with him now and again. Anyway, they were in the pub one evening and Mrs Barley came bursting through the door in a right state, proper yelling at him and saying he'd be sorry if he didn't stay away from her Frank. Sounds as if she didn't like sharing him with anyone. The bloke laughed it off but I think she put the wind up him.'

'What happened?'

'Well, nothing for a week or two. He must have thought the dust had settled and called for Frank to go to the pub with him again one Friday night. The next day he was climbing up onto a roof, something he'd done hundreds of times before, and somehow his ladder slipped and he fell.' She cast her eyes downward, shaking her head. 'Shattered every bone in his body, apparently. He died the following week – never regained consciousness. But the rumours soon started flying round that she'd helped him on his way – whether she'd tampered with the ladder or something, I don't know. Nothing was ever proved, but everyone thought she'd had something to do with it.'

I felt a chill pass through me. 'Do you know what the man was called?'

'Funny name – somebody Wisecracker or something, I think Mum said. He's still got family round here apparently, but I don't know them. He was only in his twenties, poor bugger. I mean, it could've been a co-incidence I s'pose, but no one looked at her in the same way after that. All a bit nasty, really.'

'Could it have been Wise*acre*? *Leonard* Wiseacre?'

'Yeh! Yeh, that was it. Have you heard of him, then?'

I remembered the book about Avoncote, and the man in the photograph in Mrs Barley's album. I felt slightly sick.

'Yes, I read about him in a book about the village. He was the Jack o' the Green in the May Day celebrations the same year. God, that's awful.'

'I mean, it might've all been gossip – you know how these things can get blown up. But the old woman's done herself no favours with some of the things she's said and done over the years. Like I said, just watch yourself – and the bab, if she's looking after her. Not saying she'd do anything, but you don't want to take any chances.'

I stayed with Lucy for an hour or so and then made my way home. It was a dismal afternoon, the sky white with cloud and the air damp and chill. I kept thinking about what she had told me about Mrs Barley and my stomach was in knots. I really wanted to give our neighbour the benefit of the doubt, but the more I learned about her past, the more uneasy it made me feel.

As we approached Wisteria Cottage, I looked up at Mrs Barley's windows. My heart sank. The upstairs looked a real mess, the egg having dried to a pale yellow crust splattered across each of the three panes of glass.

After what I had just heard, I was beginning to have reservations about Jack climbing a ladder to clean them.

But that was silly. Why on earth would she want to hurt Jack? All these narrow-minded rumours about Mrs Barley were making me paranoid.

I was about to wheel the pram through the gate when a sharp voice from behind brought me to a halt. I turned to recognise the woman who had claimed to see my aura, climbing from a small red car parked on the opposite side of the road. Wild-eyed and gesticulating, she began marching across the street towards me. With her flapping purple kaftan, she reminded me of a demented scarecrow. Her whole body was taut with rage.

'You! You warn that old witch I'm onto her. My nephew is doubled up today because of her. I know she's behind it – she does it every time.'

I stepped back as she continued to advance, confused by her hostility. 'What – what are you talking about?'

She stopped only feet away from Mrs Barley's front wall, staring up at the house as though she'd like to see it go up in flames. 'Just because him and his mates chucked a few eggs – it was only a bit of fun. He lost his watch out here last night. And now he's been rolling around with belly ache all day. His mother's taken him to A & E. You can't tell me it's a coincidence. That old woman's at the back of it – I know she is.'

My heart pounding, I gripped the handle of the pram with one hand and reached for Jobie with the other. Normally so placid, he pricked up his ears and began to bark. I attempted to reassure him, bending to stroke his head, but the woman's stance was unnerving. The barking ceased and he dropped to the ground, grumbling, and looked on warily.

'For God's sake, how can Mrs Barley be to blame for someone she's had no contact with having stomach pains? You're being ridiculous.'

She rounded on me. 'What would you know? You've only known her five minutes. Well, don't you ever cross her, that's all I'll say, or believe me you'll soon find out what she's capable of.'

Mrs Barley's front door opened suddenly. Her face unreadable, she began to walk slowly up the path towards us, never taking her eyes from the irate figure shifting angrily from one foot to the other at her gate, the woman's fists curled into tight, angry balls.

'Go away.' Mrs Barley's voice was calm and measured. 'You are upsetting Stina and you're causing a scene. Take a look at yourself, my girl.'

The woman stared from her face to mine. She seemed to crumple and fold in on herself suddenly, becoming shrunken and nervous. She began to back away.

'You – you're in it together, aren't you?' She waved an accusing hand in my direction. 'I knew the first time I saw this one there was something not right about her. Just you leave my family alone, Virginia Barley. Haven't you hurt us enough?'

Pale with fright, the woman retreated to the safety of her car. She glanced back towards us, then revved the engine and hurtled away. Jobie sprang to his feet once more, his tail wagging now that the episode was over.

Stunned by this confrontation, I turned to Mrs Barley. 'What was that all about? What an awful woman.'

The old lady seemed unfazed. She shrugged. 'It's as I told you. Anything happens to anyone round here, and I'm always the one they love to blame.'

'Who is she? I saw her once before, at the May Day fete, but I haven't laid eyes on her since.'

'Her name's Wendy Wiseacre. She was a horrible child and she's grown into a worse adult. Fancies herself as a bit of a fortune-teller. Her sister still lives in Avoncote but I believe she moved away from the village a few years ago, so that's probably why you haven't seen her about. Her family have had it in for me for years.'

I caught my breath. 'So – she's related to Len Wiseacre?'

She looked taken aback by my recognition of the name. 'Yes. Frank's friend, if you could call him that. He was her uncle – not that she ever knew him. He died young, long before she was even thought of. Of course, they wanted to pin that all on me, too. I may not have liked the man but I didn't want to see him dead. But any outsider coming into Avoncote has always been viewed with suspicion – they're incapable of believing anything's an accident, always have to apportion blame. You can see that – she even tried to point the finger at you.'

I felt as though shards of ice were creeping up my spine and the veins in my temples began to pulse. *Had* the woman genuinely seen something in me? I didn't want to dwell on my past, or any mistakes I may have made. But trying to attribute her nephew's illness to Mrs Barley in some way was completely far-fetched. How could anyone inflict an ailment on someone without even coming into contact with them? It was laughable.

'Are you all right, love? You look a bit shaken up. Don't you let her upset you. You've done nothing wrong and neither have I. But we both know that, don't we?'

I attempted a smile but prayed that my path wouldn't cross with that of Wendy Wiseacre again. It was bad enough that she and many of the other villagers had it in for Mrs Barley, without them lumping me into the same category. The whole incident had left me with a sense of dread.

*

Later that evening, Jack got out the ladders straight after work and cleaned the windows for Mrs Barley, with me standing below directing a torch towards the glass. Afterwards, over dinner, I told him about the altercation with Wendy Wiseacre and the saga of her unfortunate Uncle Len. He shook his head.

'That's the kind of thing she's up against, poor woman. There's not much you can do when people hold these outlandish archaic beliefs – they're so entrenched, their attitude will never change. Exasperating.'

'It seems ridiculous, I agree. I mean, you can't make something bad happen to someone without going near them – can you?' I kept thinking about all the things that Mrs Barley was suspected of having a hand in and was beginning to wonder if there was something very real at the heart of it all. I took a deep breath.

'Jack, I'm really worried – I keep thinking about that Len Wiseacre. Do you think Mrs Barley would be capable of killing someone? I mean, when I saw his picture in her album, she was obviously very pissed off about his influence on Frank. D'you reckon she'd have it in her to do a thing like that?'

He looked at me as if I had finally flipped and put down his fork.

'Look, I think she's definitely a bit strange. But murdering someone's a whole different ball game. I'm sure the police would've picked up on it at the time if there were suspicious circumstances, but clearly it was written off as a tragic accident. In a word, no; I don't think she's capable of cold-blooded murder. I mean, from everything you say, it would have been premeditated, sabotaging the ladder or whatever they're suggesting she did. Or were they trying to imply she'd made it fall with the powers of her mind?' He arched an eyebrow. 'All a bit Mulder and Scully, isn't it? No. She's a bit batty and there are some superstitious idiots who will latch on to that and let their imaginations run riot. It's so quiet round here, they probably need to drum up a bit of excitement.'

Everything he said made sense. I felt much better about it all and resolved that it was best to completely ignore local gossip. Rural communities were long steeped in superstition and rumour, and there was always some poor soul who would bear the brunt of their beliefs. I went to bed that night feeling reassured that our neighbour was just eccentric.

Why, then, was I still so troubled by Wendy Wiseacre's words?

CHAPTER 15

Weeks passed. Everything had gradually begun to feel more settled; Elodie was sleeping a bit better and I was healing nicely after the C-section. Feeling less exhausted was definitely helping me to cope and keep things in perspective. We were looking forward to our first Christmas as a family.

'I was thinking,' said Jack, looking up from the TV after I had put Elodie up to bed. 'What does Mrs Barley do at Christmas? Maybe we should invite her to spend it with us. I mean, she's done a lot to help us out these last few months. It would be a nice gesture. What d'you reckon?'

'Yes, that's a lovely thought. I bet she's spent Christmas on her own ever since she lost Frank. I'll ask her tomorrow.'

'She hasn't got any funny ideas about it though, has she? I mean, she's not exactly conventional . . .'

I laughed. 'Hopefully not. I mean, Christmas is Christmas, isn't it?'

Apparently it wasn't. Mrs Barley was in the garden hanging out washing the following morning when I broached the subject.

'Oh, that's very thoughtful of you. My own celebration actually starts with Mother's Night on the 20th – I haven't really kept up Christmas since Frank passed. The whole thing was commandeered by Christianity about four hundred years after Christ, you know – its roots are very much pagan. I celebrate Yule, the winter solstice, which will fall on the 21st this year.'

I was beginning to regret saying anything, but she added quickly, 'But it would be lovely to spend the day with you and your family. And thank you for asking me – I'll look forward to it.'

I always found the season a bittersweet time. Christmases spent with my mum were wildly unpredictable, and how things panned out would depend invariably on her current mood. I recall one particularly bad year when I was about ten. She couldn't drag herself out of bed and I spent the entire day in front of the television and ate beans on toast for my Christmas dinner. No presents had materialised. Rather than looking forward to it, I would always feel apprehensive as the day drew near, wondering what it would hold for me.

Although more calculable, Christmas with Auntie Jane was a staid affair, and with it being just the two of us, dull and even depressing for a teenager. I look back now and realise that she must have had a miserable time spending it alone for so many years, and as such didn't really make much of an effort. There was always the tiresome ritual of decorating a small, balding Christmas tree that was brought out of an upstairs cupboard and placed in the corner of the living room. We would pull a cracker at the table and exchange small gifts after dinner (she would usually buy another book to add to my growing collection; I would give her a pair of gloves or a scarf), and then settle down to read or watch the standard Christmas Day repeats on TV.

The year after I moved in with Reggie, I lied and told my aunt that I was unwell, so that I could spend Christmas with her and Luc. Reggie really went to town, decorating the flat with a huge real tree that she dragged back from town, flashing fairy lights and reams of tinsel, and a tasteless blow-up Santa that took up half the hallway. We laughed when she burned the dinner and had to resort to cooking frozen pizzas, then we ate too much chocolate and got a bit drunk on Baileys and played loud Christmas music and rowdy card games. It was the best celebration I can ever remember, although it made me feel a little guilty about leaving Auntie Jane on her own. Even more so now, when I think of how she ended her days.

I had loved every Christmas that Jack and I had spent together. Come what may, we would go for a walk in the morning to shake off the Christmas Eve hangover, and then share the cooking. Later in the afternoon, there would be a Skype call to his parents, who preferred to stay in Spain during the colder weather. But it was always fine, as we'd have had a fair bit to drink by this time and they had, too, so Sylvia was generally a bit more laid-back. Even if she hadn't been, I was usually so happy that whatever she'd said would have washed over me anyway. In the evening we would curl up together in front of the fire with yet more wine and a Christmas movie. It was my idea of heaven.

I always relished having Jack to myself at Christmas, but now we had Elodie, and although I knew the routine would be different, it felt as if we were even more complete. I was determined that our first Christmas in Avoncote would be perfect, and while I had hoped for the day to be a family occasion, I knew that including Mrs Barley was the right thing to do. She had been so good to us and I wanted to make her feel welcome and give her something to look forward to.

Christmas Day soon arrived. It was a clear, crisp morning but annoyingly I was muzzy-headed after a particularly rough night with Elodie, who appeared to have colic and couldn't be placated. We had tried giving her infant drops, and took turns walking her up and down and rubbing her back and tummy as she screamed and writhed, drawing up her little legs. Eventually she had fallen asleep out of sheer exhaustion, giving the occasional hiccuping sob.

We were still sitting up in bed when a loud knock carried through the hallway. Jack groaned. He pulled on a hoodie and went downstairs to find Mrs Barley on the step, carrying an open cardboard box.

'Don't worry, I haven't come to impose on you yet,' she announced. 'I know you're not expecting me until after midday – I just thought you might like these.'

I came down behind him, bleary-eyed. Elodie was finally sleeping as though she hadn't a care in the world and I felt like a zombie.

'Merry Christmas, Mrs Barley.'

'And the blessings of the season to you all!'

Jack relieved her of the package and peered inside. She had baked honey cakes, sprinkled with chopped nuts, and they were still warm. A delicious aroma wafted from the box.

'Something sweet for your belated yuletide breakfast.' She beamed. 'I'll see you all later. Enjoy!'

We savoured the cakes that Mrs Barley had brought, and I made a pot of strong coffee to try and liven us up. I didn't feel remotely like entertaining, but knew I needed to galvanise myself into action or the dinner would never be cooked. To his credit, Jack would always try to help, but he wasn't exactly a master chef.

'Come on, we'd better get cracking while we can. Madam upstairs will be awake again soon.'

Jack nodded unenthusiastically. Between us, we peeled and chopped and the time flew. But the effort of actually cooking the meal seemed daunting; I couldn't focus and my eyes felt as though they needed matchsticks to prop them open. I looked up at the clock. It was almost noon and Mrs Barley would be coming over shortly. Christmas was going to be a wash-out.

'I'll grab a shower before Elodie wakes. Can you entertain Mrs Barley for a bit when she comes round, if I'm still upstairs?'

Jack looked shattered himself and utterly dishevelled. His chin was darkly unshaven, his eyes heavy. He smiled weakly. 'Yes, carry on. At least we can collapse in a heap after dinner.'

'You speak for yourself. I'll still have a baby to feed.'

Elodie managed to stay asleep until I'd finished getting ready, but gradually started to snuffle and wriggle. She opened her eyes and began to look around. Thankfully she seemed happier, her face breaking into a smile and kicking her feet as I peered into the cot. Wearily, I lifted her out, then changed and dressed her in the little Santa's elf outfit we had bought. Wisps of tawny hair peeped from the sides of the tiny green hat and she stared up at me almost quizzically with her bright blue eyes. She looked impossibly cute. I took her downstairs, where voices from the living room told me that Mrs Barley had arrived.

'Oh my goodness, doesn't she look a treat!' The old woman held out her gloved hands to take Elodie. I smiled, placing the baby into her arms.

'Yes; fresh as a daisy, unlike Mummy and Daddy today. I'm sorry, I don't think I'll be much company – my brain's frazzled.'

'You poor thing. It's so hard when you're losing sleep, I know . . .' She looked momentarily distracted. 'Well then, what still has to be done in the kitchen? Point me in the right direction and I'll roll my sleeves up.'

'Mrs Barley, you're our guest. I couldn't possibly . . .'

'Nonsense! I haven't been up all night with a young baby. Let me help; it's the least I can do.'

I told her what needed doing and she was off. We looked on, guilty, but full of gratitude. I had actually made a tiramisu the previous day, so at least pudding was sorted. Mrs Barley seemed to be enjoying herself, humming as she bustled about. I lit the fire and leaned back on the settee to feed Elodie, sipping a glass of alcohol-free eggnog as I listened to my Christmas playlist with Jobie at my feet, while Jack went to get showered and dressed. It should all have felt very cosy, but I was struggling to muster any enthusiasm through my fatigue.

Soon we were all seated at the table, enjoying the fruits of Mrs Barley's labour. She was chatty and upbeat, and the meal was delicious, but I was so tired that conversation felt like a real effort. Thankfully, Jack managed to talk enough for both of us, squeezing my hand from time to time as I smiled and nodded politely, my thoughts very much elsewhere.

After dinner came the exchange of presents. Jack and I had agreed that we would buy each other something in the January sales, although he had surprised me with a pair of beautiful topaz earrings, which made me cry, both because I was touched and also because I felt guilty that I hadn't got anything to give him in return. We had bought Mrs Barley a new cardigan and some slippers. She seemed surprised but delighted. From the carrier bag that she had brought with her, she produced two parcels wrapped in brown paper and tied with red ribbon; one, heavy and solid, for Jack and myself, and another smaller, featherlight one for Elodie.

I tore the paper from Elodie's gift to find a small, old-fashioned jointed teddy, with button eyes and a tartan bow tie; well cared for, but clearly not brand new. Ours contained a black velvet drawstring bag. I opened it to find a hefty lump of unfaceted, glittering rock.

'It's amethyst. To bring you love and happiness always.' She beamed. It was a huge, violet crystal, uncut and weighty. We thanked her and I set the stone on the hearth.

It actually looked quite beautiful and I was a little choked. These were obviously items she must have already had within her home, but it was moving that she thought enough of us to want to part with them.

Later, Jack and I cleared up while Mrs Barley sat nursing Elodie. I popped my head round the door to ask if she'd like a cup of tea and saw that she had fallen asleep with the baby on her shoulder, clearly exhausted from being on her feet for so long. I crept into the room and gently prised Elodie from her arms. The late afternoon sun was dwindling and the sky beginning to dim, swathes of pink and gold draped beneath a louring blanket of petrol blue.

Cradling my daughter to my chest, I walked over to the French doors, revelling in the spectacular beauty of the sunset. Despite feeling so tired, I was momentarily captivated.

And then there he was.

Seemingly entranced, the figure stood hunched beneath the portico of the summer house staring at the shrubs, devoid of foliage and cut back to spindly stalks in preparation for next year's blooms. It *had* to be him. It had to be Frank Barley.

I let out a scream. There was an almighty clang as Jack dropped the saucepan he'd been drying and came running through from the kitchen, looking panic-stricken. The baby, startled by my reaction, began to wail.

'What is it? Is Elodie okay?'

Mrs Barley sat up with a jolt, clapping a hand to her chest in fright.

'Whatever's happened?'

270

I could hardly speak. 'That . . . that man – in the summer house . . .'

Without a word, Jack flew through the doors and down the garden. He disappeared into the entry. Jobie, thinking this was some exciting game, chased after him. We waited anxiously, but within minutes Jack had returned. Pausing to catch his breath, he leaned against the doorframe, shaking his head. The dog trotted up behind him, looking deflated.

'There's *definitely* no one out there – yet again. I'm sorry, Stina.' He wore a look of weary irritation. 'I really think it's your eyes playing tricks on you. You've had a succession of disturbed nights and it's affecting your judgement.' He looked from me to the old lady. 'Don't you agree, Mrs Barley?'

The old woman turned to me. She looked uncomfortable. 'I think Jack's probably right, love.'

'I tell you, I saw him – like the last time, and all the times before that. Why don't you believe me?'

Jack was obviously drained. He sounded unwontedly impatient, his voice rising an octave. 'It isn't a matter of not believing you – but it speaks for itself. You're the only person who ever sees this . . . this man you're on about. Think about it, huh? If he really existed, surely *someone* else would have seen him – at least once?'

I began to feel anxious. I thought of all the times that I had seen the man in Mrs Barley's garden. Jack had a point. No one had ever noticed him but me. Never.

What if he was right – what if I *was* seeing things? What if it wasn't just tiredness or hormones, or a trick of the light? I thought about my mum and remembered

271

how I would sometimes hear her ranting to herself. Had *she* thought there was someone in the room with her – someone that she alone could see? Was it possible that her psychosis was intrinsic – not caused by narcotics as Auntie Jane had always maintained, and that I too was beginning to show the same traits? I felt a sudden tightness in my chest and throat, my breathing becoming rapid as panic rose from the depths of my stomach. I thrust Elodie into Jack's arms.

'I think I need to lie down.' I turned to Mrs Barley. 'I'm sorry. I'm not feeling well. Please excuse me.'

Tears coursing down my cheeks now, I sought the refuge of our bedroom. Everything seemed to have come to a head. I curled into the foetal position and sobbed uncontrollably, my chest painful from the effort. I was *sure* I had seen someone. Was I going mad? I was so tired it was hard to think straight.

There was a sudden tap on the door. I swiped a sleeve across my eyes and rolled over to see Mrs Barley standing in the doorway.

'I hope you don't mind – Jack said it was all right to come up.'

I nodded mutely. She approached the bed, her hand outstretched. She was holding a small white cardboard box in one hand and a tumbler of water in the other.

'These are asafoetida pills,' she told me. 'They're very helpful if you're tired and emotional. I've often turned to them in times of stress. Completely safe – all natural,' she added, seeing the worried look on my face. 'Please, take some. It'll make you feel better, honestly.'

She opened the box and shook out two tiny white

balls. I accepted them reluctantly and popped them into my mouth, swigging from the glass she handed me.

'There. Just swallow.'

I gulped and shuddered as the pills slipped down my throat, then suddenly panicked. 'But what about feeding Elodie? There's definitely nothing harmful in them, is there?'

'No, no – like I said, all natural. Just you try to get a bit of sleep. I think everything's getting on top of you, isn't it? Quite understandable, after all you've been through.' She gave me a knowing look and I wondered if there was some hidden meaning in her words. It made me uneasy.

I slept for a solid two hours, until Jack woke me gently. 'I didn't want to disturb you but the baby's hungry.'

I sat up, rubbing my eyes and feeling oddly tran-quillised. He handed me Elodie, whose open mouth eagerly sought her food. She latched on to my breast as though she hadn't been fed for a week. Jack sat on the bed and took my hand.

'D'you feel a bit better?'

'I do, actually. Mrs Barley gave me something – one of her herbal things. I've slept like a log.'

He looked dubious. 'Nothing iffy, was it?'

'She assured me not – *assyfetta* or something, I think it was called. Anyway, I feel a bit more human.' I sighed. 'I'm sorry. I've been so convinced that there was someone out there – maybe you're right. I know hormones and sleep deprivation can do funny things to the brain. Maybe I need to talk to the GP.'

'Whatever you think. But I reckon given a bit of time and rest, you'll be fine. And I'm sorry too. I've felt pretty crap today. I didn't mean to snap.'

He hugged me as best he could with the baby guzzling between us, then kissed the top of my head. 'Early night for us all, I think – that's a first for Christmas Day!'

I laughed. 'Yes. Where's Mrs Barley, by the way?'

'She left just after you came up to bed. I think she was worn out, poor thing. But at least she didn't have to spend the day on her own.'

I felt bad. My little meltdown apart, it would have been a memorable occasion for the old woman. I was angry with myself, feeling that I had spoiled everything, but determined to see it as a blip and try to be more rational and logical in future.

Next year, Elodie would be older and things would have settled down.

Next year would be better.

CHAPTER 16

By the time spring came, Elodie was developing into quite a character, and with nobody else close by to help us out, Mrs Barley had readily assumed the role of surrogate grandmother. Jack and I rarely went out socially, but it was good to know we had a willing, reliable babysitter on our doorstep whose help we could call upon if we needed it. Elodie was always quite happy with Mrs Barley, and I would often leave her at Rose Cottage if I went shopping. She had her moments and was definitely a bit idiosyncratic, but as time passed, I grew to trust her and had no qualms about her looking after my daughter as Elodie clearly loved the old woman and always went to her readily. In spite of everything, I was confident that she would never come to any harm in her care.

Out of the blue, I had received a call from Maryam, Reggie's girlfriend. I was surprised to hear from her as, in spite of Luc passing on my details, she hadn't been in touch since we met at Reggie's funeral. I had thought that perhaps she was trying to move on with her life and put it all behind her.

I was pleased that she had contacted me, as I still really missed Reggie. Although we hadn't been in close contact since I had moved to Avoncote, losing such a good friend had left a huge void. Being able to talk to someone who knew her well helped me feel as if there was still a connection there, somehow. Originally, I had thought she could come to Avoncote, but Maryam had invited me over to her new flat in the city centre for lunch. I loved our cottage, but having been stuck at home for so long, I was grateful for the opportunity of a change of scenery.

'I have something for you; a keepsake,' she told me over the phone. 'Something that belonged to Reggie.'

We arranged to meet up the following Wednesday, and I was looking forward to seeing her again. I hadn't had the chance to speak to her much at the funeral, and I was interested to hear her opinion of Akhmad and all that had happened in the weeks leading up to Reggie's death. I also wondered whether any further light had been shed on what had actually happened to make Reggie fall as she did. It was all so odd.

It was a pleasantly warm April morning. I had intended to take Elodie along with me to see Maryam, but she was teething and had been grizzling constantly since the previous night. I wondered if I should rearrange, but worried that it was short notice.

I had given Elodie some Calpol and rubbed teething gel into her gums, and, still sobbing intermittently, she had finally fallen asleep in her pram. Mrs Barley was pottering in her garden as I went to peg out the washing.

'Lovely morning,' she said brightly. 'How's the little one today? I keep hearing a lot of wailing.'

'She's miserable, poor little thing. It seems to be taking forever for those teeth to come through and it's wearing Jack and me down, to be honest. We were up half the night with her again. I was supposed to be having lunch with a friend today, but I think I'll have to cancel.'

'Well, that would be a shame. You don't get out much. Why don't you leave her with me? It would give you a bit of a break.'

'That's very kind, but it wouldn't be fair on you. It's hard work when they keep crying all the time.'

'Nonsense. I can cope for a few hours – I've nothing else to do.'

I hesitated. It would be nice to have a brief period of respite and I wasn't planning on being gone all day.

'Are you sure?'

'Of course! Just pop her round in her pram when you're ready to go. I'll look forward to it. Are you taking the dog?'

'I didn't intend to, no. My friend – well, she's more of an acquaintance really – lives in a flat by the canal, and I don't think there's a garden.'

'Leave me your key, then, and I can let him out. A shame for him to be cooped up inside for hours when it's so nice.'

I felt slightly apprehensive as I left Elodie later, but Mrs Barley shooed me out of her house and told me not to worry. I left Jobie with plenty of food and water, and made a big fuss of him before leaving. I felt guilty not taking him along, but, garden or not, it really wasn't practical as I was travelling by rail. I took the train into Birmingham and enjoyed the leisurely journey, ambling past the designer shops on the way to Maryam's flat, which was some twenty minutes on foot from the station.

The apartment was part of an exclusive-looking development in a converted warehouse. One side overlooked the canal, from where a narrow passageway opened out into a smart courtyard area with a bubbling fountain and a seating area beneath a large pergola. Tall zinc planters, containing neatly clipped Buxus balls, flanked the entrance. I pressed Flat 18 on the door panel and waited.

Maryam's distinctive voice came over the intercom. 'Hi, Stina, come on up!'

I took the lift to the third floor and she greeted me warmly at the door. She looked effortlessly chic, in skinny jeans and a loose linen tunic.

'It's good to see you again. Oh, no baby with you?' She seemed a little disappointed.

'She's not too well today, so I've left her with my neighbour.'

'Never mind; another time, eh?'

She ushered me into the living area. The apartment was open-plan and impressively spacious: light and airy, with high, oak-beamed ceilings and exposed terracotta brickwork throughout. Sun spilled onto the polished wooden floor through a huge arched window, which looked out onto the canal. Everything was simply but tastefully furnished. A huge, black-and-white image of

Reggie, windswept and resplendent in a flowing white dress, was displayed on one wall. Her prized carved African tribal heads, bought from an antiques market in London some years ago, stood either side of a huge fireplace. A lump came to my throat.

Seeing my face, Maryam smiled sadly. 'She loved those heads; I'm sure you know. The photo was taken on a shoot in Tunisia last year. I had it blown up. She looks stunning, doesn't she? We were working, but had a few days off. It was a wonderful holiday, too. Please – sit.'

I sank into the soft corduroy cushions of the huge corner couch and looked around. This would all have been very much to Reggie's taste. It was awful to think she would never have the opportunity to live here.

'Let's have a drink. Maybe some wine, as you haven't got the baby in tow?'

It sounded appealing, particularly as I felt somewhat tongue-tied, so I agreed. Maryam walked over to the huge American-style fridge in the kitchen area and returned with a bottle of prosecco and two tall glasses, each containing a handful of fresh raspberries.

'We'll have lunch soon. I've made a roasted vegetable couscous – I hope that's okay?'

'It sounds delicious.'

We sat in awkward silence for a minute or two, sipping our drinks.

'So, how are you?' I ventured. 'Have you been working a lot?'

She sighed. 'I've taken a couple of weeks off. It's been so busy these last few months. I've been glad of the distraction, but I need time out now, just to get my head straight. I wanted to spend some time at home, too. Luc was staying with me for a while when I first moved in, but he's found work in a hotel kitchen in Rugby, and the accommodation comes with the job.'

'Oh, that's good to hear. Reggie always worried about him. I'm so glad he's making something of his life.'

'I think he's finally been able to move on. Not that he forgives Akhmad for his behaviour – far from it. But at least he knows the man didn't kill his sister.'

I still felt strongly that even if Akhmad had not actually pushed her physically, he was ultimately responsible. I had no doubt that his abusive, controlling behaviour and the resultant anxiety would have led to Reggie's uncharacteristic heavy drinking, without which none of this would have happened. My eyes began to well as I thought of her parting words to me the last time we had met: '*I'm a born survivor.*' The tragic irony of it all.

Maryam interrupted my thoughts. 'It's so weird, though. I keep going over it in my mind. I mean, how could she have just slipped like that? Was she rushing and not looking where she was going? I've tried to picture it a thousand times. Did something startle her so that she stepped backwards suddenly – or did she have a dizzy spell and lose her balance? Even after the post-mortem there was no conclusive explanation, so I suppose we'll never know now.'

Reggie had been athletic and graceful. How could she have fallen for no obvious reason – and sustained such terrible injuries? She had been alone – it wasn't as if she had been trying to escape Akhmad, or anyone else. As if from nowhere, the memory of the creepy little figure on Mrs Barley's side table resurged, and the way the old woman had looked at my friend with such animosity.

And then the most awful thought came into my head. *The bandana*. Something that had a link to Reggie. If that's what *had* been inside that book, it would explain why Mrs Barley would have wanted it. Couldn't a hex be put onto someone using something that belonged to them? I thought then of little Alfie's upset stomach after eating the cakes; then Sylvia, and the thread that Mrs Barley had cut from her jacket; Wendy Wiseacre's nephew. And poor baby Georgie's seizure. Was my elderly neighbour spiteful enough to have been in some way responsible for all these misfortunes?

I could hear the pounding of my blood in my ears and my mind began to race. I probably shouldn't have said anything, but the wine had loosened my tongue – and fired my imagination.

'I know this might sound wildly improbable, but do you believe Reggie could have been cursed?' I blurted out.

She sat back in her seat and stared at me as if I had gone mad. 'Cursed? You mean, like voodoo or something?'

It all came out in a rush. 'No. Well, yes, but not voodoo. The old woman next door to us is into all things esoteric – crystals, fortune-telling, that kind of stuff. There have been some really odd things happening since we moved into our cottage and I saw a weird little doll sitting on a table in her front room.'

I paused, wondering if I had already said too much.

'Go on.' She nodded encouragingly, studying me with

281

some concern: whether for me or about what I was telling her, I wasn't sure.

'Well, I read up about them when I was writing an article about local folklore. They call them poppets – witches used to make them hundreds of years ago to inflict bad luck on someone they didn't like – or worse. The thing is, I'm sure she had a piece of Reggie's bandana alongside it – Reggie had messaged to say she lost it when she came to see me. The old woman could have used it – you know, to cast a sort of spell or whatever. It's just – I know it probably sounds far-fetched, but my neighbour obviously didn't like Reggie. She's a peculiar woman and sometimes I wonder what she's capable of.'

Even as I uttered the words, I realised how ridiculous I must have sounded. Maryam remained silent for a moment. When she eventually spoke, slowly and clearly, the pity in her eyes was unmistakable. It made me feel guilty and pathetic. She had lost the most important person in her life and yet her sympathy for me in my overwrought state was tangible. She placed a hand on top of my own.

'Stina, Reggie found her bandana,' she said gently.

'What? When?'

'A couple of weeks after she came to visit you. She had her car valeted and the guys found it under the seat. They'd folded it up and left it on the dashboard so she'd see it.'

'And it wasn't – ripped or anything?'

'No, completely intact.'

Stunned, I slumped back, remembering how I'd broken into Mrs Barley's house; the things I'd suspected of her, the wild, groundless allegations I had just made. I felt terrible about it all. She was just an eccentric old woman, and she'd been so helpful, and here was I, accusing her of God knows what. Maryam must think me some kind of lunatic – and it probably wasn't far from the truth. I put a hand to my mouth, tears spilling down my cheeks.

'Stina, I think we have to accept that what happened to Reggie was a tragic accident. No one was to blame. It was sheer bad luck. I don't believe in curses or the power of juju dolls, or whatever you want to call them. Why would your neighbour wish her ill, anyway? It makes no sense. I know sometimes it makes it easier if we have someone to blame when something so terrible has happened, but I don't think in this case anyone is. I know how much you loved her, and I did, too. But we have to let it go.'

I nodded mutely, feeling foolish and hating myself for my outburst. I wondered whether she must think me slightly deranged. To think I'd had such doubts about Mrs Barley, much less actually voiced them. I felt wretched.

Maryam was still looking at me anxiously.

'I'm sorry.' I plucked a tissue from the box on the coffee table and dabbed at my eyes, composing myself. 'You're right, of course. Please ignore me. It's probably the wine – I'm not used to it. I just – I don't know, it's hard to believe that Reggie could have just slipped over. But I suppose none of us are completely on our guard when we've had a drink.'

'She was drinking a bit too much towards the end, to be quite frank. She knew she was going to have to break

283

it off with Akhmad and I think it was stressing her out – she was building up to the right moment. I should have been there for her, but as usual my job came first.'

I didn't know how to respond. She clasped the stem of her glass with both hands, looking earnest and tense as she continued to speak of Reggie and how her loss had turned her whole life upside down, reliving it all through the inquest, returning at the end of each day to the empty flat they had both planned to call home. It was clear how much the whole harrowing situation must have dominated her existence, murder or not. I lived out of the city now, cocooned in my sleepy rural village, absorbed in my life with Jack and Elodie. I didn't have reminders of Reggie wherever I turned. I thought of her often, but there was so much else to distract me.

'But Akhmad was violent towards her, wasn't he?'

'Oh yeah – he would get wound up at the slightest thing, lash out at her. It had started to get worse. Apparently, he was attentive at the beginning. Mr Nice Guy. Reeled her in, I suppose.'

'I thought something was wrong, the last time we met. It was so unlike her, though, to put up with any crap from a man.'

'It was more to do with Luc, I think. She was worried that he'd fire him and he would end up going off the rails again. I don't think for one minute that Akhmad found him a job out of any sense of altruism. The bastard was good at that – making people feel they owed him something. Manipulative. He liked the power it gave him over them.' Her face clouded. 'The same with quite a few alpha males, I guess.'

'I almost forgot. I have something for you.' She left the room briefly and returned with a large, unwieldy cardboard box, placing it at my feet. Lifting the lid, I found Reggie's beautiful Thai wooden 'mother and calf' elephant sculpture.

'She said how much you liked it. I thought you should have something to remember her by.'

I choked back tears as I remembered the day Reggie had brought it into the flat we shared. Both elephants were carved from a single block of dark wood, the mother gently guiding the calf along with her trunk. The craftsmanship was extraordinary, and it really touched me, somehow. It seemed a lifetime ago now.

'Thank you so much. I'll cherish it forever.' I struggled to get the words out.

'It's a lovely piece. Reggie had an eye for these things. I thought you were coming by car, though – will you manage it on the train?'

'I'll get a taxi to and from the station; it'll be okay.'

We chatted for a while and, in need of consolation, I drank a little more than I probably should have. Feeling slightly woozy, I followed Maryam through to the kitchen, where we perched on stools at the island to eat. The couscous, which was slightly spicy, was quite delicious.

'You must give me the recipe,' I said. 'Jack would love this.'

'Ah, yes, Jack. How is he?'

'He's well, thank you. Working long hours as ever.'

'Reggie spoke about him quite a few times. I don't think they really got on, did they?'

'No. Just a bit of a personality clash, you know. I don't think there was ever a falling-out as such.' It upset me a little to think that Reggie had obviously discussed her misgivings about Jack with Maryam. I wondered what she could have told her that she'd felt unable to share with me.

From Maryam's body language it became apparent that she knew something significant. She seemed to tighten, averting her eyes.

'What? What did she tell you?'

'Well, maybe I shouldn't say. I don't want to cause any trouble.'

I watched her face as she distractedly began pushing food round her plate, her eyes darting. Her expression worried me. I put down my fork.

'Did Reggie share something with you about my husband?'

'Me and my big mouth.' She looked up at me, almost pleadingly. 'Listen, it's hardly worth mentioning. It all happened a long time ago.'

'*What* happened? Please – if there's anything I need to know, just tell me.'

She took a deep breath. 'Reggie said that there was some girl – a vet nurse, I think – that Jack worked with, who was being a bit too friendly. She said it was worrying you.'

I wondered where this was leading. 'Yes. She worked at his surgery when we still lived in Brum – started sending him texts with lots of stupid emojis. I never actually saw her, but he said she was a bit of a sad case and he felt a bit sorry for her. But she got fixated with him – the messages kept pinging on his phone all the time, and I got pretty pissed off about it in the end. It was all totally one-sided, though. He was as glad as I was when she left and went to work somewhere else. He said it was all getting quite awkward at work, and he was always trying to avoid her.'

There was an uncomfortable pause. Suddenly, she blurted out, 'That wasn't quite what Reggie told me, I'm afraid.'

'What d'you mean?' Her tone made me feel oddly queasy.

'Reggie cared a great deal about you, you know. She knew how much Jack meant to you, and she was incensed to think that someone was trying to muscle in on your man, spoil your happiness. So, she decided to go and put the frighteners on the girl. One evening, she drove to Jack's work and waited for her to come out. But when she did, Jack was with her. They got into Jack's car and seemed to be having a heated debate.'

I sighed with relief. Reggie had obviously got the wrong end of the stick.

'He must have finally been telling her where to go. It was causing rows between us – I'd told him he needed to be firm with her and make it plain that he wasn't interested, and he was a bit half-soaked about it. Said he didn't want to cause an atmosphere at the practice. That's him all over – he doesn't like rocking the boat.'

Maryam looked uneasy. 'That's just it, though. It sounded as if there was more to it. The girl got out of the car and she was crying, in a bit of a state. She started walking off down the road. Jack drove off, so Reggie decided to see if she could find out what was going on. She pretended she was a concerned passer-by, asked the girl if everything was okay. Anyway, the girl was obviously glad of a shoulder to cry on. She confided that she really liked Jack. They'd had a one-night stand, apparently, some months earlier at a colleague's house party. I think they were both really pissed. He obviously regretted it afterwards, but she kept hoping that he might warm to her, given time.'

I felt as if I'd been punched. I couldn't believe what I was hearing. I could feel the blood pulsing in my temples and I seemed to be fighting for breath.

'It sounded as though he did actually tell her where to get off eventually, but he was pretty blunt about it. He said that she needed to find a job elsewhere, that he knew someone who would take her on and he'd put in a word, but if she wouldn't leave and continued to make things awkward for him, sending messages and, worst of all, threatening to tell you about what happened between them, he would make something up and get her sacked. Sounds as though she did as she was told.' Her face earnest, she studied me for a moment, then swallowed before continuing.

'To cut a long story short, Reggie confronted Jack about it all the following day. He was angry at first, but then quite sheepish. Said how much he loved you and didn't want to hurt you, that it had all been a stupid drunken mistake and he bitterly regretted it. She warned him that if he ever did anything like it again, he'd live to rue the day.'

My mouth was so dry I couldn't speak. I was suddenly

aware of a metallic tang, and realised that I had bitten down so hard on my lip, I had drawn blood. I sat, staring at Maryam, too stunned to respond.

'Look, whatever happened, it's all water under the bridge. Jack obviously adores you. You've got a beautiful baby and you've made a home together. I just wanted to explain what was at the root of the bad blood between him and Reggie. I'm really sorry. I should never have said anything. The last thing I wanted to do was cause you any distress.'

I sat staring at her, trying to make sense of what she had said. The room seemed to have grown even more enormous, and I was a tiny, inconsequential speck in its midst. My world had just been turned on its head. A sickening image of Jack and the faceless girl ran through my mind, like something from a pornographic film. I wanted to be sick. Eventually, I was able to form words.

'I can't believe it, that he'd be capable of something like that. Not Jack. Why the hell didn't Reggie say anything to me?'

She reached across and squeezed my hand. 'She believed Jack was truly sorry, that it had all been an ill-judged blip. He begged her not to tell you. She said it was the first time she had seen you really happy, and she didn't want to ruin your future with him. Personally, I always feel it's better never to have secrets from those we love. If the bond is strong enough, things can always be worked through. It can even bring you closer together, knowing you've overcome something like that. Please don't hate me for telling you.'

*

My earlier character assassination of poor Mrs Barley and subsequent embarrassment had been completely overshadowed by Maryam's revelation about Jack. All the way home, I thought about what she'd said; about never keeping secrets. But then, we *all* have our secrets, don't we? There are some things that we can never share, often because we're trying to protect someone from learning something that might cause them hurt or trauma. Or because we're trying to protect ourselves . . .

I fully understood Reggie's reasons for keeping what had happened from me: she didn't want to see me hurt, and for that I was grateful. But how I wished that she was still here, so that I could talk to her about it. Part of me felt guilty that our relationship had cooled because of her opinion of Jack – and now I understood what was behind it all, my anger was directed at him, not my lovely friend. But then I reasoned that Jack really *did* love me; we had something good together. We were married now with a child, and that had cemented our relationship further. I could never destroy everything we had built because of some meaningless, booze-fuelled shag that he'd had with a girl he obviously now despised. No other man had ever cared for me the way he did, nor were they likely to. I was plain and geeky; hardly a great catch. I would be a fool to say or do anything to jeopardise what we had. And there was Elodie to consider. I had grown up without a father figure. I certainly didn't want the same for my daughter.

By the time I got home, I felt calmer and more sober. I opened the back door and Jobie came bounding in, his tail furiously beating the air. We'd told him a thousand times and he knew that he shouldn't, but he couldn't contain his excitement and jumped up, putting his paws on my shoulders and licking my face as if we'd been parted for months. I had effectively abandoned him for the day, and yet he was still so pleased to see me. Such pure, unconditional love and loyalty. I wrapped my arms around him and allowed myself the luxury of a good cry, then went upstairs to take a shower and brush my teeth before going to collect Elodie.

I went round the back and looked through Mrs Barley's French window. I watched for a few minutes as the old woman bounced my daughter on her knee, crooning softly to her as she did so. Elodie looked quite contented, and not at all as though she had been missing me. My heart soared as she turned her head and saw me, beaming that gorgeous, gummy smile. The thought of what I had said to Maryam about Mrs Barley overwhelmed me with guilt. She was always so good with Elodie – how could I ever have suspected her of something so terrible? Maybe I really did need to talk to a counsellor, or even a psychiatrist. Even though Elodie was getting older and my sleep wasn't quite so disrupted, the things running through my mind seemed to be increasingly irrational.

'Hello, love. We were just singing some songs, weren't we, Elodie? Did you have a nice time?'

I hesitated. 'It was . . . bittersweet, I think you'd say. I met my friend Reggie's partner – we've never really spoken properly before. We had a good long chat. She's nice. It was so sad to think I'll never see Reggie again, brought it all back. I feel a bit emotionally wrung out, to tell the truth.'

I winced internally as I thought once again of the suspicions about Mrs Barley that had resurfaced. It was unforgivable and seemed even more ridiculous now. I wasn't about to mention the bombshell that Maryam had dropped either, nor the inner turmoil it had caused me.

'Maybe next time you see her it'll be better; a happier occasion. There's always something to remind us of the past, sadly. Time helps, but some days it's easier to bear than others.' She smiled empathetically.

'How's Elodie been?'

'Fine. She had a little cry when she first woke up, so I gave her some of her medicine. We've kept busy, though, so I think that's taken her mind off the teeth. We let the dog out a couple of hours ago. I could see him trotting up and down, and he looked quite happy.'

'How are you?' I asked, noticing the rings under her eyes were darker than usual, and she wasn't a good colour. 'You're looking a bit pale.'

'I'm fine. I've had another one of my headaches, but the paracetamol has done the trick. I'll have an early night though, I think.'

I felt even worse then. 'I'm so sorry – I hope it hasn't been too much for you, minding Elodie.'

'Not at all – she's been a real joy. You can bring her any time. She always cheers me up.'

I thanked her and, hugging Elodie to me, returned home to start on the dinner.

Elodie reclined, kicking her chubby legs and gurgling in her little bouncy chair in the doorway as I cooked. Jobie had seated himself bolt upright at her side, like a sentry.

Jack's key turned in the lock at 7.15. My stomach churned. I stood stiffly with my back to the door, stirring a pan of ready-made pasta sauce at the stove.

'How are my two favourite girls this evening?' He squatted to plant a kiss on Elodie's head, then came up behind me and peered over my shoulder at the saucepan. He smelled of coffee and disinfectant, and his stubbly cheek brushed against my own. I felt my pulse quicken, but didn't look up, focusing my attention on the stove top.

'We're okay. Elodie's had fun at Mrs Barley's.'

'How about you? Did you get on well with Maryam?'

'Yes. She's a nice girl. Very . . . I don't know. I'd say she's got a lot of integrity.' Anger started to stir in me.

'Oh? What makes you say that?' He sounded surprised.

'What, wouldn't you have expected someone who could think so highly of Reggie to have had principles?' I said, finding myself biting at his remark. I had promised myself that I wouldn't do this, that I was going to rise above it and not confront him.

'That's not what I meant. It was an unusual observation, that's all. I just wondered what made you describe her in that way.'

'She believes in being brutally honest, acknowledging our failings and learning from them; trying to be better people. She studied philosophy, you know.'

'Very commendable.' I read this remark as sarcasm, and it irritated me further.

I turned to look at him, feeling suddenly defiant. 'Do you?'

'Do I what?' He looked taken aback.

'Believe in being honest?'

293

He looked uncomfortable. I wondered if he had ever considered that Reggie might have told Maryam about his indiscretion.

'Well? It's a fair question,' I said.

He seemed to be deliberating over an appropriate response. His voice was quiet. 'I think honesty is usually the best policy, yes. But there are times when a white lie might be acceptable. Sometimes, unless it's absolutely necessary, it's kinder to bend the truth, if it would mean hurting someone; especially someone who's vulnerable and might be badly affected. Wouldn't you agree?'

I turned to face him. Jack looked straight into my eyes and the concern was etched onto his face. He had been at work for almost thirteen hours, and looked drawn and tired. He might have had a really shit day, for all I knew, but he rarely came home in a bad mood. He certainly never took it out on me, or on Elodie. My husband was kind and patient, and caring.

In spite of everything, my anger melted and I felt suddenly overcome with emotion. I could never not love him. Yes, he had made a really stupid mistake; but it was a long time ago. So much in our lives had changed since then. And who was I to take the moral high ground? I certainly wasn't perfect, either. If I were to stand in judgement of Jack or anyone else, I had to be prepared to be judged myself. I shuddered as I reflected on my own past misdeeds and had to acknowledge that some secrets were best never shared.

'I suppose so. If it meant shielding someone from real devastation, then, yes. But there would have to be a very good reason for it.'

294

'I'm glad we're agreed on that.' He heaved a sigh. Cupping my chin in his hands, he kissed me gently on the lips. 'Christ, I thought I'd done something wrong for a minute. You looked like a woman with murder on her mind when I came in.'

I smiled. 'Oh, ignore me. It's been an emotional day.'

'I don't want to upset you again, but there's something you should know.'

My stomach turned over. 'What?'

'You're burning the sauce.'

*

In spite of my determination to move on from Maryam's revelation, I kept torturing myself with thoughts of Jack and the vet nurse. It was like a scab that I couldn't resist picking. I had even started to wonder now if there had ever been any other one-night stands – or worse. After all, I'd have remained in complete ignorance if Maryam hadn't spilled the beans. I'd have sworn that my lovely Jack could never have had the propensity for infidelity. It set me to thinking then; did I really know him as well as I thought? What about all those late nights at the surgery? Was there was someone else that had caught his eye? After all, I looked such a mess these days, who could blame him? It was one more thing to plague my thoughts as I lay awake at night. I was beginning to feel that I was living under a permanent cloud for one reason or another; that I was never going to be truly content with my lot.

After a particularly bad night, Elodie was still teething and refused her morning feed, throwing her head back and screaming as I tried to offer her my breast. I was so tired that my patience was wearing thin. I gave her some Calpol and laid her back down in her cot. Mercifully the combination of her dummy and the medication gradually did their work, and she drifted off.

I went to let Jobie out after Jack left for work. Mrs Barley was out in her garden, watering the planters that sat outside her back door. Corvus was perched on the fence watching her. Seeing Jobie, he let out a shrill cry and flew off.

'Morning, Stina. Oh dear, you look as if you're carrying the weight of the world on your shoulders today. Is anything the matter?'

After Maryam told me about Jack, I had made a sort of pact with myself; that I would never share what I had learned with anyone. But I felt so low and desperately needed someone to confide in. Feeling tears begin to threaten, I tried to swallow them back but somehow it all came tumbling out.

'I found out that a couple of years ago, Jack was unfaithful to me. Reggie's partner Maryam told me. She said it was just the once, but now I can't get it out of my head. What if it happens again? What if it's *already* happening? I feel as if I don't know him any more and it's eating me up inside.'

Mrs Barley frowned. 'I'm very surprised to hear that. Are you sure she wasn't trying to cause trouble?'

'I believed her – she had no reason to lie. And it all makes sense, knowing what was happening at the time with this girl he used to work with. But I feel so gullible. And I keep going over and over it in my head. It's awful.'

'Well, I think it highly unlikely that Jack's being unfaithful to you now. Anyone can see how devoted he is to you and Elodie. I have a nose for these things.'

'Yes, but how can you know for sure? How can *I* know – if someone does a thing like that once, surely they're capable of doing it again?'

Mrs Barley put down her watering can and approached the fence. 'Listen, now. I'm very attuned to people's feelings and atmospheres. If Jack was doing anything . . . untoward . . . I'm sure I'd have picked up on it. So you can rest assured he isn't.' She reached across to me. 'Here, take my hand a minute.'

Hesitantly I accepted her gloved palm. She held my own hand for a moment, then gave me a strange look.

'I think that maybe your concerns about Jack are more rooted in your fears about yourself. You've a lot of self-doubt, haven't you? But he loves you very deeply, Stina. And what's past is past. Don't let it ruin your future. Life is too short.'

I withdrew my hand and stared at her. I felt suddenly uneasy. 'How can you possibly know – that I doubt myself?'

'Oh, it's obvious, isn't it – you've had a baby not so long ago; you're still hormonal,' she said, avoiding my eyes. 'Jack's a good man. Trust in him and everything will be fine. And don't confront him. It could do more harm than good. Least said, soonest mended – that's what I've always believed.'

I felt oddly reassured by this. But it was what she said as I turned to go back into the house that sent a chill through me.

'Everyone has their secrets, Stina. After all, there are probably things about you that you'd prefer your husband never learned, too.'

I kept turning her words over in my mind for the rest of the day. It wasn't so much what she'd said, more her intonation. Full of weight; full of inference. Somehow Jack's blip didn't seem so significant any more. Maybe that had been her intention: to shift my focus. If so, she had succeeded.

That night I awoke with a start, shocked into wakefulness by a nightmare that seemed all too real. Cold beads of sweat pricked at my temples; my whole body was rigid with fear. I could hear my heart, thudding through my head like a jungle drum beating out a warning. It was a dream I had had countless times in the past: I was a teenager once more, returning home with leaden feet that dreadful day to find Auntie Jane dead in the hallway. But this time my surroundings began to blur. I realised that I was standing in my neighbour's summer house. And the cold, unseeing eyes that stared up at me from the ground weren't those of my aunt.

They were Mrs Barley's.

CHAPTER 17

It was a glorious, tranquil Sunday in early June. Such a memorable, happy day. There had been no further sightings of Mrs Barley's intruder and I was beginning to think that they had indeed all been caused by a weird hormonal interlude, some sort of temporary insanity. Things seemed more settled all round – Jack and I were getting on well, and since Elodie's sleep pattern had improved, so had my own. I was feeling upbeat and optimistic. Thinking back now, I see it as the calm before the storm. All too often, an unpleasant memory seems to be preceded by a joyful one; as though something out there takes glee in luring us into a false sense of security.

Jack and I had enjoyed a leisurely walk into Stratford that afternoon. We took a picnic and spread out a blanket on the grass, beneath a tree close to the river, a stone's throw from the Royal Shakespeare Theatre. Jobie was on his long lead, straining to reach the swans that wandered, aloof, across the cool turf, almost as if to taunt him, and into the rippling Avon. Jack took Elodie down to the water's edge and they threw our leftover crusts to the clamouring birds. There was a vibrant atmosphere and the tourists were out in force. We enjoyed ice creams and eventually ambled home, Elodie worn out from her excursion and sleeping in her pram.

Later that evening, with Elodie tucked up in her cot, we sat, sipping wine and watching as dappled shadows cast by the leaves of Mrs Barley's birch tree danced on our living room wall. Gradually, the sun's last rays dwindled to nothing, disappearing behind the swaying silhouettes of distant poplars.

How grateful I was for our blissful new life and our daughter. And how, knowing what some women had to put up with, I appreciated my wonderful husband and the fact that he had chosen me, with all my flaws and foibles, to share his life. I had managed to overcome my doubts and fears of losing him, accepting that his little fling was no more than that. He constantly reminded me how much he loved me and our life together, and I had finally allowed myself to believe him; to trust him once more. I felt better than I had done in months.

I watched as he stretched out his tanned legs, pushing back his hair as he reclined in his seat. He turned to me and smiled, his eyes shining. I wondered if he had any notion of how gorgeous he was, how my heart still leapt at the sight of him. I rarely instigated sex, probably through fear of rejection, but felt so much love and sheer lust for him for him at that moment the urge was irresistible. I pulled him to me and we made love there and then, without a thought for anyone or anything else.

Inebriated and content, we fell asleep on the sofa, our limbs entwined.

*

Deep into the night, a heavy thump on the wall disrupted our slumber. I was on my feet almost instantly, my heart pounding. Another bang. I shook Jack hard.

'Wake up! There's a noise coming from Mrs Barley's – something's wrong.'

Blearily, Jack sat up, rubbing his eyes. He staggered to his feet. 'Wait here. I'll go and see what's happened.'

Mercifully, the spare key that Mrs Barley kept under the potted geranium outside her back door was still there, so Jack was able to let himself in. After a few minutes, he was back, his face grave.

'Mrs Barley's had a stroke,' he said. 'I've called for an ambulance. They'll get here as soon as they can. It's not looking good, Stina. She's in a bad way.'

I felt my insides drop. The thought of anything happening to her filled me with dread. She had come to mean so much to our little family.

Jack kept a vigil from our window for the ambulance, while I stayed with Mrs Barley, holding her hand until the paramedics arrived. One side of her face had dropped and she seemed very confused. She was struggling to speak. As they carried her into the ambulance, I fought back tears and offered up a silent prayer to anything that might be out there to bring her safely back to us. It was too awful to contemplate.

*

Mrs Barley's recovery was remarkable, astounding the doctors, who, convinced she wouldn't make it through the night, had prepared us for the worst. It had been a hellish time. Yet less than three weeks later, she was sitting up in bed, pleading to go home.

Jack and I took Elodie to visit her, bringing freshly cut irises, which we remembered were her favourites. She was thrilled to see us.

'Hasn't she grown!'

Her voice was slightly slurred, her smile lopsided. She stroked Elodie's plump, velvety cheek, accentuating the paper-thin, mottled flesh of her own hand.

'Mrs Barley, whatever happened there?'

For the first time, probably owing to the absence of the fingerless gloves, I'd noticed a deep scar running along the outer edge of her palm. She withdrew her hand defensively.

'A dog . . . bit me,' she said, abruptly.

Her lips tightened. Any remaining colour in her cheeks drained away, and I was taken aback by the hostility of her expression, which invited no further questioning. I shot a look at Jack, hastily changing the subject.

'Everybody's amazed by how well you're doing,' I said. 'You'll be home in no time. We've been feeding the lovebirds. I'm sure they miss you.'

Mrs Barley softened, smiling weakly.

'And I them. My little darlings.' She leaned back on her pillows. 'Have you seen Corvus?'

'He was sitting on the summer house roof yesterday. I did throw him some bread but I'm not sure if he ate it.'

'He'll be wondering where I am, I imagine. We've been friends a long time, he and I.'

Making conversation proved taxing for her. Soon, Mrs Barley's eyes began to close and she drifted off. We crept from her bedside, pausing to speak to the nurses before leaving.

'It's awkward,' explained the ward sister. 'She's much improved, but we can't discharge her if there's no one at home. It would definitely be better for her mental state, but she really isn't in a position to look after herself yet. There's always the option of a convalescent home while she recuperates . . .'

Jack squeezed my hand gently. I needed no prompting. I thought of everything that Mrs Barley had done for us. And I thought of Auntie Jane.

'We'll do it,' I volunteered. 'I'm at home all day with Elodie, anyway. Mrs Barley has been so kind to us. It's the least we can do.'

'That's very good of you. It'll be a long slog, as she needs physio – and someone will have to bring her back here for that, and for check-ups to see how she's progressing. It'll be quite a responsibility. Are you sure?'

I nodded resolutely.

The nurse smiled. 'Well, if you could start by bringing a few things in for her from home, that would be useful. She needs clean nightclothes and underwear – and her slippers, as she'll be able to get out of bed soon. I believe you already have a key to her house?'

*

I felt like an intruder as I went up the stairs to Mrs Barley's bedroom that evening. I had had no previous

303

cause to venture beyond the kitchen and living room, and felt slightly uncomfortable as I rifled through the tall chest of drawers to find the items requested by the hospital.

The room, as I would have expected, was immaculate, although the air smelled musty; the type of odour you might associate with old belongings. It was more conventionally decorated than her living room, making me wonder if this was how things had been in general when Frank was alive. I couldn't have imagined him approving of spirit balls and pagan symbols, somehow. The furniture was polished mahogany, making everything seem dark and rather gloomy. Faded pink roses adorned the walls. A small vase of dried flowers sat on the windowsill, flanked either side by two porcelain Beatrix Potter figurines – Peter Rabbit and Jemima Puddle-Duck. They made me smile.

On one side of the kidney-shaped dressing table sat an old-fashioned vanity set with hand-mirror, hairbrush and comb; on the other, a threadbare green silk make-up purse, a cream leather jewellery box, and a jar of Pond's vanishing cream, which I remembered Auntie Jane using. In the centre stood an old sepia photograph in a silver frame of a young, smiling couple, their arms wrapped round one another. I wondered if it was a picture of Mrs Barley's beloved parents. The only concession in evidence to Mrs Barley's wiccan leanings was a large lump of rose quartz and one of her small, faceless dolls, propped upright on the bedside cabinet.

The room was stiflingly warm, but a sudden shiver ran up my spine. It was a disquieting sensation. I became convinced that I could feel a presence and, fearful that I was being watched, whipped round, fully expecting to see Frank Barley observing my actions from the doorway. There was no one there. I sighed with relief, my pounding heart rate gradually slowing. My imagination was running wild again.

I took the underwear and some bed socks from the shallow top drawer and put them into the carrier bag I had brought along for the purpose. I noticed several pairs of the fingerless gloves the old lady always wore, and grabbed some of those, too. Her meticulously ironed nightdresses were in the equally shallow drawer beneath, the lower three drawers deeper and reserved for bulkier items. I thought a bedjacket or something similar would be a good idea, and went through the drawers below to look for one. I recognised the fine knit of a pale green cardigan she often wore. As I pulled it out, the thread of one of the buttons caught in a crack in the corner. Cursing, I tried to winkle the button from the gap. As I did so the base of the drawer lifted. It had a false bottom.

Beneath the thin layer of hardboard was a crinkled sheet of tissue paper, yellowed with age, enveloping whatever was beneath. Cautiously, I peeled it away. I stepped back for a moment, stunned at what had been revealed. It was a layette of old-fashioned baby clothes. There were several of everything, all neatly folded. Muslin cloths, towelling nappies. Tiny vests, cardigans; bootees, bonnets. Old-fashioned romper suits with blue smocking; dresses, some trimmed with pink silk rosebuds, some with seed pearls. All faded white, some flecked with iron mould, all painstakingly crocheted and trimmed with silk ribbons and pearly buttons. And a beautiful knitted shawl, edged with lace.

I sat back on the bed and stared in disbelief at the contents of the drawer, my mind whirring. Had Mrs Barley lost her babies? Or had she wanted them so badly, prepared for them and never fallen pregnant? Is that what she'd meant when she said they 'weren't blessed'? I couldn't possibly ask her. If she had wanted me to know, she would surely have volunteered the information. I had done nothing wrong but felt suddenly guilty, as though I had seen something I shouldn't have.

Reeling from the discovery, I carefully replaced the base of the drawer. As I picked up the hard board, my fingers brushed against something stuck to the rough underside. Turning it over, I discovered a battered pale blue envelope, taped to the board by each of its corners. Handwritten in faded black ink was one word: *Ginny*. I knew it must be for Mrs Barley; *Virginia* Barley, although I never felt right addressing her by anything other than her formal title. Burning with curiosity, I paused for a moment, but then thought better of opening it. It would have been an invasion of her privacy – and being so well concealed, it was clearly meant for no one's eyes but her own. Hurriedly taking the items I had come for, I descended the stairs and left the house, locking the door behind me.

Glancing down the path, I saw what looked like a crumpled black refuse sack on the ground, heaped in front of the summer house. As I approached, I realised with horror that it was Corvus. His head lolled to one side, the black beak slightly ajar. It looked as if his neck had been broken. My insides reeled and I let out a shriek of horror. It felt like a warning; an ill omen. I couldn't bring myself to touch the bird and rushed back to my own house, leaving the lifeless body for Jack to dispose of.

I was only glad that Mrs Barley hadn't been there to see him.

I wondered how the poor creature had come to meet such an unpleasant end.

*

Two days later, I paid a visit to the corner shop. It was a beautiful, sunny Saturday morning and Jack had taken the whole day off, which he rarely did. I thought we might have a nice lunch, and fancied some of Judy's lovely olive bread and tasty nibbles from the deli counter. Leaving Jack to watch Elodie, I crossed the street, only to hear someone calling my name. I turned to see Lucy pushing a pram, Alfie trotting at her side. I hadn't seen her for weeks. She made her way over and I was pleased to see that she looked much better; less tired, and she'd gained a little weight.

'It's been ages! How are you?'

I smiled and patted the beaming Alfie's chubby cheek. 'We're all fine, thanks. How are things with you?'

'Oh, *so* much better now that I'm with Mum. She works part time, but on her days off she takes over with Georgie at night and I can actually get some sleep. Sorry I haven't been round. I'm not going to lie – I was quite down for a good while, but I'm starting to feel a bit better. I'm well rid of the arsehole.' She inclined her head in the direction of the cottage she had shared with Eddie. 'He's moved that floozy from the pub in with him. She's bloody welcome to the sod, as far as I'm concerned.'

I wondered how long it would be until the floozy was passed over in favour of someone else, but said nothing.

'Anyway,' she went on, 'I'll burst his bubble soon enough – I'm filing for divorce and I want my share of that house, so he'll have to sell.'

'Good for you. It was your home too, after all.'

'I'm looking forward to seeing his face when he's served the papers!' She laughed: a little bitterly, I thought, but with good reason.

I thought of Eddie's permanently sour expression, and remembered Lucy's despair. It felt immensely satisfying to think that he would get some sort of comeuppance. Yes. What goes around definitely comes around, in the end.

'You're looking well, by the way. How's Georgie?' I peered into the pram. The baby was sleeping, but his cheeks were rosy and well rounded.

'He's been fine, thank God. No more episodes; not yet, anyway. A proper little gannet – eating us out of house and home.' She looked over towards Rose Cottage. 'Mum said the old dear's in hospital. She all right?'

'She is now. It was touch and go for a time, but she's making a good recovery, thankfully. Due to be discharged soon.'

Lucy nodded, but I suspected she wasn't really too concerned about Mrs Barley's welfare. 'By the way, did you ever see anything of that bloke again – you know, the one you saw in the garden?'

I felt oddly light-headed. 'Not for a while, no. I had

thought I'd heard something once or twice next door, though, since Mrs Barley was taken into hospital, but you know how these old houses are; all creaking floor-boards and window frames. But I was round there the other day and had this really odd feeling – as though someone was watching me.'

'Oh, dear.' She shuddered. 'Ooh I've gone all cold.' She lowered her voice. 'Hey, you don't think there's someone squatting in there, do you?'

I was still certain that any intruder was more likely to be not of this world, but thought she might think I'd gone round the twist if I said as much. I recalled one occasion as a child when my mum had actually collected me from school, I'd overheard a woman at the gate saying behind a cupped hand, 'That one's a couple of sandwiches short of a picnic.' I didn't want anyone to say the same of me.

'I hope not,' I responded. 'I mean, I think there would've been some sort of evidence if there was someone actually staying there. Probably just my imagination.'

'Why don't you get Jack to go and have a look, if you're concerned? Just in case.'

I remembered the sensation of being watched when I'd been in the cottage the other day, and wondered if my instinct had actually been right. The hairs on my arms prickled at the prospect. If I could only convince Jack that there was a presence in the house. It seemed the most likely explanation, given that no one else had seen the man. Not everyone is sensitive to ghosts. I wasn't entirely comfortable with the idea, but maybe I was more receptive to it for some reason.

We chatted a little longer and parted company. I went to buy my groceries and returned home. My appetite had vanished.

Jack was making his way around the living room on all fours in monster guise, pretending to chase a squealing Elodie. He looked up as I came through the door.

'What's up?'

'I've just seen Lucy. She's set me thinking again, about that . . . that man I saw in the garden. Jack, I had the weirdest feeling when I was in that house. I really think Rose Cottage might be haunted by Frank Barley.'

He stopped in mid-crawl, his head dropping. I thought I saw him roll his eyes.

'I mean, if there had been an actual person in there, surely we'd have heard noises; the loo flushing, that sort of thing. I didn't mention it before but I really felt quite spooked – as though I wasn't alone.'

Jack sighed. He pulled himself to his feet. 'We've had this conversation before. I thought you were over that.'

'Well, I'm not! Just because I don't keep talking about it doesn't mean I don't still stand by what I think – and what I saw.'

'What you *thought* you saw.' His voice was quiet, his expression weary.

'For God's sake! *You* didn't see the photo. I want you to come round there with me now. I'll show you the album. You can look for yourself. I've described the man I've seen to you often enough and he's Frank Barley to a T.'

I shut Jobie in the kitchen, and, scooping Elodie up, frogmarched Jack down the garden and up Mrs Barley's path. We went through the French doors and into the living room. I rooted through the sideboard. Spotting the old photo album that Mrs Barley had shown me, I handed it triumphantly to the exasperated Jack.

I looked around uneasily as he sat in the armchair, turning pages. He raised an eyebrow.

'Christ, Mrs Barley was a looker in her day.'

'Yes, never mind that.' Placing Elodie on his lap, I took the album from him and leafed through to the section containing Frank.

Cold fear swept through me. The man's face in every picture had been scribbled out with red ink. It was bizarre – and chilling.

'What is it?' Jack stared at my open-mouthed reaction. In stunned silence, I handed back the book. He frowned. 'What the hell's happened there? That's a bit bloody creepy, if you ask me.'

'Creepy and downright malicious. Who would do such a thing? Mrs Barley will be devastated.'

Jack pulled a face. 'You don't think – I mean, she couldn't have done it herself, could she? You know, in a fit of pique or something. She can be a bit, well, odd . . .'

I stared at him, incredulous. 'Mrs Barley? Never. She worshipped that man. Her whole life revolved around him.'

He looked a little sheepish. 'It was only a thought. The alternative is really worrying.'

'D'you think it can be restored?'

'It's doubtful. The pen's gone right through the paper on some of them.' He shook his head.

'You'd better hide it before she comes home. If the

old girl adored him as much as you say, when she sees that, it'll be enough to give her a relapse.'

But who could have done it – and why? My mind darted to all sorts of explanations but none seemed plausible. The possibility of there being an unwanted and very solid house guest in Rose Cottage seemed, increasingly, a more likely explanation. I could have been in that house alone with a psychopath.

'Should we call the police?'

'And say what?'

'I don't know – isn't that criminal damage or something?'

'Maybe, but there's no sign of forced entry or anything. I mean, if you hadn't taken the thing out to look at it, we'd have been none the wiser. And technically we're trespassing.'

He had a point. Jack went to look in every room before we left the house, but there was no obvious sign of recent habitation.

'Maybe we should install a security camera at the back, point it at Mrs Barley's gate,' he said. 'I don't like the thought of you here alone when I'm at work. I'd say this is down to someone completely unhinged.'

'Not a ghost, then.' The realisation made me shudder. This was almost certainly stamped with the hallmark of somebody with an axe to grind, not a phantom. And as the saying goes, we have far more to fear from the living than the dead. I was angry with myself for having been so blinkered, so swept along by the fanciful notion of the man being Frank Barley's ghost, that I hadn't been prepared to consider the more rational – and likely –

alternative, in spite of the fact that I would never previously have entertained the idea of there being a supernatural explanation for his appearance. It all seemed obvious now. How could I have been so foolish?

'*Definitely* not a ghost.'

We locked up and took the album home. I felt suddenly frighteningly vulnerable and was massively relieved when Jack, now on a mission, managed to find someone to fit a security camera and floodlight that same afternoon. And I tried to convince myself that, even if Jack wasn't home all the time, I always had Jobie . . .

*

Over the next few days, we were extra vigilant, checking the footage from the security camera and watching the house next door like hawks. But there had been no sign of anyone. It was baffling. I almost wished the man would put in an appearance; when Jack was home, at least. It was the fear of the unknown. At least if we could confront him, we might discover his identity and hopefully gain some understanding of his motives. He was proving frustratingly elusive.

Mrs Barley's release from hospital was imminent. Her precious garden was beginning to look neglected, since Bob had been unwell himself, and hadn't visited during her absence. We decided to tidy things up before her return.

I mowed the lawn, while Elodie dozed in her pram, beneath the overhang of the summer house's roof. Jack pruned and weeded the borders, taking care to replace each marker in its original position – rose, iris, violet, sweet william. Jobie, typically frenetic, darted about like one possessed, sniffing everywhere like a bloodhound. He wasn't usually allowed into Mrs Barley's garden and it was obviously all very exciting for him.

We paused for lunch and went indoors. Suddenly, the dog hurtled through the back door, panting excitedly and covered in soil.

'Jobie! What've you done?' I cried, rushing outside. To my horror, Jobie had burrowed a huge hole in Mrs Barley's flowerbed.

'*Bad boy!* No!' I was too late. Mrs Barley's magnificent damask roses lay crushed and strewn across the path.

We stared helplessly at the devastation that our pet had wreaked. Before we could stop him, the dog resumed his frenzied digging, triumphantly raising his head to reveal a small bone between his teeth.

'Shit! Look at the mess he's made. What can we do?' Turning in desperation to Jack, usually the voice of reason, I was shocked to find his complexion drained to an unearthly pallor.

'Jack . . . ?'

'Stina, that's no animal bone.'

Perplexed, I scanned his ashen face. 'What d'you mean . . . ?'

'I'm certain . . . it's human.'

I almost retched. What the hell had our dog uncovered?

My heart hammering, I knelt beside Jack to examine the decimated flowerbed. There were numerous bones of varying lengths – but all of miniature proportions; tiny, porous, filigree-like twigs. Tentatively, I raked back the soil with my hand, revealing a larger, more rounded object.

I recoiled in horror.

It was a tiny human skull.

'I'm ringing the police,' said Jack, eventually.

*

The doorbell chimed.

We showed the young policeman responding to our call into the garden. Mutely, he made notes, nodding occasionally, before retreating to his patrol car to relay the information to his colleague.

The forensic team arrived and cordoned off the cottage. Their blue and white tape seemed incongruous around Mrs Barley's privet hedge and front gate. In disbelief, we watched the proceedings from our living room. It felt completely unreal. They continued to work by flashlight beyond dusk, painstakingly brushing away soil and putting samples into clear evidence bags.

'Bit grisly, this one,' remarked one officer, passing by the open window. 'Appears there are around three bodies. Babies. We'll know more once we get everything back to the lab.'

CHAPTER 18

Four minute skeletons were discovered in total, in three quite clearly separate graves. Apparently, it wasn't possible to determine their gender conclusively, as they had been so young. Preliminary tests suggested that the three smallest were not full-term foetuses and so may never have drawn breath; two had been buried together in one grave, probably twins. But horrifically, the largest, which was identified as the most recently deceased, would have been at least three months old. The baby had sustained a fatal head injury, delivered, the pathologist confirmed, by a heavy blunt instrument.

They had lain, undiscovered, for maybe forty to fifty years. Curiously, each had extra digits – some on their hands, some their feet.

I gasped, remembering Mrs Barley's scar. It made me feel quite nauseous.

'What d'you reckon?' I said.

Jack shrugged. 'I don't know what to think. The police

have gone to interview her. It's just horrible, knowing that we've been living next to this in blissful ignorance. I can't get my head round it. I'm wondering if there are any more out there. It's fucking sick.'

An invisible hand seemed to grip my intestines. Our rural idyll had become irreversibly tainted.

Thankfully, a thorough excavation of the whole garden over the next couple of days revealed no further remains. It was heart-breaking to look out and see Mrs Barley's beautiful plants torn out and discarded, the turf ripped up, everything trampled irreverently and in disarray. Even the summer house had been pulled apart. I felt numb. I desperately wanted to speak to the old woman, to gain some understanding of what had happened. But then, would she have wanted to tell me?

I thought about my own past and shuddered. There are some secrets we'd all prefer to take to the grave.

*

Mrs Barley never saw her home again. Her distress at the police's line of questioning brought on a second massive stroke. She never regained consciousness. I tried to console myself with the thought that she was now at peace and with her beloved Frank once more. In spite of the uncertainty about how the baby had died and whether she could have been involved in some way, I felt utterly bereft. I didn't want to think ill of her.

DNA tests had confirmed that she was definitely the babies' mother. Knowing how good she had always been with Elodie, I couldn't believe that she was capable of harming any child, much less her own. Maybe in my subconscious the old woman had been a replacement for Auntie Jane – a second chance to repay the help and support that I had been given as a child and had, if I was honest, failed to reciprocate.

She'd had her faults, I knew. But in her better moments, Mrs Barley was warmer, more caring – maternal, even – than Auntie Jane had ever been. And now that she had gone, I would never be able to do everything that I had intended to do, to care for her in her hour of need, after all the help that she had given us. The old lady's life had been tinged with sadness, something I understood all too well. She had become like family to me: more of a grandmother to Elodie than Jack's mother. More than my own mother could ever be.

There were so many unanswered questions. I could understand only too well why the three smaller babies had been buried in the way they had. If they had been the result of a late miscarriage, they would never have been allowed a proper funeral in those days. However premature, they would have been no less cherished, their loss equally devastating. Keeping them close to home might have been a huge comfort to a bereaved mother. But it seemed that the mystery surrounding the death of the infant with the fractured skull would remain unsolved. It was all very unsatisfactory and had left a dark cloud hanging over us.

And then it dawned on me that it was no coincidence that they had been buried in the flowerbed. Obviously, no grave marker could be used and their resting places had been marked with a plant to acknowledge their brief existence. Rose, Iris, Violet. And the largest, the boy: Sweet William. It was all so sad.

In spite of everything, Jack and I felt duty-bound to arrange the old lady's funeral. I remembered her mentioning once that she had arranged for Frank to be 'taken home' to be buried. My heart sank as I realised that it would take some research to find out exactly where 'home' had been. I felt strongly that she should be laid to rest with her husband, but there was the possibility that we might not be able to locate the grave. In the meantime, if we were unable to find out, we needed to have something in place. I contacted a local funeral company and explained the situation.

It was a busy period and the funeral director explained that we might have to wait nearly three weeks anyway, which hopefully would give us enough time to find out exactly where the Barleys came from. We set the ball rolling by provisionally booking the local church and left everything else to the undertaker. They had branches country-wide and therefore, for an extra fee, were prepared to transport the body if necessary.

With regard to the cottage, things appeared to be complicated, as there was no will in evidence. Mrs Barley had told me that she had no living family, and we knew no more than the fact that she hailed from a small village in Dorset. Apart from Bob, no one that we were aware of had ever visited her in all the time that we had lived in Avoncote, and it begged the question of what would become of her possessions.

But a solicitor's letter arriving a few days after her death left us completely stupefied. Some months earlier,

Mrs Barley, confirmed to be of sound mind, had contacted a local legal firm to express her last wishes. Apart from a small pecuniary bequest to Bob for his loyalty over the years, we were the only other named beneficiaries of Mrs Barley's entire estate.

At first, we were in denial, feeling that someone was sure to come out of the woodwork to say that there had been a terrible mistake; that she had a long-lost niece or a nephew with a legitimate claim to all her worldly goods. But a visit from tall, poker-thin Mr Lewis, the kindly, slightly harassed-looking solicitor dealing with her affairs, confirmed that the document was indeed legitimate and that, since the majority of what she had left seemed to be tied in with Rose Cottage and its contents, there were a few formalities to be completed at their end before everything could be finalised.

We sat around our dining table, staring in disbelief at the document Mr Lewis placed before us. I noticed his eyes scanning the room and wondered if he thought we could probably benefit from a little financial assistance.

'Mrs Barley plainly thought very highly of you both,' he had told us. 'She told Mr Brain, my colleague, that you were quite the nicest young people she had ever met. There is a little money, but obviously the property is the main asset. We have been paid in advance for our services, therefore it should all be very straightforward.'

'I can't get my head round any of this,' Jack told me, shortly after Mr Lewis had left us. Dazed, we sat together in our living room, staring out at the now ruined garden next door. 'A whole house and everything in it, and we'd only known her five minutes. To be upfront, I'm really not sure how I feel about it. I mean, what are we going to do with it? After the bones turning up, it's all left a very nasty taste.'

'We're going to sell it, eventually. It's a no-brainer. You have to admit, it's the answer to our prayers, financially at least. We can use the proceeds to get all the work done on Wisteria Cottage, and hopefully there'll be some left over besides. But I think we could do with a holiday – once the funeral's behind us, maybe we can get away for a while. Even if it's only to a little caravan somewhere by the sea. A change of scenery might be just what we need.'

'You're right. A few days away might help to put a bit of distance between us and everything that's gone on. It's such a shame. We ought to feel over the moon, but every time I look out of the window, that's all I can think of now. It makes me feel ill.'

'I know. The whole situation keeps going round and round in my mind. I still can't believe Mrs Barley would've been capable of hurting her own child, though. And she still adored Frank – surely no mother could feel like that about a man who had harmed her baby. But from everything we've heard, there were only ever the two of them at the house. It's mind-boggling.'

Mercifully, details of Frank's final resting place and the deeds to the grave in Dorset had been left with the solicitor, too. It simply remained to pass the information on to the funeral director and they would then liaise with their branch in the area. It sounded as if pretty much all we would need to do was choose hymns and pertinent Bible readings, and turn up on the day.

We set about sifting through Mrs Barley's things, setting aside anything that looked saleable, taking other things to the charity shop in the town or the local recycling centre.

The jewellery box on the dressing table contained mainly costume jewellery – nothing of any particular value other than sentimental.

I couldn't bring myself to part with the baby clothes. I had bought a little white-lidded wicker basket, lined with silk, and took it up to the otherwise empty bedroom one humid Tuesday afternoon late in July, when Jack was at work. Leaving Elodie sleeping under the shade of the pram's parasol in our garden, I carried her monitor with me so that I could hear if she awoke. I was reassured to hear her soft, rhythmic breathing.

The bed had been disposed of: nobody would accept anything too old to have fire-retardant labels attached. It was a shame, since it was perfectly serviceable. We had donated the mahogany furniture to a local charity shop supporting a baby hospice, which seemed fitting. I gently packed the clothes into the basket, handling everything with as much tenderness as I'd have held the babies themselves. I wondered if any of it had ever been worn, or whether after its painstaking creation, everything had waited in vain to be shown to the world.

Of course, the letter was still there, attached to the sheet of hardboard. I stared at it for a moment, wondering if I really wanted to know its contents. My heart began to race as, with quivering fingers, I peeled away the tape that had secured the envelope's position for God knows how long. Finally holding the paper in my hands, I hardly dared open it. Steeling myself, I took a deep breath and lifted the flap.

The thin sheets of paper within were a faded blue, the words written in black ink, in a neat cursive hand. There was a date at the top – 27th December 1980. It began with the line, '*My darling Ginny*'.

I stopped suddenly. I don't know why, but I had a strange feeling of foreboding. These were the words of a dead man, intended only for the eyes of his beloved, and part of me didn't want to know how they would play out. Once viewed, I wouldn't be able to unsee the content.

I read no further, stuffing the pages back into their envelope and into my jeans pocket. It could wait for another day. Or maybe never. I had already learned enough secrets to last a lifetime.

Composing myself, I took the basket and went back downstairs. I checked on Elodie, who was stretched out contentedly, arms above her head, her eyes still tightly shut. Back in my own house, I pulled the letter from my pocket and tucked it safely into the jacket flap of the book about Avoncote. I decided to make a pot of tea.

Jobie had been wandering happily in and out of the open French doors. Elodie was still asleep on the patio just outside. Suddenly, the dog began to bark loudly, something that jarred as it was so rare. I hurried out of the kitchen in time to see him leaping up at the fence, where a man – *the* man – stood, apparently mesmerised, staring at him from Mrs Barley's garden. He was in the exact spot where the babies' remains had been uncovered. I was astounded to see Jobie baring his teeth, and growling in the most menacing fashion. I had never seen him react to anyone in this way before. Seemingly unperturbed, the man lifted his head, fixing me for a moment with intense, emotionless brown eyes. Something in them made my blood run cold. I felt with the utmost conviction that I was in the presence of something – *someone* – evil.

Everything seemed to be happening in slow motion. Without a word, the man turned and walked briskly out of the garden, disappearing into the entry. Jobie sprinted down the path, whining and scratching at the gate to be released. Disturbed by the commotion, Elodie began to cry. At once, Jobie came bounding back up towards me, panting. His front paws on the handle, he peered into the pram, then up into my face, his tail thrashing. It was as though he were seeking approval. I realised then that this wonderful animal had acted to protect my baby.

'Good boy. You're *such* a good boy.' I had never been so glad to have him at my side and took his face in my hands, roughly scratching the fur behind his ears, which he always loved.

Grabbing Elodie, I flew back into the house, followed closely by Jobie. In spite of the heat, I was shivering. I think I was in shock. With trembling hands, I flung the doors to and locked them. I wanted Jack; to feel the comfort and protection of his strong arms round me. I felt unnerved. Who knows what might have happened if Jobie hadn't been there?

I just didn't get it. The man looked exactly like Frank Barley. There was no mistaking the resemblance from the photographs that I'd seen. I tried to shake the memory of his baleful expression, but it was burned into my consciousness. The thought of those malevolent eyes made the hairs stand up on my arms.

And then I remembered the security camera. From where it was positioned, it should hopefully have captured a clear image of him. I would wait for Jack and we could examine the footage together. I had no desire to look upon that face again alone.

*

It was some hours before Jack arrived home, by which time I was a little calmer. Elodie, clearly oblivious to the drama of the afternoon, had fallen asleep after her feed and was snoozing peacefully upstairs in her cot.

Unable to conceal my agitation, I greeted Jack at the door.

Seeing my expression, the colour leached from his face. 'What's happened?'

'We need to look at what the CCTV's picked up. He was there again – in next door's garden.'

'*Who* was there?'

'*The* man – the one who looks like Frank Barley.'

Incredulous, he stared at me. For a moment, I really believe he thought I'd finally lost my mind. He seemed to be struggling to remain composed, but rather than shouting, he lowered his voice.

'If you're sure you saw someone, why the hell didn't you ring the police – or me?'

'I . . . I don't know. I couldn't think straight. Please, just play the footage.'

We went into the living room and, his face stony, Jack sat at the table and booted up his laptop, which was linked to the camera. I stood behind him, staring in trepidation at the screen as he scrolled on fast-forward through the film. Suddenly, he paused the footage.

'There – see him?' I said.

The blurred outline of a man was frozen on the screen, his hand on Mrs Barley's gate. Jack pressed 'play' once more and my heart began to race. I watched as the man I had seen earlier walked up the path and stopped abruptly, staring at the ground. The remainder was as I had experienced it first-hand, with Jobie's heroics plain for all to see. But of course, the coldness of the man's eyes wasn't adequately represented by the slightly grainy quality of the film. His face, however, was plain enough.

Jack turned to me. He spoke quietly, his complexion suddenly pale. 'I'm sorry that I doubted you before. I mean, all that talk of ghosts threw me off track. To think you've been in that house by yourself . . .' He bit his lip.

I peered at the image before me. There was no denying the fact that the man looked *exactly* like the pictures I'd seen of Frank Barley.

'So, any thoughts as to who he might be?'

'That's what I intend to find out,' Jack said. 'I'm going to call the police and tell them we've got a prowler. They'll have to manage without me at the surgery. I'm not leaving you and Elodie on your own here until he's caught.'

*

Two plain-clothes police officers, a middle-aged man and a younger woman, arrived within the hour. They watched the CCTV footage with interest.

'You've got a good dog there,' the woman remarked.

I smiled. 'He's wonderful. I don't know what I'd have done without him today.'

'And you say this is definitely the same chap you've seen before?' The man scrutinised me from over the top of his steel-rimmed glasses. I felt uncomfortable.

'Yes. He's been out there a few times, but that's the closest I've ever got to him. As I said, he looks exactly like the photographs of Mrs Barley's late husband.' I wasn't about to divulge that I had long believed the man to be an earthbound spirit.

'But as far as you know, Mrs Barley had no surviving family?'

Jack spoke up. 'Not to our knowledge, no. But then again, we knew nothing about the babies. She was a bit of an enigma, to say the least.'

'It would certainly seem so.' The man raised an eyebrow. 'Well, particularly in light of the recent discovery of human remains, I think we can probably stretch to some surveillance of the property. Rest assured that we're taking this very seriously. We thought we'd hit a wall, but it's possible that this individual has some knowledge that might help us with our inquiries.'

Jack looked at me, then turned back to the police officer. 'What – you think he might've had something to do with what happened there? But he doesn't look that old. I mean, unless he's got a painting in his attic, he would've only been a child when those babies were buried.'

The policeman gave him a wry look and I wasn't sure he'd understood the allusion to *The Picture of Dorian Grey*.

'From everything you've told us, it seems strange that he's always been so focused on the area where the skeletons were found, even before their discovery. A bit too much of a coincidence, if you ask me.'

The two officers left with a promise that a couple of constables would be deployed shortly to keep an eye on the house, which seemed to put Jack's mind at rest. In the meantime, we had been advised not to enter the property until further notice.

I had a horrible feeling that worse revelations were to come. I kept looking out into the garden, wondering exactly what had happened in the Barleys' home all those years ago. Remembering the photo album, the evident frenzy with which every image of Frank Barley had been destroyed, I wondered whether it had been the work of this doppelganger. But what on earth could have motivated him to act in such a way – and what else might he be capable of?

*

With an unmarked police car containing two bored-looking policemen watching the house, Jack was mollified to an extent, and decided that he would risk going into work after all. Three days had passed without further event. I was restricted in that I had been advised not to leave home without good reason, and *certainly* not without informing the officers first; plus I couldn't make any further progress in Rose Cottage. It was beginning to feel claustrophobic.

After lunch, while Elodie was sleeping, I sat down with a coffee to check my emails. A message had come through from my editorial contact at *Avon Life*, asking if I'd be interested in writing another article for the magazine. I hadn't written a thing since Elodie's birth, and seriously wondered if I'd be capable of applying myself with everything that was going on. I was deliberating over my response when the phone rang out, making me jump.

'Stina Mason? Conrad Lewis here, dealing with Mrs Barley's affairs?'

'Oh, hello, Mr Lewis. What can I do for you?'

'I wonder if it would be possible for you to come into the office – at your convenience, of course. There is something I would like you to see.'

It seemed like a valid excuse to escape the four walls for a while and I didn't hesitate. Thankfully, Jack had ridden his bike into work that morning and left the car. I gathered up a drowsy Elodie and stuffed a few of her necessary accoutrements into a bag, before putting Jobie into the kitchen. He looked up at me, his eyes doleful.

'I'll be back soon, don't worry.'

I informed the policemen that I had an urgent appointment with my solicitor and strapped Elodie, now fully awake, into her car seat. I couldn't imagine what further information Mr Lewis could have to impart and wondered what it might be that he wanted to show me. It all felt very cloak-and-dagger.

The solicitors' office, 'Brain, Lewis and Lewis', was a narrow Georgian townhouse, situated in a small row of shops, some ten minutes' drive from Avoncote. It was on a quiet side street, just outside the village of Shottery, famous for being the home of Shakespeare's wife, Anne Hathaway.

Mr Lewis, impeccably dressed and upright as ever,

greeted me at the door and showed me through the wood-panelled reception into a small, stuffy room overlooking a tiny courtyard to the rear of the building. Bouncing Elodie on my knee, I sat in front of his green leather-inlaid desk, watching the abundance of dust motes dancing in a shaft of light that poured through the sash window.

He looked flustered.

'Mrs Mason, I have something for you. I'm terribly sorry, it appears to have been previously overlooked; I'm not sure how.' From his sheepish expression, I wondered if he had been reprimanded for his error by the practice's senior partner, Mr Brain, whose formidable heavy-browed countenance glared down from his portrait just inside the entrance.

'Mrs Barley left explicit instructions that this was to be handed to you in the event of her death. It has been in our safe for several months now. I – we – must have missed it somehow, when we were going through her other documents.'

I accepted the large, sealed brown envelope. Tearing it open, I discovered a lengthy letter on several sheets of cream paper, handwritten in neat blue ink.

The opening line read: *'My dear Stina, There is something that I feel I must share with you.'*

Dumbfounded, I looked up at Mr Lewis. He smiled, looking a little uneasy.

'I have no idea of the contents, only that it's clearly not something for public view. Maybe you would prefer to read it in private.'

I nodded and thanked him, replacing the pages in the

envelope. I drove home, my mind whirring. Elodie fell asleep once more in the car.

I waved to the bored policemen to let them know I had returned, then went straight upstairs to put Elodie into her cot. I let Jobie out into the garden and made myself a cup of tea. My senses electric with anticipation, I sat down at the table to read the letter.

CHAPTER 19

My dear Stina,

There is something that I feel I must share with you.

You may recall that I told you Frank and I hadn't had any children. I'm afraid I wasn't entirely honest with you. When we moved to Avoncote, I was pregnant. We weren't married, and of course in those days, it was highly frowned upon. We talked about what we should do and came to the painful conclusion that we ought to give the baby up. I gave birth at home, to a baby boy, and the next day Frank drove back down to Dorset to leave him with my Auntie Ivy, my mum's younger sister, who lived on a farm. She was still a relatively young woman, only in her late thirties, and she and her husband had never been able to have children. They were good, kind people. It broke my heart to part with him and I cried for days, but I thought it was for the best. We were very young and had little money coming in when we first moved, and thought that the baby would have a better, happier life in Dorset.

I was devastated, of course, and it took me a long time to get over parting with my son. But as time passed, the pain of losing him lessened and I gradually became used to the idea. We settled in to Rose Cottage and Frank was starting to make enough money for us to be comfortable, and well, things had started to look up.

When our little boy was four, my aunt's husband died and she was struggling to cope, both with her grief and the running of the farm. She asked if our son could come and live with us – for a while, at least. I had mixed feelings about it, as I had managed to put it all behind me. I didn't want him to come only to lose him all over again when he had to return to Auntie Ivy. But Frank persuaded me to let him stay. Where's the harm? he had said. If anyone asks, he's just a little cousin come to visit for a while.

If only I'd known. Joseph – for that's what they'd named him – was a strange child. He was my own flesh and blood, but I couldn't take to him at all. I don't suppose being separated from him for all those years had helped. He was secretive and sullen, and didn't want to talk to us. On more than one occasion, I woke up in my bed to find him staring down at me, a peculiar, almost hateful expression on his face. One day I discovered him in the garden, crouching over a tiny bird that had fallen from its nest, just a fledgling, a featherless, helpless little thing. He was prodding at it with a twig. Before I could pull him away, I watched in horror as he stood up suddenly and stamped on it with all his might. He looked up at me, and the glee and malice in his eyes turned me cold. It is a terrible thing to say about my own child, I know, but he looked evil. After that, I could barely bring myself to look at him.

Frank was out at work a lot and didn't see as much of Joseph as I did. He tried to persuade me that he was only a little boy, that we should make allowances for the recent disruption in his life. But in my heart, I knew that our son wasn't right. I tried to treat him well, really I did, but I'm sure he must have sensed that I didn't like him. The sly looks he gave me, the secretive behaviour. He may have only been a child, but there was something deeply disturbing about the way he acted.

After about six months, Auntie Ivy was starting to feel better, and rang to ask when we were going to take Joseph back to her. She was completely alone now and obviously missing his presence. I couldn't get rid of him soon enough. I felt I had failed – my aunt clearly loved the boy and I wondered if he was a different child when he was with her. Maybe it was my fault – perhaps subconsciously he was reacting to my rejection of him. Whatever the reason, I felt a massive sense of relief when Frank took him back to Dorset.

Joseph didn't know, of course, that we were his real parents – I thought it would be wrong to tell him. He had always thought of Auntie Ivy as his mother, and to all intents and purposes, she was.

Time passed and we settled back into a routine. I thought of Joseph from time to time, but was glad that he was far away. The memory of how he would stare at me with his strange, coal-dark eyes made me shudder. Outwardly, he resembled Frank, but those eyes seemed to harbour something wicked behind them. There appeared to be nothing of his father in his character. It was as though there was something missing, something not connected properly. I hoped that he would outgrow his odd behaviour and surly manner, and develop into a decent human being. But three years later, we were dealt a blow when my aunt became seriously ill suddenly, and we had no choice but to bring the boy back to live with us once more.

I can't begin to tell you how life changed for us – and not for the better. With age, rather than improving, Joseph's behaviour grew more erratic and unpleasant. We felt duty-bound to shield him from the world, or more to the point, to protect the world from him. We kept the boy in the house most of the time, only letting him play in the garden when we knew the neighbours were out. I attempted to educate him at home, but he wasn't receptive to anything I tried to teach him. He was prone to aggressive outbursts, both verbal and physical. He was quite a big lad for his age, and sometimes he would lash out at me without warning, a vicious punch or a sharp kick. I grew fearful of his irrational rages and where they might lead.

He seemed to take a perverse pleasure in inflicting pain and injury, and I discovered several mutilated frogs and mice hidden in his room, poor creatures that had clearly fallen victim to his sadistic tendencies. The worst was the neighbours' poor cat. I think there may have been more, but I couldn't be sure. As you can imagine, it was extremely disturbing and I wondered what else he was capable of.

I don't want to go into every terrible thing that he did. It is far too painful. But what I will say is that we felt it necessary to take him to see a psychiatrist. Of course, we told no one that he was our child, just that he was my young cousin. We had never done anything through official channels, and there would have been too many questions asked. But even at the age of nine, he was worryingly manipulative, saying all the right things, and the baffled doctor told us he could find nothing obviously wrong with him. He lived with us for almost two years, until Auntie Ivy was well enough to take him back. She was quite insistent that he return to her. I could only assume he was a different child when not under our roof. It was quite bizarre.

By this time, our lives had been irreversibly damaged. We had no further contact with Joseph, and although we tried to put the experience behind us, Frank was never the same again. He was filled with hatred for our son, whose actions had cast a shadow over our whole existence. I think it was only Frank's strong faith that had stopped him from beating the boy within an inch of his life before he finally went back to my aunt in Dorset.

Stina, I am so sorry that I didn't tell you about Joseph. Selfishly, I suppose I thought it reflected badly on me – on us. Out of the blue, he reappeared recently and it has brought everything to the fore again. He has been visiting me regularly as he has found a job in the quarry, where Frank once worked. I know you, and probably others, have seen him. I expect you will think it odd, but to explain who he was would have opened a whole can of worms that I really didn't want to reveal.

My son seems changed now, a shadow of himself. My son. The very words have a bittersweet ring to me. He has been sorting out Frank's things, sifting through them all to help me. It's something I've put off for far too long. After all, he was his father. Joseph spent a few years in a psychiatric hospital, and after being discharged, moved from Dorset to Warwickshire. He's still under the doctor, but medication and therapy seem to have helped him see the error of his ways, and kept him on an even keel. He's never married and lives alone, only about four miles from Avoncote. I actually pity him. I genuinely believe he regrets how he behaved. Maybe it was all a reaction to his circumstances. I suppose he was just a child. But I can never fully forgive his actions, and the devastation he caused us. And because of what happened, I don't want him to

inherit my home, the home I shared with Frank.
Because Frank would never have forgiven me for
that. I'll never understand why Joseph did what he
did all those years ago.

But I'm certain you'll see it from my point of view.
You know better than anyone, we never really know
what's going on in someone else's head, do we?

I put down the letter, shocked. I turned her words over
in my mind, piecing together this new revelation with
the 'apparition' in the garden. And then I remembered
the old photograph in the magazine – the young boy
staring solemnly down from the window. So, the person
who, for all that time, I'd been convinced was Frank
Barley's restless spirit was, in fact, his son, who was very
much alive. Judging by the evidence in the photo album,
their hatred was mutual. Joseph had obliterated every
image of his father, as if he wanted to wipe any evidence
of his existence from the face of the earth.

It was obvious now: the noises in the attic, the man's
voice in the old lady's bedroom. Had he been helping
her at all – or just trying to find anything that might
incriminate him in some way, in order to dispose of it?
The latter seemed more plausible. Maybe he had still
been looking for something in his more recent visits to
the house. I wondered then if he actually had a key – if
she'd even given him one. I shuddered to think that he
could have walked in at any moment when I'd been there
alone.

Mrs Barley must have been a very troubled woman,
keeping this to herself for all those years. I knew only

too well myself what a long-held secret could do to someone, how it could eat away at you. I wondered how she could have been so uncannily accurate about me and it left me with a dark, restless feeling; like someone walking over my grave – isn't that how the saying goes? It was as though she had been able to see into my very soul.

I wondered now about the baby, little William, for that is how I had come to think of him. That is how I'm certain his mother must have thought of him, too. Was it possible that Joseph was responsible for his death and that this was the 'terrible thing' that Mrs Barley felt unable to share in her letter? It was unthinkable.

But how would it have affected a child, keeping him behind closed doors, locked away from the outside world like a dirty secret? Maybe the Barleys had done it with the best of intentions, but it had been a very unhealthy arrangement. I felt completely torn about the whole thing.

CHAPTER 20

As we now had a confirmed date and time for the funeral, I rang to discuss the finer details of the ceremony with the vicar of the Barleys' local parish in Dorset. I was not prepared for what I was about to learn. And how everything that the people of Avoncote had ever believed about Mrs Barley – Jack and myself included – had been so far from the reality.

'From the information passed on to the undertaker, she was quite emphatic about wanting to be interred with her parents and brother,' he said. 'There aren't any details about other specific requests, however; no mention of preferred hymns or Bible readings. It isn't the type of thing you usually bring up in general conversation, is it? I don't suppose she discussed her feelings on such matters with you?'

'I'm sorry – I think there must have been some sort of mix-up. I'm certain she would have wanted to be

341

buried with her husband. They were completely devoted to one another.'

There was a noticeable inhalation of breath from the other end of the line.

'I'm not aware of any spouse, Mrs Mason. To the best of my knowledge, Miss Barley never married. She and her brother kept themselves to themselves when they lived here in the village, from what I'm told. Their parents passed when both of them were still quite young – I suppose it had brought the siblings very close. I did meet Frank Barley – just the once. Miss Barley and her brother attended their aunt's funeral, a few years before Mr Barley's decease. The aunt had a son, I recall – not quite right, by all accounts. I think he had some sort of mental issues. Finished up in a psychiatric hospital. An awful shame.' There was a pause. 'I delivered the aunt's memorial service; and the service after poor Mr Barley . . . erm . . . passed away. He'd seemed a quiet chap; rather serious, I remember thinking. He must have been a very intelligent man. His sister was telling me that he won a place at Oxford to read Mathematics, but turned it down for some reason. Such a waste. Deeply religious, and a keen gardener too, I learned. A man after my own heart. Miss Barley herself found him in their summer house, apparently. Terrible shock for her. A tragic business – he'd hanged himself, you know. I recall the undertaker remarking that he'd had an extra toe on each foot. Strange, the little things one remembers . . .'

*

I disconnected the call. I had a horrible, sick feeling in the pit of my stomach. Our unexpected bequest now felt even more like a curse than a gift. All I could think at that moment was that we would have to sell Mrs Barley's house immediately – maybe even sell our own beloved Wisteria Cottage; get as far away as possible from the sleepy backwater of Avoncote and its sinister connotations forever. I wasn't sure I could stand living there any longer. From infanticide to incest – and now the terrible tragedy of a suicide, all right on our own doorstep.

All this time I had naively assumed that Frank Barley's had been a natural death. It felt as though we had become unwittingly embroiled in the making of some horror movie, one that I wanted no part in.

Still reeling from the shock of what I had learned, I went upstairs and took out the letter that I had found under the old woman's drawer. I needed to read it now, to find out if there was anything else Mrs Barley had omitted. I felt sure that its contents would offer further clarity. I sat on the bed, reading and rereading the words on those pages, realising that all the clues had been staring me in the face and I had missed them.

Jack appeared in the bedroom doorway, jiggling Elodie on his shoulder.

'There you are. I wondered what you were up to. What's wrong?'

Without a word, I passed him the letter, my hands quivering.

His brow furrowed. 'What's this?'

'You need to read it. I've just been speaking to the vicar in Dorset. I didn't want to believe what he told me, but reading between the lines, it's here in black and white.'

Jack handed Elodie to me and sat beside me on the bed. Silently, he began to read the words that I was still struggling to digest.

27th December 1980

My darling Ginny,

I'm sure you know how I've been feeling – and that this has been building for many years now. I've thought long and hard about it, but I can't live with myself any longer. We opened Pandora's box when we declared our love for each other. We knew what it would mean for us, how people would react, and we were prepared for it. And at first, moving to Rose Cottage felt like a clean slate, the chance of happiness in a place no one knew us. But what has happened in the years since has been far worse than anything I could ever have imagined. Our fresh start was only the beginning of the nightmare. The pain is too much to bear. Everything keeps going round and round in my head endlessly – I feel sick when I think about it all.

We may have had different beliefs, but we have always been two halves of the same person. We both know it. But you are the strong one. You have always been able to hold your head up, ready to spit the world in the eye and defy anyone who dares to speak ill of us, or look at us as if we're the Devil's spawn. I can't even cope with that these days, much less the knowledge of what he did. The product of our union, our love, and he is Satan himself. There's no other word for it. But he's a monster of our making. Rotten to his very core. I know now that he should never have been born. The girls being taken from us was an act of God. We should have known that we weren't meant to have our own children. It was never to be.

Even though he is no longer living with us, the memory of his suffocating presence and his shocking deed haunts me still, every waking hour. We have been punished for our unnatural love. God has passed judgement on us and we will pay the price for as long as we live. I blame myself. I should have had more self-restraint and walked away from you. It may have been hard at first, but we could have moved on eventually. Maybe then we'd both have had the chance of happiness with someone else and none of this would have ever happened.

I know how hard it has all been for you, too, but at least you have been able to put everything behind you, focus on the future. I'm too worn out with torturing myself about it, too beaten down by my guilt. I need to find peace and this is the only way.

I will always love you. And I'll be waiting for you. Stay strong until we meet again. I know you'll be able to carry on.

Forever yours,

Frank

'Jesus Christ.' The colour had drained from Jack's face. 'Who'd have thought it?' He put down the letter and turned to look at me, his hand reaching for his throat.

I felt empty as I stared at the piece of paper resting between us. 'I don't know how to feel – what to think. But whatever they may have done, the Barleys paid for it in the worst possible way. I suppose no one can help who they fall in love with. It's just how they choose to deal with it, and it seems they stumbled from one horrendous mistake to the next. At the end of the day, the only ones who really suffered were them – and poor little William.'

Everything made sense now. The wording of Frank Barley's letter had not spelled it out exactly, but it was blatantly obvious why he had lived under such a cloud. Taking his own life must have been a blessed release. His whole existence, particularly as a man of religious conviction, would have been overshadowed by their last taboo and its shocking ramifications. It was feasible that Joseph, as the result of an incestuous relationship, was damaged in some way by his unnatural genes. Perhaps this explained, if not excused, his behaviour. Maybe the other babies would have had some sort of problems too, had they survived. The thought made my head swim and I didn't want to dwell on it.

I thought of Mrs Barley – but then, she hadn't been *Mrs* Barley, had she? The person that I'd believed her to be didn't really exist. At that moment, it seemed like such a betrayal. I felt I'd never really known her at all. So many half-truths; so much that no one outside their insular little world had been privy to. The slow realisation of everything that had gone on in the Barleys' home made my stomach roil. The times I had blithely left my

346

precious daughter in the old lady's care, not knowing that her estranged, unstable son could visit at any time. I thought of little William's fate and swallowed down the bile that had risen in my throat.

But then, after the initial shock, I began to rationalise: who was I to pass judgement? I wasn't the person she had thought I was, either. I wondered if anyone was ever really who they professed to be. All of us show only the faces that we want people to see; we are composed of many layers, and choose only to peel them back to reveal our true colours if and when we see fit.

*

After a few days, and the opportunity to fully digest our discovery and reason everything through, we concluded that we would stay put in Avoncote; for the time being, at least. It was our plan to let out Rose Cottage for a while, with a view to using the income to make some improvements to our own home. More governed by practicality than me, Jack had tried to persuade me that we could knock both cottages together to create a more spacious home, but I couldn't get my head round the idea of living in a house where a baby had been murdered. He agreed reluctantly to maybe selling it on at some point in the future, but for the time being we settled on the rental idea. I was happy enough with our own home, even if it was a bit on the small side. And there were only the three of us, after all.

We attended Mrs Barley's funeral, booking into a B & B in the little Dorset village she had once called home. It was only for the one night, so Jack had asked a colleague to take care of Jobie (and Mrs Barley's poor lovebirds, who had now become a permanent fixture in our home) for us until our return. The service was a muted affair, with only Jack, Elodie and me, plus two sweet-looking elderly local ladies, who had apparently known the Barleys from when they were children.

After a couple of hymns and a perfunctory eulogy inside the old church, we traipsed to the graveside while the vicar delivered the final words of the ceremony, committing Mrs Barley's soul to eternal rest, and watched solemnly as the coffin was lowered into the ground. Dappled light shimmered through the trees, a soft breeze ruffling the white lilies laid on the ground that had adorned the casket. The only sound was that of the birds, twittering as they foraged and swooped tirelessly from hedgerow to branch to feed their demanding offspring. There was an undeniable air of tranquillity and calm. The old woman was at peace now, and with her beloved Frank once more.

In spite of everything, I cried silently. Her life had been undeniably tragic, and the only people left to mourn her were little more than strangers who had known her for only a tiny fraction of her life. It seemed pitiful.

It was a temperate, mellow afternoon, and had it not been for the occasion I would have loved to stay longer in the area. Apart from its proximity to the sea, the village was not unlike Avoncote, with its old church and cobbled streets nestling in a dip amid rolling countryside; quaint, slightly wonky cottages and a small solitary grocery store in front of its green. There was no wake to attend, so we pushed the pram slowly back to the B & B, both of us lost in our own thoughts. It felt very much as if a chapter in our lives had closed. But now we had to look to the future.

*

With the funeral behind us and now that everything had been cleared from Rose Cottage, we were able to take stock of what needed to be done in order to make it more attractive to prospective tenants. While the house was old-fashioned, that was part of its charm. Mrs Barley had always maintained her home very well, so on the advice of the letting agent, we bought a huge can of emulsion and washed the interior walls in magnolia paint to freshen it up. Only days after the man from the agency had called to assess the property, I looked out of the window one Monday afternoon to see that a *To Let* sign had been erected in the front garden. I was apprehensive but also rather looking forward to seeing who our new tenants (and more importantly neighbours) would be.

I reflected on the past eighteen months and everything that had happened since our move to Avoncote. I had been through the trauma of losing my best friend; the physical and emotional upheaval of pregnancy. Making an unwanted and shocking discovery about my husband. And then there were the revelations about everything that had taken place at Rose Cottage. I thought about Joseph Barley, who had disappeared without trace since his mother's death. We had changed the locks to the house as a precaution, although I couldn't imagine him returning. There was nothing here for him any more. I wondered where he could have gone, and whether he felt remorse for his actions and their repercussions. Or if in his own mind none of it was really his fault.

For a while, it had been as though I was on the edge of a precipice mentally. In spite of it all, I felt I had grown as a person, and now that I had Elodie, I was gaining a different perspective on life. It was so important to live for the moment, not to dwell in the past. It never did any good, wallowing over things that couldn't be changed. Mrs Barley's own existence had become so small, so aimless since the loss of Frank, as though a part of her had died with him. It obviously hadn't been helped by the vicious gossip which, I'm ashamed to say, influenced me too. I realise now how irrational I had been, believing such superstitious rumours, allowing myself to be sucked in by the whispers that had circulated for so long. Any previous notions I'd had about curses and spells now seemed risible. My only defence is that I was hormonal, and Reggie's death had affected me badly, too.

I wondered if the new people moving into Rose Cottage were looking for a rural haven, somewhere to flee their past. As had its former inhabitants. I understood only too well the Barleys' need to escape, to attempt to start afresh. Maybe the old woman had recognised it in me; she had certainly been astute enough to know there was something that troubled me. Perhaps she really was a witch of sorts. In the nicest possible way. She certainly meant us no harm; I was sure of that, looking back. Now that I was less tired and more focused, I might even write about her, set the record straight. Her life could have been so much happier after Frank's death if the villagers had given her the benefit of the doubt. There are two sides to every story and she had never had the opportunity to express hers. Maybe I could be the one to do it for her.

It had been my own dream to shake off the past when we moved from the city. To become Stina, the doting mother, the good wife, the accomplished writer. Maybe my own suspicions of others, particularly Mrs Barley, were rooted in the fact that I realised from personal experience no one could really be completely trusted. Everyone was trying to bury something, with varying degrees of fear of that something being unearthed.

I thought of my own mother, on whom I'd effectively turned my back. After much deliberation, I'd decided recently that I would bite the bullet and go and visit her again. I'd spoken to her consultant, and it seemed she had been more settled of late. I had thought very long and very hard about it, but losing Reggie had made me realise the importance of acting while the opportunity was still there. My mum wouldn't be around forever and I didn't want to look back and regret that I hadn't at least tried to see her again. She was the only living link to my childhood now, even if I'd prefer to forget much of it.

I thought guiltily too of my great-aunt. Of her final miserable months. And of the worst thing I had ever done in my entire life.

*

I hadn't been home for some weeks and my conscience was pricking me. I knew that Auntie Jane was unlikely to have been further than the corner shop, nor would she have had any visitors. Recently, my studies and social

351

life seemed to absorb every waking hour, although I knew I ought to make time to go and see her. But my guilt was born of a sense of duty rather than love.

I wasn't prepared for her mood as I walked through the living room door that afternoon. The television was blaring loudly; some old black-and-white film. Her eyes flickered as I entered the room but didn't leave the screen.

'Oh, good of you to call.' The sarcasm in her tone was biting. She was sitting in her customary armchair, fingers drumming the cushion.

'I'm really sorry, I just seem to be so busy these days.'

'Too busy to pick up the telephone and check if I'm still in the land of the living? Nice to know you're obviously *terribly* concerned about my welfare. You're only the other side of the city, not in Timbuktu.'

'I said I'm sorry, Auntie. How are you?' I sat down in the armchair opposite hers, glancing round at the unusually untidy state of the room, the sideboard thick with dust.

'I'm fed up, that's how I am. Stuck here; day in, day out. I'm an old woman, in case you hadn't noticed. Can't even do my housework any more with these stupid hands.' She spread her fingers to demonstrate the arthritic knots in her joints.

'Couldn't you get somebody in? Lots of people have homehelps these days. I could make some enquiries for you . . .'

'Why should I have to pay someone? And besides, I don't want some stranger rooting through my things. You get all sorts doing those jobs.'

'There are lots of reputable agencies out there. They

352

employ people who've had all the proper checks, to make sure they haven't got criminal records.'

'No. Not interested,' she countered tersely. She rose from her seat and hobbled towards the door, throwing me an icy look. 'If you'll excuse me, I need a lie-down.'

'But I've only just got here.'

'Well, I want a rest. You know where everything is. Make yourself a cup of tea – if you can find some milk.'

I heard the creak of her footfall as she climbed the stairs. I felt irked. She must have known what university would be like, that I wouldn't be able to drop everything and rush round to see her every five minutes.

I sat for a moment, then thought I'd better show willing and clean up, since I was obviously persona non grata. I tidied the room and damp-dusted everywhere, then pushed the vacuum cleaner round. As I turned off the cleaner, I heard her thumping on the ceiling.

I went out into the hallway. 'Are you okay up there?'

'I'm trying to have a nap. How am I supposed to sleep with you making all that bloody din?'

'I thought you'd like me to make myself useful while I'm here.'

'So that's my lot, is it? Do a bit of hoovering and then clear off for another couple of months?'

I sighed. She could be prickly, but wasn't normally quite so cantankerous. I went up the stairs. She had gone into the bathroom, so I waited on the landing. I heard the toilet flush, then she appeared in the doorway.

'Come to say goodbye, have you?'

'I was just going to ask if you needed anything – I can get a bit of shopping in, if you like.'

'I could do with the fridge stocking up and someone to make me a decent meal. I've been living on microwave muck for weeks. I can't chop stuff properly any more, you know that.'

I glanced at my watch, realising that I was likely to have to write off the rest of the day if she needed me to do a major shop and cook her something into the bargain. She must have noticed the look on my face.

'Oh, I see. You've only pencilled me in for an hour. Got something more interesting to do later, have you?'

'It's not that, I just . . .'

'My old mum used to say, one good turn deserves another. I brought you into my home, put up with your shenanigans, fed and clothed you. And this is all the thanks I get. Just like your bloody mother.'

My hackles were beginning to rise. I tried not to react.

'I'm very grateful for everything you've done for me,' I said quietly.

She stuck out her chin scornfully. 'Grateful? Well, you've got a funny way of showing it. I should have known how you'd turn out, shown you the door when you got pregnant. Just as well you lost the thing. God knows what the neighbours would have thought, me having a slut and her piccaninny under my roof. I'd have been a laughing stock.'

The recollection of her, putting my baby into the fire as though it were a piece of rubbish, suddenly flooded my mind. All the hatred and resentment I had tried to bury for all those years came to the surface. 'You loathsome old *bitch*!'

Engulfed by rage, I pushed her. It wasn't even a proper

354

shove – she was so unsteady on her feet, even if I'd just prodded her, I'm sure she'd have gone down like a skittle. I remember the look of horror on her face as she fell, her arms flailing feebly as she groped the air, the dull thud as her head hit the banister. She toppled forwards, tumbling and clattering from step to step.

Aghast, I stared down as she lay, motionless, at the foot of the stairwell. I was rooted to the spot. Eventually, collecting my thoughts, I tentatively descended the stairs and peered down at her crumpled, contorted body. A small trickle of blood had pooled at the corner of her mouth.

I know I shouldn't have left her there, but she was obviously dead. There was nothing that could be done for her. What would be the use in calling for an ambulance?

Panic set in. My heart was pumping so hard it felt as if it might burst out of my chest. I became disorientated, and sat back down on the stairs for a moment, my mind racing. I'm ashamed to say my thoughts were only for my own welfare. What would happen to me? Would this be considered manslaughter – or even murder?

I had come in through the back door – no one would have seen me, and the neighbours were away. If I waited until dark, I could slip out without being noticed. And so that was exactly what I did.

*

It took all my nerve, but after three seemingly interminable days, I returned. I knew I had to face the music eventually. Karen, the woman from next door, accompanied me into the house. When we 'discovered' Auntie Jane, she was distressed, but kind and sympathetic. It worked out for the best, I suppose, having a witness to my feigned horror. Well, not entirely feigned – but obviously I knew what would confront us as we entered that dark hallway.

Karen's thoughts were obviously for me and how this was all going to affect me, a vulnerable young woman with no family. She tried at once to shield me from the sight of my aunt, took me round to her house, and hugged me to her in the most protective fashion. She sat me down and made me a cup of strong, sweet tea for the shock, then phoned the police. In the immediate aftermath, I think I felt every bit as guilty for deceiving her as I did for my actual transgression.

There was apparently no evidence of a break-in or foul play, and the inquest into the old woman's demise concluded accidental death. Which it was, in a way. Although I cannot deny that, at that precise defining moment, I hated her with every fibre of my being, wanted to wipe her from the face of the earth. Afterwards, with the trauma of the inquest over, I was relieved initially to be able to put it all behind me, move on with my life and forget the whole sorry incident.

But of course, you can never truly bury something like that. Every night when I close my eyes, I see Auntie Jane's face, feel the reproach and anger that she must have felt towards me; must still feel, even from beyond the grave. I'm tortured by the thought that one day there will be a knock at my door, that all these years I have been under observation, that some covert investigation has brought new evidence to light and my crime has been discovered. However irrational, I live in dread that the time will eventually come for me to be made accountable for my actions.

After what I had done, I could never judge Jack for his moment of weakness. One drunken, uncharacteristic act on his part; something he was unlikely ever to repeat. That is how I see it. Nothing compared with my own appalling secret. I sometimes wonder how he would react if he knew he were married to a killer. For that is what I am; I can't hide from the fact. Whether he would ever want anything to do with me again. He might even take our daughter away, refuse to let me see her. It's possible that he could actually be fearful of me, of what else I might do, since I'd been capable of committing, and then concealing, such a shocking act. Of course, I would never harm him or Elodie. My actions were the result of a split second of madness. I'm sure Jack would never do anything to enrage me in the way that my aunt did, to push my buttons and tip me over the edge, make me act in such an uncharacteristic fashion. Surely nothing could make me act in such a way ever again.

But regardless, I could never tell him, of course. To risk everything we – I – have would be insanity. It's a chance I will never take.

And so you see, I can fully understand Joseph Barley. In a way, I even pity him, in spite of what he did. I wonder if he had any inkling of his parentage and whether it would have influenced his behaviour. Maybe we are all products of our childhood, our actions and reactions shaped by events over which we have had no control in our formative years. It has made me even more determined that Elodie should have the best, most stable childhood possible; that she should always feel loved and protected, clever and beautiful. It is my mission in life to ensure that she grows into the happiest, most confident and well-adjusted human being that she can possibly be. That she can fall asleep each night without a hint of regret, or a care in the world.

Those long nights when sleep evades me, I often think of the legend of the Flying Dutchman, the captain of a ghostly ship condemned to spend all eternity sailing the seas as punishment for daring to defy God, and bringing certain death to anyone who sees him and his spectral crew. I wonder if, never having paid for my wrongdoing, once I have passed from this life to the next, my restless soul, too, will roam the earth for years to come, in penitence for the terrible thing that I have done.

ACKNOWLEDGEMENTS

First and foremost, huge and grateful thanks to my wonderful editor, Rachel Faulkner-Willcocks, who saw the potential in this story and has rooted for it all the way. Without her expert advice and input, this novel would never have come to fruition. Her support and guidance is greatly appreciated. Thanks also to Helena Newton for her meticulous copyedit. Many thanks to the lovely wider team at Avon. There is so much going on behind the scenes to bring the reader the final polished article and all credit to those unsung heroes working away in the background who help this happen.

Enormous gratitude to all the authors and bloggers who I have come to know over the past few years – it's been a huge learning curve and your help and support have been invaluable. The Writers' Community really are a brilliant bunch.

Thanks as always to my husband, Mark, and my children, without whose support and encouragement I couldn't have carried on. This has been a particularly tough year and I am so grateful that we will all be able to spend time in one another's company properly again soon.

And last but by no means least, a massive thank you to every reader who has bought and read this book – I really hope you have enjoyed it! You help to validate my existence as a writer.